The Dragoneer

Book 1: The Bonding

A Dragons of Cadwaller Novel

By Vickie Knestaut & Danny Knestaut

The Dragoneer Series

The Untethered Trilogy

The Wisdom of Dragons Series

The Dragonjacks Series

The Dragoneer

Book 1: The Bonding

A Dragons of Cadwaller Novel

The Dragoneer

Book 1: The Bonding

A Dragons of Cadwaller Novel

Vickie Knestaut
&
Danny Knestaut

BL Books

First electronic publication by BL Books 2018
First trade paperback publication by BL Books 2020

Copyright © 2018 by Vickie Knestaut & Danny Knestaut
All rights reserved. No part of this publication may be reproduced, stored or transmitted in any form or by any means, electronic, mechanical, photocopying, recording, scanning, or otherwise without written permission from the publisher. It is illegal to copy this book, post it to a website, or distribute it by any other means without permission.

This novel is entirely a work of fiction. The names, characters and incidents portrayed in it are the work of the author's imagination. Any resemblance to actual persons, living or dead, events or localities is entirely coincidental.

First edition

Cover by covermint designs

ISBN: 9781679123627

For Kayla

It's hardly an adventure without you.

Acknowledgement

Special thanks to Michael O'Brien for help and feedback.
We appreciate it!

Part I

The Bonding

Chapter 1

Ulbeg flicked his tail and caught Trysten across the shins, knocking her and the two buckets she carried off balance. Water sloshed across the stall floor. Trysten sighed and straightened herself, then emptied what was left of the water into the dragon's trough. She turned and patted his flank. "It's okay. I feel it too. No need to apologize."

The emerald green dragon dipped his head, brushing his muzzle against her sleeve as if to say thank you.

She moved on down the center aisle of the weyr, picking up empty water buckets on the way. The dragons watched from their stalls as she passed. Ahead, a deep red female flicked her wings out, then drew them back. Straw skittered across the weyr in her wake. The dragons were unsettled. They knew Trysten's father was coming, paying a visit for the first time since the accident.

In the middle of the weyr, she stopped before a gold dragon. The dragon lowered her head to meet Trysten's outstretched palm.

"He's coming, Elevera," she whispered to the dragon. Her palm touched the small scales along the dragon's muzzle. The entire length of Elevera's head was longer than Trysten's arm. Despite the tension in the weyr, Trysten smiled when Elevera nuzzled her palm. Not that it wasn't a happy day. Ignoring protests from herself, her mother, and Galelin, the village healer, her father had decided he'd had enough of his bed and was going to the weyr. He was still dragoneer of Aerona weyr, and Aeronwind needed to see him, to know that he could stand once again.

Trysten closed her eyes and listened. The soft hush of a brush against leather whispered through the dim shadows. Her breath slowed. She could hear her own heartbeat in her ears, but around it, the whispered song of the dragons rose like smoke up to the vaulted roof. The quiet, rushing breath, the shift of leathery skin, a quick click of a jaw, a flick of wings all added to a shifting, whirring song, a whispered chorus as the dragons spoke with each other in quiet and subtle cues that few ever noticed, let alone understood as Trysten did.

Her fingers curled a bit beneath Elevera's golden muzzle as she picked out the individual notes and rhythms of the song. The dragons were excited, pleased to know that Mardoc was coming back. But woven through their song a deep, barely audible rumble rolled, a noise that Trysten imagined the heart of a mountain might make. Expressions of concern, of sadness deepening into sorrow. The sorrow was new.

Trysten's blue eyes snapped open. She peered into the next stall. There, Aeronwind, the iron-gray dragon that led and held the horde together, her father's dragon, lay curled in a ball upon a heap of straw. She no longer seemed the indomitable, timeless and majestic beast that Trysten had known her to be all her life.

Trysten jumped as around her the tones and notes of the dragons drew together, collapsed from a rolling, swirling song and fell into a single, pulsing beat. One breath breathing. Every dragon breathed in unison as if under a single mind, honed and at the ready as the dragoneer entered the weyr.

The sudden absence of the song left Trysten disoriented. Her own breath ceased, and her fingers clutched slightly at Elevera's muzzle as if she might grasp the song and pull it back to her. Oh, how she had enjoyed the time in the weyr while her father had been confined to bed, and how guilty she felt for that. But the dragons only sang when he was absent. Now that he was back, she would miss their ever-present song while she did the morning chores. Her hand dropped away from the face of the gold dragon. Trysten touched her fingertips to her breastbone to remind herself to expand her lungs again, to draw the air on her own, to breathe without the dragon horde.

She looked back to the entrance of the weyr. A dark figure stood silhouetted against the morning light. Leaning on a crooked walking stick, her father limped into the building, looking as if he had trekked a long distance, even as far as the mountains that lay gray and blunt along the horizon.

Her breath caught to see him struggle so. She looked away, back to the shadow-strewn stalls and the dragons that still responded to him as if he were the powerful, commanding man that he had been at the beginning of the past fighting season. Even as he limped along on a twisted leg, he was still the dragoneer, the one who had bonded with and rode mighty Aeronwind, the alpha. The horde still responded to him as his own heart did, beating in time, obeying as long as life coursed through him.

The horde did not sing for her father or any other dragoneer. It breathed as one. It thought as one. It stood as one, waiting for the dragoneer's next command. She would miss that song when she became the dragoneer.

Her throat tightened at the thought and at the memory of that awful day she first told her father she wanted to be the next dragoneer. She blinked hard and drew a long breath through her nose as if she might strike up the song and nudge the dragons to sing, but they would not as long as their dragoneer stood in the weyr.

Her father turned toward the hopper.

"Let me get that for you," Trysten said as she hurried toward him. If she beat him to the hopper, he'd give her less grief. If he got there first and gripped the handle of one of the feed pails inside, she wouldn't get it away from him until it sat empty outside Aeronwind's stall.

"Mind your place," Mardoc said.

Trysten stopped. Her father continued on to the hopper, pulled the door open, and surveyed the pails inside. He leaned forward and inhaled several times, judging the fitness of the meat. He hefted a pail by its wooden handle, and gripping it in his left hand, limped forward, leaning on the staff in his right hand.

"If Mother saw you—"

"I'd tell her the same thing," Mardoc said. His back straightened a bit as he approached. Enough light remained behind him that Trysten couldn't make out his features, but she could still see the pain on his face despite his effort to hide it.

The strain of being out of bed weighed on him far more than he cared to let on. Trysten turned her attention from him to the hopper. This was all about proving that he was still vital, that he was still capable of caring for his dragon. It was what the dragoneer did, and as long as he and Aeronwind both lived, it was his duty to care for the dragon that held together his horde.

"Tell Paege that the hopper is nearly empty," Mardoc said.

Trysten nodded to the side of the weyr that bordered a small pen. "It's already being taken care of."

Mardoc stopped and lifted a heavy eyebrow, visible even in the shadows. "And how do you know that?"

Trysten glanced to her father's goatskin boots. The right foot still twisted out at an odd, unnatural angle. She closed her eyes against the memory of seeing his leg when she ran to him in the field. When Aeronwind bellowed a noise that sounded like an entire blizzard condensed into half a minute.

They had argued that day before he left for training exercises. Argued about her wanting to be dragoneer. The argument weighed on her as heavy as the weight of his dragon on his crumpled leg. She couldn't have known how the exercise would end, yet she felt guilty. Why did sticking up for what she wanted always seem to hurt him?

"Trysten," Mardoc said.

She looked up at him, wide and thick as a wall. The walking staff made him seem smaller. Even if she didn't look at his feet, the staff always invited her to look down, to see how even her father, the dragoneer, was vulnerable in the end, and his mighty dragon, there behind them, lay curled on a bed of straw, dying.

"Did someone tell you that more feed is being prepared?" Mardoc asked.

Trysten shook her head. Her blonde braids shifted against her vest.

"Then how do you know?"

"The dragons know. They can smell it."

Mardoc shifted. His grip on the staff tightened momentarily. It betrayed the grimace that he tried to hide in the shadows. She shouldn't keep him from his work. She reached for the handle of the pail. If caught off guard, she could slip it from his hand, and he would follow along behind her, berate her for taking it while secretly feeling relief.

Her hand wrapped around the handle. She tugged. Mardoc's grip tightened.

"They can smell it?" he asked. "How do you know this? Did you ask them?"

She waited for a little noise, a hint of a chuckle hung at the end of the question. None came.

The best thing to do would be to let go of the pail. She gave it another tug, added a slight twisting motion as if the pail were a root needing pulled from the rocky soil.

"How do you know?" Mardoc asked.

Trysten looked up at her father. She had grown accustomed to the light and could almost see his eyes in the shadows of his thick eyebrows and bushy beard.

She swallowed. Her heart flitted in her chest as she thought of telling him the truth, again. He hadn't believed her weeks ago when she told him the first time that she could hear the dragons. Not just their songs, but what they thought. Though it wasn't quite as simple as that. They did not think in words. They did not think in sound at all. Or maybe they did. She couldn't ask them. She had no words for it. She just knew. The first time she had told him, he had laughed and passed it off as the romantic imaginings of the dragoneer's daughter. But he did not laugh when she insisted again that she would be dragoneer one day soon. She worked with the dragons every morning, cleaning stalls, dragging buckets of food and water until her muscles ached. She had few romantic notions about them.

"The way they act," she finally said. "They're impatient. They fidget. They can smell the blood."

Mardoc peered into the shadows, over his daughter's head. His brow furrowed. His eyes squinted as he searched the shadows for evidence of this himself.

He shook his head. "No. They're just nervous. Aeronwind's injury has shaken us all."

With his staff, he attempted to brush her aside, gently, and continue on. Before thinking it through, Trysten stepped away, out of his path, and as she did so, she twisted the handle on the pail again. With his weight shifted to the staff and his shattered right leg, he let go rather than risk toppling over.

Trysten stepped back half a step to prevent her father from recovering and reaching out for the pail. He continued on as if she had done nothing more than exactly what he had willed her to do.

"Strike a light there," Mardoc called back.

One of the weyrmen lit a lantern and hung it on a post outside of Aeronwind's stall. With a glance between Mardoc and Trysten, he then disappeared into the shadows again. Soon a brush whispered against the leather of a saddle.

Mardoc stopped before Aeronwind's stall, set the staff aside, and planted his elbows atop the half-wall. The lantern light fell on his dragon, her breath coming in slow rumbles.

Sensing the dragoneer's presence, Aeronwind opened one gray, cat-like eye and uncoiled her long neck to stare at him leaning against the stall. If a dragon could smile, then Aeronwind would be smiling to see Mardoc on his feet. Trysten felt the dragon's joy and relief as Aeronwind extended her neck to the dragoneer. A forked tongue flicked out and landed on the back of Mardoc's hand as if patting it. Then a sense of sorrow took the dragon. Guilt shook her for not being stronger, not being mighty enough to hold her rider up and protect him. Aeronwind's regret flooded into Trysten. She covered her lips with the tips of her fingers and blinked away the sudden wetness in her eyes. Mardoc reached out to his dragon as if her drooping head was nothing more than an invitation to scratch her snout.

"There, there, my lady. See? I'm all right." He scratched at the small scales that covered the dragon's snout.

"I'm right as rain. A few more days of rest, and then we'll be up in the air again, you and me, putting terror back in the hearts of hawks."

Trysten swallowed hard and glanced at Elevera. The dragon's dark brown eyes did not reflect Mardoc's reassurances. Instead, Trysten saw only concern and deep resolve. The horde's beta dragon knew that Aeronwind would not recover.

"I brought you a morsel or two," Mardoc said. He began to stoop, to reach toward the ground, and then stopped. He cocked an eyebrow at Trysten, who, reminded of the pail, placed the handle over a hook in the wall. Mardoc reached in, removed a fist-sized chunk of meat, and held it out to Aeronwind.

The dragon plucked the offering from Mardoc's hand with a delicateness that betrayed her size, nearly that of a small cottage. With a flick of her mighty head, the meat was gone. Her eyes tracked from Mardoc's hand to the bucket.

Trysten pulled in a deep breath in unison with the dragons, and their power and strength coursed through her as well. Elevera stirred in her stall. She swept her head down, reaching behind Mardoc, but not enough to take meat from the pail. The stalls were merely suggestions, a place to shelter the dragons. If they wanted to leave, smash open the hopper, or even exit the weyr and terrorize the livestock around the village, nothing could be done to stop them. They obeyed the alpha, and the alpha always honored the dragoneer to which she was bonded.

Trysten reached for a piece of meat in the pail.

"What are you doing?" Mardoc asked.

Trysten froze, her fingers inches from the food. "I was going to give Elevera—"

"Paege should feed her."

Despite herself, she let out a short breath that betrayed her frustration.

Mardoc chose another piece of meat and fed it to Aeronwind. "Do you understand? They must bond. They must be ready. The fighting season will be on us soon and ... We've already discussed this, Trysten."

Heat flushed over Trysten, baked off her skin and made her scalp itch. The urge to tell him *no* crowded at the back of her tongue and reached for her teeth, ready to wrench her mouth open and spill it. To the wilds with it. She would tell him again, then and there, that she would be the next dragoneer, that she would enter the consideration and take the title and carry on the family tradition even if he didn't have a son.

But then her father offered another bite to Aeronwind, and as the dragon gulped it down, he reached up and ran his fingers along the side of her neck. Though turned away from her, Trysten could see enough of his face to know that he felt just as bad as Aeronwind did. He felt as if he had failed her. He should have been stronger. Should have had legs of iron to withstand her weight. Should have leaped off her back, or done a better job of flying. As far as he was concerned, their broken bones were all his fault.

The declaration dried up on Trysten's tongue. It could wait. There would be time enough to hash it out again. The fighting season was months off yet. It was Mardoc's first day out of their cottage since the accident. Surely she could wait until tomorrow.

As Mardoc took his hand away, the dragon stretched and lowered her neck, prolonging the physical contact between the two as long as possible.

"Have you seen Galelin?" Mardoc asked. He glanced back at Trysten as if to assure that it was she to whom he spoke and not the dragon.

"Yes, a bit ago."

"Tell Paege to bring him around. I would have a word with him."

Trysten nodded.

Mardoc gave Aeronwind another bite, then turned back to Trysten once again. "Is there something you need, Little Heart?"

She blushed at the nickname. She was not Little Heart anymore. She was no longer a little girl. She was ready to be the dragoneer. Soon. Regardless, she turned and started up the central aisle of the weyr to look for Paege.

Chapter 2

Trysten found Paege and Galelin at the opposite end of the weyr, and both showed surprise to hear that Mardoc was there. As much as she liked Paege, she glared a bit at his surprise. The dragons across the weyr all breathed in unison, betraying the fact that the dragoneer was there, among them. It was obvious to her, and it should have been obvious to Paege as well.

"Father wants a word with both of you."

"How is he?" Galelin asked as he peered off into the gloom between himself and the open doorway. "Is he walking? He's walking, isn't he? Surely he didn't have the weyrmen carry him down on a litter, did he?"

She shook her head. "He has a staff. He leans on it a good bit, but he's here under his own power."

"By the wilds, that man should be in bed!" Galelin spat, then tottered off on his creaking knees toward the head of the weyr.

She turned to Paege. "And he told me to tell you to make sure the hopper is stocked, and that he wants you personally to feed Elevera."

Paege nodded, then began a slow walk behind Galelin. "The weyrmen are in the pens now with their knives."

"I told him as much."

Paege's gaze traveled over her briefly, searching for something, as if he hoped to catch a glimpse of how she wielded a particular trick, a sleight-of-hand. He had begun to let his hair grow out, and he had ceased shaving since her father's accident. His beard was not coming in well, not nearly as full as her father's, or even that of the men in the village. It did not suit him. She missed his smooth face, his full smile. Not only for the scraggly beard, but it seemed that the weight of twenty dragons had been placed on his shoulders after the accident.

"How are things going?" Trysten asked, and then she looked ahead. She knew the answer and she didn't want him to see that she knew.

Paege let out a small sigh, one that would not befit a dragoneer. "It's coming along," he said after a few seconds. "I'm getting the hang of things. I'm making progress with Elevera."

Trysten stifled a grin. Elevera felt differently, but she did not want to delight in the dragon's indifference to her friend. No one, not even Paege, expected her to become a dragoneer. No one expected that of any woman anywhere. It was the way of things. Or so said her father.

Ahead, Mardoc and Galelin exchanged a few words. After a moment of tense silence, a moment in which Paege slowed his pace even further, Mardoc glanced at the two of them and then turned away. With the staff at his side and the weight of his broken body hurting more than he cared to let on, he hobbled up a set of stairs and into his den.

Galelin opened the door to the stall and slipped inside. Trysten and Paege followed.

Aeronwind lifted her head and watched as the three people entered. Galelin lowered himself to his knees, his joints popping the whole way. He landed in the straw with a soft grunt and began to examine the dragon's bandaged and splinted foreleg. With shaky, trembling hands, he undid the knots that secured the bandages. Aeronwind let out a low rumble, a groan.

Across the weyr, the other dragons picked up the sound. They passed it around. They added their own rhythms, their own sounds to it, and it swelled into a song that threatened to entrance Trysten. Her own breath began to fall into the rhythm, and her head threatened to spin with dizziness.

"How does it look?" Paege asked Galelin.

Trysten straightened her shoulders and grasped her wrist behind her back, shaking her head to clear it of the dragons' anxious song.

The Dragoneer: The Bonding

Galelin shook his head as he began to unwind the cotton bandages. "Not good, young man. Not good."

Paege drew in a sharp hiss of breath. How much of that was dread for the dragon, and how much of it was dread for the role that Mardoc wished to thrust upon him?

Trysten crouched, careful not to obstruct any of the light falling from the lantern.

"There's a good bit of drainage here. And it's not a healthy color," Galelin continued. He looked up at the dragon that stared at them with half-lidded eyes. A groaning rumble escaped her, a sound of disgust. Galelin shifted his posture. One puff of flame, and Aeronwind could incinerate them both. But staring into the dragon's gray eyes, Trysten knew it was nothing more than Aeronwind's disgust at herself, for allowing herself to become injured so severely.

Galelin returned his attention to the wound before him. "I'd say that our lady's humors are out of balance." He leaned forward. His brow and nose hovered over the wound where bone had pierced the scaly skin. He inhaled deeply, squinted his eyes, then sat up again.

"The humors are definitely out of balance. What we have here is an excess of pustulence."

Galelin looked up at Trysten, then Paege. He extended his hand to the young man.

Paege took the healer's hand, then hauled him to his feet. Galelin dusted his palms together. "There's nothing to be done for her but to try and balance the humors. Lay off the meat. Feed her some vegetable matter. Give her lots of water. Keep that bandage clean at all costs, young man."

Paege nodded.

"If you will excuse me, then, Mardoc has asked to see me in his den. If you need anything further..." The healer approached the stall entrance.

"Wait," Paege called and took a step toward the man. "Aren't you going to dress Aeronwind's wound?"

Galelin turned back with a raised eyebrow, his lips cocked in half a smile. "Me? Young man, every person in this village knows that Mardoc favors you above all to succeed him." Galelin nodded as if agreeing with himself. "It will serve you quite well as a dragoneer to know how to dress a dragon's wounds. For reasons unbeknownst to me, hordes fly into battle with neither sense nor a healer. You saw me pull that dressing apart. You can put a fresh one together. But if you get into trouble, as I said, I will be in the den."

Trysten gritted her teeth and knitted her brow as the healer turned away. His nonchalant attitude toward the severity of Aeronwind's wounds bothered her. He had essentially said in his own way that there was nothing he could do but offer up the wounds of a doomed dragon for the new master to practice dressing as if Aeronwind were nothing more than a chirurgeon's ceramic doll. She stepped toward Aeronwind's head, then reached up to press her palm against the dragon's muzzle, against the scaly cheek. Aeronwind twisted her head up and away, curled her neck around the other side of her body, leaving Trysten there, her hand outstretched into space, staring up at Elevera in the next stall.

"She doesn't have much faith in my ability to dress her wound, does she?" Paege asked.

Trysten's hand dropped to her side. The dragons all knew. It was no secret to them that Aeronwind was not healing. The scales around the wound swelled outward. The exposed flesh was red and angry where the scales had been pushed away by the snapping bones. Greenish-yellow pus oozed from the corners and stained the bandage Galelin had last wrapped around the leg. The balance of humors was too far gone. It could not be corrected with all of the water and fresh vegetables in the kingdom. Aeronwind was dying.

It seemed impossible that such a beast could ever die, but there it was, a fatal injury. Now did not seem like an appropriate time for her to assert her will. Her father was in pain, and his dragon was mortally wounded, but there had never been a more necessary time. Once Aeronwind passed, Elevera would become the new alpha, and the human bonded with her would become the new dragoneer.

Trysten looked up at the gold dragon again. Instead of watching Paege's every move with interest, Elevera stared directly into Trysten's own eyes.

Her fingertips slid down the scales of Aeronwind's side, over the stiff ridges and the leathery wings, past the fold of flesh stretched taut near the foreleg, held out stiff and rigid between the splint.

Paege pulled the old bandage out and wadded it into a ball. He stood, walked to the back of the stall, and shoved the used bandage into a pail before flipping open the lid of a trunk. He rummaged around inside before bringing back a fresh fold of linen and a clay jar of salve prepared by Galelin.

"How long do you think she has?" Paege asked as he knelt beside Trysten. His voice was low, hardly more than a whisper.

"I don't know." A second later, Trysten added, "But you'll be ready," and it surprised her to hear the words pass her lips.

Paege snorted. "Ready? By the wilds, I can hardly get Elevera to notice I exist, let alone form any kind of bond with her. Even now, she's more interested in you and what you're doing than she is in me. I will never have the bond with her that Aeronwind and your father have."

A twinge of guilt sparked through Trysten. But then, why should she feel guilty? It wasn't her fault that Paege and Elevera hadn't bonded. Trysten and Paege had grown up together, had often been playmates as children, but Trysten, as the daughter and only child of the dragoneer, had grown up in the weyr. She had spent more time with the dragons than she had with most people. It would only be natural that she should have more of a bond, more of a connection with them.

She shook her head. To the wilds with feeling guilty. What was best for the horde was all that mattered. If Paege would be a better dragoneer, then he would be chosen. If Trysten proved to be the better choice, then how could her father tell her no?

Paege gently lifted the dragon's foreleg, and Aeronwind let out a long groan. A ripple effect threaded through the horde. The song drew out, became muddied and slowed. The sound of it squeezed Trysten's heart. The alpha's suffering was the horde's suffering.

She reached under the broken leg and pulled the wad of linen strips through. As Paege began to lower the leg, she told him to hold it in place. He did so without question, and she proceeded to wrap the linen around the leg as she had seen Galelin do for dozens of other battle wounds and accidents.

"You're even better at this than I am," Paege said.

Words of comfort and encouragement sat on her tongue, but she would not get anywhere acting like the women of the village were supposed to act.

"Do you want to be the dragoneer?" she asked.

Paege did not respond right away, and so she started to let the question go, to pretend she had never asked.

"It is my duty," Paege said.

"Your duty?" she asked.

Paege nodded. A lock of dirty blonde hair fell onto his forehead. Most of the hordesmen wore their hair tied back when they flew into battle.

Paege's hair was short enough to single him out, to show anyone from any distance that he had been a weyrman and a stable hand for longer than he had been a hordesman.

"The horde needs a dragoneer." He glanced up at Elevera.

"But why does it have to be you?"

Paege would have shrugged and jostled his grip on the dragon's wound, but he had always been kind, considerate. She liked that about him, and so he held his hands and arms steady for Aeronwind's leg.

"Who else would it be?"

A flash of color passed over Trysten's face. "So that's it, then? There's no one better suited, and so it just falls to you, does it?"

"No, no," Paege said with a shake of his head. "I'm sorry. I didn't mean it like that. I meant that... Well, since your father doesn't have any sons, and since your family has nearly adopted me since my own father's death, then it falls to me. It is my duty. The horde must be kept, and the kingdom's borders must be secure. So for King, country, and family, I will be the dragoneer."

Trysten pulled a small knife from her pocket and cut the linen from the larger piece. Paege lowered the dragon's leg gently then tied the bandage in a knot.

"Besides," Paege said as he sat back on his heels, "what else would I do? Be the village healer?" He flashed her a lopsided grin.

"If you don't want the position, Elevera will know."

The grin fell away as he turned his attention to the bandage before them.

"I know. But I want the position. I really do. It's only that..." He shrugged, then shook his head. "My father would be proud of me if he could see me now. His son, a dragoneer, leading the horde into battle, into glory and defense of the kingdom. But, to be honest," and he leaned in toward Trysten as if to whisper, as if anything he told her could be hidden from the dragons, and for a flicker of an instant, she wanted to stop him, to press her fingers against his lips and stop up the words before they came out because he didn't know about her, about the dragons, about the connection she alone seemed to have. It was unfair, but she dared not tell a soul.

"Between you and me," Paege continued, "I want the position more than you can imagine. But, I'm afraid that I just can't do it. I try... I try hard to do what your father tells me, to form that bond and connection that he talks about. I find myself holding conversations with Elevera in my head."

Paege let out an embarrassed chuckle, and his cheeks flushed. He shoved a lock of hair out of his eyes and her heart lightened for him. "To tell the truth, I've even been caught muttering to myself out in the market or someplace, trying to believe that she can hear me, or that she even cares to hear me, though I know she can't. She won't. But I have to pretend, you know? The fighting season... And everyone is counting on me to be the one who defends the village, the one who keeps the kingdom safe from invasions. Above all that, I know my father would be..." Paege swallowed hard. He bent over, undid the knot on the bandage and tied it again. Aeronwind shifted beneath his attention.

"I know he would be so proud of me, but he would also be equally disappointed if I failed. And after he gave his life in defense of the village, how can I turn my back on him? How can I say to his memory that his sacrifice was important, but not important enough for me to honor by following—or even surpassing his footsteps, you know?"

Trysten took a deep breath. She thought she knew him, but she had no idea. She had assumed he was trying to be dragoneer only to please her father, who had become like a father to him as well.

"I didn't know that it meant so much to you," Trysten said.

Paege shrugged again and looked up to Elevera. "It doesn't matter, does it? Whatever is best for the horde, right? Either Elevera will accept me or she won't."

The words weighed on her in an odd way, feeling both like lead weights and warm winds, pushing her up while pulling her down. She agreed exactly. What was best for the horde was what was best for the village. Yet to see her friend resigned to disappointing his father tore at her. She wished to place a hand upon his shoulder, to comfort him, but when she glanced at Elevera out of the corner of her eye, she felt like a thief, guilty, as if she had stolen the dragon away from him.

But he knew it. What was best for the horde. And if it were best for the horde that she should be chosen, then she would be. There was no reason to feel guilty for that. No reason at all.

Chapter 3

Paege pushed himself to his feet. "Well, I better get back to work. I won't ever earn Elevera's respect by moping around here, will I?" he asked as he peered up at the golden dragon.

Elevera made no movement, no indication at all that she'd heard or understood. Her predator's eyes had flicked to him when he moved. They flicked back to Trysten when she stood a few seconds later.

As Paege went off to the pen to help prepare the food for the day, Trysten climbed the set of wooden stairs to her father's den and slipped inside. Heat from a small stove brushed cold from her shoulders that she hadn't been aware was there. In the next room, on the other side of the small receiving room, Galelin stood before a table and spoke in hushed tones. Mardoc, appearing to ignore the healer, sat in a chair on the other side of the table and studied a scroll from the collection that had gathered in a basket since his injury.

Galelin glanced back at Trysten, then returned his attention to Mardoc. "I see that arguing with you will get me nowhere."

"I always knew you to be a wise man, Galelin," Mardoc said without looking up.

With a huff and a shake of his head, Galelin exited the room. Mardoc looked up. His eyes bored into the back of the man who dared leave before the dragoneer had dismissed him.

"A pleasant evening to you and your mother," Galelin muttered as he brushed past Trysten.

Once the door shut with a rattle behind her, Mardoc sat back in his chair. He ran his calloused, thick hand through his beard. "Is everything all right downstairs?"

Trysten nodded and approached the doorway to her father's chambers. The heat of the fire stayed behind. It pushed at her back and dared her on.

"Is there something on your mind?"

She opened her mouth, paused, then asked, "How is Paege coming along?"

Her teeth snapped as she clenched her jaw shut. That was not at all what she had meant to ask.

Mardoc folded his hands together and laid them on the table. His brown eyes considered them for a moment. "Paege will be ready when called upon."

He nodded once, a bit of punctuation to state that the line of thought was done and over with.

Trysten swallowed. Her eyes darted to the window behind her father. The glass had been a work of labor from the village's glass blower. He had worked many hours to provide the clearest glass possible for the window in the dragoneer's den. Still, it warped the view of the mountains slightly. They were gray, without depth. The shepherds in the hills beyond were nearly invisible, blotted out by the slight blurs and ripples in the glass. The world outside was distorted, yet her father's sole purpose was to keep it orderly, to keep things exactly as they were now.

He would resist her bid to be dragoneer. He would resist it both as dragoneer and as her father. And though he would never say such a thing to her outright, she had overheard him discuss the matter with her mother. The lack of a son bothered him. The title of dragoneer had been in the family for many generations, and it was about to slip away from him. He was the end of the line. Or so he thought.

Trysten pulled her shoulders back. It would not be easy to convince her father to change, but no dragoneer ever backed down from a fight or fled a necessary confrontation.

"Things look grim with Aeronwind," she said. "Galelin says that the humors in the wound are unbalanced."

Mardoc nodded again. "So I've been told."

"He had Paege dress the wound after he himself took a mere glance at it. He said that Paege needed the practice. Galelin has given up on Aeronwind. He thinks she can't be saved."

Mardoc gestured at a chair on the other side of the table. "And how did Paege do?"

Trysten sat, and despite herself, she gazed about the room. She had been here many times as a girl, and the room had always looked so big and intimidating with its charts hung on the wall and a fortune of books along a shelf.

"Paege did fine," Trysten said as she returned her attention to her father. "He knows how to dress a leg wound, but the matter at hand is that Aeronwind will not last much longer, and there is some concern that Paege may not be ready to bond with Elevera when her time comes."

Mardoc sat back in his chair and steepled his fingers together. The proximity to the window hid a bit of his face despite the solid, gray clouds outside. "Paege will be ready. When Elevera's time comes, she will do what is best for the horde. It is instinctual with them. She will bond with Paege. They will both be ready."

Trysten shifted. "I know that what is best for the horde is what should always be done, and though I would like to see Paege be the next dragoneer, I can't help but wonder if there might be someone better suited. Wouldn't it be better for the horde if there was someone who already had a strong relationship with Elevera?"

Mardoc lifted an eyebrow. "Such as?"

Trysten's hands clenched the wooden armrests of the chair. He was supposed to have agreed with her, and not immediately challenge her for a name. Wilds. She had not prepared the case for herself yet, and here he was already demanding a name.

She glanced out the window again, to the glass-blurred landscape of mountains and the press of winter storms that held back the soldiers of the Western Kingdom. Being the dragoneer was so much responsibility. It was about leading the force that kept the Gul mountain pass empty and free of enemy soldiers when the fighting season began. It was not something to take lightly. Should she back off, regroup, take a day or two to build her case gradually before dropping her own name?

She recalled the look in Elevera's eyes when she stared at Aeronwind. Despair and pride mingled in a way that Trysten could barely wrap her own mind and heart around. The way dragons felt things was so huge. It was eight different feelings all at once. But it was clear to her that Elevera was ready, that she was standing by. Aeronwind would not last much longer. Now was the time.

Trysten sat up and looked at her father. Her knuckles whitened against the chair arms. "Me. I want to—I will be the next dragoneer."

"This again. You?" Mardoc asked. His steepled hands collapsed. He placed his hands in his lap. "You want to be the next dragoneer? You want to replace me?"

His head drooped a bit at the last as if in utter disbelief.

Trysten nodded. "I already have a rapport with Elevera. She knows me. She trusts me. She will bond with me when the time comes."

"You?" Mardoc repeated, then shook his head. "No." The corner of his mouth jerked up. It was either an aborted grin or a twitch of his lips. "No. It can't be. There are no female dragoneers. There never have been. It's always been a position held by men. The alpha dragons will not bond with women. What you ask simply can't be, though I do admire your courage for stating such a thing in the first place."

Trysten leaned forward as if she might escape the heat creeping up her face. "How do you know dragons won't bond with women?"

"How do I know?" A grin creased Mardoc's face. "Well, I know my history, Little Heart." He gestured at the hand-copied books on the shelf. "It is the duty of a dragoneer to be well-educated, to know history and geography. And I know in all my studies, in all the times I've spoken with others, a woman has never been a dragoneer. It just doesn't happen. It's not because I don't wish it, but because it just doesn't happen. The alphas won't allow it."

To the wilds with that. It wasn't at all that alphas wouldn't allow it. Trysten knew it. She knew it from Elevera. They had a connection. They had a bond already that was as strong as any bond between her father and Aeronwind. It only needed for Elevera to become the alpha for it be cast as a true bond. Such a connection need only be proved to her father. Once he was forced to see for himself the relationship between her and Elevera, a future dragoneer and her mount, he would have to recognize that his excuse belonged to the wilds.

Chapter 4

Trysten pushed herself up out of her chair. When she didn't turn away, when she didn't retreat to the door, Mardoc's eyes widened.

She took a deep breath. "It is the right of anyone in the village to compete in the consideration, is it not?"

"Yes, but Paege is already—"

"Then I formally enter my name into the consideration. I, Trysten, daughter of Mardoc and Caron, wish to become the dragoneer."

Mardoc didn't respond right away. He let out a long, slow breath through his nose and folded his hands on the table before him. "I would dismiss any hordesman from consideration for interrupting me, but you are not a hordesman. You are a stable hand. You are not even allowed to be a hordesman."

Her father leaned forward and placed his elbows on the table, "But this cannot come to pass. You will only complicate things. I cannot deny the connection that you seem to share with Elevera already, but it takes more than familiarity to be a dragoneer. It is a bond between dragon and man that transcends all other relationships. It requires a level of strength and will on the part of the dragoneer that women just don't have."

Heat rushed over Trysten's face. It trickled down her back until her skin itched with irritation.

"This isn't about my attitudes or beliefs," Mardoc said as he held up a hand. "This is just how things are. The dragons require this. If you wish to be upset about it, then you must direct your ire to the dragons in general and to Elevera in particular. This has nothing to do with me."

Trysten drew in a deep breath. "Are you denying me a chance in the consideration?"

Mardoc sat back again, then shook his head. "It is not my place to deny you this. It is the law. The law states that the consideration is open to any man who can make the declaration."

"Have you ever denied anyone else before?"

Mardoc rubbed the top of his right thigh. His gaze dropped to the table top and the basket of scrolls still awaiting his attention. As if coming to a decision, he looked back up to her.

"I have never rejected anyone who was qualified."

Trysten straightened her back. "I am qualified. I'm as capable as any of the other hordesmen. I can ride a dragon. How many hours have I spent riding the courier dragons with Mother? I can shoot a bow. How many hares have I shot since mother taught me the bow? What else is there?"

Mardoc glanced away. Finally, he gave his head another shake. "Do you understand what you are asking, Little Heart?"

And suddenly there was her father, trying to talk sense and reason into his ram-headed daughter. The dragoneer was gone, placed for the time being behind his other title. This wasn't the dragoneer who was denying her rights, but rather, it was her father.

"I am asking for my right, as a member of the village of Aerona, to defend my village against those who would see it harmed."

Her father lowered his face slightly, stared at his hands as he clasped them together again. "Being the dragoneer is about more than defending your village. I applaud your desire, and should the troops from the Western Kingdom ever make it this far, then I would expect nothing less than to see you on the front line, shoulder to shoulder with the other hunters drawing back their bows. But being the dragoneer is not about defending the village. It is about defending the entire kingdom. It is leading the dragon horde into battle. It is about maintaining the horde."

Her father leaned back in his chair. A quick whisper of pain twisted his face, then faded away as he rubbed his right knee.

"Being the dragoneer means defending against all enemies, including other alphas who would steal our horde away. It is about keeping the horde from absconding. It is about running the weyr and keeping order. It is a dangerous position."

Trysten nodded. Her gaze fell to his twisted leg. "I have seen so. First hand."

Her father wiped his hand down the length of his beard. "There is a lot that rides on this position. This is not playing soldier when the village comes under threat. Should Aerona fall, then so falls one of the first lines of defense against the Western Kingdom. The responsibility that rides on the dragoneer's shoulders—on my shoulders—" Mardoc said as he thrust his index finger into the bottom of his beard where it covered his breastbone. "This responsibility is not to be taken lightly. It is not negotiable. It is not about to change because a young girl takes a notion."

"I am not a young girl," Trysten said through a tense mouth. "I am half a year older than Paege."

Her father sat back in his chair and rubbed at his right leg again. Whether intentional or not, his brow furrowed a tiny bit. Lines appeared at the corners of his eyes. Pain lay just beneath his features.

"This isn't about your age. This isn't about your gender. This is about duty, about *my* duty. Aeronwind, as much as it pains me to see this, will pass soon. And though my heart may always be at the peak of the fighting season, I am not too full of either pride or ignorance to admit that I can no longer hold a saddle the way a rider must hold it. It is time for Aeronwind and myself to step aside, but my duties are not complete just yet. I must find my replacement. Someone who understands the severity of this position. Someone who the dragons will respect and work with. These are my primary duties, and after last year's fighting season, now is not the time to let some romantic notion of a warrior princess cloud my judgment."

Her father leaned forward again, and it was obvious that his leg pained him to the point of distraction.

"There will be a consideration, as there always has been. But Paege will win that consideration. My mind is already made up. Other hordesmen will one day, perhaps, make worthy successors if called upon, but Paege will be my successor as dragoneer of the Aerona horde, and as your father, I ask you to not make this more difficult. It is hard enough on Paege to win the respect of Elevera without having to also contend with your notions. Please. Accept my wishes and cease this foolishness before you endanger the horde."

Trysten took another deep breath. "Would it not endanger the horde to make a dragoneer of someone who is not ready?"

"Paege will be ready. You have my word. I will see to it. I, more than anyone, know the importance of this."

"It is my right to participate in the consideration. I have grown up in this village, and I am of age," she said.

Mardoc let out a long sigh. He slumped further back in his chair and rubbed again at his leg.

"It is not a right. It is a right only for men, so says the law." He nodded to the books on the shelf.

"Prove it."

The edge of Mardoc's eye twitched. "Prove it? I need not prove it. I am the dragoneer. It is my duty to know the laws I am sworn to defend."

Trysten nodded to the books. "You say it's in there, then show me."

Mardoc considered her a moment. A slight grin spread out beneath his beard and mustache. "Once I show you that the consideration is only for men, will you then promise to let this go?"

Trysten swallowed hard, her pulse pounding in her head. She flexed the fingers that gripped her left wrist. Dare she gamble on this one thing? Why not? If it was supposedly impossible for women to bond with alpha dragons, then why would there be a law forbidding something that couldn't happen? Besides, what other choice did she have? Her father was a man of his word. If there were wiggle room in the old laws, then she would have it.

She nodded.

"You are a good girl, Trysten. A smart one. I admire that you are willing to let the law be the law. How could I allow anyone to be dragoneer who would ignore the laws once they became an inconvenience?"

He pointed to one of the leather-bound books on the shelf. "There. Fetch me that one... Fourth from the end."

Trysten stepped up to the shelf and pulled out the book indicated. She handed it to her father.

Mardoc split the pages open to a section near the back, then placed it on the table. His eyes darted back and forth over the neatly lettered laws scrolled out on the parchment pages. With a delicate touch, he turned back several pages, then stopped. He placed a finger beneath a line and left it there.

Trysten stepped up behind him and read over his shoulder.

...Furthermore, the Consideration will be made up of those men who fall under the protection of the weyr, and who have formally proclaimed a desire to serve as their weyr's dragoneer.

The bottom dropped out of Trysten's stomach. She read the law again. "No."

Her father's hand closed the book gently as if putting the book as well as the argument to rest. His palm remained on the leather cover. "We had an agreement."

"But that doesn't make *sense*," Trysten said. "Why would there be a law forbidding me to do something that I'm not supposed to be able to do in the first place?"

"To keep overly ambitious young women from hurting themselves and endangering others, I assume."

"No." Trysten shook her head as she stepped back from the table as if to put some distance between herself and the laws. "They don't mean 'men' as in *men*. It is to mean *people*, all people in the village. Whoever wrote it down wrote it down wrong. They *had* to have. Why else would they forbid women if women can't even—"

"That's enough, Trysten. We had an agreement."

"No," Trysten said with a shake of her head. "That's not what they meant. Show me where it says that women aren't allowed to participate. Show me where women are strictly forbidden!"

"That's enough!" her father said. His knuckles blanched slightly as his hand clutched the book. "The law forbids it, and so I forbid it. Both as the dragoneer, and as your father."

"My father? No, I'm of age. I went through the rites. I'm an adult, and you can not—"

"You are an unmarried woman, then!" Mardoc said as he turned in his chair with obvious effort. His face burned red. Despite the chill back in his den, away from the fireplace in the receiving room, beads of sweat dotted his brow. "I am responsible for you, regardless of your age, until you are married and have a family of your own. You are not to be part of the consideration, and even if you were to participate, it would not matter because as the dragoneer I am telling you that Paege will succeed me, and my decision is final! I will not have you complicating things to satisfy some whim of yours. It is for the good of the weyr, the good of the village, and the good of the kingdom that I tell you no! And even if you can't get it through that stubborn head you inherited from your mother, I'm telling you no for your own good as well."

Trysten's mouth fell open. She took another step away from him. He gripped the back of his chair. His other hand lay flat against the table, ready to push himself up. The book continued to lay in the middle of the table, looking wholly innocuous and innocent and not at all like the trap that had just swallowed up her dreams.

She shook her head. "I am of age. I am under the protection of the weyr. I made the formal declaration. Nowhere does it say women can't be in the consideration. You have to consider me."

"Take it up with the next dragoneer. This conversation is over. Your father tells you no, and that is final."

Her head hummed with fury, enough that the room appeared to vibrate slightly as if the entire weyr were a great bell that had been dealt a blow with a heavy iron mallet.

Her hand fell to her side. "It is your duty to protect the law. And what is the kingdom—"

"Don't you speak to me of duty, Trysten. I have given everything to uphold this kingdom." His right hand slipped from the table and came to rest on his twisted leg. "I am your father, and no law lies above that responsibility. You will not be chosen, and your presence would only complicate the current situation. That is final."

Trysten swallowed hard. Her hands balled into fists. She turned and ran from his den, bolted through the receiving room, and thundered down the stairs as if to crumble the entirety of the weyr beneath her feet.

Chapter 5

Their cottage stood empty. Mother was nowhere in sight, and neither was her bow, which normally hung above the mantel. She must be out hunting hares alongside the river.

Rather than wait for her mother's return, Trysten hurried out into the lanes of the village. Villagers called out as she passed to ask how her father was doing. Word was out that he had gone to the weyr for the first time since the accident.

At the edge of the village, Trysten descended a path along a slope. Below, the River Gul burbled as it rushed over its stones and away from the Cadwaller mountains, eager to escape from the Western Kingdom and hurry on out to the wider rivers of the eastern plains. In the tall grasses that straddled the river, Trysten caught sight of her mother near a copse of bushes. She held her bow in one hand, and an arrow nocked in the string with her other hand. She considered the base of a bush, waiting.

Trysten plunged into the grass. The sound of the leaves rustling drew Caron's attention. She lowered her bow, slipped her arrow back into the quiver, and came at a jog through the grasses.

"What is it?" Caron called. "Has something happened to your father?"

Trysten's jaw tightened at the question. Once she reached her mother, she stopped and leaned forward. Her hands rested on her knees as she panted.

"Trysten?"

"I told… I told Father… that I want to be in the consideration."

Caron lowered her bow to her side. Her shoulders slumped. "Oh, Little Heart—"

"Don't!" Trysten snapped. "Don't call me that. I am of age now. And it's my right. It's my right to be in the consideration. I am under the protection of this weyr."

Caron's face softened along with her shoulders. "But women aren't allowed to participate in the consideration."

"It doesn't say that women *can't*. It doesn't say anything at all about women. But he says that women can't even *be* dragoneers, that we can't connect with dragons like the men can. But he's wrong! And if women can't bond with the alphas, then why is there a law to forbid it? It makes no sense! But he won't even let me try! He's already decided that Paege will be the next dragoneer. He's already decided it before the consideration has even begun."

Caron lifted her palm in a manner to suggest Trysten calm herself. "It is his choice to make."

Trysten resisted the urge to stomp her foot, to let out a frustrated grunt that would undermine her claim to be of age. She peered over the long grass, whipped and whirled into rolling patterns of shifting green by the winds cast from the winter storms in the mountains. Between the gusts, the River Gul babbled, let out a low chuckle as if amused by her simple, inconsequential frustrations.

Trysten looked back to her mother. "But he won't even let me try. That's the worst part. He's still holding the consideration, and most of the hordesmen will compete, but he won't even let me try. How fair is that?"

"It's not fair at all. But it is life." Caron reached out and touched her daughter on the side of her shoulder. "Your father is the dragoneer. It his duty to choose his successor, just as his grandfather chose him."

Trysten shook her head. "His grandfather didn't choose him. Aeronwind did. It's the alpha who chooses the dragoneer, and Elevera isn't going to choose Paege. He's not… He doesn't know the dragons like I do. He doesn't… *feel* them the way that I do."

Caron's hand dropped back to her side. "You think Elevera will choose you?"

Trysten looked away again. Heat flushed over her face. "Why are you choosing his side? Don't you think it's unfair that he won't let me try out just because I'm a woman?"

Caron didn't respond right away. "I think it's fair that he doesn't want to see his daughter hurt. I think it's fair to not want her to suffer like he has, especially for nothing at all. Paege will be chosen. The dragoneer knows the dragons better than anyone."

Trysten lifted an eyebrow and glared at her mother. Caron cracked a grin, then attempted to smother it.

"What?"

"Nothing," Caron said with a shake of her head. "It's just that you remind me of your father with that expression."

The raised eyebrow dropped away. Trysten did her best to adopt a stony, impassible face.

"If the dragoneer is the one who knows the dragons best, then I should be dragoneer."

Caron frowned and looked up the hill, to the long, arched hall of the weyr.

"Can you talk to him?" Trysten asked. "I just want a chance to compete in the consideration. I want to show him what I can do. If he wants to choose Paege, that's his right, but he has to let me compete. Please, Mother. Talk to him."

Caron returned her attention. A gust of wind stirred several loose ends of blonde hair about her face, wisps not long enough to be caught up in the braids she wore.

She shook her head. "I can't, Little Heart."

"Why not?"

"Because it is his decision to make. The other hordesmen are owed the right of the consideration. They've flown with your father into the fighting season. You have not. And since you will not be chosen regardless, I can see why he would not want to risk you, or even the safety of another dragon. Especially after what happened to Aeronwind."

Despite herself, Trysten's mouth fell open. "How could you say that? How can you side with him? Don't you think it's unfair to be kept out of the consideration? Why don't the laws apply to me—to us—just because we're women?"

Caron shook her head. "It's not because you're a woman; it is because you are his daughter."

Trysten shook her head and planted her hands on her hips. "That's not true! So if any other woman in the village were to make a declaration, he'd let her into the consideration?"

Caron's gaze fell to the grasses between them. Whether she found an answer there or not, she looked back at Trysten. A stiff gust pushed her back, and she leaned into it, refusing to let the wind make her shift a foot forward and brace herself.

"I don't know, but probably not. Your father has sworn to uphold tradition. He has sworn to uphold the things that make the kingdom what it has been for centuries. These things are important to him. He puts his life on the line every time he takes the village sword and flies off into battle. He would die for these things, for everyone in this village. For anyone in the kingdom. How can you expect him not to take our traditions seriously?"

Trysten glanced up to the weyr, then out into the space between the village and her mother. A man and a woman led a mule along the seemingly endless road that ran down into the low plains. The mule was weighed down with packs and bags that swayed with each of the animal's steps. How long had it taken that couple and their mule to come from the mother city to trade goods for Aerona's wool and knitted clothing? It would do her no good to descend into the mother city and seek out the Dragon Master. He would do nothing to help her cause anyway. If she couldn't find an ally in her own mother, then there was no ally to be had.

"Here," Caron said as she presented the bow.

Trysten took it without thinking, without questioning. Her mother then slung the strap of the quiver over her head and held it out to Trysten. "I am sorry, and I wish I could help you, but you were born in the time and place in which I was ready to give birth to you, and there was nothing that could change that. The world may be unfair, but it is not immutable. Join Paege. Support him. Become his closest ally. Use your special bond with the dragons to support him. He will need the help. Perhaps he will make a hordesman of you, and when the time is right, you may yet have a chance at being dragoneer."

"When Paege dies?"

Caron glanced up at the weyr. "Or Elevera."

Trysten shivered at the thought. She then held up the bow and quiver. "And what am I to do with these?"

Caron nodded at the brambles behind her. "Take your frustration to the hares, then bring dinner back to the house."

Trysten let out a sigh lost to the wind as Caron stepped past. She stopped, reached out, and drew her daughter into an embrace.

"It's not fair, Little Heart. Not at all. But if life was fair, what would you have to strive for?"

"I'd strive to be a better dragoneer," Trysten said, her voice muffled in her mother's woolen vest.

A grating, clacking noise peppered the wind. Trysten and Caron turned to look up at the weyr. A minute later, Elevera, gold against the gray clouds, leaped out of the end of the hall and into the air. Though they were too distant to make out the rider, Trysten knew it was Paege. Behind him, several more dragons took to the sky. The multicolored dragons contrasted greatly with the gray of the clouds, and Trysten's heart nearly stuttered to a stop in awe as she watched the patches of color climb and shift, writhe and rise, circling back, forming a wide ring of dragons and riders in the sky.

Caron stepped back. "I plan to make enough stew to feed all the weyrmen. Hunt accordingly." She began her return to the village between glances at the sky.

Elevera twisted her wings, nearly went sideways, and began to spiral back down to the village. She then folded her wings back and started to plummet. The other riders did the same, but none of the other dragons were as bright or as large as Elevera, and so they were little but the fading tail of a shooting star.

A shout and a snap pierced the wind. A dole of doves poured out of a pen and rose into the sky like smoke that would not dissipate. Elevera tucked her wings further back and dropped even faster. Her neck stretched out long and straight as if to make an arrow of herself, and the heights above served as the string that snapped her into her downward motion. At the top of her back, just beneath where her neck met her shoulders, a man clung to her, his feet buried in the stirrups of his saddle. His hands were tucked underneath him, but Trysten knew he had the reins twisted up around his wrists. The reins were more about keeping him in the saddle than they were about giving the illusion of control over a beta dragon.

With a flick of her wings, Elevera darted to the side of the dole, then snapped her wings open wide. She swooped down and around the dole.

The doves, startled by the dragon below and then before them, shifted and began to climb to their right. More dragons fell from the sky and snapped their wings open to startle the doves into different directions, herding the dole to where Paege had indicated.

Trysten's breath caught at the display. If the sun had broken through the clouds and shone on the outstretched wings of copper and silver, maroon and emerald green and a pale blue, she would have dropped to her knees beneath the power of such a sight.

It was *her* place. She had grown up in the village and never had she stepped foot beyond the pastures that swaddled it. But it was not her home. Her home was up there, in the air and skies. The sight of it filled her with a longing that brought an ache to her teeth and dampness to her eyes. Her toes curled inside her boots as if trying to slip free of the constraints of gravity.

Elevera swung around, flapped her wings and gained altitude. She spread her wings, tilted to catch the wind, and let it thrust her back, careening toward the doves like a net. At the last minute, she flapped her wings once and shifted her body in a fluid, serpentine motion that sent the doves scattering to the south. Two of the smaller dragons dropped down and sent the doves flying to the east again.

Trysten glanced at the bow and quiver still clutched in her hands, then up at the dole of doves spiraling in a tight knot under the harassment of the dragons.

It was a lucky day to be a hare, and not so much a dove.

She slung the quiver over her shoulder and headed for the weyr on the hill above.

Chapter 6

The weyr was mostly empty when Trysten arrived. Likely, the weyrmen stood outside watching the sport with her father. The stalls, too, were mostly empty, though a few dragons remained behind.

Trysten jogged down the aisle to survey the mounts that remained. She stopped before the stall of the green dragon that had tripped her that morning. He was a courier dragon, a bit larger than a horse, but small even for a male. He was mainly used for errands, for flights to the mother city and back. He was a brilliant, emerald green, but he had never demonstrated the ability to assert himself like the other, larger dragons in battle exercises. She had seen him in flight, however, and what he lacked in brawn he made up for with speed and nimbleness.

"Want to take a flight, Ulbeg?" Trysten asked.

The dragon flicked his head slightly as if he understood.

Trysten grinned, then retrieved riding gear from a nearby rack. The dragon stood in his stall and watched as Trysten threw a saddle blanket over his back and smoothed out the wrinkles. As she reached for a stool, the dragon crouched, going down onto the elbows of his forelegs. Trysten's eyes widened a bit at the gesture as if the dragon not only understood but was impatient to get underway. Trysten patted the dragon at the base of his neck, just above where it met the shoulder. The scales beneath her hand were hard, tough, and warm, like living stone.

Ulbeg let out a soft sigh, nearly a hiss. Trysten threw the saddle up and over the dragon's back. He immediately stood and cleared access for her to reach the straps and buckles that would keep the saddle in place no matter what maneuvers the dragon made in the sky.

A man cleared his throat.

Trysten looked up. A weyrman named Bolsar stood at the head of the stall, arms crossed over his chest. "I don't think your father would approve."

Trysten returned her attention to the straps and buckles. "I'm just getting Ulbeg ready."

"For what?"

Trysten glanced at the man again. He appeared to be irritated as if his time were being wasted.

"For a flight."

"And who will be flying him? Your father left us orders that you are not permitted to be around the dragons until after the consideration."

Trysten's brow hardened at that news. Her teeth clenched. Her hands drew the slack of the leather straps through the buckles with a little more force than necessary. The well-oiled straps creaked. Ulbeg didn't budge.

"Surely that doesn't apply to Ulbeg? Who would fly him in the consideration?"

"I don't care who does what with him. Your father said you are not to touch any of the dragons. Now please step out of there before I have to go fetch him."

Trysten fed the tongue of the next strap through the buckle. To the wilds with it. She wanted her father to see her determination.

"Fetch him, then."

"He's out supervising the games. They're running a round of dole herding."

"I saw."

"Wait," Bolsar said. "Why do you have a bow and quiver? What is it that you think you're going to do?"

"I think I'm going to take Ulbeg for a flight. If you want to tell my father, then I suggest you step to it. I won't be in here much longer."

"Now Trysten, if I have to go out and fetch your father while he's supervising the hordesmen, you know how irritated he'll be," Bolsar pleaded with her as if she were a child.

Trysten tightened the next buckle. "I don't plan on hiding from him."

Bolsar took a step forward. Ulbeg swept his head down past the weyrman. Trysten looked up in time to see the light and the shimmering heat of a small puff of fire as Bolsar backpedaled a few steps. His eyes grew wide, and his face pale. He glanced from Ulbeg to Trysten and back.

Ulbeg lowered his head and held his jaw open. Another hiss escaped the normally meek dragon.

Trysten reached out and placed a hand along the base of the dragon's neck, as much to calm him as to reassure herself that it was there, that she had seen Ulbeg fend off the weyrman with the threat of fire. Would he hurt Bolsar if the man tried to physically stop her from taking the dragon?

"Did you...?" Bolsar asked.

Trysten's hand dropped away from the dragon's neck and resumed the practice of buckling up the saddle. "I'm taking Ulbeg for a flight," Trysten said. "You best go tell my father."

Bolsar stood a moment more and then took off down the aisle. He'd have help in a mere few minutes.

With renewed concentration, Trysten finished strapping up the saddle. Again, when she bent down to grasp the stool and bring it close, the dragon lowered himself to his elbows.

"You're too kind, Ulbeg. A real gem, you know that?" She patted the dragon on his neck, thrust a foot into the stirrup and pulled herself into the saddle.

Ulbeg rose almost the moment Trysten's bottom hit the leather. The dragon trotted forward in the awkward way of dragons as she hurried to fasten a leather strap around herself that held her to the saddle.

Ahead, several weyrmen advanced down the aisle at a trot. At the sight of Trysten and Ulbeg, they shouted for her to stop and for Ulbeg to stay. The dragon snapped his wings open as he tossed his head. The muscles in his shoulders writhed beneath Trysten, and she clenched the lip of the saddle before her and leaned her weight forward as she dug in with her heels.

In response, Ulbeg folded his wings along his back and lowered his head. A second later, he crouched. The muscles of the dragon shivered with pent-up energy, a barely-restrained excitement.

A weyrman pointed back to Ulbeg's stall. "Take him back there now, Trysten. Bolsar is seeking out your father. You don't want to make things worse for yourself, do you?"

Trysten cocked an eyebrow at the man. Though it was true that she didn't want to make things worse for herself, she didn't see how following his orders would make anything better. Her father had already told her as much when he insisted that she would never succeed him as dragoneer. No, if he would not allow her in the consideration, then this would be the only way to show him and the other hordesmen what she could do on the back of a dragon.

With a spur from her heels, Trysten leaned forward and rested her weight on the lip of the saddle. Ulbeg crouched. His wings flipped open with a snap that whipped the air back. The weyrmen paused.

"Ulbeg!" one of the men called out. He held his hand up, his palm out at the end of his arm almost as much to brace himself as to command the dragon to remain still.

"Fly," Trysten said and patted the dragon on his neck.

Ulbeg leaped off the floor of the weyr. His wings beat down and back. Trysten's fingers curled around the lip of the saddle. She crouched closer to the back of the dragon's neck as he took to the air, undulated briefly, then brought his wings back up and thrust them down again.

Two of the weyrmen broke from their stance and rushed to either side of the promenade. The weyrman who held up his hand stood his ground for a second more, then dropped to the floor as the green dragon flew past. His wingspan barely cleared the promenade, but the smaller dragon was able to manage the tight quarters before he reached the open door at the end of the vaulted hall.

Gray sky and dragons waited beyond.

Chapter 7

With a roar, Ulbeg shot into the sky and aimed for the horde. Trysten allowed herself a small glimpse of the ground below. At the edge of the weyr yard, a small group of men pointed at her and Ulbeg. It was Bolsar, and before him stood her father.

Trysten eyed the dole of doves, which was little more than a swirl of dust kept aloft by the circling dragons and their broad, sweeping wings. The distance between them and Ulbeg bled away quickly. Trysten hadn't given the dragon any commands, yet he aimed straight for the center of the dole as if he wanted nothing more than a dove for himself. She tightened the grip of her thighs on the saddle as she reached for her bow. The snugness of the strap about her waist reassured her that she would stay in her seat. She slid an arrow from the quiver, slotted it in the string, and drew back to take aim at the doves.

The swirl of dragons had widened as the others took notice of Ulbeg and Trysten. The knot of doves began to loosen with the diverted attention of the dragons and their riders. Several doves broke away.

"That's it!" Trysten yelled into the wind. "Faster, boy. Faster!"

They were close enough to see Paege motioning from the back of Elevera. He signaled for the hordesmen to draw their dragons back around, to resume formation. The horde tightened up, drew in. The doves responded in kind.

Then the horde formed a ring around the doves, a flying wall of dragons that blocked Trysten off. Two of the smaller mounts broke from formation. One rose up, and the other dived down to keep the dole from fleeing in either direction.

With her heels, Trysten motioned for Ulbeg to go up. The dragon rose higher. Paege tried to respond by commanding the hordesmen to slant the circle, to present a wall to Trysten. The nimble Ulbeg climbed faster than the others, however, and then with a downward kick from her heels, Ulbeg arched his back, tucked his wings, and began a controlled dive.

Trysten yanked back on the arrow, took aim, and let it fly. As she reached for a second arrow, the first one arced down and disappeared into the cloud of doves. A dove fell from the sky.

She slotted a second arrow into place and let go. The arrow sped away as the circle of dragons started to break. The cloud of doves began to scatter. Still, the arrow found a mark and another dove fell from the sky.

By the time she reached back, grabbed a third arrow, and slotted it into the bowstring, Ulbeg dove through the dissipating ring of dragons. A flurry of feathered wings beat in panic all around her. Ulbeg snatched a bird from the sky. Gray feathers streaked back from his jaw.

She twisted around in the saddle. Her left heel dug into Ulbeg's side as she sought purchase. The dragon flipped his right wing out full and allowed the air's resistance to swing him around sharply to the right. Trysten lifted the bow to the sky and scanned the calamity behind them. The hordesmen had broken formation. Doves scattered in every direction. No clear shot presented itself. She returned the arrow to its quiver.

As she did so, Elevera cut a sharp, undulating turn through the air above. The large dragon began to descend toward her and Ulbeg. She dropped hard and fast. Paege lifted a fist into the air and flung it about in a circle to signal for everyone to form a holding pattern.

Trysten's eyes flicked down to Elevera's face. A sudden sensation of both joy and envy struck her. Trysten grinned broadly. With a tug on the lip of the saddle and a kick of her heels, she sent Ulbeg back up into the air, after the closest dove.

As Ulbeg climbed, his wings beating as if the air itself were but a ladder to be scaled, Trysten scanned the ground for her father. Already, two weyrmen ran through the pastures in the direction of the doves she'd taken down. How nice it would be if a little sun shone, so that she might see the shadows of the dragons on the ground, sliding over everything. As a girl riding with either of her parents, she was entranced by the sight of the dragon's shadow shimmering across the ground like a fish flying beneath the undulating waters of the River Gul. Unlike the fish, however, the dragons were not contained by river banks. They owned the air. The sky. While on their backs, Trysten felt like there was nothing she couldn't do.

Elevera dropped down before them, wings spread wide and claws extended. Despite herself, Trysten let out a little yelp as Ulbeg dove to avoid colliding with the larger beta dragon. He banked back and began to spiral to the ground. As one of the subordinate males, he wouldn't dare disobey the beta's order to go to ground.

Trysten glanced up. She couldn't see Paege atop Elevera, but the gold dragon held her place and drifted in lazy circles above Ulbeg. She didn't even bother to look down and make sure her orders were being followed.

Below, the weyrmen had forgotten the fallen doves. Instead, they ran to the spot of pasture where they expected Ulbeg to touch down.

Ulbeg would likely pay a price for disobeying the beta, and Trysten would certainly pay a price for defying her father. But this was her chance to show them all what she could do, and it would likely be the only chance Ulbeg ever had to show what he was capable of as well.

"How about it, Ulbeg?" Trysten yelled into the wind. She patted the dragon's neck. "Want to make the most of it?"

Ulbeg tossed his head back, up at Elevera, and let out a growl and a shot of flame, a puff of smoke that indicated his dissatisfaction.

Trysten grinned. "That's my boy!"

She slung the bow over her shoulder, then gripped the lip of the saddle and yanked up with all her might as she raked her heels up and back along the dragon's side. Ulbeg let out a roar and thrust his wings down with power that surprised Trysten, coming from such a small dragon. He rose back into the air.

Below, the weyrmen trotted to a stop and pointed up.

Above, Elevera let out an answering roar, deeper and louder and longer; a peal of thunder that meant nothing but business.

"Not today, lady!" Trysten hollered up at her beloved dragon. She kicked Ulbeg's side again and yanked on the saddle's lip, driving the dragon up as fast as he could go.

Elevera swung out in a wide half-moon, then tilted her wings at an angle. She soared down in a smooth arc and made her way toward Trysten and Ulbeg. Her jaw dropped open, and she let out another roar.

Ulbeg answered. Flame licked over his snout as he climbed into the wind.

Above, on Elevera's back, Paege pointed at Trysten, then swung his hand down to the ground over and over, emphatically gesturing for her to land. The tassels on the shoulders of his leather riding armor streamed out behind him as his mount picked up speed.

Trysten gasped. Paege looked like the dragoneer in his armor, atop Elevera. He was still too far away for Trysten to see his face, but she imagined it to be stern, full of confidence and assurance. He was giving an order, and there was no one in the village, no one under the protection of the Aerona weyr, who would dare disobey an order from the dragoneer.

Well, almost no one.

As Elevera approached, she spread her wings and reared in the air. Her tail flicked out and lashed to make herself appear as big and menacing as possible.

The muscles beneath Trysten shifted. The left wing stiffened. Ulbeg was about to defer, to swing away and take to the ground after all.

"No you don't!" Trysten hollered. She released the lip of the saddle and thrust herself forward. Her arms wrapped around the dragon's neck as her heels dug in and pushed back. She kicked again with the sides of both of her boots to make sure Ulbeg understood.

But before she finished, the dragon had straightened out and regained his posture as if the signals weren't necessary. He plunged forward, let out an answering roar, and swerved only at the last second. He undulated and dipped down to avoid colliding with Elevera. As he passed beneath her bottom claws, he reached out with his jaw and nipped Elevera's tail in passing.

"Wilds!" Trysten gasped. Her eyes widened at such a show of defiance. What trouble had she gotten Ulbeg into?

A shuffle of air and the leathery flap of wings above and behind her indicated Elevera was moving. She glanced back to see the dragon drop, using gravity to quickly regain the speed she lost in her display of might.

Now was Trysten's chance.

Still clutching Ulbeg's neck with her arms, she tugged to the left as she dug in with her right heel. The dragon turned sharply, and as if he knew and agreed with her idea, curled tightly in the air, then dropped as Elevera spread her wings wide to catch the wind off the mountains and push her back up to Ulbeg's elevation.

The beta dragon's surprise hit Trysten like a blast of snow as Elevera turned and eyed Ulbeg.

The wind off the mountains was no longer sufficient for Elevera. She pushed her great wings down, shoving the air and the altitude beneath her as she climbed to meet Trysten and Ulbeg. At her shoulders, Paege still motioned for Trysten to land as if she simply hadn't noticed his command.

Seconds before crashing into the larger dragon, Trysten pulled up on Ulbeg's neck. He set his wings out straight and tilted them up slightly. They slid right over the heads of Elevera and Paege as the gold dragon roared and Paege ducked.

Trysten whooped. She raised a fist to the air and sat up, her back straight and tall. With her other hand, she gripped the lip of the saddle and spurred Ulbeg to curve upward on his momentum and bank to the left.

The momentum, in addition to Ulbeg's size, allowed him to climb higher than Elevera, who still rose into the air while twisting her neck back to watch them.

With a shove on the lip of the saddle and a downward kicking motion against his sides, Trysten sent Ulbeg diving once more, this time at an oblique angle that would rob Elevera of a chance to defend herself.

Ulbeg let out another roar. Flames licked over his snout again. Wisps of heat passed over Trysten's face and her broad grin. As cold as it was in the air, the hammering of her heart and the sparks of excitement leaping through her muscles kept her warm and going.

Elevera attempted to twist herself around, to orientate herself so that she might flip onto her side and present her claws to Ulbeg and Trysten. With a flick of his wings, Ulbeg slid through the air. The smaller, more nimble dragon matched her maneuvers.

They approached close enough for Trysten to see the wide expression of shock on Paege's face. He knew she had him. If this had been a real aerial battle, then she, on her courier dragon, would have the dragoneer at her mercy.

To finish the exercise off, she gave a snap to either side of Ulbeg's neck with the butts of her palms. Before she did so, however, the dragon already leveled out his flight. As they shot past, Ulbeg twisted, folded his wings up, and slipped past by mere inches over the top of Elevera from her right flank to her left shoulder.

Great joy flooded Trysten, and she knew without having to look that Ulbeg had succeeded in snatching one of the tassels from Paege's uniform. He was done. She and Ulbeg had won.

She turned to the ground and looked in her father's direction. Even if she couldn't begin to see his face from this altitude, she wanted to picture it, to imagine the warring looks of anger and pride on his face.

Rage engulfed Trysten. It wrapped around her like the fingers of flame from a sudden fire, and then pain wracked her. She gritted her teeth and clenched the lip of the saddle as Ulbeg's muscles writhed beneath her. He let out a roar. His spine bucked. It was his tail. Even before she glanced behind her, she knew it was his tail.

It swished back and forth behind them in agitation. She couldn't see what had happened, but looking back into the face of Elevera as she spread her wings and began to slope back down to the weyr, Trysten knew and understood that the beta dragon had nipped Ulbeg as they slipped past. She had taken a bite of the smaller dragon's tail.

No damage was evident, but Ulbeg still swung the tail back and forth, much like Trysten would shake her finger if she had accidentally hit it with a hammer.

She glared at Elevera.

Elevera turned away, and Paege, one tassel remaining on his left shoulder, stared a second longer and then turned away as well.

The triumph of her victory dissipated into the thin air and gray clouds.

Paege signaled for the horde to return to the weyr. Above, the dragons and their riders began to break formation and drift down to the edge of the village, toward the long, vaulted barn that dominated Aerona. No longer corralled by the dragons, the doves scattered toward each corner of the sky.

The horde descended. Below, the weyrmen and her father returned to the weyr as well. There was nothing more for Trysten to accomplish in the sky. With her heels, she urged Ulbeg to circle around once and then descend to the yard.

Chapter 8

Once Ulbeg touched the dirt and stone in the wide yard outside the weyr, Trysten dismounted and leaped the small distance from the stirrup to the ground. She laid a hand upon the dragon's side and turned her attention to his tail. He held it up slightly, near the end, curling it up a bit like a dog's tail.

The gray light of the sky caught a wet patch near the end of the tail. Blood trickled from a few spots where the dragon's scales had been broken.

"Oh, Ulbeg," Trysten cooed. She stroked the dragon's side. "I'm so sorry."

"What in the wilds did you think you were trying to do!" Bolsar yelled as he trotted into the yard. "My word, it's a miracle you didn't get yourself or someone else killed!"

Ulbeg swung his neck around at the man's agitation. His jaw opened, and he appeared ready to issue a hiss.

"Come on," Trysten said as she turned her back on the weyrman. "Let's get you fixed up." She reached under the saddle and pulled out a length of leather that would allow her to lead the dragon, as long as the dragon was willing to be led.

"Trysten!" Bolsar yelled again, his voice much closer.

She led Ulbeg toward the weyr. As they approached, some of the younger weyrmen who had gathered at the doorway to watch the antics now stepped aside. They eyed Trysten in silence. One of the young men swallowed and glanced up at Ulbeg who held his head high. For the wilds, Trysten wished she could read people as well as she could read dragons.

She kept her gaze stone-faced and focused ahead as she gave the lead a tug to hurry Ulbeg along.

With a whoosh of air and a long, low growl, Elevera landed in the yard behind them. Ulbeg and Trysten each looked over their shoulders. Elevera spread her wings wide and reared up on her hind legs. Paege, clinging to the saddle, looked both frightened and angry as the large dragon ignored his own orders, and instead, tried to reassert her dominance over the smaller male.

Ulbeg hung his head and looked away. He gave a slight shake, kind of like a dog might do to dry itself. Trysten glared back at the gold dragon.

"Behave yourself!" she called across the yard. "He was following my orders."

Elevera dropped onto all fours. Her wings folded back into themselves, and Paege looked positively relieved.

"What was that?" Bolsar called as he trotted up to Trysten.

"Nothing," she said as she turned away.

"I would have a word with you, young lady," Bolsar said. He attempted to step before Trysten's path.

"It'll have to wait a minute. Ulbeg has been hurt. Elevera nipped his tail."

Bolsar crossed his arms before himself. "I thought I saw that. Elevera told him to return to the ground. She can't allow one of the horde to ignore her. She's the beta, soon to be alpha. It's more important than ever that she maintain dominance among the horde, and you, young lady, aren't helping a wild thing by encouraging such behavior."

Trysten fumed. Ulbeg's own fire seemed to rise in her. "Where's Galelin?"

"Galelin?" Bolsar glanced over Trysten's shoulder as if just now realizing for the first time that the old dragon healer might be needed. He shook his head. "And why did you take this dragon out of all the horde? He's not built for battle. He's far too small to be out sparring with the others."

Trysten turned back at the younger weyrmen still gathered and gawking at the weyr door instead of watching the other dragons drop into the yard.

The dragons were always to come first, and they should have rushed out to take Ulbeg from her, and the other dragons from the other riders, and lead them all back to their stalls. The weyrmen stood frozen by inaction as if waiting to be told what to do.

"Go," Trysten yelled back to them. "Find Galelin and tell him to come to Ulbeg's stall. He's been hurt."

The young men traded glances amongst themselves.

"By the wilds, young lady!" Bolsar said as he planted his fists against his hips. "I am the head weyrman around here. You will address me before you order my staff around."

"Now!" Trysten yelled at the young men.

They all turned to Bolsar, who glared back at them. A young weyrman took several steps toward the yard, then peered back at Bolsar. The man gave a grudging nod, and off he went.

Bolsar stood his ground for a moment. He stared at the dragon's tail where blood darkened the scales. He shook his head, then trotted forward.

"I'll take him," he said as he reached for the lead. His gaze shot up to the dragon as if to check whether or not Ulbeg might object to him again.

Trysten clutched the lead tighter and gave another tug.

"Trysten! I'll take Ulbeg. You, you are in deep trouble. Your father is livid. You should wait for him in his den."

Ahead, Aeronwind lifted her head and watched them over the half-wall of her stall.

"Trysten!" Bolsar grabbed the lead. Ulbeg whipped his head around and issued a growl.

Bolsar let go. He stepped back. His gaze looked wild and unsure as he looked back and forth between the dragon and Trysten. She glared at him as well. The dragons always came first. They should see to Ulbeg before meting out her punishment. At least when Elevera tried to pull rank, it was among her own kind. Bolsar was nothing but a frustrated stable master who was miffed that a girl wouldn't listen to him.

She looked back to Aeronwind, who now rested her head atop the half-wall. She stared at them with mild curiosity as if wondering how Ulbeg had gotten mixed up in all of this ridiculousness with the humans. Ulbeg himself hung his head low and looked a bit chagrined as if he, too, was starting to realize that perhaps he had gotten a little carried away.

Trysten reached out and patted the dragon on his neck. She pushed her shoulders back. No, they hadn't gotten carried away. The nip on Ulbeg's tail needed to be addressed, but it wasn't serious. And if her father had let her join the consideration, then she wouldn't have had to take such rash actions. Taking Ulbeg out to spar with Paege had been her only way to stand up for herself.

As Bolsar went on about what a reckless stunt it was that she had pulled, Trysten reached out and patted Ulbeg on the neck again. "I'm so sorry. I didn't mean for you to get hurt."

Ulbeg bobbed his head once as if he understood.

Chapter 9

Once Trysten had Ulbeg in the stall, she searched the faces milling about the weyr for that of Galelin's. The healer was still not in the weyr. Bolsar stood outside the stall, arms crossed, brow scrunched.

"Wait here," Trysten said and gave Ulbeg another pat on the neck. As she left the stall, Bolsar stepped back and turned slightly toward the other end of the weyr, where the stairs to her father's den waited.

Instead of heading to her father's den, Trysten went the other direction.

"Where do you think you are going?" Bolsar called after her.

"Ulbeg needs help, and I don't know where Galelin is," Trysten called back.

"He's on his way. You best get up to your father's den before you make things worse for yourself or the weyr."

Trysten opened a cabinet in a storage area in the center of the weyr. She pulled out some linen and salve. As she carried these back, she caught sight of her father limping along, through the other end of the weyr, among the hordesmen leading their dragons back to their stalls.

He said nothing. He made no motion. He merely maintained eye contact and kept moving at a steady pace with his cumbersome staff, and Trysten's heart nearly snapped for the sight.

He should have been leading Aeronwind, his dragon, with his shoulders back and straight, his chest broad and seemingly as tough as the dragons he led. The man heading toward her was still strong and willful but broken as well. By the wilds, she had been reckless. Not only with Ulbeg, but with her father. He'd been through so much since the accident. And here she was creating havoc and chaos while he worked toward a smooth transition.

She dodged into Ulbeg's stall and fell to her knees beside the dragon.

"Bring me clean water," Trysten called over her shoulder.

"What?" Bolsar asked. "I'm not a weyrboy—"

"Bring me some clean water for this dragon's wounds!" she snapped.

Bolsar glanced from Trysten to the foot of the hall, where her father and the other hordesmen were. He grumbled, then moved on.

A moment later, he returned with a pail of water and plunked it down beside Trysten. Water sloshed over the sides and wet the leg of her pants. While Bolsar slunk back, she plunged some strips of linen into the water, wrung them out, and began to wipe away the dried blood on Ulbeg's tail.

"How is he?" her father asked from the head of the stall.

Trysten peered over her shoulder. Mardoc's staff leaned against the stall's wall. His left hand gripped the top edge. His face was solid and expressionless.

"Elevera gave his tail a nip. It's nothing serious."

"I told her to wait for you—" Bolsar began.

"Quiet," Mardoc said. "Now, Trysten, why did Elevera give him a nip in the tail?"

Trysten took in a deep breath, and beneath the scents of hay and dirt, she hoped to bury the urge to sigh.

"He disobeyed Elevera's orders." She dunked the strip of linen into the pail and began to wrap another strip around the wound.

"Leave it," Mardoc said. "I want Galelin to take a look."

"It's nothing serious."

"I said to leave it. Galelin is the horde healer. I want him to look at it."

Trysten dropped the length of linen to the ground. She pushed herself up and turned around.

"If you would have—"

"Why should I have given you a chance? We have already discussed this. I have already given you my reasons and told you why you cannot be the dragoneer. And so what do you do? You disobey my orders. You act with reckless disregard for yourself, your father, and that poor dragon there, not to mention Elevera and Paege. You put yourself in danger. You put all these hordesmen and their dragons into danger. What were you thinking when you shot those arrows? You could have hit any—"

"But I didn't."

"You got lucky. But your luck ran out, didn't it?" Mardoc nodded to Ulbeg's tail. As he did so, Galelin squeezed through the crowd of hordesmen and weyrmen gathered around the dragon's stall.

Although heat flushed up Trysten's neck and face, she held her chin up. Her jaw tightened. She took a deep breath and tried to stretch out her lungs, which felt bound in tight leather strips.

"Ulbeg is injured because of your stubborn recklessness," Mardoc said. "And because of your ignorance. What were you thinking by taking this dragon out? Ulbeg is too small for battle exercises, much less sparring. He has no experience. He doesn't know how to participate. If he did, he would have known to go to ground when both Paege and Elevera ordered him to. You endangered him and yourself as well."

Galelin gave a small shove and moved Trysten out of his light before he knelt next to the injured dragon's tail.

"You have shown me and all the hordesmen and all those out watching your stunts that I was well within my own rights to deny you a saddle in the consideration, even if the law didn't already forbid it. You have proven that you lack the judgment and the experience to fly with the hordesmen, let alone lead them."

Trysten swallowed hard. The words rained down upon her, and she wanted nothing more than to lean back, to place a hand on the haunch of the dragon and steady herself. Instead, she lifted her chin just a fraction higher.

"You are banished from the weyr, Trysten. You are not to set foot in here again unless you are with me. Do you understand?"

A wave of dizziness threatened to overtake Trysten. Her heart fluttered at the sentence. "If you had—"

"No," her father said with a single shake of his head. "Hordesmen do not offer excuses, and if you wish to pretend that you can be one, then you can pretend to act like one. Leave. Go back home. I will speak to you further there."

Trysten stood a few seconds more. Despite herself, despite her effort to lock her eyes on her father's and not look away, she let her gaze slip to the other men who stood about with hands on their hips or arms crossed over their chests. Each of them appeared angry and agitated. Bolsar himself looked as red as she felt, as if he was not only angry at her for ignoring him, but also at Mardoc for denying him the opportunity to dress her down himself.

"Go."

Trysten glanced back at Ulbeg. The dragon returned her stare, then shifted in the stall.

"Easy, fella," Galelin called.

Trysten took another deep breath, then looked down the line of stalls, past the dragons that occupied them. The dragons themselves stared down at her and ignored the weyrmen who busied themselves with wiping down the dragons or polishing saddles.

Everything was really a mess now. Trysten's shoulders slumped. There was no way in all the wilds that her father would let her fly now. Her chances of becoming the dragoneer were done for. It was a broken dream. And the thought of it slammed into her and threatened to sap the strength from her knees. She would not falter, would not fall, though. She would not give these men the satisfaction of seeing her break.

Trysten stepped through the stall. The hordesmen cleared a path for her. Her father regarded her with a face that barely concealed his disappointment. And it was the sadness behind the disappointment that made it worse. He had been through so much, and she had defied and embarrassed him in front of the entire weyr. Her jaw clenched. She swallowed hard. An apology unfurled in her belly like a newly hatched dragon unwinding itself.

"Wait," Galelin called from inside the stall.

Everyone looked to the healer as he emerged from the stall, bits of straw stuck to his knees.

"I believe this is yours," he said. He held out the tassel that Ulbeg had snatched from Paege's shoulder.

A quick grin crossed Trysten's face. As she reached for the tassel, she glanced at her father. He eyed the tassel as well, and all traces of sadness and disappointment disappeared from his face. All that remained was stone as he clamped down even harder upon what ever emotions he felt.

From there, she looked at Paege, who stood several feet away. Redness flushed through his cheeks, and for a second, Trysten felt sorry for embarrassing him as well. They had grown up together. They had been friends since as long as she could remember. Never did she wish to embarrass him in front of all the hordesmen and half the village.

But a lopsided grin rose on his face as he met her eyes. He nodded quickly, curtly.

"Don't you all have dragons to see to?" Mardoc bellowed across the weyr.

Men scattered like a dole of doves. Mardoc considered her, then the tassel again, and snatched his staff from its spot against the wall. "I will see you at home."

Trysten stifled her grin. She took the tassel from Galelin, then turned away. As she walked down the aisle, her grip tightened on the braided, woolen tassel. It brushed against the side of her thigh as she walked, and then she could do no more to hide the grin. Even if she had forever ruined her chances of becoming the dragoneer, no one could deny that she had shown prowess in the air that few others could demonstrate. She had taken the tassel from the beta rider, and she had done so with a small dragon who was more used to flying missives to the mother city than flying maneuvers through the air. There would be talk in the village, certainly, and in none of that talk, could anyone take away the tassel she now clutched.

As she passed Elevera's stall, she glanced at the dragon. A mixture of emotions tore at her—pride for her achievement, sadness at her banishment, and frustration that things couldn't be better, that her father couldn't let her compete for the title on her own merit.

Elevera bowed her head as Trysten passed. She lowered it past and beyond the stall's wall, until her head was lower than Trysten's and nearly in her path. Trysten reached out to pat it and then realized what the dragon was attempting to convey. She almost snatched her hand back. Surprised, she looked back to her father. He stood near Ulbeg's stall, with Paege, and his face was tired and tight with a look of concern as Elevera bowed in a show of deference.

Chapter 10

As soon as Trysten burst into her cottage, she held the tassel up. "Mother! Look what I have."

Her mother turned away from a table at the end of the room where she had been adding spices to a pot. Her face grew long, her eyes wide.

"Where did you get that?"

"Off of Paege's shoulder."

Her mother appeared confused. Her eyebrows settled down over her gaze. "You snatched it off his shoulder?"

Trysten gave a quick shake of her head. Her braids flew side-to-side. "No! Ulbeg snatched it off his shoulder. In the air. I was riding Ulbeg. Paege was riding Elevera."

"You were in the air? You and Paege? And Ulbeg? The small, green male?"

"I took him out. I wanted to show Father what I could do, that I could ride with the hordesmen. At first, I just wanted to shoot a few doves out of the air, but Paege and Elevera tried to force us down, so I took his tassel. Elevera didn't like that one bit, and she gave Ulbeg a nip on—"

"Where's your father?"

Trysten's grin faltered. "He's in the weyr."

Caron nodded. "I assume he knows then what you did."

"That was the point. I wanted him to see that I could ride as well as any of the hordesmen."

Caron shook her head. "Trysten, your father told you that you were not allowed to participate in the consideration. What made you think that taking a dragon out without permission would make anything better?"

Trysten held up the tassel a fraction higher as if her mother hadn't quite seen it well enough to know what it was, what it meant. "Ulbeg took this from Paege. If it had been the final consideration, I would be dragoneer. I took it from him on a courier dragon, even."

"The title does not automatically go to the one who wins the games."

"I know, but... But I wanted to show him... I wanted to show them all that I could win. It isn't fair that they keep me out of the consideration."

Caron sighed, then shook her head.

"Mother," Trysten said. Her hand and the tassel it clutched fell to her side. "I thought you would be proud of me. I beat the hordesmen. I beat Paege. I showed them that a woman could fly just as well—better, even, than any of them."

Caron took a deep breath. She picked up her dish again, considered it, then put it back. She turned to Trysten. "I am thankful that you didn't get hurt. Or that no one else got hurt. But you disobeyed your father. You disobeyed the dragoneer. That is not anything that I can be proud of, Trysten. You are my daughter, my little heart, and I love you more than anything, but I cannot be proud of your willfulness when you endanger yourself and others. Out here, we have to rely on one another and to respect the wishes of those who are in charge of our safety. It is the only way we can live this close to the mountains. You ignored your father. You ignored the village dragoneer. And by the looks of things, unless you have a string of hares hidden behind your back, you ignored me as well."

Trysten flapped her arms at her side in frustration. The tassel snapped against her calf. "Mother! By the wilds! Doesn't anyone care? If we rely on the dragoneer to keep us safe, then shouldn't the best rider be the dragoneer?"

"There's more to being a dragoneer than stealing tassels from other riders. Your father takes the lives of the hordesmen into his hands at the start of each fighting season. If they are to survive, they must follow his orders to the end, and he must be able to count on them to do as he says. If they don't, any one of them, or all of them, could be killed. And if they are killed, there is little to stop the armies of the Western Kingdom from crossing the pass. Do you understand, Trysten?"

She swallowed the urge to grunt in frustration. "Understand? I understand that this is unfair. If someone had denied Father something he should have, then he'd go take it. He wouldn't stand by and do nothing. He'd act. He'd do exactly what I did."

Caron gave a short nod. "He would. But he's the dragoneer. You are not."

"Why not? What's wrong with me being the dragoneer?" She held up the tassel. "I've proven myself."

The door opened behind her. Trysten dropped the tassel to her waist.

"Why do dragons obey us?" Trysten's father stepped inside the cottage and shut the door, snapping the floor with his staff.

Trysten looked over her shoulder.

"I asked you a question," Mardoc continued as he proceeded to the table before the hearth. He sat hard in his chair. Its wooden legs cracked the floor, and his face tore itself into a terrible grimace as his eyes squeezed shut. He took a deep breath, grasped his right knee, and rubbed it a bit. Caron took several steps forward, then stopped as if she were a dog on a rope.

"Trysten?" her father asked again.

She looked to the floor. Might there be someplace to hide, someplace to escape that look? She wasn't sure why the dragons obeyed them. She had hints, got impressions from time to time, but why they stayed in the weyr and responded to the commands of humans was lost on her. She shrugged.

Caron finally stepped forward and took the staff from her husband. She placed it in the corner of the room. "Can I get you a bowl of stew?"

Mardoc nodded. His eyes remained focused squarely on Trysten. "The dragons obey us because there is a bond that is formed between the dragoneer and the alpha. There is a relationship there. It is deeper than anyone can know. It is unlike the relationship I have with your mother, or even with you, and you are a part of me. The relationship I have with Aeronwind is beyond love. It is beyond loyalty. It is formed by the last bonds shared between the gods and us. It is the last reminder of their work, of their labor, of the gifts they left us before all was destroyed. Aeronwind obeys me because she cannot stand to disappoint me, and she trusts me because she knows that I will never hurt her needlessly or carelessly. And since she obeys me, and the other dragons of the horde obey her, then they obey me as well. The horde cannot turn on its alpha. The horde is one heart, one mind. The horde cannot turn on Aeronwind any more than your hand can decide on its own to tear out your heart."

Trysten glanced to the floor. This was true. Elevera felt deeply about Aeronwind, and she felt deeply about Mardoc precisely because he belonged to Aeronwind.

"Trust is the heart of what it means to be a dragoneer." Mardoc reached down, placed the butt of his palms on either side of his chair, and shifted his position. His face wrenched into pain again and Trysten found herself gritting her teeth and holding her breath.

"How can I name you as dragoneer if I cannot trust you to obey me?"

"But you wouldn't even let me try."

"To what end? Aside from it being against the law, you did try today. You tried even though I forbid it. You shot arrows into a formation. Those arrows could have pierced a wing. They could have killed a rider."

"I wasn't even close—"

"You were lucky. A sudden gust. If Ulbeg had lurched or shifted unexpectedly at the moment before you released an arrow, then your shots could have gone wide. They could have hurt someone, or worse. That was bad enough, but you ignored Paege's order to ground. He was flying beta. He is the horde's commander. When in the air, you always obey the horde commander. To top it off, after Elevera tried to ground Ulbeg, you egged him on. You have damaged that bond of trust between Ulbeg and Elevera. She will be the new alpha before long, and Ulbeg will depend upon her as all the dragons depend on the alpha. You damaged that trust by forcing that dragon to act against the wishes of the beta."

"She what?" Caron asked. "She forced Ulbeg to act against Elevera? How is that possible?" She studied Trysten, then looked at her husband.

Mardoc held his hand up, stopping Caron's questions. "This is why I denied you a chance to compete. I feared that something like this would happen. You don't act in a respectful manner toward the dragons. You never have. I know it is my fault, and I often looked the other way, but I see now—"

"What do you mean I don't treat them in a respectful manner?" Trysten's blood sparked through her veins. Few things could dig under her skin and explode like such an accusation. "I..." Words failed her. How could she defend against something so obviously false? "Those dragons..."

and her mouth hung there, her jaw open and slack like a branch broken from a tree, but not quite snapped clean.

What had she to lose? Trysten straightened her back. "I hear them. I look into their eyes, and I know what it is they are feeling, what they are thinking. I know them better than anyone in the village knows them. How can you say that I don't respect them?"

Mardoc leaned forward a bit. "I didn't say that you don't know them. You've grown up in the house of dragons. I would expect nothing less from you than familiarity. But perhaps it is such familiarity that led you to this action, that you convinced yourself that you could do what you did, that you were in the right when all you have done is complicate an already difficult situation in addition to injuring Ulbeg and threatening his position in the horde. We need every dragon. What if Elevera rejects him when she becomes alpha?"

"She won't."

Mardoc raised an eyebrow. "And how is it that you can be so sure of such a thing?"

"I know her. And she knows me." Again the words trailed off. How could she convince her father that she knew? Elevera would not reject Ulbeg because Trysten would not allow it. But there was no point in saying such things. To her father, it was the ravings of a young girl, nothing more than a flight of fancy. He wouldn't believe her because to do so would be to admit that she had a connection with the dragons that he did not, and his connection to the dragons could not be surpassed. He was the dragoneer after all.

No, it was best to let it drop. And so her hands fell to her sides again. Her gaze scudded to the floor before her father's feet. There was nowhere to go. There was nothing to say or do at this point. It was all over. She had taken her chance, and she had succeeded in proving herself, but still, it wasn't enough.

Mardoc sighed. He planted an elbow on the table and wiped his palm across his mouth before running his fingers through the length of his beard. "Trysten, I want you to know that I love you. You are my daughter. You are my family. I am not upset with you as much as I am upset with your actions. You disobeyed my order. You took a risk that could have injured you. It could have killed you. And it did injure one of our dragons. It may be a minor injury, but it is an injury all the same. I want you to see that this is exactly why I have forbidden you from the consideration, not as the dragoneer, but as your father. It may not seem like it, and you may not believe it, but I know you better than I know any of the dragons out there. You are a strong, smart, young woman, but along with those vibrant characteristics comes stubbornness, willfulness. These are characteristics that need to be tempered. They will be tempered with age, but as you have demonstrated today, that age is not today's age."

Trysten looked up at her father and willed herself not to shed a tear. She blinked back the water gathering in her eyes.

"My decision stands. I hope with some time and reflection, you can see the wisdom of my actions."

Trysten nodded. She swallowed hard against the knot in her throat. "I'm sorry. I didn't mean for anyone to get hurt."

"I understand. If a nip on the tail is the worst that comes of this, then it will be well-worth the lesson. You may go," her father said with a nod to the door.

As Trysten turned, her mother called out. "Trysten, little heart, I am still waiting on those hares."

Trysten's shoulders slumped as she reached for the door handle. "Yes, Mother," she said. "I'll go get them now."

The truth was, venting her anger and frustration through the bow sounded like a good idea.

Chapter 11

Trysten stood upright as she clutched the shaft of an arrow that still held the hare it had pierced. From the corner of her eye, she caught sight of Paege descending the slope from the village. He moved at a relaxed pace along the trail. His eyes were locked on hers, but nothing about his demeanor or movement showed that he was in a hurry. He also wasn't slinking up to the bank of the river as if he were looking to offer her an apology, either.

"How's the hunting?" Paege called out.

"I preferred the doves," Trysten called back as she grabbed the hare's skull and pulled her arrow free. She laid the hare in a pile with two others and wiped the shaft of the arrow with a rag. She turned away from Paege, slotted the notch of the arrow back onto the string, and scanned the brush for movement as she took several steps forward.

"I wanted to let you know that Ulbeg will be fine," Paege continued. His voice was closer. The grasses rustled as he moved through them at a quicker pace.

She glanced over her shoulder, and Paege immediately slowed. He was out of his riding armor, wearing wool pants and a dark green sweater that Trysten's mother had knit for him for the peace season celebration the year before. "I knew he would be. Elevera just wanted to check him. You should fly him more often. In the battle drills, I mean. He enjoys it."

Paege closed the remaining distance between them. "He's a bit small for battle."

Trysten reached down and rubbed her palm over the braid that stuck out from the waistband of her pants.

Paege's eyes followed the motion. He nodded as color flooded his cheeks.

"My father doesn't allow me back in the weyr. Not until you're the dragoneer."

Paege's facial features crunched up a tiny bit, a wince. "I told you to go to ground. I didn't want this to happen."

"Why didn't *you* go to ground, then?" Trysten asked.

Paege ran his tongue along his teeth. "How could I? I'm supposed to be leading the horde now. Or soon." He glanced behind himself as if to see whether the distant mountains had snuck up on him while he wasn't looking. "Galelin says that Aeronwind won't make it to the next fighting season. And even if she did, your father..." His gaze fell as if mentioning Mardoc's injury was an insult to Trysten.

"How can you lead the horde if a courier dragon can take your tassel?" Trysten regretted the comment as soon as it left her mouth. She swallowed as Paege winced, struck by her words.

He took half a step back as if recovering from a blow. "I didn't want to hurt you. It wasn't a real battle. It was just an exercise. Ulbeg wouldn't stand a chance if Elevera decided to force him down."

Although the tang of regret hung on her like wood smoke, Trysten cocked her eyebrow. Her lips parted. She closed them again, and then looked toward the weyr.

To the wilds with it. "So you had that much control over Elevera? You could keep her from forcing Ulbeg to ground?"

Color flushed over Paege again. His fair skin betrayed every flicker of emotion that ran through him. He was like an ember that blushed with the slightest breeze. He looked straight at her. The hazel of his eyes became a hard gem, rather than the colors of the soft lichens that grew upon the stones. "It will come. Not all of us have the advantage of being the dragoneer's daughter. Some of us didn't grow up around these dragons, and we have to work a lot harder."

"Paege, you at least get to work at it. You are expected to be the dragoneer. It is being handed to you, and my father won't even let me into the consideration. At least you get to work hard. I'm not allowed to work at all!"

Paege drew in a deep breath. His mouth tightened. It was similar to an expression that he would get when they were younger, when he had had it with her teasing and was about to storm off home after swearing he was never going to play with her again.

He reached up and tucked a lock of hair behind his ear. "Are you going to tell me it isn't fair?"

Trysten's grip tightened on the bow. She would want Paege to go away if it meant she could head up to the weyr and slip into Elevera's stall, to curl up against that great, heaving chest of hers. If she could lay her head against that wall of muscle and hear the whoosh of air through her lungs and feel the smooth scales on her cheek, all would be better. Everything would be tolerable. She was cut off from that, however. Cut off until Paege succeeded her father. Oh! Her brows furrowed a bit. He was a clever man. The sooner Paege could bond with Elevera, the sooner Trysten could see her as well.

A look of concern grew on Paege's face. It caught her off guard. It wasn't what she normally expected once he started to look frustrated. It was new in him, something she hadn't seen before. It was adult enough to be eerie.

"I'm sorry." Trysten shook her head. "I know it's nothing personal. I know you're just doing what you have to do. I don't mean to take it out on you."

Paege nodded. A slight grin crept onto his face. "If it were up to me, I'd allow you into the consideration. By the wilds, after the way you flew today, I'll be begging you to join my hordesmen."

Trysten grinned. "My father wouldn't care for that."

Paege shrugged. His smile widened. "Once I'm dragoneer, who's going to tell me no?"

The thought of flying with the hordesmen thrilled her. She had gone for flights before, for pleasure or to locate lost sheep, but those flights had been steady, regular. The flying done on the back of Ulbeg this morning had been different, like dreaming of flying for all of her life, and then one day discovering that she could actually fly. Though she had used her heels and the lip of her saddle to control Ulbeg, it felt as if the motions were nothing more than empty gestures to be completed as a matter of ceremony. Ulbeg had responded as if he were an extension of her legs and arms. She needed to do no more than think of taking to the sky, of pushing up toward the belly of the clouds before the might of Ulbeg was propelling her upwards.

"Will you do it?" Paege asked.

"Don't make me wish for the Western Kingdom to breach the pass."

Paege glanced over his shoulder again as if checking on the pass. Clouds swirled around the hidden peaks. The ceaseless winter storms that formed the border between the two kingdoms still raged. The enemy remained bottled up, and Paege was safe for the time being.

His attention shifted to the hill above them. "Is that Yahi?"

A woman trod steadily down the path. The wind off the mountains whipped her dark hair and scarlet dress off to the side and highlighted her bony frame.

"Trysten!" Yahi called. She lifted a thin arm and waved.

"Yahi!" Trysten called back.

The woman continued to pick her way down the slope. Once she reached the bottom of the hill, she watched the wind press the grass into undulating shapes that rolled over the meadow between herself and the mountains. Whether she saw what she was looking for or not, she tucked her long hair back behind her ears and picked her way over to Trysten.

"I saw your flight today!" Yahi said through a great grin. "Half of the village saw it, I think. That was incredible!"

Her eyes flicked to Paege, who returned a thin smile that betrayed his discomfort. He glanced to the tassel in Trysten's waistband as the wind stirred it.

"Thanks," Trysten said. "Half the village saw it?"

The older woman beamed and nodded. "Word was out that your father had gone to the weyr today, the first time since the accident. I think everyone was curious to see what the horde would do in response. No one expected you, though! Surely you gave Paege a run for his life."

"I'm afraid I was acting a little foolishly," Trysten said.

"Nonsense! That was a brilliant bit of flying! And it was on the back of Ulbeg, was it not? I thought he was a courier dragon. It surprised me to see him in the air. For a short while, word was out that we had a new dragon in the horde, though I don't know how we could get one without everyone noticing."

Trysten blushed. "No, it was Ulbeg. I..." Trysten let out a puff of frustrated breath. "Thanks, Yahi. I appreciate it, but it really was nothing. I shouldn't have even done it. I'm afraid I didn't really do anything more than make a nuisance of myself."

Yahi grinned, then glanced at the mountains. She studied them for a moment, then turned her attention back. Her grin faded.

"Is everything all right?" Paege asked Yahi.

She nodded, then pushed her hair back behind her ears again. The wind immediately lifted it out and sent it whipping about her head. "I think so. Something is going on in the clouds. They look different than usual."

Trysten turned her attention to the clouds as well. They looked solid, like a batch of gray tallow just before it hardened. They looked the same as they always did in the late winter.

"How so?" Paege asked.

Yahi tucked her hair behind her ears and studied the clouds a minute longer. She shook her head. "I can't say at the moment. Something is changing."

Paege shifted his weight. He planted his hands upon his hips, then folded his arms over his chest, restless. "Do you think we'll have a longer season of peace this year?"

Yahi didn't answer right away. Finally, she shrugged. "Who is to say?"

Paege let out a slight grunt. "I'd like to think *you* would. You are the cloud reader after all."

"I read the clouds only when they have written what they want to say, only when they've decided to make their minds known. Now..." She glanced over her shoulder at the mountains and then scanned across the sky and down to the distant horizon forever across the eastern plains. "For now, the clouds are but a poet struck by thought. They are thinking. What they will have to say will come when they decide."

A gust of wind slammed into the three of them. Trysten gritted her teeth as chills shook her. Paege rubbed his arms briefly. Yahi tucked her hair back behind her ears only to have it blown free immediately afterward.

"Well," Paege said as he planted his hands back on his hips. "I should get back to the weyr." He reached out for Trysten's hares. "Are those for the dragons?"

Trysten smacked his hand away. "They're for my mother, who is going to make sure your weyrmen don't starve."

"Oh, they're *my* weyrmen already?" He grinned, but then the grin faded as Trysten failed to react.

"Trysten, Yahi," Paege said with a nod, and then returned to the trail.

Yahi watched him go a moment. "He's still to be the dragoneer?"

"Who else would you expect?"

"I would expect the one who can ride like you rode Ulbeg today." Yahi gestured at the tassel.

"My father says Paege is to be the next."

"Because he has no son?"

"Because I'm reckless."

Yahi shook her head. "Men are reckless. War is their invention. What is more reckless than war?"

Trysten shook her head and looked up toward the weyr. What she wanted to say wouldn't fit through her mouth.

Yahi touched Trysten on the shoulder. "The clouds mind us. They watch over us in the absence of the gods. They record all, and they are preparing for a great change. It is a change that has been coming for some time. Your father never had a son, and now this accident that has made him the first dragoneer in a score of generations to not die in battle, but rather to live long enough to name his replacement and see that one succeed him. The clouds are heavy." She nodded to the sky above. "They are watchful. A new chapter will begin this year. Watch."

Trysten peered at the sky. The clouds looked as thick and featureless as they had for weeks since the last winter storm had covered the highlands with snow and left a clear, blue sky to dazzle them all before the dry winds off the mountains ate the snow up and left clouds blanketing all.

"You flew well today," Yahi said with a nod. "You flew like I've never seen another fly, and as cloud reader, I can assure you that little takes place in the sky without my knowing. Be ready, dear. A new story is about to unfold."

Yahi turned around. The mountains and the wall of clouds continued to hold the Western Kingdom back, but they did so ominously. It wasn't a favor, but rather a taunt. They would lift that wall one day soon, and the hordesmen of the Western Kingdom would stream through the Gul pass.

Without a further word, Yahi followed in Paege's footsteps. Her skirts billowed behind her, and the wind pushed the hair from her face. At any minute, she looked as if she'd lift off the ground, take flight, and sail on up to the clouds that she regarded as living beings.

Chapter 12

A pounding on the cottage door woke Trysten from her sleep. She sat up in bed.

"Mardoc!" Bolsar yelled from outside. "Mardoc!"

Trysten slipped out of bed and rushed into the front room. Orange and red embers in the hearth betrayed the late hour. She cracked open the cottage door. Bolsar stood outside with a lantern.

"Where's your father? Tell him to come to the weyr quick. Aeronwind has turned."

"What is that?" Mardoc called from behind Trysten.

Bolsar pitched himself onto the toes of his boots as if to shove his words over Trysten's head. "Come to the weyr, Mardoc! Aeronwind has turned."

"Fetch Galelin," Mardoc commanded from the bedroom door.

"I just came from Galelin's, sir."

"Good man," Mardoc said. "I'll be right there."

Bolsar hurried off. Trysten shut the door and bolted into her room to make short work of getting dressed. As she emerged from her room and crossed to the front door, Mardoc called out. "Where are you going?"

"Aeronwind is in trouble."

"You are barred from the weyr."

Trysten turned to her father. Caron knelt before him and guided a boot onto his twisted foot.

"Father," Trysten pleaded, "if she is to die—"

"She is not going to die," Mardoc said with a shake of his head. "At least not tonight."

"Mardoc," Caron said as she tightened the buckles on his boot. "What harm would there be in letting her see Aeronwind? Our time with her is short. She means as much to Trysten as she means to you."

Mardoc locked eyes with Caron for a second and then inclined his head slightly. "All right," he said to Trysten. "This one time. You are not to interact with any of the other dragons, understand?"

Trysten nodded, then fled out the door.

Inside the weyr, several lanterns glowed around Aeronwind's stall. A small crowd of weyrmen and hordesmen gathered. Elevera watched with obvious interest.

"Trysten," one of the weyrman said as he looked up. "You are not to be in here!"

"My father is coming right behind me," she said as she jogged up to the stall. "How is Aeronwind?"

She reached the head of the stall and peered inside. The dragon lay curled in a loose ball. Her sides heaved in rapid, short breaths. With each exhale, a low groan escaped her.

"It's not good, I'm afraid," one of the weyrman said. He removed the cloth cap from his head.

"Let's not dig the poor girl's grave before she is dead, shall we?" Galelin asked from where he crouched upon a short stool next to the dragon's broken leg. His sleeves were rolled up, and his forearms covered in an oily substance. A long scar snaked its way up from his inner wrist to just before his elbow. The greasy substance made the scar appear pinker than the surrounding skin, puffier.

He wiped the sweat from his brow with the cuff of his rolled sleeve. "She's having a bad spell, but I think she'll pull through. She's a tough old girl. She's taken down many a Western horde. It'll take more than a mere pustulence to bring this one down. She'll be fighting in the season yet."

Trysten studied Aeronwind's face. Her eyes were closed. It was unusual. The dragon seemed never to sleep, never to cease watching. Trysten got no sense from the alpha, no indication of how the dragon felt or what she thought. All that came to Trysten was a feeling of uncomfortable warmth, of a wish for a cool breeze, the flow of air beneath wings.

Trysten glanced up at Elevera. The gold dragon met her eyes. She lowered her head the slightest bit, and Trysten was flooded with a feeling of sadness. Woe. It was enough to make her grasp the half-wall before her knees gave out. And there, underneath the woe, discernible only after the woe had broken over her like a spring flood, Trysten found resignation. Defiance. Elevera wanted Aeronwind to know that she was ready. She assured her alpha that the horde would be fine, that she would take care of it, see to it, keep it together.

Aeronwind was dying.

"What's going on?" Mardoc cried from the end of the weyr.

Several men trotted down to meet the dragoneer, to tell him of the new development.

"Galelin?" Mardoc asked.

"In the stall, of course."

Trysten took a deep breath. She gripped the top of the wall and raised her face to the gold dragon once again. Was she sure? Elevera glanced to Aeronwind, then back to Trysten. Soon. Elevera would step up soon.

Trysten's breath stalled as her heart fluttered. It nearly paced up and down her breastbone as the implications hit home. Elevera would be thrust into the role of alpha soon, and if she wasn't ready to bond with Paege, or he wasn't ready to bond with her, then Elevera would abscond. She would leave the village. She would either go wild or latch onto another horde, one with an alpha who could sway her. But worse yet, if Elevera absconded, the horde would follow her. The village would lose all twenty-one dragons, and not one would remain to offer up any kind of defense if the hordesmen of the Western Kingdom came screaming through the Gul Pass.

She had to tell her father.

Mardoc slipped past her and into the stall. He surveyed his dragon. Trysten couldn't see his eyes.

"How goes she?" Mardoc asked.

Galelin sucked in a deep breath as he straightened his back. "The pustulence has taken a turn for the worse. She is fevered."

Mardoc gripped the staff with both hands. "Is this the first fever?"

Galelin studied the wound, then gave a slow nod. "The first that I know of."

"Is there anything you can do to stave off the next one?"

Galelin regarded the wound a moment more, then lifted his hands as if suddenly remembering that he had them. "A new compound. I sent word to the Dragon Master in the mother city. His healer sent me some new herbs to try in a salve. I've tried to get her to drink cool water, but she will have none of it."

Bolsar crossed his arms over his chest and nodded. "She tastes battle in the waters."

"Battle?" Galelin asked. His face twisted into a look of incredulity. "What does battle taste like?"

Bolsar's Adam's apple bobbed. He lifted his chin slightly. "Blood. Like iron. It gets in the water ahead of the start of the fighting season. It's what opens up the passes. Don't tell me you've never tasted it in the river?"

"I think you're confusing it with fish pee," Galelin said.

Amid a smattering of chuckles from the hordesmen, Bolsar's hands fell to his sides. He flushed and stepped forward. Mardoc lowered his staff so that the tip of it landed against Bolsar's chest and stopped him.

"Is there nothing more you can do?" Mardoc asked Galelin.

Galelin considered the wound again. The light from the various lanterns appeared to get stuck, mired in the greasy liniment that the healer had slathered upon the dragon's leg. He shook his head. "It's in her hands now. These herbs are supposed to draw the fever out, balance the humors."

Galelin leaned forward a bit and held his open palms over the wound as if warming them on a fire. "But that's the thing with dragons. Their humors run to the hot side as it is. It's why they breathe fire and seek out the cold of the sky. It keeps them balanced. If these herbs do their job, they might sustain her until she can get on her feet again, at least long enough to take wing and feel the sky."

Mardoc lifted his face to the front of the weyr, to the end that looked out over the mountains. Trysten saw in his face that he was calculating what it would take to ferry snow and ice back from the frigid peaks. But then the dragoneer in him eclipsed the man desperate to save that which he loved. He shook his head, glanced at Elevera, then on to Aeronwind. His head inclined, and in the space of a few seconds, he appeared to age twenty years.

He looked about the men gathered around the stall. "Back to bed, men. I will see after Aeronwind."

The men stood a moment longer before breaking up. They slowly dispersed like a dollop of milk in water before Mardoc turned his attention to Trysten. "You, too. Tell your mother that I will be holding a vigil in here tonight."

Trysten looked up at Elevera. A flash of sorrow and resignation washed over her again. She swayed on her feet, then drew a deep breath.

"Is something the matter?" Mardoc asked.

"It's Aeronwind. She isn't doing well."

"She's in capable hands," her father said. He straightened his back, and a little of his strength returned as if he were assuring himself as much as his daughter.

"No, it's worse than we think it is. She isn't..." Trysten swallowed hard, then took another deep breath. "She's worse than we think. She isn't going to last long. The pustulence is too deep. It can't be drawn out any more. It's in her bones."

"Have we been studying the healing arts when not raising a ruckus?" Galelin asked as he sat back and planted his forearms upon his knees.

"I know this," she said to her father, ignoring the old healer.

"And how do you know this? Galelin makes a good point. I know you have spent most of your life with these dragons, but I haven't noticed you spending that time in the study of their physiology."

Trysten glanced at Elevera again. Dare she tell her father? If only Elevera could speak up. Or if only her father could listen. But telling him the truth would only further rob her of credibility. There was nothing she could do but hope for the best.

She hung her head.

Mardoc clamped a hand on her shoulder. It was heavy and strong and reassuring, like a solid post in the middle of a rushing river. It was something she wanted to cling to.

"Aeronwind will be fine. We have herbs from the Dragon Master himself. I know you love her, and so do I, but I will spend the night here to make sure she is all right. Go. Tell your mother the news, and of my plans."

Trysten let out a sigh as she studied Aeronwind, who lay curled loosely in the hay, her shattered foreleg held out before Galelin.

Mardoc squeezed her shoulder. "Go."

Trysten nodded, then looked at her father. His eyes were rimmed in red. They betrayed the strength in his grip and the solidity of his stare.

She walked away. The aisle to the entrance of the weyr had never felt longer.

Chapter 13

The following morning, Trysten and her mother found Mardoc in Aeronwind's stall. He slept with his back against the dragon. His body rose and fell with each of the dragon's fevered breaths as if he were being rocked.

Caron called for him, and when he woke, she presented a tray that bore the breakfast they had prepared for him.

Mardoc tore into the fresh bread and eggs, assuring Trysten and Caron that Aeronwind would be fine. Her breathing was a little easier, a little less labored. The fever was being transformed into a vapor by the herbs. He could smell it. Sharp and hot. It cleared the head if inhaled deeply.

Trysten glanced up at Elevera and nearly expected the golden dragon to shake her head. Instead, she stared back with resignation and sorrow that threatened to drop Trysten to her knees.

She excused herself and worked her way past the hushed conversations of the weyrmen, who fell silent as she approached and concentrated on the work of feeding the dragons.

At the back of the weyr, Trysten entered the bunkhouse where the hordesmen lived. There, in the cramped dining hall, she found Paege at a table in the center of the room. The men ate mostly in silence as they stared at their plates. The boisterousness which they frequently displayed during meals was absent, and their collective silence was larger for that absence. They looked as if they were preparing for a wake rather than another day of training.

Paege looked up from his plate and stood as if expecting a summons. When Trysten did nothing more than cross the room, he resumed his seat on the bench.

"I need to talk to you," Trysten said.

Paege glanced about at the other men at the table, then back at her as if waiting for her to indicate something.

"Alone," Trysten added.

One of the men made a quick, quiet comment to another, his words hidden behind the back of his hand. The other man stifled a chuckle that brought a glare from Paege as he stood.

Paege ushered Trysten to the bunk hall. It sat empty. Neatly made bunks lined the walls. It was a level of care that Trysten hadn't expected to see.

"What's wrong?" Paege asked as he shut the door to the hall.

"It's Aeronwind. She's not doing well."

A bit of color dropped away from Paege's already pale face. He gave a curt nod. "So we've heard."

"No," Trysten said and shook her head. "You don't understand. My father thinks these herbs from the mother city will heal her, but they won't. She's dying. She's dying more quickly than what Galelin or my father thinks. She's going to pass the horde on to Elevera sooner rather than later."

Paege leaned back some. His shoulders rested against the closed door.

Trysten took a deep breath, a little frustrated that she had to spell it out for him.

"My father won't believe me, but you have to talk some sense into him. He'll listen to you. You need to be ready when Aeronwind passes, or we'll lose the horde. We don't have the kind of time that he thinks we have."

More color fell away from Paege's face. He was downright pale. Surely none of this was such a shock to him.

"Do you understand?" Trysten asked.

"More than you would believe. Have you spoken to Yahi today?"

Trysten's shoulders slumped slightly. She shook her head.

"She says the clouds are preparing to break soon. Spring will come early this year."

The bottom fell out of Trysten's heart. An early Spring meant an early fighting season. What awful timing.

Paege nodded as if agreeing with Trysten's unspoken thoughts.

Her heart fluttered. "Oh, Paege. I'm so sorry."

Paege let out a long sigh as his gaze drifted over Trysten's head and out beyond the rear wall, out beyond the eastern plains. "It is what it is. There's no need to be sorry."

He looked back at Trysten. "But I'll be ready. I have to be."

His expression lacked reassurance. He was the boy she had grown up with. The patchy beard and the hair caught in the awkward place between short and long highlighted how out of place he was. When growing up, he had spoken of being a hordesman like his father, but more often, he spoke of carpentry. He had helped build a number of cottages, helped put an expansion on the weyr. He was far more comfortable holding a hammer than holding the reins of a dragon.

Yet, here he was, hardly more than the boy she had known, and already he was willing to do what he had to do to secure the horde and protect the village. The fighting season loomed, now mere weeks away if Yahi was right, and like most cloud readers, she usually was.

By the wilds, here he was willing to give up everything for the village, and here she was feeling sorry for herself because she couldn't be the dragoneer, she couldn't earn what she wanted more than anything, while it was being handed to a man who would take it as a responsibility, rather than a passion. But there was little room to quibble now. She had to do her part and tell him what she knew.

Trysten took half a step closer to Paege. His back stiffened, and he pressed himself even harder against the door as if bracing himself for an attack.

"You have to be ready, Paege. You have to bond with Elevera. I... " She glanced to the floor briefly, then back up at him. "I can sense what Elevera is thinking. What she's feeling. She knows that Aeronwind won't survive long. She knows that her time is coming soon. If you aren't ready to bond with her—"

"I know," Paege interjected. "Believe me, I know full well what is at stake here."

He swallowed hard and glanced at the rafters. "I lay awake at night and wonder how in the wilds I'm going to pull this off. I have the whole village, the whole horde depending on me, and I can't seem to even *touch* the kind of bond that you share with Elevera, let alone form anything like what is between your father and Aeronwind."

"It's just a matter of time. I'll stay out of the weyr, and you can put in some extra time with Elevera. You'll do fine."

"No," Paege said with a shake of his head. His eyes shone. "No, you don't understand. It's not going to happen. I *can't* do it. I can't bond with Elevera. She won't have me. Dragons are sensitive, right? They know what's in the hearts and minds of their riders. Look at the way you handle her. Look at the way you handled Ulbeg! By the wilds, Trysten, *you* should be the dragoneer. Not me."

His words pierced Trysten in ways that arrows and blades never could. She nearly grabbed Paege's arm to keep herself from reeling under the blow of his words.

"Don't deny it," Paege said. He rubbed the butt of a palm beneath his eye. "I know it. I know it's never going to happen between Elevera and me. She can sense that I don't want to do this. I don't want to be a dragoneer. I don't even really want to be a hordesman. If it were up to me, I'd do almost anything else."

Paege inhaled sharply, then turned his face to the ceiling, as if it were the best he could do in his effort to hide it from Trysten.

"Even now, I bet Elevera knows I'm in here telling you this. But what else can I do? Your father is keen on choosing me. I was hoping after yesterday that he would see that I'm not fit. But he only spoke of my need to train harder. And then Yahi brings us this news this morning about the fighting season and everything is happening too fast, and by the wilds, Trysten, I am *not* prepared for this! I'm scared to death that the horde is going to abscond when Aeronwind dies, and there is nothing I can do about it."

Trysten stepped forward and pulled him into an embrace, held him as he sniffed softly into her shoulder.

Her grip tightened as her mind raced. At this point, there was no way her father would entertain the idea of her being the dragoneer. And with the news of an early fighting season combined with a fever from Aeronwind, her father would only double down on his belief that Paege ought to succeed him. He would put everything on Paege as time dwindled.

The best thing to do would be to help Paege be ready. It was what the village needed. It was what Elevera and the horde would need.

Trysten gripped Paege by his forearms. Her hands slid down until she held his. He looked almost anywhere rather than make eye contact with her.

"Look here," she said, and Paege finally met her gaze.

"You will be ready." She squeezed his hand. "I have a special connection with Elevera. We have had it since I was a little girl. I will work with her. I will work with you both to make sure that you are ready to assume the title when the time comes. We will not lose the horde. We will be ready when the Western Kingdom comes. You have my promise. Do you understand?"

Paege swallowed hard as he nodded, and then his nod became a shake of his head. His bangs fell before his eyes. "How? How are you going to do that? She knows that I don't want to be the dragoneer. She is never going to bond with me."

"She will. I promise. Elevera is as concerned about losing the horde as you are. More so. She wants to bond with you. We just have to... work out the rough spots."

She spoke with the best of intentions, but she couldn't help the voice inside that also called out for Paege to tell her father all of this, that he didn't want the title, and that he felt Trysten should have it.

She shook her head, silenced the voice. There was no point in dwelling on it. The horde came first. The village came after that. There was no time for what she wanted, as without the horde or the village, there would be no place for her. Without these things, nothing she wanted mattered. Helping Paege live up to the dragoneer's expectations was what she must do, to be true to her duty, and to be true to herself.

"Thank you," Paege said. "Thank you so much."

His expression had calmed and grown bland. He was not exactly convinced or hopeful, but it appeared that he at least believed he had an ally. And his admission seemed to have taken a great weight off his shoulders, even if it had served to place a burden on her own.

It was worth it, however. For the horde. And for the village. For Paege, and for her father as well.

She left the weyr.

Chapter 14

Borsal glowered at Trysten as she walked into the weyr that afternoon. She held up the basket she carried, then pointed at Aeronwind's stall. Borsal considered her a moment, then nodded before returning his attention to the saddle he had been repairing.

The synchronous breaths of the dragons pulsed against Trysten as she walked down the central aisle. Their breathing was heavier, more rushed than usual. A tension hung heavy in the air, and it tasted of copper, of spent lightning.

Her father remained in Aeronwind's stall, holding his vigil for the dying dragon. Aeronwind's breathing seemed easier than it had that morning. Enough so that Trysten glanced up at Elevera with the hope that a corner had been turned, that the older alpha dragon was indeed on the mend. Elevera, however, continued to regard Trysten with a solemn expression that filled her with resignation and grief.

"Trysten?" her father asked.

She glanced at her father. His back rested against the sleeping and fevered dragon.

"Mother and I fixed you lunch." She held the basket up. "She said I could bring it to you."

"I appreciate it." He nodded at an upturned box off to his side. A cold lantern and an empty cup sat upon the makeshift table.

Trysten placed the basket upon the box. She plucked the towel off the top of the basket and handed it to her father. As he spread it across his lap, she handed him a bit of mutton and some carrots in a dish.

Her father held the dish before himself and inhaled deeply. "It smells wonderful. Thank you."

"How is she?" Trysten asked with a nod at Aeronwind, who slept with her neck curled around so that her head rested near the dragoneer's feet.

Her father did not respond, but instead plucked a carrot out of the dish and popped it in his mouth.

Trysten handed over a slice of bread, a knife, and a fork. "Can I get you some more water?"

Mardoc nodded as he sliced into the mutton while chewing the carrot.

When Trysten returned, she filled his cup from a pitcher, then sat on the edge of the box. "I heard about Yahi's prognostication this morning."

Her father looked up from his dish. "Don't you worry, Little Heart. Paege will be ready. I will see to it."

Trysten regarded Aeronwind's expressionless face. In her earliest memory, she recalled standing at her mother's feet and looking up. The wall of the stall appeared to be immense. The vaulted ceiling of the weyr may as well have been the top of the sky itself. And there, staring down at her from nearly the top of that sky was the gray face of Aeronwind as if she were a goddess checking on the mortals. There was such an overwhelming sense of emotion. The memory crashed through her like an impossible load dropping through the bottom of a lightweight basket. Now that same dragon's face was blank and empty as if the spirit of the dragon had already fled, but the shadow of such a strong, magnificent spirit proved to be enough to leave the body breathing, the heart beating, the fires of life still smoldering.

A sob caught in her throat. In the back of her mind, she considered again telling her father about Paege's desires, about his concerns, about his belief that it was she who should succeed her father, and not him.

She reached down, plucked up a strand of straw, and picked at the end of it. Now was not the time.

"Father, I've been thinking."

Mardoc lowered his fork to the dish with a clink.

"I want to apologize for what I've done, for my actions the other day."

His expression was curious, trying to decide where she was going.

"I was wrong to disobey your wishes," she glanced to the dish of mutton. It was hard enough to lie to him. She couldn't look him in the eyes and do it as well.

"I see now, that for the good of the horde and the village, Paege needs to be made ready to accept his responsibilities." She looked back at him. He appeared to be shocked. Her eyes flicked up to Elevera, who watched in silence. Curiosity baked off of her like a great fire.

"If you will allow me to be in the weyr again, to work with Elevera again, I promise you that I will do whatever I can to help Paege and Elevera bond."

Her father resumed a slow chewing of his lunch. He swallowed, then poked at the piece of mutton with his fork as if searching for something.

"Might it be best for them both if you kept your distance?"

Trysten's breath stopped. Her heart hammered against the bottom of her jaw. She meant to protest but managed only instead to give her head a slight shake.

Her father cut another chunk off the mutton. As he did so, his gaze fell on Aeronwind as if he expected her to snap one eye open, to sniff the air and lift the big block of her head for a bite of his lunch. She did not move, and soon, Mardoc appeared disappointed, though Trysten couldn't imagine him disappointed in Aeronwind. Not ever.

"Perhaps Elevera is merely a bit confused. She has known you for your entire life. It's only natural that she should be familiar with you. But Paege, you understand, never really got to know her until after his father died. And between you and me," Mardoc said as held the fork up and gestured between the two of them while a piece of mutton remained speared on the tines, "I suspect that part of Paege's issue is that Elevera was his father's mount. I'm sure that riding her would naturally bring up some things for him. It was on Elevera's back that his father died."

Trysten gripped her knees. She recalled seeing Paege's father ride her, seeing him care for her, but she never knew that he had died in flight on Elevera's back. She knew he had been killed in battle, but somehow, that was someplace distant as if battle was a foreign city. She glanced at the dragon next to them. How could she have not made that connection?

Mardoc took his next bite and laid the fork on the dish. He appeared to consider the dish as he chewed. Finally, he shook his head and looked up at his daughter. "Don't get me wrong, Little Heart. I'm delighted that you have come around to seeing things my way. It shows true wisdom and an open mind on your part. But I think the best thing for Paege, and the entire horde at this point, is for you keep your distance. Give those two space to work things out. They will come together in the end. You will see. I know dragons better than I know anything else."

Trysten stared at her father a few seconds longer and considered whether to tell him how Paege felt, about the dangers they faced when Aeronwind died. But it would do no good. His faith in Paege was unshakable.

Without waiting for him to finish his lunch, Trysten left. She walked out of the weyr and into a shower of fat, heavy snowflakes that blurred the scenery about her.

Chapter 15

By the following morning, a few flakes still drifted out of the gray sky. The storm had dumped several inches of snow overnight. The clouds had edges to them now, layers. Trysten looked behind herself. The snow betrayed her by showing her footfalls around the base of the hill. Still, it seemed unlikely that anyone would follow her into the foothills. She had told her mother that she was going for a walk and perhaps would do a little hunting. When her mother made a comment about the snow and cold, she had merely said that she couldn't sit around the cottage, and since her father wouldn't let her back in the weyr any time soon, she'd walk off her frustration and make herself at least a little bit useful with the bow.

A shiver ran down her. She rubbed her arms beneath the cloak she wore over two sweaters. When she had first approached Paege about meeting in secret to train, he hadn't been keen on the idea, to say the least. But he came around. He saw the wisdom in her argument. Hopefully, he didn't get cold feet and leave her out in the foothills. He couldn't necessarily give her a ride back to the village without raising the suspicions of her father, but a little time on the back of a warm dragon sounded delightful. Especially to her cold feet.

The silhouette of a dragon sailed over the top of a hill. Trysten rocked gently from side-to-side as the rider scanned the hills and dales below. The dragon flapped her golden wings, changed her course, and began to glide down.

A broad grin spread across Trysten's face. Unlike birds, who always looked as if they struggled with the air, as if they pushed it down beneath their wings or glided over it as one might glide across ice, Elevera appeared to dominate the air, to be the reason it existed. The air pushed her up. It parted for her. When she neared the ground, she threw her wings up and back and shoved them forward again as she extended her claws. Billows of snow lifted and fled as she touched down.

As she settled on the ground and folded her wings behind her, Paege waved from the saddle. He at least appeared dressed for the part. His leather riding armor was well-oiled. The traditional tassels of wool hung from his shoulders and from the crown of his helmet. A woolen scarf the color of Elevera braided with the yellow and blue colors of Aerona's crest gave him the look of a true hordesman, and with mild embarrassment, Trysten had a flash of herself as a maiden come to illicitly meet her boyfriend before he flew off to battle.

She cast the silly image from her mind. She was there to meet Paege, the boy she grew up with. She was there to help him bond with Elevera. She was there to save the horde and the village. Duties of a dragoneer.

She approached Elevera and Paege. The snow crunched beneath her goatskin boots. It both dampened and echoed the sound of her footfalls. The hills rising around them trapped the noise, and it felt like a pit for a moment, as if she might never get out.

Elevera let out a snort. She swung her head low in greeting, then let out a long sigh before shuffling her feet on the spot.

"I'm glad to see you, too," Trysten said as she approached the dragon.

"You weren't followed?" Trysten asked of Paege.

He shook his head. "And neither were you. But your tracks through the snow make you easy to find."

Trysten reached out to the dragon. Elevera rested her scaly chin in Trysten's palm. She grinned, then recalled why they were there and drew her hand away. Elevera pulled her head back as if struck.

Paege glanced at the sky, then back to the hill they had just flown over. "I told your father that I thought I could benefit from a bit of solitude with

Elevera. Give us a chance to get to know each other without the interference of others."

"And I suppose he accepted that."

Paege nodded. "He thought it was a great idea. But I have to admit, I don't like lying to him."

Trysten sighed. "I don't like it either, but what else are we supposed to do?"

He shrugged. "I don't know. Maybe he's right. He is the dragoneer."

He looked up at the back of Elevera's head for a second. She turned her head around on her long neck and stared back at him until he looked away, toward the horizon again. He let out a sigh. "Maybe I should just refuse. Maybe I should tell your father that I can't do it. I can't be the dragoneer, and he has to get someone else."

Trysten took a deep breath. Despite the cold that bit at the back of her nose and the top of her throat, a fire rose in her. By the wilds, she wanted nothing more than what he was being handed, and here he sat considering whether he should refuse it. What if he did just that? What if they went to her father and told him simply that Paege refused to do it, that another must be selected. With Aeronwind's health flagging and the fighting season coming early, to whom would he turn? Might he relent and let Trysten have the title?

She swallowed. She blinked away the cold. No. He would not give the title to her. He would pick another of the hordesmen, one that he favored over the others.

They would have to start over from scratch, training a new hordesman to bond with Elevera.

"We don't have the time. The fighting season is coming. I'm afraid if you wanted to have cold feet, you should have developed them sooner. You should have told my father the truth back when he first approached you."

Paege's gaze fell to the ground. A gust of wind stirred a whirlwind of snow that raced off between the hills. Elevera shuffled her feet, flicked her wings. Snow was not something that dragons cared for.

"Then I suppose we should get down to business, then," Paege said.

Trysten nodded. She approached Elevera and held her hand up to Paege. He patted Elevera's neck. She knelt down onto her elbows while Paege grabbed Trysten's wrist and pulled her up. The riding saddle didn't accommodate two riders, and so Trysten sat on the border of the blanket that stuck out from under the back of the saddle.

Paege yanked on the lip of the saddle. Elevera stood, then launched herself into the sky with a great push of her wings. Without stirrups or straps to help keep her in place, Trysten wrapped her arms around Paege's torso.

The dragon undulated slightly beneath them as she climbed into the air. Once she reached the tops of the hills, she spread her wings wide, twisted to her right, and slid back down into the dale before she caught a breeze channeled between the two hills. With another twitch of her wings, they were lifted into the air on the back of the wind. Elevera beat her wings some more, searched for other currents, for more air forced over the hills as it fled the distant mountains. Soon, they circled high in the sky, among the twirling flakes of snow. Off in the east, the village of Aerona was visible as a patch of flecked brown among the white foothills. Small twists of smoke lifted from various buildings, the largest one being the weyr.

Her grip on Paege tightened. How vulnerable the village looked from this height. It sat in the open, among rolling plains of snow-covered heather and grass for as far as she could see to the eastern horizon. To the west, the mountains sat thick and dark, tops shrouded by clouds until a great, golden wing of leathery flesh eclipsed the view for a second.

Trysten's envy bubbled through her veins, sped up, and grew sharper. The hordesmen always made themselves out to be so brave, as if they were sacrificing so much to be hordesmen, to be the dragon riders ready to fling themselves headlong into battle at a moment's notice. They never talked of this, of the trade they made. Yes, they flew into battle, but most of the year, they rode on the backs of dragons and called it training. They lived in the sky. They were the equals of birds. Such a life was no sacrifice.

Elevera pushed them higher and higher yet until the village became barely discernible through the swirling snow. The ground itself was fuzzy, little more than fog. If Trysten fell off, she'd drop into a mist and fall forever, according to the view she held now.

The cold bit into her. The chill ached in her cheekbones. Her hands tingled despite thick, woolen mitts wrapped around Paege's midsection. She leaned forward some, shifted, and immediately Paege's posture went tight and rigid beneath her.

"Send her through maneuvers," Trysten called above the breathless wind.

"What kind of maneuvers?"

"Please keep in mind that I'm not strapped down," she replied.

Paege nodded. He sat a moment more, then leaned into the lip of the saddle. Elevera's wings leveled out, and they drifted in the sky, wobbling back and forth in the breeze.

Paege gave a short kick of his heels. Trysten felt the movement pass through his body, the way his torso moved as she buried her raw face into his back to warm her cheeks. Out of the corner of her eye, she saw his knee dip as he ordered Elevera to descend. And then the dragon tilted her wings forward some as she drew them in. They began to descend. A breeze hit them hard, and Elevera fell into a wide spiral. Normally, such a maneuver would have thrilled her, but the snow and the height, the cold and the lack of ties all left her stomach lurching, nauseous.

Elevera stretched one wing out while twisting the other. They sailed down. Paege leaned forward on the lip of the saddle. Elevera drew her wings in further. Their descent increased. It felt as if they were dropping. Trysten peered over Paege's shoulder. The snow-covered ground rushed at them. It appeared so soft and gentle. Off on another hill, a smattering of small, gray specks moved among the snow. Wolves.

Trysten tapped on Paege's shoulder, then pointed to the wolves. Suddenly, Elevera threw out her wings and lifted the right. They careened off in the direction of the wolves. Trysten gripped Paege tight and clenched her jaw as speed pushed her down against Elevera's spine. She was mostly safe on the dragon's back, as long as she didn't try and fly upside down, but the speed was still a little unnerving.

The dragon let up some.

"What is she doing?" Paege yelled over his shoulder.

"What is who doing?"

"Elevera! What is she doing?"

"Aren't you the rider?"

"I told her to descend. She's acting on her own right now."

"Are you giving her directions?"

"I'm trying!"

The dragon spread her wings wide. She released a ferocious roar as they came upon the wolves. A blast of fire escaped her jaw and dissipated above the scrambling wolves.

"By the wilds!" Paege cursed.

Elevera tipped to her right and spun around in a quick, tight circle.

"Paege!" Trysten screamed as she clutched his torso.

"It's not me! She's on her own."

Elevera straightened out and left the pack of wolves to flee across the hills.

As Elevera's flight leveled off in speed and altitude, Trysten sat up and peered over Paege's shoulders to see where his hands rested upon the lip of the saddle. She then wrapped her hands around his shoulders so that she might feel if he gave any additional orders through the saddle's lip.

"What are you doing?" Paege asked.

"Tell her to go up."

Paege pulled back on the lip of the saddle. Elevera's wings began to flap, and she climbed toward the sky.

"Harder," Trysten called.

Paege scraped his heels up along the dragon's side. Her wing beats grew more furious. She undulated slightly as she powered up into the sky.

"Level off."

Paege flicked his calves, enough to make his heels bounce off the dragon's shoulders. She immediately leveled off.

Trysten placed her cheek against Paege's back and stared across the hilltops and on to the mountains. They seemed closer now as if they had sneaked up on them during the excitement. The mountains were trying to surprise them, to get within striking range, then let loose a horde of Western dragons.

Trysten pulled a breath from the sky, and it hurt. It sat in her chest hard and sharp. The air slipped right back out of her lungs, too cold and thin to hold onto. She wrapped her arms around Paege's torso again, then thought of dropping down, of a full-on dive. She pictured the matted plains and the white snow rushing toward her.

Elevera's wings folded in.

Paege screamed as they dropped from the sky. He jerked and pushed against Trysten while fighting to regain control of the falling dragon. He yanked on the saddle's lip and kicked with his heels to convince her to level off.

Despite the hammering of her heart and the tremble in her cheek where she felt fear rumble through Paege's chest, she continued to imagine the ground rushing up, coming for them, ready to smash them like an insect.

Then she pictured Aeronwind. She pictured the great, gray wings like clouds made tangible, made into something one could touch and stroke. She pictured the wings folding out, the dragon streaking over her as it came out of a dive, the tail straight and flowing behind her, like the tail of a comet.

Elevera's wings snapped out. The bottom of Trysten's stomach dropped as the dragon streaked across the hills. She opened her eyes and peered over the dragon's side. The tops of hills and twisted bits of shrubbery zipped by mere yards beneath the dragon's claws.

"For all the sky!" Paege panted. He yanked back on the lip of the saddle and raked up on Elevera's sides with his heels.

The dragon began to lift, to trade some of her momentum back to the sky, but then Trysten imagined her going to ground. She pictured the great, golden wings spreading out wide and upwards, the claws taking the ground as if she were claiming the very land as her own.

Atop the next hill, Elevera settled to the ground.

"What in the wilds is wrong with you!" Paege yelled at Elevera.

Trysten swung her leg back and over the dragon. She slid off and dropped to the ground with a little hop. "It's not her. It's me," she called up.

Paege furrowed his brow as he peered down at her. "You?"

"I... can't explain it."

"Well, by the wilds, I sure can't!"

"She's responding to me."

Paege glanced from Trysten to Elevera, who stood in the snow and waited for the next command, the next desire to cross Trysten's mind.

"How do you mean she's responding to you?"

Trysten took several steps back in the crunching snow. Elevera's gaze followed her. By the wilds, was her father right? Was it best for her to put some distance between herself and Elevera, allow the connection between Paege and the dragon to strengthen without strain from her?

She tugged at one of her braids.

As if working something out for himself, Paege placed the palm of his hand against the back of Elevera's neck, then flicked his heels against her shoulders. Elevera ambled forward several awkward steps. Once he removed his palm from Elevera's neck, she stopped and turned her attention back to Trysten, giving the impression that she was seeking approval.

"For all the sky!" Paege spat. "Look at her! It's like she's only following my commands because she thinks it might impress you. This has nothing to do with me, does it? I will never bond with this dragon!"

Trysten glared at Paege. Was it too late? Her gaze went beyond him and to the mountains, solid and ominous as close as they were now. If she held her breath, might she hear the roar of Western dragons in the canyons already?

She shook her head. It was apparent that she had a special bond with Elevera. Might she use that to their advantage? Her insight might be exactly what was needed to convince Elevera that she needed to bond with Paege for the good of the horde.

Chapter 16

Trysten approached Elevera. She held up her hand as if reaching for a high object. On cue, Elevera lowered her head and nuzzled her palm. Trysten stroked the top of the dragon's snout.

"I've been around these dragons all my life. And with my father, no less. I just have a relationship with them formed by time. That's all. I can teach you what I know."

Paege glared at the mountain range. His frustration would be a barrier to the dragon.

"Dismount. I want to show you something."

Paege considered her command a second, then swung his leg over Elevera's neck and slid down her shoulder to land in a crouch on the ground.

"Come here. I want you to look right into Elevera's eyes."

Paege approached slowly and stared up into the dragon's eyes. Elevera continued to gaze at Trysten as she dropped her hands to her sides. Elevera then dipped her head a bit more, as if she might seek out and nudge Trysten's hands back into action. The dragon paused as Trysten moved her hands behind her back.

"This isn't—" Paege began.

"Quiet!"

She took a deep breath, then imagined Paege's hazel eyes. Her own eyelids began to drift shut as she pictured the dark pupils, the flecks of gold in the green of his eyes. The way his eyes always appeared to be searching.

Elevera shifted her gaze to Paege.

"Good girl," Trysten muttered.

"What was that?"

"Nothing. Are you staring into her eyes?"

"Yes."

"What do you see?"

"What do you mean, 'What do I see?' I see Elevera's eyes."

"You're not making this easy," Trysten said.

Paege shifted. "It's not easy."

A cold breeze rattled them all.

"Look into her eyes. Tell me… Tell me what you feel."

"Cold."

"Paege," Trysten said with a sigh.

"Well, what am I supposed to be feeling? I'm cold. And I'm frustrated. And I'm worried. How in the wilds am I going to keep the horde from absconding? I can't do it. Your father may be a great warrior and dragoneer, but he did a lousy job of picking his successor."

"Stop!" Trysten commanded.

Elevera flicked her gaze back to Trysten.

"That's your problem," Trysten continued. "You're too caught up in yourself. You're only paying attention to what is going on inside of you. You need to open yourself up. Focus on the dragon. Focus on Elevera. You have to be paying attention to what she feels."

"What she feels? How do I do that?"

"You see it in her eyes. It's there."

"You're kidding me."

Her face no longer felt bitten by the cold. "Do you want to bond with this dragon or not?"

Paege glanced away. Color flushed his cheeks. "I'm sorry, Elevera," he called to the dragon. "Look at me. Please."

Elevera continued to stare at Trysten. She resumed picturing Paege's eyes, and then the dragon turned her attention back to Paege.

"Now, pay attention. Look into her eyes. Watch. Tell me what you see. Tell me what you feel. Describe it. No matter what comes into your head, no matter how silly it sounds or feels, tell me about it."

They stood in silence a few moments. The wind ruffled them, batted at their ears. A slight hissing sound came from the snow as it fell in wind-driven waves and added to the several inches on the ground. Nearby, a flutter of great, feathered wings gave away the approach of a bird of prey, and then it was silent as it fell atop its quarry, no longer hidden by the snow and the great, empty expanse of the hills.

Paege shook his head. "I don't know what you want me to say."

Trysten inhaled a deep breath. "I already told you what to say."

He shook his head again. "And I already told you what I feel, but it is apparently not what you wanted to hear."

As Trysten began to extend her hand to the dragon, Elevera turned her head from Paege and nuzzled her palm again. She cupped the point of the dragon's chin and held it.

"I look into her eyes, and I see... curiosity. She is wondering what is going on here. What are we up to? This is unlike any of the other things that humans have made her do. She's a little amused. She's cold, though. And she's a little impatient to take to the sky."

Trysten's brow furrowed slightly. "And she's worried. She wants to get back to the weyr and check on Aeronwind."

"That's a fine idea," Paege said.

"She's worried."

"You said."

"No," Trysten said with another shake of her head. "She's worried about something else as well. She's worried about..." She let her words trail off as she was flooded with images of the horde, of the dragons flying away, fanning out as they sought a new alpha.

"About what?" Paege asked.

"About... my father. She's worried about my father as well."

Elevera lifted her chin from Trysten's palm.

Paege rocked back once on his heels. "How can you tell all of that?"

Trysten shoved her hands into the pockets of her over-sweater. Paege's bangs were starting to look damp where they stuck out from beneath the edge of the leather helmet.

She shrugged. "I can. It's there, in her eyes. It's the way... The way her eyes shift. You know how you can enter a room sometimes and just know what mood people are in by the way they are sitting?"

Paege stared as if waiting for her to explain herself.

She turned back to the dragon. How did her father do it? He had always written off her insight in the past when she had alluded to it, referred to it as the fancies of a young girl with a powerful imagination. But there was no doubt that he was the dragoneer, that the entire horde acquiesced to him, saw him as their leader and master. How did he do it if he couldn't sense what they were feeling or thinking? There had to be a trick that he used. If she knew what it was, then she might be able to use it, along with her own abilities, to encourage the relationship both Paege and Elevera needed to keep the horde together.

She turned to Paege. "How does my father do it? What does he tell you to do?"

Paege, still staring at Elevera, shrugged. "I don't know. He tells us to form bonds with them by interacting with them. We do a lot of exercises."

He brushed the damp bangs off his forehead. The cold had settled into his cheeks, and they were a vibrant red now. They would be cold to the touch if she took off her mitten and laid her palm against them.

"He tells us to think of the dragons as extensions of ourselves. He says that we can't think about them as if we are riding them. They're not horses. They're not tools. When we're riding, we have to be aware of them. We have to know where every part of them is in relation to ourselves, like how you always know where your feet and your hands are in relation to yourself. And we have to feel them like we feel our arms and legs. We have to pay attention to their movements. We have to be able to tell with our thighs how they are shifting, what their wings are doing, how they are changing their postures."

"How do they feel?" Trysten asked.

Paege's eyebrows lifted slightly. "You know. It's that shift. You feel it under your saddle, and against your thighs. That pressure."

"I mean the dragons. How do they feel?"

"What do you mean?"

Trysten glanced at Elevera again. "It's how you tell how they feel. You look at someone..." she turned her attention back to Paege. "You look at him, and you take all of him in, and you know how he feels by the way he stands, the color of his cheeks, how one boot is buckled tighter than the other."

Paege glanced at his feet. He lifted his left foot slightly, then chuckled. "I was in a hurry."

Trysten turned back to Elevera. "I imagine you were overwhelmed."

Paege let the silence answer for him.

His response was surprising. Trysten had not imagined that her father would be one to encourage deep relationships with the dragons. She'd never really given it any thought before, as to how he coached the hordesmen, but she had always assumed that he coached them to have a commanding presence, to make their will known to their mounts. And the dragons went along with it for the sake of the alpha, who went along with it for the sake of the dragoneer. But when he was a boy, how had her father managed to bond with Aeronwind? Might he have a bit of her gift in himself? Was it where her talent had come from? If so, why did he hide it? Why did he dismiss her so easily when she indicated that she understood the dragons on a deeper level?

The only way to know would be to ask him straight out.

"We should call it a day," Trysten said.

Paege took a deep breath. "You know how it feels? It feels like we haven't accomplished a thing. In fact, I think I feel worse now than I did before we came out here. I felt good coming out here, you know? She responded to me just fine. She did what I asked. It was almost effortless to fly out here and find you. But seeing what I've seen now, I think it was her in control all along. It was her who wanted to come out here and find you. The fact that I was ordering her, or instructing her, was merely coincidental. I was telling her to do something she was going to do anyway. Seeing how she behaves when you're around, though, it just makes me feel like this is hopeless."

He cupped his hand around the back of his neck. "What am I going to do? I look at the way these dragons behave around you and your father, and I am never going to be able to manage that. If you two can't coax these dragons into listening to me, what hope do I have?"

Trysten placed a hand on the back of his shoulder. Paege rubbed at his neck, then allowed his hand to fall to his side. He glared at the snow between himself and Elevera. His shoulders heaved in a sigh. He glanced back at Trysten. "We have to come up with a better plan. We have to figure out how to make your father listen."

Trysten lifted an eyebrow. "Listen? Didn't you accept the role?"

Paege peered into the sky. "You know how it is with your father. It's not so much that he asks for your opinion as much as he tells you what your opinion is."

Trysten nodded. He did have that quality about him.

"What was I to do? When it comes to something this big, this important, I can't just do what I want to do. I have to do what is best for the horde, for the village. What I want comes second."

Trysten crossed her arms over herself and rubbed them under her cloak. "But yet you're telling me that we have to do something different?"

"For the sake of the horde, we do. I'm not trying to get out of my obligation. Believe me, I'm not looking forward to the shame of being passed over, of knowing how incredibly disappointed my father would be in me for blowing this. Seeing me take the new alpha's saddle would have been the proudest day of his life. I have no doubt about that. I don't remember much about him, but I remember that. He wanted me to grow up and follow in his footsteps. He wanted me to ride dragons. He lost his life defending the kingdom. He gave up everything for me, for all of us. How do I repay that, you know? It seems so selfish to not follow in his footsteps, as if I think his sacrifice isn't worth repaying."

Trysten opened her mouth to respond but didn't know what to say.

"And then there's your father," Paege continued. "He treated me as one of his own. He made sure that my mother and I had enough to eat, that our cottage was always in good repair. She told me many times what a wonderful man your father was. That he honored my father and his service. That we owed everything we had to your father. How was I to tell him no? Again, it's not like he asked, as much as he told me that I would follow him. And after his accident and all…"

Paege drew in a sharp breath.

"You know," Trysten said, "we need things in the village other than dragoneers and hordesmen. There are others who are needed, who have services and skills that are just as indispensable, and they all give. They all contribute to the village in their own way."

Paege looked away. "Yeah, I doubt the village would fall if we were suddenly without a blacksmith."

Trysten shrugged. "Who would make the buckles for our saddles? Or the tips for our arrows? Or the blades with which we slaughter the food for the dragons or the food for ourselves? Who would make the spits on which we cook our meat?"

Paege shook his head, but Trysten continued. "You know what I mean. This is a small village. One on the border of the kingdom. We all depend on each other to survive. You needn't be a hordesman, or even a dragoneer, to give back. You just have to be yourself."

Paege's jaw clenched and flexed as if chewing on his words. "That sounds all fine and good to hear you say it..." He glanced back at Trysten. "But it doesn't address the bigger problem. What do we do when Aeronwind dies? Can you look into Elevera's eyes and tell me what she feels? Can you tell me that she is going to feel like bonding? That she is going to obey my every wish and command and use her position among the horde to make sure the other dragons serve us?"

"They don't serve us," Trysten said. "They're not beasts of burden. They're not mules with wings. They live with us. They work with us. The alpha gets satisfaction from the pride that the dragoneer feels. That is what keeps the horde in Aerona. Aeronwind wants to make my father proud. She cares for him. She cares for him because he..." She recalled her father sitting in the stall, his back against his dragon with his twisted leg sticking out before himself. The look on his face, when he thought she wasn't looking, set her back some. It was the closest thing to helplessness she had ever seen on the face of a man she thought capable of moving the whole world if the whim took him.

"My father cares for Aeronwind in a way that he cares for no one else. He loves me, and he loves my mother, but there is something about him and that dragon. They fly together into battle. They depend upon one another. Aeronwind has kept him alive, has kept his family safe. She has selflessly thrown herself into battle when called upon. That's what's missing here, Paege. You have to care about Elevera. You have to care about her like you've never cared for anything else before."

The words yanked at her throat as if each one was knotted to a piece of twine attached to her heart with a loop of steel. Each one was a part of her, a morsel of her that she handed off to this man who didn't appear capable of understanding. What did he care about? What would he give his life for?

Paege turned his face slowly toward her. Breath billowed out in a cloud from his parted lips. His nose glowed with the cold. His eyes were bright and shining in the gray light and bored straight into her. He sucked in a deep breath, and if it were there for her to grasp, Trysten would have clutched at a pole, a rail, anything solid as if she might be sucked in, or blown over by the words she feared he would say.

Her fingers curled into a fist, and that was the best she could manage unless she reached for Elevera.

Then he turned away, and he stepped toward Elevera. He approached her and reached up to grab the edge of her saddle, leaving Trysten standing there weak and wobbly in the snow, wrung out from what had almost happened, which she wasn't quite sure about. What she did know for sure was that she would not ask Paege to tell her what it was he cared for more than anything else.

Paege stuck a foot in the stirrup, then pulled himself up and onto Elevera's shoulders.

"We should be getting back. You've got a distance to walk. We'll give you a ride to where we found you."

A little relief flowed through Trysten. The fact that he had said *we* instead of *I* was an indication that all was not hopeless or lost.

She approached Paege and offered her hand. He helped her up onto the dragon's back, and as Elevera shuffled in the snow to take advantage of the wind, Trysten wrapped her arms around Paege and laid her cheek in the space between his shoulder blades.

How had things come this far?

Chapter 17

Shivers wracked Trysten by the time she entered the village. The snow had stopped some time ago, and the clouds had begun to bunch up, to show their edges and soft corners. It appeared at times that the sun might even pop through, but it never did. If the sun was going to come out, it wouldn't be until the next morning.

Back at the cottage, she changed clothes and warmed up by the fire as her mother sat on the other side of the hearth and worked on her knitting. She had asked Trysten about her walk but didn't push it too far. Both of them ended up staring into the fire, moving only to stoke it, add wood, or pour a cup of tea from the kettle on the hob.

Once warmed, Trysten helped her mother make dinner, and though she offered to take another basket to her father, Caron said she would take it this time.

After Caron departed for the weyr, Trysten donned her dried over-sweater and cloak and headed off to a cottage a few doors down. There, she knocked on the door, waited, and was relieved to see Galelin open the door a crack, and then tug at the collar of his sweater.

"Is something the matter with Aeronwind?" he asked.

Trysten shook her head. "I haven't seen her all day. My mother just went to visit her and my father."

The wrinkles in Galelin's brow deepened. "What is it then, my dear?"

"I have questions. I want to know a few things about dragons."

"Oh," his head bobbed as if it were the most natural thing in the world that she showed up at his door when she never had before. "Come in, then. I'll try to answer what I can."

He stepped back and allowed the door to swing open. Trysten stepped inside. All about the man's cottage sat piles of books and baskets filled with scrolls. Her jaw dropped. It was an absolute prince's fortune in books and scrolls, and here Galelin kept it all in a cottage not quite as big as her own.

"Can I get you something to drink? A cup of tea, perhaps?" As the man shuffled over to his hearth, Trysten noted the smell. His whole cottage had the sharp smell of old books, a slight mustiness that she had only ever smelled before when she stuck her nose to the pages of the volumes in her father's den. She had expected that his collection of a dozen or so books was the greatest in the village. Galelin had at least a hundred and maybe more.

"What are all of these?" she asked as she waved an absent hand toward a stack along the back of a table.

Galelin paused as he reached for the kettle, then straightened his back. His spine cracked as he twisted around to see what she had gestured at. "Why, those are books, my dear."

Trysten let out an exasperated sigh. It had already been a long day. "What are they about?"

Galelin reached for the kettle again. "Oh, a little of this, a little of that. As the dragon healer, I'm expected to be a bit of a scholar. One never knows when a little geography or a little alchemy might come in handy. Even knowing a little bit about art is helpful from time to time."

"Art?"

Galelin carried the kettle over to the table and placed it on an iron trivet. From a shallow reed basket, he produced a trembling sheaf of parchment and held it out to Trysten. She crossed the room and took it. Among sketches of plants and what appeared to be the interior of a fish, she examined a drawing of Aeronwind's wound, next to what appeared to be the skeleton of a healthy dragon.

"These are amazing," Trysten said as she turned the parchment over and found even more sketches.

"It's not art. Not like the greats of old. But studying their work does help an old healer communicate better. I was able to show my friend in the mother city Aeronwind's wound with more clarity and much less time than if I had to tried to use words alone."

He grinned at his own cleverness, then turned his attention to a teapot and a small dish of dried leaves. "Now, what was it that you came here for? Certainly not to brighten an old man's day, and definitely not for a cup of tea that could be had in any home in Aerona."

Trysten glanced at the parchment once more, then placed it on the table. "I wanted to ask you about the bonds between humans and dragons."

"Oh?" Galelin picked up the kettle and filled the teapot. Steam leaked up and out, and his hands lingered a second over it as if sampling the warmth.

"What is responsible for that bond? Why do humans and dragons bond at all? What causes it?"

Galelin scooped several spoonfuls of leaves into the teapot. "Concerned about young Paege, are you?"

Trysten's shoulders sunk a bit. "More like I'm concerned about the horde."

Galelin's lips turned down at the corners for a few seconds. "It is troublesome. An absconding horde is never a good thing. Especially before the fighting season. And dear Yahi says, if I heard correctly, that the fighting season will visit us early this year."

"You know more about dragons than anyone in the village. Is there anything you can do to help foster the bond between Paege and Elevera? I'm... concerned that they aren't taking to each other."

Galelin flashed a crooked grin. "Do you think your father has asked the same of me?"

Trysten's jaw dropped. It hadn't occurred to her that he would ask. She had assumed that he knew best, or that he at least thought he knew best.

Galelin's grin widened, and then he shook his head. "Well, he hasn't, your father. The man is dragoneer. You can't have him going around acting like there is something he doesn't know. It wouldn't do now, would it?"

He picked up the teapot, brought it to his face, and inhaled the steam deeply.

Trysten sighed. "He thinks that Paege and Elevera will bond, but I have my doubts. He doesn't..." she paused. There was no reason to try and protect his feelings now. This was too important. "Paege doesn't care for Elevera the way that he should. You know how it is. That relationship between—"

"Between you and Elevera?" Galelin asked.

"Between my father and Aeronwind."

"Ah, yes. A man and his dragon." Galelin poured the amber-colored tea into two cups. "The mythical idea that man can be married in a figurative sense to the wilderness of this land. It is at the center of our mythos that something as noble and powerful as a female dragon can be made to mind a mere man—a pitiful creature without the benefit of scales, wings, or the breath of fire. It makes us feel as if the gods themselves had granted us our position on this land, doesn't it?"

Galelin shook his head. "No matter. I may have studied philosophy some, but I am no philosopher. I am merely a dragon healer."

"Can you help me secure the bond between Elevera and Paege?" Trysten asked.

"Sit." Galelin motioned to a stool at the table.

As Trysten took her cup and sat at the table, Galelin sipped from his own cup, then nodded as if passing approval on the tea. "I can do nothing for Paege and Elevera. I have heard of potions, of concoctions said to create a bond between any person and any dragon, but I suspect that it is a matter of fancy over a matter of fact. Anything that can be achieved through a mixture of herbs and elements is a matter of alchemy. The bond between your father and Aeronwind is beyond alchemy. It is a matter of soul."

"Soul?"

Galelin nodded. "Soul. What is it that causes any two persons to fall in love?"

Trysten stared at Galelin until she realized he was waiting for a response. She shrugged.

A wide grin spread over the man's face and framed his ramshackle teeth. "Ah, to be young enough to be ignorant. You have the whole world ahead of you, waiting to be discovered. But that is not what you came to know."

He cupped both of his hands around his tea, then took a sip. "There is in people, a hollowness. An emptiness. It is… If you had studied art, and you had seen the vases that are made by the masters of Tylu, you would see what I mean."

Galelin picked up the scrap of parchment he had shown her earlier before plucking a stub of charcoal from its resting place between the edge of the table and the wall. He sketched an elaborate shape, like an inverted teardrop with a flower blossoming from the top of it.

"This in no way does these vases any justice. It is purely for demonstration. But what makes these vases incredible is not so much the shape of them, but where the shape ends. It is the emptiness that surrounds them that defines their shapes, their curves, the very things that a person's eye lingers upon. Understand?"

Trysten glanced up at Galelin. "Maybe?"

He grinned again. "No matter. I don't wish to bore you. Just suffice it to say that as we grow up, experience shapes us like hands that will shape wet clay into a pot or vessel. But where the hands draw the borders, the edges, the walls of the pot, there is emptiness. People are like that. Our experiences shape us, but also leave empty areas that define our edges, that give us our definitions. Now, a vase is quite content to sit upon a pedestal and be admired by a wealthy patron or some fool. But a person, aware and alive, in possession of a soul, is not content to let these empty areas be. We try to fill them. We try to find complementary shapes. We like to fit together. It makes us feel like we belong, understand?" Galelin held his hands up and threaded his fingers together.

Trysten nodded. That bit she believed she understood.

"Your father is a man of ambition. He was shaped that way by his grandfather. The lines that define him as such leave in him an emptiness that he feels keenly. Your father has always pined for an equal, and in your mother, he found such. Your mother is a strong woman, as capable and strong and willful as any person of either gender. She compliments your father's shape. Likewise, Aeronwind compliments your father's shape, and he compliments hers. But a vase, taken from the kiln, can never be molded again, and I'm afraid that by the time your friend is old enough to be dragoneer, he is old enough to be taken from the kiln, to be fired and fixed in the shape that he is. You cannot force him and Elevera to be together. It can't be done."

Trysten shook her head. "But something has to be done. If those two can't bond, the horde will abscond."

Galelin nodded as if agreeing with her assessment of the weather. "It happens."

"It happens? No! It doesn't happen here. It can't happen here. The fighting season is coming. The hordesmen of the Western Kingdom will push through the pass on the first clear day. We can't be without the horde to protect us! You have to do something. You have to help me save the horde!"

Galelin took another sip of tea, then shook his head. "There is nothing to be done. Believe me. I have studied this subject far and deep, ever since I was a young man."

Wistfulness fell off his statement as if a puff of dust had billowed up around a memory touched for the first time in a long time.

Trysten placed her cup on the table.

Galelin slapped his palms against his thighs. "Well, my dear, I'm frightfully afraid that I have done very little to help you, have I? But at the very least, I hope you are warmer and less thirsty than when you first arrived. Is there anything more to be done?"

Trysten sat a moment longer. How could he give up like that? There was always something that could be done.

"Are you sure? If I could just get Paege to…" She trailed off, letting go of the end of the sentence as if flinging it into the open, a frayed bit of rope that she hoped the old healer would catch and knot off to another line of thought.

Galelin shook his head. "Paege may try the best he is able, but in the end, a relationship cannot be forced. The best he or any of us can do is to make ourselves available. To open up our empty curves so that others might recognize the inverse of themselves and see whether or not they might fit."

Trysten sighed in frustration. The options available were few.

"Thank you for the tea," Trysten said as she stood.

"Any time, my dear. Any time. It is always a pleasure to have someone such as yourself as a guest in my cottage."

Trysten's brow furrowed a bit. "How so?"

"Why, the dragoneer's daughter. I've always admired the people who could bond with dragons. I have wished for such a gift myself all my life, but I've had to settle for being a healer. Still, I must admit, that if a man can't have his dream, then there is a certain amount of satisfaction in watching others have it for him."

"You wanted to be a dragoneer?"

Galelin nodded as he placed his cup next to Trysten's. He then pushed himself up off the stool and strode to the door. "My father was Wiglin, Dragoneer of the weyr Drowlin. I was his eldest son."

Trysten's eyes grew wide. "You were the eldest son of a dragoneer?"

"Have you ever heard of Drowlin?"

She shook her head.

"My father died fighting the Western Kingdom. He took an arrow through the throat. The alpha brought me his body." The matter-of-fact tone of the admission chilled Trysten.

"It was quite a fright, of course. I was 17 years old at the time. The hordesmen of the Western Kingdom had prevailed that day. We lost half our horde and all but one of the hordesmen. The alpha, Tillin was her name, came to me, and I will never forget the look in her eyes as she dropped to the ground before me, my father still limp and strapped to her back. There was such a look of... expectation in her eyes. She wanted something from me."

Galelin's gaze traveled to the top of the wall behind Trysten. She steeled herself from turning around, from looking for herself.

"And then," Galelin said with a shrug, "she turned away from me as if whatever it was she sought was clearly not before her, and so she wished to find it elsewhere. She crouched, as dragons do, and then it hit me then and there what was about to happen. I remember it like it was yesterday because, to be honest, I lived these moments over and over yesterday, as I have today, as I am now. Time stretched out as if time itself wanted to give me every chance possible to right the egregious wrong about to take place. I threw up a hand as if wildly hailing Tillin might stop her. I opened my mouth to issue a command to stay, to flat out beg her not to leave."

Gaelin let out a sigh, thick and weighty, like a bag of soil whose burden he wished to put down.

"She leaped into the air. She spread those great, magenta wings of hers and beat them down as if pushing away from me, my failure to bond, and all of Drowlin. And as I watched her heave into the air, there was my father upon her back still, bent over backward, his arm cast out and waving back and forth as if waving goodbye, and that was the last I, or anyone in the Drowlin weyr, ever saw of her or the remainder of the horde. Drowlin fell to the Western Kingdom the next day. But I had gone the evening before."

Trysten let out a slow breath. "I'm so sorry. I had no idea."

Galelin held up a hand and shook his head. "Of course not, of course you didn't. It's not something that most people in the village know. Your father. I assume your mother knows as well. That's it."

Trysten's back straightened. "And you're telling me?"

"I spent many, many years, decades, studying dragons and everything else to discover what I did wrong, what I might have done differently to save the horde and my father's body. I wanted to know the depth of my shame. And I eventually discovered that there was nothing I could have done at all. I was not open to Tillin. I was not ready to accept her as my bonded one. I saw my father dead upon her back, and I completely shut down, shut myself off from her and myself as well. It took some time to realize this, but there was nothing I could have done. I was a 17-year-old boy who just saw his father and his future murdered by an advancing army. I am, as I have always been, utterly human."

Heat flushed across Trysten's cheeks. "So you're saying I shouldn't blame myself if the horde absconds?"

Galelin's bushy eyebrows lifted in surprise. "What? No, that's not what I'm saying at all, my dear. What I'm saying is that you cannot force a bond between a human and a dragon. I admire young Paege, who is doing the best he can given the circumstances handed him. The fact that he even gets on the back of his father's former dragon at all is quite admirable, but he cannot bond with Elevera. Elevera will not have him, because he will not have her."

Trysten' shoulders slumped. "So what are we to do?"

Galelin opened the door to his cottage. "My dear, we do what we have to do." The old man stared steadily into Trysten's eyes.

Trysten glanced between the doorway and Galelin. It hardly seemed like the simple answer that Galelin presented it as. His posture, however, clearly indicated that the conversation was over.

Trysten took a last drink of her tea, then stood, thanked Galelin for the tea and his time, then stepped back out into the mud and snow of the lane. She glanced to the sky. Above, the clouds rolled in shifting patterns of gray. Beneath them, dragons wheeled and swooped in the sky. Among them slid the large, golden form of Elevera. Trysten's heart both thrilled and sank at the sight of her. What could she possibly do to save the horde?

She glanced at the weyr a few doors away. It seemed that there was very little else to do except trust her father and Paege.

After a few days, Aeronwind's fever broke. Mardoc placed his vigil on hold and returned home to sleep and eat. Trysten met Paege in the foothills twice more, and though she tried hard to show Paege how to handle Elevera, it eventually ended in frustration. He was adept at issuing commands, but Elevera only listened and obeyed when Trysten wished her to obey. Though Paege took her advice without argument or complaint, Trysten was left with the sense that she had only made matters worse between them. Paege felt a bit betrayed, she imagined. He knew, or at least suspected, that the commands Elevera obeyed were not his, and he was right.

The morning after their last training session together, the sun broke through the clouds in the east. The light across the hills drew Trysten out of bed and to a window where she squinted into the pink and red dawn. Still in her nightshirt, she stepped outside to peer at the mountains. The block of gray that hung over them remained. But the clouds above had definition. Edges and contours. For a second, she thought she saw a spot of deep blue in a shifting patch.

"Good morning," a neighbor cried.

Trysten glanced back at the older woman who lived in the next cottage. She flashed a quick grin and a wave.

The woman turned to the mountains as well. She surveyed the wall of rock and clouds as if waiting for a dispatch, for distant word. "Looks like we'll have some sun today, doesn't it?"

Trysten nodded. A tight band held her lungs and prevented her from responding. She glanced at the mountains again, and the band around her chest grew tighter.

Chapter 18

Later that day, when Trysten brought in several hares taken from the meadow by the river, she found her mother once again at work over a large meal. She turned to Trysten, and when she didn't comment on the number of hares, Trysten knew something was wrong.

"Aeronwind has taken fever again."

Trysten drew in a sharp breath. Though it seemed impossible that Aeronwind would recover from her injuries, she had hoped that they would at least level out, allow Paege and Elevera—mostly Paege—to develop a bond.

The hares strung together on a cord fell to the floor. "Does Galelin know?"

"He's at the weyr, with your father, I suppose."

Caron turned to the piles of vegetables and roots before her. "I was preparing a dinner for the hordesmen."

Trysten placed her mother's bow and quiver above the mantle. She then moved to hang the hares from a peg on the wall above the table.

"What are you doing?" her mother asked.

Trysten paused, her hand outstretched, her knuckles blanched where the weight of the cord pressed against her fingers. "I was going to hang these up here."

"And then what?"

Trysten's shoulder slumped a bit. "I want to see Aeronwind."

"Clean those first. When you're done, I'll have something for you to take to your father. No one will enforce your banishment if you're bringing your father something to eat and drink on his vigil."

A grin crossed Trysten's face as she lowered the string. "Thank you."

Caron returned her attention to the carrot before her. After a few slices, she stopped and looked back at her daughter. "Your father is trying everything he can to protect the weyr. You understand that, right?"

The grin disappeared from Trysten's face. "If that were true, he would let me be the dragoneer. I can bond with Elevera."

Caron set her knife aside. "What makes you so sure of that? That you can bond with her?"

"I know." Trysten's back straightened. "I know."

"Yes, but how do you know?"

Trysten glanced away, to the cooking utensils hanging from a row of pegs in the wall.

"It takes more than confidence to be the dragoneer," Caron said. "If confidence were all there was to it, then you would certainly have the position."

"I can learn everything I need to learn. And Elevera already knows—"

"Elevera doesn't have to convince anyone of her ability, or her value."

Trysten's head shifted back a tiny bit on her neck. "What do you mean by that?"

"Only what I said. What Elevera knows or thinks or feels is not at issue here. This is about her rider."

"I don't understand, then. What are you getting at?"

"There are other qualities to a dragoneer. We talk about bravery and skill. We celebrate it in those who ride the dragons into battle, but there are other qualities necessary."

"Such as?"

"What do dragons think of honesty?"

"Honesty?" It had never occurred to Trysten. After her mother mentioned it, she thought back and couldn't remember a single time that a dragon had felt like someone was lying.

"I don't know," Trysten said, then clamped her jaw shut before adding, *I've never asked them.*

"I'll ask you again," Caron said. "How do you know that you could be a dragoneer?"

Trysten took in a slow, deep breath as her mind raced. Not saying something that no one would believe anyway was not a lie by omission. It wasn't a lie at all. She wasn't saying anything that was untrue, and she wasn't withholding anything that would be recognized as truth.

"I just know."

"How do you know?"

"Mother…"

Caron returned her attention to the work before her. "Paege may have difficulty with the dragons, with earning their faith, but he is always truthful."

"Always?" Trysten lifted an eyebrow.

Caron nodded quickly as she picked up a turnip and began slicing it into thick chunks.

Trysten went to cross her arms over her chest, then recalled the line of hares hanging from her hand. She settled for cocking a hand upon her left hip. "Does father know then that Paege doesn't want to be dragoneer?"

Caron regarded her daughter a second. "Yes," she said, "he does. And your father also knows that Paege is willing to do it anyway because it is what is best for the weyr."

A scowl darkened Trysten's face. "Well say it, then. What is wrong with me? Why won't he let me be the dragoneer?"

"Have you asked him?"

Trysten nodded sharply.

"Then you have your answer. Your father is a dragoneer. He is honest in all things."

A sharp bushel of words bubbled up in Trysten's throat, scratched at her chest to be let out, to fly from her mouth like a dozen arrows shot at once from her bow. Instead, she slung the hares over her shoulder, took the skinning knife from its place in the block, and stormed outside.

When Trysten returned with the skinned hares, her mother presented her with a tray that held a bowl of stew, a hunk of bread with a bit of goat cheese, and a large mug of tea. She took the offering to the weyr where several of the weyrmen acted to stop her, but after a glance at the tray, let her go as she made her way back to Aeronwind's stall.

There, her father once again sat on the floor with his back against the great dragon, who breathed fast and shallow. The air above Aeronwind's nostrils shimmered as if exceptionally warm.

"I brought you some lunch," Trysten said. She held up the platter.

Her father's eyes were red, rimmed with sleeplessness. When he moved, a grimace passed over his face, and his right hand clutched his right knee.

The look nearly brought Trysten to her knees with helplessness. She glanced up at Elevera, who regarded the scene from above, from the end of her long, graceful neck of gold. Her face creased in concern. Where was Paege, if Elevera was in her stall? Ought he not be out practicing with her, pretending to bond with the dragon who would not have him?

"Thank you," Mardoc said, his voice rough and sandy. He cleared his throat, then motioned at the wooden chest by his feet.

"How is Aeronwind?" Trysten asked as she entered the stall.

Mardoc nodded slightly and said nothing.

Trysten placed the platter where indicated, then glanced back up at Elevera. "Where's Paege?"

"Out with Galelin," her father said. He extended a hand to her, and she gripped him about the wrist and pulled him to his feet. "I wanted Galelin to spend some time with him, teach him a bit about dragons and dragon lore.

Elevera swung her head out toward the aisle. She let out a huff, a bit of a rumble, then shuffled her feet in the straw. Her wings flicked up and then back. An answering disturbance came from several of the other dragons, and the noise shuffled down the aisle of the weyr. Trysten's skin crawled. The hairs on her arms stood on end.

Mardoc grabbed the edge of the stall with one hand, then raised the other above his head as he stretched.

There were so many things Trysten wanted to say to him. She wished to unpack them from herself and swing them like sacks of grain into her father's stomach. She demanded answers, or would, but ended up saying nothing at all because she couldn't say it all at once.

"What good has your mother made this time?" Mardoc asked.

"Is it because I'm a girl?" Trysten said, then straightened her back. "A woman?"

Her father raised an eyebrow. A bit of straw stuck out from the bottom of his beard, and she pictured him curled up on his side, sleeping beside his dying dragon. She wanted to reach out and pluck the bit of straw away and then hated herself for wanting to do it. None of the other men in the weyr would do it. But then again, should she aspire to such attitudes? Shouldn't they aspire to hers?

"I beg your pardon?" Mardoc asked.

"If I were your son, would I be the dragoneer?"

Her father's shoulders slumped. He looked down to the plate of food. Longing filled his face. His jaw flexed, and his eyes appeared to grow heavier as if they were becoming too much of a burden, too much of a bother to do anything with.

"If you were my son," Mardoc said as he studied Trysten, "then I would be the worse off for not having such a daughter."

Trysten's brow furrowed. "What does that even mean? That's not an answer."

Mardoc shook his head. "I suppose not. I'm afraid I don't have an answer. If you were my son, would you behave the way you did the other day, taking Ulbeg into battle practice without my permission and against Bolsar's orders?"

"Would I have to? If I was your son, that is?"

"Who has that answer? Where would you find it?"

Trysten glanced up at Elevera, who looked away as soon as Trysten made eye contact. Again, she shuffled her feet. Her tail swished and landed with a soft thud against the side of the stall. Something was in the air of the weyr.

"We're going to lose the horde," Trysten said. "Paege can't do this. He can't open himself up to Elevera like he has to, like I have. When…" Trysten gestured at Aeronwind. "When it's time, we'll lose it all. We'll lose everything."

It was Mardoc's turn to straighten his back. "No such thing will happen here. This is my horde, and I will pass it on as I see fit. Aeronwind has chosen me, and it is my duty to see that her horde has succession."

Trysten took a deep breath. "Elevera has chosen me. Can't you see that? She wants me to be the dragoneer. Not Paege. If you know these dragons like you say you do, like the dragoneer is supposed to, then surely you can see that. So why won't you pass the title on to me? Is it because I'm your daughter?"

Redness flashed across her father's face. He let go of the stable wall and stood upright and tall as if his twisted leg had found itself braced and rigid with a sudden flush of anger. "What I can see is that my child, regardless of gender, is too envious, too jealous to take on the role of a dragoneer.

Trysten, you are too rash. You don't think. You don't stop and consider the consequences of your actions. You act without considering others. I have forbidden you to enter the weyr, to mingle with the dragons, and I have asked you to give Elevera and Paege space in order to bond."

Trysten flinched.

"And yet you insist on meeting with Paege in secret among the foothills."

Trysten's stomach twisted.

Mardoc nodded. "I know these dragons. You cannot meet in secret with Elevera without me knowing. Consider that whatever the dragons know, I know as well."

"By the wilds, then, how can you not know that Paege isn't ready for this! I can…" She clamped her mouth.

Her father lifted an eyebrow. "You can what?"

"See it from a mile off. He's not comfortable with her, and she knows it. He doesn't fit. It's not who he is."

"That is for me to judge. Now, tell your mother thank you for—"

"You!" Trysten called and pointed at Elevera. The dragon lowered her head slightly as if leaning in to give Trysten her undivided attention. "I am giving you an order. I am telling you to accept Paege. For the good of the horde. You have to accept him and keep the horde here."

"That is enough!" Mardoc commanded.

"You owe it to Aeronwind. To my father. You owe it to the village. We cannot exist without you—" Trysten's voice cracked, and she clenched her eyes shut.

"Trysten!" Her father snapped.

She swallowed hard. "You have to listen to me," Trysten said. When her father reached for her, she stepped out of his range. He teetered a step, then caught himself on the stall wall. She thundered around Aeronwind's unconscious form and wagged her finger up at the large, gold dragon that towered over them. "You know you have to. You know it. I am telling you that you have to accept Paege! Do you understand?"

"Trysten!"

"Elevera?" Trysten asked, and the dragon blinked her large, brown eyes, and the world filled with such a cataract of emotion that it threatened to sweep Trysten away, to throw her against all kinds of rocks and stones she had no idea existed up until that moment. A thousand different sensations and feelings whirled about her and left her heart feeling as if it were made of onion skin paper. Each beat threatened to crumple it up, leave it knotted and wrinkled and bouncing down to the bottom of her chest. She swayed, then reached for the wall herself.

The world fell sideways as the dragons ruffled. They growled and murmured and shuffled among the straw. Wings snapped and shifted and sounded like wind looking for a place to lay in the swaying, sighing grass.

The avalanche of feelings knocked her feet from under her, rattled her bones, and left her lying still, clinging to her breath upon the floor of the stall, unconscious.

Chapter 19

Caron poked her head into Trysten's room. "How are you feeling, Little Heart?"

Trysten heaved a sigh into her lap. She glanced out the window, to the gray sky and the cold rain that slicked the glass. "Fine."

"Then you can receive a visitor?"

"Who is it?"

Her mother drew her head back. A second later, Paege stepped into the room, looking a bit sheepish and scraggly beneath his mop of hair and his patchy beard. He glanced at the floor before the foot of Trysten's bed.

She drew the cover over herself.

"How are you feeling?" Paege asked. He looked up at her, made eye contact as if he had been waiting for her to cover her nightgown all along.

"I'm fine. I don't need to be here. I'm not sick or anything."

Paege nodded. He moved to the window, then placed his fingertips to the glass before peering outside. He stared as if looking for something, as if standing in her room while she was in bed in her nightgown was the most natural thing for him to be doing. And how dare her mother just leave him in here, alone with her.

Finally, his eyes fell away from the glass and landed upon the sill. "Your father has named me the dragoneer."

The statement didn't quite register. It whirled around in Trysten's head, looking for a place to fit. She gasped. "Aeronwind?"

"No," Paege said and glanced up at her. "No, Aeronwind is fine. Well, no, she's not fine. I mean, she's alive."

"Then how…"

Paege turned his attention out the window again. He squinted into the gray light, and his face looked pale as if he was ill along with Aeronwind. "It's a formality thing. Your father said that I'm the one most qualified for the title, and since he cannot ride anymore, that he should name me as the acting dragoneer, in case Yahi's prognostication comes true and the Western Kingdom breaks through the pass early."

Trysten's fists clutched the covers. Sweat tickled her palms, and her heart fluttered in her throat as she struggled to breathe normally.

"So that's it," Paege said as he turned to her and spread his arms out at his sides. "I am the new dragoneer. The dragoneer of Aerona weyr. There was even a ceremony. I wanted to invite you, but your father said you were ill."

Breath leaked from Trysten. It bled from her. She might have to scramble, to clutch and claw to get it back.

"Elevera?" she asked, then closed her eyes as the room swirled with the ghosts of hundreds of conflicting emotions.

"Are you all right?" Paege asked. "Shall I get your mother?"

"Elevera?" Trysten repeated.

Paege stood in silence for several heartbeats. "She's the same as always."

A breath came to Trysten, thin and reedy. "She obeys you, then?"

Paege's shoulders shifted back some. His chest came out in an act of bravado that betrayed the coming statement. "Your father assures me that the connection will come. Our relationship will deepen. But I am the dragoneer. She will respect that."

Trysten turned to the window. The light was too bright. If Paege weren't in the room, she'd sink down under the quilts and covers and wrap herself up, tuck herself away from the world. Instead, she took in another breath. She closed her eyes and focused on drawing in a lungful, or at least enough to give her congratulations to him.

"Are you sure you're all right?" Paege asked.

"Congratulations," Trysten said. "I'm quite proud of you."

To Trysten's surprise, Paege plopped down on the foot of the bed. He planted his elbows on his knees and stared out the window a few seconds before turning his attention back to her. "I want to thank you. For what you did. For what you tried to do."

"And what was that?"

He looked back out the window. "You know. The training. The attention. I heard you commanded Elevera to obey me."

Heat flushed over Trysten's face. She stared into her lap. "I didn't mean..."

"It's all right. One of the weyrmen heard you. He told me... He told me everything you said."

Trysten shook her head. Heat baked off of her face. "Paege..."

"No, that's all right. You don't have to apologize for telling the truth. It's true. All of it." He looked back at her. "But what am I to do? What can I do? The horde is in danger. The village is in danger. Your father thinks that I'm the one. He thinks I'm the one who can save everyone else. I hope he is right." He looked back at the window.

"He is the dragoneer," Trysten said, unsure of what to say, and so falling back on the old admiration that she had held when she was a girl.

"No. I am the dragoneer, now. I'm supposed to go visit the armor guild and be fitted for new armor. It doesn't seem real, does it? And the worst part is, that the one person, the one person who would be enjoying this, who would be bursting with pride, is my father, and he's not here to see it."

"I'm sure he's here in spirit. I'm positive he's proud of you."

Trysten wrestled another cold, damp breath from the air around her. "My father knows what he's doing. He wouldn't have named you dragoneer if he didn't think you could do it. It is his job to preserve the horde. He doesn't take his job lightly. He knows what he's doing."

Paege glanced back at her. "You don't really believe that, do you?"

"Why wouldn't I?" She pulled the cover up a little closer to her chin.

Paege sat up straight. A hint of a grin teased at the corners of his lips. "Because that would be a first for you is why."

Trysten stared at Paege for a moment, long enough for the hint of his grin to fade away. He leaned forward, onto his elbows, and wove his fingers together. The bed creaked with his movement. For a split second, Trysten stifled the urge to kick him, to just draw her leg back and plant her heel in his ribs. Instead, she drew her legs up under her as she sat upright. She took a deep breath. This wasn't his fault. He didn't ask for any of this.

But he wasn't refusing it, either.

"Well," Paege said, then stood. "I was on my way to the armor guild. I just wanted to stop by and give you the news and check on you. I'm glad you're feeling better."

"I'll go with you."

Paege's face widened, startled. "What? No, that's not necessary. They're supposed to just be taking measurements. And it's cold and wet—"

"I'm tired of being cooped up in here. I'm going with you. If you'll step outside and wait, I'll get dressed and be with you in a few seconds."

Paege glanced at the doorway as if Trysten was speaking to someone else.

"Really," he said as he returned his attention to her. "It's not necessary."

"Out," Trysten said and pointed to the door. "Wait for me."

"What? Wait. You can't give me orders. I'm the dragoneer now."

The look on Trysten's face stopped his joking. He blushed, then turned away. "Right." He pointed at the door. "I'll just be out there. With your mother."

He exited the room, and as the door shut behind him, Trysten fell back against the head of the bed and peered at the ceiling. A hollowness opened inside her as if the ground she had walked on all her life was suddenly but a shell with nothing underneath. A hint of her fainting spell came upon her. She recalled briefly bits and flashes of what she felt, of the dragons, of their states and their thoughts and the power of their emotions pulsing through the weyr like thirty flocks of birds flying in every direction all at once, zipping around and through each other.

By the wilds, what had she done?

Chapter 20

Jalite opened the door to the armor guild and grinned when she saw Paege.

"Oh, get in here. Out of the rain!" She rolled her hand and motioned them in.

"Congratulations!" the woman continued as they stepped inside. She caught Paege up in a great hug, and he appeared both lost and embarrassed. His eyes bulged slightly as he glanced back at Trysten.

"We're all so proud of you!" Jalite said. She released Paege, then glanced back at her children, Assina and Talon, both nearly the same age as Trysten and Paege.

"Congratulations," Assina said.

Talon smiled politely and nodded once.

Jalite ushered them through the cottage and to a large room that had been added onto the back. She offered them each a cup of tea, and before they answered, she sent Assina away and told Paege to remove his cloak and tunic.

"We need to measure you for your armor. Take off your outerwear. You can't go into battle with armor that is too tight or too loose," Jalite said with a shake of her finger as if ill-fitting armor were nothing more than a careless habit.

Paege blushed and glanced from Jalite to Trysten.

"Come now," Jalite said. "No time to be modest. We must get your armor started. We've heard about the early fighting season. My! It's as if the clouds themselves can't wait to throw you at the Western Kingdom. Oh, how they will rue the day you took to the skies, won't they?"

Paege gave a slight, limpid nod, then undid the clasp at his cloak. Talon, Jalite's son, took the cloak, shook it once, then hung it from a row of pegs along the wall. Among the pegs were various pieces of the dragoneer's traditional uniform. Trysten stepped over and admired the work. There were cabled sweaters knit at a small gauge with fine yarn. She plucked the corner of a shoulder and pulled it out to look at the back of the sweater. A cable formed of dragon tails twisted up the spine, then split off just before the shoulder blades. Over each shoulder blade, the cables formed sleek dragons with sprays of cable work forming wings.

Trysten inhaled deeply and resisted the urge to bury her nose in the wool and search for the scent of her father. It struck her how she hadn't seen him since she fainted in the weyr, and it seemed like he was gone now as if he had died or gone away and left Paege in his place. A pang of loss rang through her like the peal of an old, sorrowful bell.

She glanced over her shoulder. Paege stood in the middle of the room, stripped down to nothing more than a blush and his pants. Assina and Talon worked together measuring his arms, shoulders, chest, and waist, Assina chattering the whole time.

"Arms up," Assina said, then tapped Paege's elbow. He lifted his arms, then after a glance at Trysten, turned away so that she couldn't see his face.

Trysten lifted her hand to her mouth and realized she was grinning. She tried to imagine her father in such a situation, young and half-dressed and being fitted for his armor. She couldn't imagine it. His armor seemed like something he had been born with as if it had always been and always would be on him.

Trysten examined more of the room. She came across a leather helmet fitted atop a wooden ball. One of the colorful braids of the hordesmen hung down from the rear quarter of the helmet. The other braid was half-finished. A piece of twine tied off the end and kept it from unraveling before someone could pick it back up again. An urge passed through Trysten to continue it, to feel the wool slip through her hands like rough, coarse hair. She reached out and cupped the unfinished braid in her hand. What would she do with herself now?

She glanced at Paege. It had never occurred to her that she would not be the dragoneer one day. It was something that had always waited for her in the future, as certain as the mountains on the horizon. And now here she was, and the mountains were no longer in front of her.

"We'll have to get one of Elevera's scales in order to match that up," Assina said. "The dragoneer always has braids that match the scales of his mount. If you bring us in one of Elevera's scales, discarded, of course, we can match the color and dye the yarn for it. I can't wait to see it! Elevera is such a beautiful dragon."

Assina turned her attention to Trysten. "I imagine the tassels on the helmet and the shoulders will look a lot like your braids. Elevera is about that color. If you were the dragoneer, we wouldn't even have to put braids on the armor, would we?" She glanced at Talon, who paid no attention to her.

The statement cored Trysten. She reached up and touched her braids. Her hair certainly felt much softer, much smoother than the wool yarn used for the helmet and shoulders. She turned her attention back to the helmet, in part to hide her face from the siblings as well as Paege. She moved on. A hank of dark blue yarn hung from a peg on the wall. It was damp. She pretended to study it, her anxiety growing. What would she do now from day to day?

She drew in a deep breath, then let out a sigh. She would be like Galelin. She would pick up his calling, his studies, and learn all that she could about dragons and hordes. She would learn history and art and philosophy and anything and everything she could so that she might look back at these last few days across the onion skin stack of years and try to see where she had gone wrong, how she had managed to give everything away. Just give it away.

A flash of Elevera's eyes intruded upon her, hit her hard like a chill, like cold feet crossing over her grave. She reached for the wall to keep from falling over, gathering a fistful of the damp yarn in the process.

"Careful!" Talon called. "It's still wet."

Trysten took a deep breath. She willed herself to stand upright, solid upon her feet as she released her hand and looked at her palm. A tint of blue dye colored her palm and fingers. "I see that."

"Trysten?" Paege asked.

"I'm all right," she said.

"Oh, fish and birds!" Assina gasped. "Get her something to wash that off with, Talon."

Talon hurried from the room with a parting glance at Trysten.

"Here, have a seat," Assina said as she rushed over to a table and snatched up a stool.

"No," Trysten said and held out her blue palm. "I'm fine."

"She's been a little under the weather lately," Paege said. He crossed his arms over his chest. Goose flesh prickled his arms.

"I can imagine," Assina said. "You poor thing. With your father and Aeronwind and all. I bet it's been hard."

Trysten gritted her teeth. It wasn't hard. It wasn't anything like that. What was hard was giving everything up for the good of the horde, for the village, for the people in it, including Assina and her brother. She was not some quiver-legged lamb just dropped in the field. She was ready to ride Elevera into the face of the Western Kingdom. She was ready to be iron. To be flight. She was ready to be the dragon streaking across the sky, diving into the withering tail of the winter blizzards. She was not a frail blossom ready to wilt under the heat of misfortune.

Talon came back with a bucket that smelled of fermented fruit. He placed it on the table and gestured at it as if presenting something special. "Wash your hands in here. Scrub hard. Most of it will come off."

Trysten peered into the bucket. The water sloshed back and forth. A shapeless form warped and slipped across the surface. The reflection of herself in the turbulent water struck closer to home than she ever would have imagined.

Chapter 21

On the way back to her cottage, Trysten watched the shadow of herself pass over the puddles in the lane. She imagined the reflection shimmering, rippling, distorted into nothing with each step of her boot as it sunk into the mud and squashed whoever it was that she was now; that faceless, dark figure.

She sucked in a deep breath and raised her face to the sky. It was a solid, uniform gray again. The rain fell steady, in large, cold drops. If it kept up much longer, flood waters would drive the hares up onto the sides of the hill. It would make for easier hunting. Perhaps that is what she would do. She would be the huntress. She would spend the day, dawn to dusk, with a bow in one hand and an arrow in the other. She'd catch whatever she could and sell the meat and fur. And when the fighting season came, and the land was bathed in the sun that brought the rock heather to flowers the color of pink flesh, then she would lift her head to the sun and sky, to the shaded underbellies of the dragons, and she would wish them success and victory knowing that she had given everything she could to see that the weyr survived.

"I'm really sorry," Paege said.

"For what?"

"For all of this. For everything that's happened."

Trysten tried to respond, but the hush of the rain and squelch of their boots sucking at the mud robbed her of thought as if the cold had numbed her brain.

"I'm sorry for not stopping it," Paege said. "I should have done more, but I didn't really think it would go this far. I didn't believe for one minute that I'd actually be named dragoneer."

As if on an unfortunate cue, the owner of the tavern called out his congratulations to Paege as he hurried past, a package tucked under his arm. Paege flashed a grin and waved back as Trysten pulled the edges of her cloak closer.

"You were expecting my father to come to his senses?"

Paege didn't respond right away. "I was expecting you to... be a little bolder."

"What?" Trysten stopped and turned on Paege. "Bolder? You were waiting for me to be bolder?"

Paege looked off to the mountains. "What was I going to do? I couldn't tell your father that I can't be the dragoneer. He wouldn't listen to me. Besides, like I already told you, it wasn't like he was asking me. He was definitely bestowing the honor upon me. It doesn't really feel like I get a say in the matter."

"So what, then? You needed me to come down, swoop in and rescue you from your fate? Is that it?"

"No," Paege said with a shake of his head. "It's... Look, I don't want to fight about this."

"Is that an order, your Highness?"

"Knock it off."

"What? You can't handle the pressure of being the man in charge now?"

"I can't handle being the dragoneer. I can't handle Elevera. You know that. Your command to her didn't work. She doesn't give a wild hop about it. She tolerates me. She listens to me only because she knows you want her to. She knows that you're the true dragoneer. Not me. And you know it, too. And I know you know it, so that's why I expected you to... to..."

"To what?"

"To care! To take charge."

"I did take charge!" Trysten yelled. "I hopped on Ulbeg's back and took your braid, right? And what did that get me? And I tried to take charge and teach you how to ride her, but you're so... closed up that Elevera can't make any connection with you. You're like a block of ice to her, Paege! She might as well be carrying a snowman around on her back for all the more you connect with her."

Paege's posture straightened, became as solid and hard as the ice she accused him of.

Trysten's shoulders slumped. "Paege, I'm sorry. I didn't mean it like that."

"Which is why you said it?" he said in a tone that matched his posture. "Because you have a habit of going around and saying things you don't mean?"

Trysten's mouth flopped open. No words came. She remembered what her mother had insinuated about her and honesty. Perhaps she wasn't always honest because honesty brought that look to Paege's face. His jaw shifted. His eyelids squinted the tiniest bit, her eyes hard and sharp as the flint in the exposed beds of rock along the river's edge.

He shook his head. "That's fine. I can't be mad at you for telling the truth."

Paege turned and began to walk away.

"Paege!"

He kept walking. Trysten's feet refused her commands to carry her forward, to close the distance growing between them as if they knew it was better that she didn't. She would just hurt him again. So she stood and watched Paege move away until he turned the corner and left her with nothing but a lane filled with bits of gray sky and dark fragments of her faceless reflection.

Chapter 22

Wild dreams drove Trysten from sleep. With a cry, she sat up in bed.

"Trysten?" her mother called in the dark.

"Something's wrong. With the dragons. Something's wrong." She flung back her blankets and searched for a pair of riding trousers in the dark.

Rather than ask her to explain herself, her mother went to the fire in the main room and lit a candle, meeting Trysten at the door to her room.

"I'm going to the weyr," Trysten said. "Please don't try to stop me. I must go." Without saying a word, Caron nodded once. Trysten crushed her in a brief hug then hurried out of the cottage.

Cold air smacked Trysten when she stepped outside. She drew a deep breath and felt the frigid air erase the warmth of sleep from her lungs. She blinked once, then looked up into the sky. Patches of stars shone through rents and breaks in the deck of clouds.

She ran to the weyr and flung open the door. A knot of weyrmen stood around Aeronwind's stall. The breathing of the dragons was different. It wasn't the solid, uniform hush of air that filled the weyr whenever the dragoneer was present. Their breath held no rhythm, no unison. The sound of it was quiet, barely audible. Chaos flooded into Trysten's veins as she rushed down the aisle.

Bolsar glanced at her approach. Rather than say a word toward her, he returned his attention to the stall. "Your daughter is here."

"What's the matter?" Trysten called, then pulled up short outside the stall.

Her dad sat upon the footstool. He leaned forward until his chest was nearly between his knees. His forehead and palms rested upon the chest of Aeronwind. It appeared that Trysten was too late, that the great alpha dragon had died. Her wings drooped. The edges of them laid against the ground. She appeared to list further to her left side than she had before. Her eyes remained closed, and her scales lacked a luster. As Trysten peered back and forth along the bulk of the dragon, she noted rapid, shallow movements of the dragon's chest. Aeronwind lived. For now.

"Our lady has taken a turn for the worse, I'm afraid," Galelin said from the rear corner of the stall.

"Do something," Trysten commanded.

Galelin shrugged. "It is out of my hands. By the clouds and sky, only the highest can have her now."

"No," Trysten said. "We're not ready."

Bolsar placed a hand upon her shoulder. She ripped it away and spun nearly about. Elevera stood in the next stall with her neck stooped, curved. She stared at Trysten, then peered down at Aeronwind. The breathing, the asynchronous tones of it, all rushed at her, and she felt as if she were being pummeled. She took a deep breath and turned back to her father, who still sat with his head against the dragon's chest.

"Where's Paege?" Trysten asked.

"It isn't necessary," Galelin said with a shake of his head.

"Necessary for what? What if he wants to say goodbye?"

"He's had his chance," Bolsar said. "We all have. It will do no good to have the whole wild village in here wringing hands."

Trysten glanced down the aisle, past the dragons who stirred in their stalls. The whole weyr felt unsettled, on edge. The hand wringing wasn't only on the part of the villagers.

She glanced back at Elevera. It felt like placing her hand near the embers of a fire on a cold night. It felt good for a brief second but quickly became too much. There was too much there. Everything all at once until her breath locked up, her heart skipped, and the room swam beneath her.

Paege had to be here. He had to be present for this. If he shared this with Elevera, it would hopefully be enough.

No one called after her as she raced to the back of the weyr. She crashed through the door that separated the hordesmen's quarters from the weyr. The scant light that fell in behind her quickly faded into the dark and left her to stumble through the tables and chairs and benches that littered the hordesmen's dining hall. She barked her shins and cracked her knees. She swatted at the dark and knocked aside what she could before she reached the other end of the hall. There, she flung open the door to the bunk hall.

Several candles had already been lit, and a couple of the nearest hordesmen were getting out of their bunks.

"What do you want?" the nearest man asked.

"Where's Paege?"

The man looked her over as if trying to assess something, to come to a decision.

"Paege!" Trysten hollered.

Paege rolled out of a bunk at the end of the hall. He stood in his bare feet with his bare chest. Instead of a nightshirt, he wore a pair of loose-fitting short pants. "What is it?"

Trysten hurried forward several steps, then paused and turned back a bit, as if ready to bolt through the door. "Aeronwind. She's about to die."

The silence in the hall grew profound in the shadow of her words. It towered up and over all of them. The hordesmen glanced at each other, and then all of the glances found their way up to Paege, who still stood at the head of the bunk hall.

Whispers broke out. One man questioned how Trysten knew. Another flat out asked what Mardoc would do. Trysten's gut tightened. She drew up her spine and clenched her fists as the whispers grew in number and volume. The hall filled with the sound of men who were unsure of what to do, of what was coming. It was the sound of a horde without an alpha.

"Where's Galelin and Mardoc?" Paege called out, loud enough to drown the whispers and tamp them into ashen silence.

"With Aeronwind. In her stall. Galelin says there's nothing more to do. But it's her time. She is departing. Soon."

Again, the whispers came.

"How soon?" Paege asked, his voice loud and forceful in a way she had not heard before. It stirred a sense in her chest. He might pull this off yet.

"Tonight. Hours. Minutes."

"Lysu," Paege called to one of the men. "Take half the men out to spread the word. Let the people know the vigil will be tonight. Tennin, you take the other half of the men and work with the weyrmen who are here. See to the other dragons. Keep them calm, make sure they are fed and watered. Make sure every man, woman, and child you see has something to do, something to keep their hands busy. I want to see no idleness at all this night. Do you understand?"

The eighteen men stood along the aisle that ran through the bunk hall. They stared at Paege, then turned back to their bunks and began to pull clothes from beneath their mattresses and begin dressing.

A tense sigh escaped Trysten. She had not expected such a display from her mild-mannered friend. Relief soaked into her shoulders. In his orders, she heard a hint of the commanding presence of a dragoneer.

As soon as Paege dressed, he trotted down the hall. The commanding expression that he wore earlier had disappeared. Now he looked concerned, worried. He looked like the old Paege that she had always known.

"How's Elevera?" he asked.

Trysten turned away from him and hurried back toward the weyr.

Paege soon caught up and grasped her elbow. "How's Elevera?" he asked again.

"The dragons are unsettled. All of them. The whole horde. Can't you feel it?"

Paege looked ahead as if the feeling might be something large and garishly colored plopped right in the middle of the weyr's central aisle. "Will she accept me?"

Trysten swallowed hard. Tears welled in her eyes and added to the wealth of things making it difficult to look at Paege. "I don't know."

She turned from him and trotted into the weyr. A new sensation hit her. Cold like the first winter wind off the mountains, and then hard and prickly like the air after a violent, dry thunderstorm. The goose flesh raised on her arms, and the air smelled both burnt and cold.

As they stepped before Aeronwind's stall, the breathing of the whole horde ceased. The silence was more complete than anything Trysten had known, almost deafening if not for the thundering of her heart in her ears.

Mardoc raised his ashen face to the vaulted ceiling. His fingers curled into claws, like a dragon's claws without the scales. Even he had stopped breathing. His chest was as still as Aeronwind's.

Trysten sucked in a breath to call out to her father, but she found she could not. The words were pressed against something in her. She stood with the words trapped inside her as a single tear fell from the corner of her father's eye and slipped into the dark tangle of his beard as if seeking to hide.

An anguished cry fled her father. Tore from him, shredding itself upon his bared teeth.

Trysten stumbled back a step. Her hands flew to her own mouth, clamped down over it as her father cried out and his hands curled and raked down over the side of Aeronwind's body. His eyes squeezed shut as if the life left him as well.

Up and down the aisle, from Ulbeg to Elevera, the dragons let out a long, dry hiss to match her father's cry. Trysten trembled. She shook and shivered, and if she weren't so scared, so panicked, she'd turn and cry out for them all to stop it. Stop it, *please*.

Her father's head fell forward. He landed against the inert form of Aeronwind. His shoulders heaved, and a great sob escaped. He lifted his hands and planted them back against his dragon's side, and he clutched at what he could. His hands worked, curled, patted, stroked and clawed at the hide as he sobbed and sobbed into the dragon's side.

Galelin stepped forward and placed a hand upon Mardoc's shoulder.

Trysten began to rush forward. Paege grabbed her shoulder as Bolsar stepped before her.

"You should not be here," Bolsar said. "It is not for a man's family to see this."

"What?"

"Leave him. He needs to grieve. This is a private thing between a dragoneer and his alpha. It is not to be shared with his family."

"What?" Trysten repeated.

"It's all right," Paege said as his grip on her shoulder tightened. "They told me about this. They told me to expect it. This is how it's supposed to go. How it happens."

Trysten whirled around, ready to thrash Paege for his comment. She stopped. He stared up at Elevera. She followed his gaze.

The last of the hiss escaped Elevera, and the horde followed suit. Silence collapsed upon the weyr, and all of them were stranded upon her father's sobbing. Elevera turned her attention, swept her graceful head and neck from Aeronwind and Mardoc to her.

Trysten wrenched herself free of Paege's grip and fled the weyr.

Chapter 23

The night dug its fingers into Trysten and rattled her, gripped her muscles and shook her bones. She lifted her face off her knees and hugged her legs tighter, trying harder to draw the heat in. The rock she sat on dug into her butt, but she didn't care. With the sleeve of her sweater, she wiped tears away from her eyes and stared up at the tatters of clouds and the riot of stars beyond them. It looked as if the old world had been torn away, just ripped off the surface of the village, and underneath, or up above, as it was with the case of the sky, bits of bone shone down through the dark muscle of whatever hovered over them, whatever saw fit to see things turn out as they had.

It wasn't fair in the least. None of it. Yet as soon as she thought it, she saw her father crying, sobbing. That wasn't her father at all. It was some ghost, some demon left in his body after Aeronwind's death. Then there was Elevera's expectant stare, wanting something, and wanting it from her.

She didn't have it. Whatever it was that Elevera wanted, whatever it was that Trysten needed in order to make her father believe that she should have succeeded him, she certainly didn't have it. It wasn't in her.

On top of that, there was Aeronwind. Poor Aeronwind. She had known. She knew that it was her fault that her dragoneer was injured, that he could no longer ride after she broke her leg and fell on him upon landing. How awful it was for her to die feeling like such a disappointment. Whether Aeronwind was concerned about Elevera's ability to succeed her, Trysten couldn't tell.

All of it, however, was just awful. It was terrible that it happened to them, out here in the middle of nowhere with the fighting season bearing down on them.

She studied the mountains. How much longer would it be before the first of the hordesmen from the Western Kingdom came across? And how would they ever be ready for them?

Trysten wiped her palms across her face. At least it was out of her hands at this point. There was nothing to be done. If Elevera was unable to find what she needed in Paege, and the horde absconded, then there was nothing Trysten could do any longer.

A small spray of rocks tumbled down the path off to Trysten's left. She peered into the darkness. A familiar form walked along the path, then made her way through the marsh grass. Without a word, Trysten's mother climbed up on the rocks and sat beside her daughter in the dark. Together, they peered at the clouds and stars and listened to the river burble as a lone trail lark let out a series of low, long whistles that sounded like it wanted to tell the mountains of its profound disappointment and loneliness.

"I wasn't supposed to be there," Trysten finally said.

Her mother didn't respond right away. "I didn't think Aeronwind would pass tonight. It usually takes a third fever for a dragon to succumb."

Trysten hugged her legs tighter. "She felt awful for hurting Father. He lived to ride."

"He lived to ride her."

"I've never seen him like that. Oh, Mother, he just..." Trysten slumped sideways into Caron. Another sob escaped her and dropped into her mother's lap. Caron wrapped her arm around her daughter and pulled her close. Trysten buried her face in Caron's shoulder. She smelled of burnt candles and wood smoke as she stroked her daughter's hair until Trysten's sobs subsided.

Trysten pushed herself upright, then wiped her eyes on her sleeve again. "It was so awful. All of it. I've seen dragons die before, but not like that. They all... They hissed. They stopped breathing when Aeronwind did, and then they all began to hiss, and it sounded so awful. It sounded horrible as if..."

The words stopped off there like a ragged trail that dwindled into a bit of nothing, into solid scrub and rock heather that stretched as far as the eye could see. There were no words. Words were for humans. The hissing had filled her with a sense of the world shifting. It sounded like the noise that might fill the air if the entire mountain and the foothills and plains were all dragged across the lands that stretched out beyond the horizon. It sounded as if the world had been relocated, and the feelings that came with it...she didn't know how to describe them to her mother.

There was something else among it. Something she couldn't put her finger on. So much had been thrown at her. The emotions and the thoughts of the dragons had threatened to overwhelm her, and she waded through it as fast and hard as she could looking for any indication of what it was that Elevera was going to do. Would she take Paege as her bonded human, as her dragoneer or not?

"You might find this hard to believe, but I do understand," her mother said.

Trysten quivered in the press of the cold night. She wasn't quite sure how to respond. How could her mother even begin to understand?

"Emotions run high at these times. It must have been frightening to see your father undone like that." Caron tightened her grip upon her daughter.

"Your father has always had to keep up an image of strength, of being made of stone. He had to be the mountains himself."

"Why?" Trysten asked. "He didn't have to do it for the dragons."

Caron stroked her daughter's hair. "No, that is true. He did have to do it for the men, though. For the hordesmen. They put such an air of mysticism about it, don't they? They make it out as if your father must eat iron and spit rust in order to be the dragoneer. He had to be perceived as the most able, most fierce warrior in the land in order to be the one chosen to ride into battle on the back of the alpha."

Trysten listened to her mother's heart. It throbbed far away, under layers of wool and cotton, muffled and hidden behind so many curtains. It seemed so distant, unlike when she had been a girl and able to curl up in her mother's lap and listen to that sound whenever she wanted.

"It's not like that," Trysten said.

"No. But they pretend it is. And now they have a problem. Paege isn't the kind of person one would expect to be the dragoneer, is he?"

"In the bunk hall, when I went to get him, he started to give orders. He started to sound like Father."

Trysten heard her mother smile.

"I'm sure your father has been coaching him. It was the hordesmen who responded to Paege, and not the dragons, right?"

Trysten gave a slight nod.

"These hordesmen not only fly into battle under the command of the dragoneer but also on the backs of the dragoneer's dragons. He controls the alpha, and the alpha controls the dragons."

"It's not that way," Trysten said. "Not entirely. He doesn't control the alpha. She just wants… It's hard to explain. It's not just a matter of wanting to please him, to make him proud, but there's also a… They are protecting him. They see us as rather silly and weak and ridiculous. They protect us so that we will build them shelters and bring them food."

A slight sound escaped Caron. Trysten wasn't sure what it was, what it meant.

"Is that what you think?" her mother asked.

Trysten placed a hand upon her mother's knee and felt the firmness and the warmth. It wasn't a matter of what she thought.

"Well," Caron continued, "it's not the allegiance of the dragons Paege has to worry about, but rather the allegiance of the hordesmen. A dragon's faith is unbreakable. Men, however, are fickle. Projecting an air of authority, of being larger than life is one way to assure these men that your father was worth following into battle. If they placed their lives in his hands, he would care for them like a dragon, lead them true, and bring them home to the cottages they have defended. It's all an act. Posturing."

Trysten recalled the look of utter and complete anguish on her father's face.

"But you know what the true secret is, don't you?" Caron asked.

Trysten nearly snorted. "If I did, I would have told Paege. He needs the help."

"I know your father better than anyone thinks. I can imagine his response when Aeronwind passed. Your father is a very passionate man. I'm sure it tore him apart to lose his dragon. The fact that he could feel that loss so deeply, so keenly is why Aeronwind chose him."

Trysten swallowed hard. That statement did not help her feel any better about Paege's abilities.

"Dragons are amazing beasts. The legends say that when the gods made these lands, and they wanted someone to admire them, to appreciate their work, so they made the Originals. But these people, the Originals, felt emotion too strongly. Too keenly. They were overcome with the beauty and the harshness of the land, and the beauty and the harshness of themselves, the creations of the gods.

"The gods became fearful of their new creations. They had not expected such passions. They knew that among the gods themselves egos existed that would use the Originals, stoke their passions, fire them up until they could be turned into an army. And that army could turn on all of the gods and destroy them.

"So a hail of lightning fell upon the land. It shattered the paradise the gods had built, but it also split their creatures in two. The passion and emotion gave rise to the dragons, and the ambition and reason gave rise to humans."

It was an old story that Trysten had heard before, but she dared not interrupt her mother. She was quite content to listen to the story, to listen to the sound of Caron's voice.

"People like your dad are a little more like the old ones, the Originals. They have it in their blood. They can draw up some of the passion of the ancients, and that is what the dragons respond to. It is what I imagine you saw tonight. It is also why the title is almost always passed down from father to son."

"But not daughter?" Trysten asked. She pushed herself up out of her mother's lap and wrapped her arms around her legs.

They sat and listened to the river, swollen with rain. They listened to the trail lark and the wind that would start to tell of something it had seen far away, but then fall quiet as it realized that no one really cared. All of Trysten's focus was on her mother, on her response.

"There's nothing that forbids it," Caron finally said.

Trysten huffed. "Nothing except Father."

"He loves you, you know."

"What does that have to do with anything? With this?"

"Everything. You have to look at it from his side. He..." Caron grabbed Trysten's knee and squeezed. "We know you are a special girl, Little Heart."

"Don't call me that. I'm not little. Not anymore."

In the starlight, Caron's grin was visible. "Oh, dear, until you are older than me, you will never outgrow that name. But your father knows that you… you feel things on a very deep level. You feel things deeper than him, even. And he worries about you. He worries because what dragons feel is so large and…"

Caron gave her daughter's knee another squeeze. "To be frank, we worry about where you will put it all. How do you make room inside yourself for what the dragons feel?"

Every bit of Trysten felt as if it were plunged into ice. Her breath stopped. Her heart struggled, staggered in her chest. She glanced at the dark blades of grass before her as they stirred in the last of the wind's tepid tale. How much did her mother really know? How much did her parents know?

"I questioned your father's refusal to let you even participate in the consideration, but after your fainting spell in the weyr, I knew that he had made the right decision. You are unlike many of the people across this land. There might not even be another like you alive today. I can see that your empathy toward the dragons runs as deep as any since possibly the Originals walked this land or the land that was. But you are not one of the Originals. You are human. And you have the limits of a human. Your father is concerned about what would happen to you in the heat of battle when passions run at their highest, their hottest."

Trysten drew her legs closer to her. A shiver ran through her. The wind spoke up. It whispered into the grasses a muffled story of a young woman, a warrior princess who flew into battle on the back of a dragon, and the mere mention of it sent goose flesh across Trysten's arms.

"This isn't about you alone, Little Heart," her mother said. "This is about the village and the kingdom. Your father feels things far more deeply than he will ever let on or admit to, and that includes fear. He is frightened of what would become of you in battle. He is frightened of that first. Beyond that, he is frightened for the village and the kingdom. What would happen to the horde if you became overwhelmed in battle?"

Trysten shook her head. "I wouldn't."

"It is not for you to decide. Your father is your father, and so what becomes of you is the responsibility of us both. But he is… He was the dragoneer, and it was his decision to make. The dragoneer is the dragoneer first. Before he is your father, before he is your friend, before he is your husband even, he is the dragoneer. The horde comes first, and the village soon after.

Trysten looked to the weyr. Its dark shape obscured the stars at the top of the hill. Soft light from torches and lanterns lapped against the stone wall. All seemed quiet. She thought of Galelin's story, of how the Drowlin weyr lost its horde. His telling made it seem as if it had all happened in the blink of an eye. Above, in Aerona, everything seemed calm. Peaceful, even. Surely she had been worried about nothing. Elevera had probably done what was necessary for the horde and bonded with Paege.

She shook her head. It would take a while to think of him as the dragoneer.

Trysten glanced at her mother. How much did her mother and father know about her ability to hear the dragons, to feel them? They knew more than she had assumed, but how deep did their true understanding go?

As Trysten considered how to word it, how to ask it, her mother patted her on the knee. "Come along, Little Heart. One thing that death teaches us is that life goes on. There is a burial feast to prepare."

Trysten took a deep breath, then let it all go. It had been a tough night. And her mother was right; there was a lot of work ahead. She pushed herself off the rock. Her mother slipped to the ground beside her and drew her into an embrace. Trysten buried her face in her mother's shoulder and thought of what she had said about all of the emotions not being able to fit inside her. It was closer to the truth than Trysten had first realized. Standing among the reeds near the river's edge, she felt like a sack stretched out of shape by some ungainly thing forced inside her. She thought of Elevera's eyes, and the way she stared at her, and the look of expectation. What she wanted would not possibly fit inside Trysten, but Elevera had wanted it anyway.

She shuddered.

Caron patted her on the back. "Everything will be fine. This is life unfolding. That is all it is. You'll see."

"I suppose so," Trysten said as she pushed back away from her mother. She wiped at the corners of her eyes again, and then the two of them started up the trail for the village.

Chapter 24

At the head of the trail, a sense of ill-ease struck Trysten. It left a taste on the back of her tongue; cold and bitter like metal. She glanced at the weyr, at the people milling about outside of it under the lights of torches and lanterns. Their chatter had an edge to it, a strained anticipation.

Dread fell into Trysten. Something more was going on than villagers simply mourning the passing of the alpha dragon. Something wasn't going right, and she feared it was the bonding. Elevera was preparing to abscond.

"Mother..." Trysten whispered.

Her mother stopped and slid an arm around Trysten's shoulders. They stared at the scene before them. A few stragglers joined those outside the weyr. In animated gestures, the villagers told the newcomers what was happening. On the breeze, Trysten caught mention of Aeronwind and Paege. The dragons. Lee, the baker, waved a wild hand at the weyr. Whatever was going on wasn't welcomed.

Caron's grip tightened around Trysten's shoulder. If she truly had the blood of the ancients coursing through her, if she had an ability to connect with the dragons that no one had had since the time of the Originals, then she could stop Elevera before she absconded. If Paege could not, then she would.

Caron's grip fell away as Trysten plunged across the yard that separated the hillside and the weyr. The people milling about called to her, asked of her father, of Paege and Elevera. They passed along condolences for Aeronwind, and then they parted as she plunged through. Muffled pardons and apologies trailed behind as she brushed past people and penetrated the crowd as it grew tighter and denser as she approached the weyr's opening.

With a drop of her shoulder and a slight shove, she cleared the last barrier and stepped into the central aisle of the weyr. All about her, dragons shuffled and groaned in their stalls. A few of the smaller ones turned tight circles. Wings snapped open and shut. Bits of straw skittered across the floor beneath the brush of quick, brief breezes.

At Elevera's stall, Paege stood among a knot of hordesmen and weyrmen. He donned her father's helmet. The great, gray braids that had fallen over her father's shoulders when he rode Aeronwind now fell over Paege's shoulders, and they appeared so much larger, like thick ropes meant to tie him down, to restrain him. He lifted his hands to Elevera, lifted them over his head and held them apart as if pleading. The rear corner of the weyr flickered with light as a dragon released a stream of fire.

A quiver shook Trysten's knees. This would not go well. She had never witnessed a succession before, but the dragon's tenor suggested that it was not going as it should. A restlessness rippled through her, crawled beneath her skin. Tightness drew over her lungs. The whispering and tongue-wagging of the crowd behind her grew in pitch.

A dragon of the lightest silver color drew up on her back legs. Her wings snapped open wide as she clawed at the air. A spurt of fire slipped through her maw. When she dropped forward, she clutched the stall gate. The wood cracked. The top set of hinges was torn from the post with a groan.

A weyrman rushed to the stall and waved his hands helplessly.

The sky. The dragons all thought of the sky. They searched for sky, for something they believed would be there. It called to them so strongly that Trysten glanced back, over the heads of the people she had grown up with. There, she expected to see a strange light, a new sun in the sky. A new kind of light. Darkness held, pinned into place with a few bright stars visible over the trembling ends of a few torches lifted over the heads of the crowd.

Trysten shifted her feet. The sky, the sky. She would charge outside, spread her wings, and take to the sky. Her arms twitched.

A man screamed.

Trysten whipped around. The weyrman who had tried to calm the silver dragon now lay upon the ground several feet away. He clutched his upper arm with his left hand as he struggled to prop himself up on an elbow. Several others gave the dragon a wide berth as they ran to the fallen weyrman. A spurt of fire roasted the air where the man had been a second before rolling away.

No. This would not happen. She would not permit the horde to abscond. It wasn't possible. It wouldn't happen.

But how would she stop them?

A great roar escaped Elevera as if to answer the challenge. She swept her head at Paege. He leaped back to avoid the dragon's teeth by inches while several others around him dove to the ground. She roared again, then reared and spread her wings. They appeared to have grown in size since the last time Trysten had seen them, since Aeronwind had died.

The dragon's gaze fell upon Trysten. *The sky. Take to the sky!*

Trysten clenched her fists and stamped a foot. No! They would not leave. She forbid it. She would do what she had to do to keep the horde in the weyr. Nothing would stop her. Nothing.

Chapter 25

Trysten stormed down the aisle. She clenched her teeth and tightened her fists against an urge to rear back on her feet, to fling her wings open and roar. Elevera's thoughts and feelings blasted into her, harder than ever before, as though the dragon's mind and heart together were a great fire, a fire blazing higher even than the roof of the weyr. And Trysten marched forward, steadfast and steady into that great rolling heat that only she and Elevera felt. The press and intensity of it threatened to set her own heart and mind ablaze, send hot, burning waves through her, across her chest, up to the base of her throat, the ends of her jaw, and the thoughts and sudden wild emotions of Elevera and the horde crashed across her, threatened to overwhelm and douse and drown her in a thundering river of fire.

"Get her out of here!" Bolsar shouted, struggling to his feet beside Paege. As he pointed a finger at her and motioned for the weyrmen to grab her, the attention of the entire horde channeled through her. They were watching, listening, drawn to her suddenly as if she were the sky, vast and blue, and the one thing in it that they wished to find.

The weyrmen were no match for her.

Elevera roared again. She threw her golden head high until the roar erupted into a howl that crashed against and threatened to loosen every stone and plank in the weyr. The men clamped hands to their ears and hunched over as if expecting the howl to collapse, to tip and fall upon them like a toppled pillar of stone.

Trysten rushed forward, called into the whirlwind of noise and wild emotion, and abandoned need.

The weyrmen summoned by Bolsar crashed into her.

She twisted, lunged. In the panic to answer Elevera's call, she launched a fist into the face of one of the men. He spun away, but someone else snatched up her arm.

"No!" She hollered. "Let me go!"

"Trysten!" her father shouted as she fell and landed hard upon her back. Her breath burst from her, and for an instant, she expected to see it geyser up in fire, smoke winding its way around the column of flame.

"Let her go!" her mother screamed from the end of the weyr. Trysten arched her back, kicked, snapped her torso left and right, but the weyrmen held her down. They clamped their arms down on hers as their faces reddened in the lantern light.

"Get her out of here!" Bolsar yelled again. "She's upsetting the dragons."

"No!" Trysten howled. "They're going to abscond!" Her breath didn't come out hot enough, hard enough. It didn't blow these men away as the wings of dragons snapped all about her like a crackling fire.

"Let her go!" Mardoc bellowed. "Now!"

The weyrmen glanced back at their former boss. As they did so, the dragons roared. All of them. All at one time. The air shivered, and the roars pitched into howls like Elevera's. All of the dragons together built into a great crescendo, a piercing noise of loneliness that threatened to peel away everyone's skin with a sound of longing.

An answering howl pushed at the back of Trysten's teeth. The urge stole her breath from her, came from nowhere, from someplace so deep inside her that it felt to be beyond her as if she were but a gate for a trumpeting call. She curled up, her knees rising over her torso as she let out a groan through her teeth that were clenched so tightly she felt they might shatter. The men let her go to pitch themselves back on their heels and clamp their hands over their ears as they glanced at the howling dragons in terror.

Elevera peered at Trysten. Her gaze pushed into Trysten, passed through her skin and muscle as if it were fog, past her bones, brushing them aside like river reeds. Trysten gasped as she let go. Let go of everything. She released her hold on all that she held to be true, all that she knew, everything that made her who she was. She was not Trysten, not the daughter of Mardoc and Caron, not the friend of Paege or the young woman who wanted to be dragoneer more than anything. All of it dropped away from her, floated from her hands. It lifted from her skin as if washed away by the River Gul. Nothing was left except Elevera's eyes and a sense of wanting and need that cored Trysten's world.

She embraced it and faded into the longing. She became it.

"Elevera!" Paege yelled. "No! Stop!"

The men who had tackled her grabbed her arms and tugged, but then dropped her and fled as Elevera charged forward, her maw wide and rippling with fire. The dragon drew up before Trysten. Her great head swung back and forth in a challenge.

Silence fell upon the weyr. Silence, and then the song of dragons as each began to breathe again. Their raspy, dry breaths filled the weyr and overran the stunned space before they fell into a single, synchronous rhythm.

Paege approached. As he came closer, Elevera hissed at him, lowered her head and raised her wings in an attack posture. Paege held up a hand, out to Elevera, then stopped. He removed the helmet from his head and crouched slowly at the edge of the dragon's striking distance.

Trysten's breath came in gulps. All of her felt limp, empty, her muscles wrung out and stitched back onto her bones.

Paege held the helmet out to her briefly, then said, "I believe this is yours." He placed it on the ground, and after a glance at Elevera, rolled the helmet in her direction.

Trysten rolled onto her side. Paege stood upright, in his hordesman outfit, as his dragoneer armor was still being worked on. The look on his face was solid, expressionless. She searched it for relief, for regret, for any sign at all to betray what he felt.

Her eyes fell to the helmet. What he felt was there, in the helmet that he had passed on to her.

She pushed herself to her knees, then picked up the helmet and held it before herself. At Aeronwind's stall, her father stood and grasped the half-wall. His own expression was also blank, as solid and uncommitted as Paege's. He was watching her, waiting to see what would happen next. Behind him, Galelin stood and wiped tears from his eyes and did his best to quell a sob behind his grin.

Trysten rose to her feet and held the helmet before her. At the end of the weyr, the villagers crowded around the entrance. Some even spilled into the aisle they were expressly forbidden to be in. No one stopped them. The hordesmen and weyrmen all watched Trysten.

She turned to Paege again, and before asking if he was sure, she stopped herself. This wasn't about what he wanted, what her father wanted, or even what she wanted. This was about saving the horde. This was about being the dragoneer.

Trysten took a deep breath, then lifted the helmet and donned it. It sat loose about her head, and it smelled of her father.

Paege, standing before her, bowed his head and dropped to one knee. The act startled her, but then she recalled what it meant, how the villagers knelt to the dragoneer upon his return from battle. Upon *her* return from battle. She looked at her father. Galelin had placed a hand upon her father's shoulder. Mardoc stood a moment longer. His face darkened to a shade of red. He opened the stall door.

Trysten's hands clenched. No! He could not do this! He could not take this from her now!

The stall door opened with a creaking complaint. Beyond, the mass of Aeronwind lay, still and growing cold, her fire gone. Mardoc stepped through, out into the aisle, and then after calling Galelin to his side, he took the dragon healer's arm and lowered himself to one knee.

Trysten's hand flew up to her mouth as she choked back a sob. She drew in a deep breath through clenched teeth as Galelin followed suit. Around the weyr, the hordesmen and weyrmen each bowed their heads and dropped to a knee. She met her mother's eyes as outside, the villagers all paid honor to their new dragoneer.

Part II

The Second Horde

Chapter 26

A sharp snap of wood upon wood woke Trysten. She sat upright in bed. Her father stood in the middle of the room, leaning against his staff.

"It's time to get going."

Trysten closed her eyes against exhaustion. It had been such a late night whirled with both excitement and sorrow, triumph and mourning. Secretly, she had hoped that being dragoneer meant that she could sleep in a bit, at least this once.

"Aeronwind awaits," her father added.

Trysten rubbed the sleep from her eyes with the butts of her palms. She threw back the blankets from her bed.

"Your mother found you a uniform to wear for today. You will pay a visit to Jalite when we get back and be fitted for your own."

Trysten had also secretly hoped that her father's days of telling her what to do were over. She was the dragoneer now. But on the other hand, he knew what to do. Trysten did not have the experience of being a hordesman to guide her in protocol.

Her father left the room, and Trysten dressed in a hurry. The uniform her mother had laid out upon her dressing table was a bit large and clearly made for a man, but still, it felt magical to pull on the gold and blue sweater with spiraling cables down the arm. It smelled of straw and a bit of sweat and sky. It was a garment that had seen action, that had logged a lot of time between the flesh of a warrior and his leather armor, which Trysten picked up and slid over her head. She tugged at the hem of it and admired the look of it, the contrast between her brightly colored sleeves and the dark leather that covered her chest. The village seal of a dragon twisting around a stone was embossed over her heart. A wide grin spread over her face as it sunk into her sleep-addled head that this was hers. She'd earned it. She was the dragoneer.

She picked up her father's helmet and carried it into the other room. Her father sat at the table and chewed on a piece of bread spread with lard. Trysten sat at the table beside him, in her place. Her mother placed a cup of tea and a slice of bread before her as well and gave her a huge smile.

"You look so nice in that uniform," her mother said. "I was hoping it would fit."

"It will do for the burial procession," Mardoc said around a mouthful.

The joy fled the room as if sucked into a bellows. Caron turned away and busied herself with her knitting.

"Your primary duty today is to lead the procession to the burial mounds, to lay the first stone, and to lay the last stone while staying busy between those two events. Do you know where the burial mounds are?"

Trysten nodded. She had ventured out to them with Paege when they were both children. She had found it to be an eerie, disturbing place, and hadn't been back since, but she remembered the trail, and whenever she passed the trailhead, she recalled the experience with chills.

"That's good. You will take Paege as your commander. Keep him close, and he will tell you what you need to know. The place of the fallen is at the rear of the procession."

Trysten winced at the term. It made her father sound disgraceful for doing nothing more than outliving his mount.

"After you lay the last stone, there will be a moment of silence, and then you will lead the procession back to the village. There will be a feast waiting for us."

Trysten nodded. She recalled the burial feast from past deaths. They had been all-day affairs in which everyone in the village dropped whatever one was working on and instead spent the day preparing food. Although an air of mourning underscored the day, as a child, Trysten had enjoyed the novelty and excitement of it, of the whole village coming together to serve a giant meal along what looked to be miles of tables lined down the central aisle of the weyr.

She recalled the ringing bells, the clanging that announced the return of the hordesmen. She had rushed to the village's edge, Paege in tow, and there she saw her father looking so tired and exhausted, and she recalled thinking how odd it was for him to look that way when she had spent the day having fun and sneaking treats.

Over her breakfast, Trysten stole a glance at her father. Exhaustion already clung to his face. Dark sacks hung beneath his eyes. The look of anguish upon his face last night, when Aeronwind finally died, appeared to have wrung his face out and left it limp, ragged.

He hadn't congratulated her yet. He hadn't thanked her for saving the horde. She had written it off as grief and shock. Would it come? Did it matter? She was the dragoneer now, and there was nothing anyone could do to change that. She had done what she had to do.

By the time Trysten and her father arrived at the weyr, the weyrmen had already removed the wall and gate of Aeronwind's stall and constructed a platform beneath her body. It consisted of six poles running right-to-left down the length of her body, and then three poles running front-to-back. The sight of such a mighty beast laid out upon a platform, to be carried over stones and trails by hordesmen instead of her wings, nearly brought tears to Trysten's eyes. When she glanced at her father and saw the exhaustion stuffed and imperfectly concealed behind a stoic look, she wanted to draw him into an embrace.

Her father nodded at Aeronwind. "You will take the central pole; the one in front. Let's be on our way."

Galelin approached and placed a hand upon Mardoc's bicep. "How are you this morning?"

Mardoc shrugged off Galelin's hand. "I'll be fine."

Galelin shot a quick glance and a nod at Trysten as if to assure her that he'd look after her father. The gesture struck her as both touching and insulting. Her father didn't need looking after like a dawdling old man, but at the same time, with his twisted leg, she wasn't sure how he'd make it to the burial mounds and back.

"If you're ready," Mardoc said with a glance to Trysten.

She looked about the weyr. The hordesmen gathered around Aeronwind's stall looked from Mardoc to her, then back. A bit of heat flushed over her cheeks, and she joined the others in looking toward her father.

One of the hordesmen cleared his throat.

Trysten glanced back. Paege crouched down and grasped one of the poles that ran beneath the deceased dragon. He gave a slight nod to the front of the platform.

Trysten pulled in a deep breath through her nose. She checked on her father once more, who no longer looked so weak and helpless. He could have at least told her what was expected of her, what the protocol was. It wasn't her fault that she had been excluded from funeral processions in the past.

She pulled her shoulders back and walked to Aeronwind's stall. As she did, the breathing of the dragons around her pulled into a single, unified breath. It was a sign that her father was at the weyr, and then it occurred to her that it was that way no longer. It was a sign that *she* was at the weyr.

Several of the hordesmen took up positions around the platform as she approached. Their stares pressed against her, prodded her like iron rods. It unsettled her a bit to look in their eyes and not know their thoughts or what they felt as easily as she could look into the eyes of a dragon and know the same.

At the head of the stall, Trysten stepped before the front of the platform. As she turned around, a few more of the hordesmen left the ranks of those gathered around the stall. A few, standing in a tight knot, stared at her a second longer, and then looked back to her father who kept his eyes locked on hers, his weight resting on his staff. Galelin stood behind him and to the side. If he had climbed up onto her father's shoulder and crouched, still and pert as a gargoyle, it wouldn't have surprised Trysten much at all.

The stragglers looked back to Trysten. She crouched and wrapped her hands around the rough-hewn length of log that formed the center brace for the funerary platform. Leather creaked and fabric rustled as the hordesmen behind her all crouched and grasped the posts that ran perpendicular to the central brace.

"Ready?" Trysten asked as she looked at the stragglers.

A few looked to her father before taking up positions around the platform. On the count of three, the hordesmen heaved, and the platform rose from the ground. Trysten gritted her teeth and pulled, and once she had the post above her waist, she shifted her hands and pushed until the post rested upon her shoulder. The weight felt like it would drive her into the ground like a stake beneath a mallet. How she was ever to make it to the burial mounds, she had no idea. But she would do it. It was her responsibility. Not only as dragoneer, but as someone who loved her father and who saw past the stoic mask and glimpsed the twinge of grief when they lifted the body of his dead dragon onto their shoulders.

"Forward," Trysten called out, and the weight of the platform propelled her out of the stall. They maneuvered the tight corner with their load, then proceeded out of the weyr and onto the wide path cut through the rocky landscape with Aeronwind upon their shoulders, her father and Galelin in the rear. The bright sunlight promised to heat the day quickly.

Chapter 27

By the time the first burial mounds came into view, Trysten's back and shoulders screamed with pain. Her sweater and leather armor felt hot and heavy. As the procession passed among the cairns piled up on either side of the trail, a shiver ran along her spine despite the heat. She recalled being here as a girl and feeling as if she and Paege had ventured to the edge of the world. The cairns stood tall and silent, wide as small mountains themselves. In some of the older ones, stone heather had taken root among the rocks. The emptiness of the graves amplified the emptiness she felt from the dragon behind her. It left her feeling hollow and alone even among the procession.

When they cleared the existing cairns, she led the hordesmen off the trail and over the rocks a short way. Once they were a respectable distance from the trail, she called for the others to lower their load. She crouched as the weight of Aeronwind pressed down on her. Finally, with relief, she lowered the post off her shoulder and set the funerary platform among the stones.

She stood and stretched, pressing her hands into the small of her back. Slight groans escaped some of the hordesmen as they stretched as well. Waterskins were opened and passed around. Bits of cheese and dried meat were shared beneath the sun. As the wind blew in from the north, the sweat evaporated from her skin and left a chill in its place. In silence, they rested and watched Mardoc and Galelin bring up the rear. They had fallen behind, but not by as much as Trysten had feared. She wanted to go out to her father, to meet him, to bring him a skin of water even though a half-empty skin sloshed at Galelin's side. But it would only embarrass her father, so she stayed put.

As Mardoc and Galelin stopped at the outer edge of the group, Trysten walked a short distance off, picked up a rock, and carried it back to Aeronwind. As she crouched beside the dragon, her back ached and her knees throbbed. She placed the rock next to Aeronwind's head.

At her feet, Aeronwind's head lay motionless. For a brief moment, Trysten expected or hoped that the dragon would lift her head up, rest her chin upon the stone and gaze out at the mountains.

Paege stepped up to her. "Move her head. She should face the village."

Heat flushed over Trysten's cheeks. Half of the hordesmen stood. The other half remained seated on stones or the ground. Her father and Galelin were among those still standing. An open water skin remained clutched in Galelin's hand as if he had offered it to Mardoc, but had yet to take the hint that Mardoc would have none of it.

All of them stared openly at her.

How long would this go on? How long would it take her to learn all she needed to know?

She crouched again, slid her fingers underneath Aeronwind's jaw, then lifted. The head was heavier than she had expected, and the sensation of her fingers sinking into the yielding, leathery flesh under the jaw filled Trysten with an odd feeling. It wasn't a dragon. It was Aeronwind, but it wasn't a dragon. She didn't want to touch it. But still, she straightened her knees and dragged Aeronwind's head forward and to the dragon's left until the head faced to the north, toward the village and the River Gul.

After she placed the dragon's head back on the ground, she moved the rock. The sensation that Aeronwind would move her head had disappeared. The dragon was lifeless, empty. Would a human body feel the same way? Her stomach sank. Finding out first hand was inevitable.

As soon as she stood, the rest of the hordesmen scattered and selected stones from among the dirt and heather and brush and grass that littered the plain. Even her father clutched his staff with one hand and stooped to pick up a fist-sized stone. The men brought their stones to Aeronwind and placed them around the dragon. On they went, piling rocks up and over Aeronwind's body until the men and Trysten had to climb over the stones to cover Aeronwind's back. As the work progressed, and the sun climbed over the sky, Trysten's mind shut off, became blank. She thought of little but where to get the next stone and where to place it. She stopped on occasion to drink water, to pour a little on her hands and wash away the dust and grit and blood that gathered as the stones tore at her flesh.

Finally, the men stepped back, forming a ring around the cairn. Trysten selected a cap stone, a large, flat one the size of a platter, and hefted it up. Her breath came hard and fast. Despite the cool weather, sweat prickled her forehead. Step by step, she climbed over the stones packed around Aeronwind's body. At the top, she peered over her shoulder. Her father stood near Aeronwind's head. He leaned upon his staff more than usual. His shoulders heaved. He panted. It wasn't the work so much as the strain, the pain perhaps, of all he had been through. Physical and emotional. She had no idea what he had been through the last couple of days. She'd have to remember that. Someday she might be in his shoes, relinquishing the title to a child of her own.

She let the weight of the stone flex her knees as she crouched atop the cairn and allowed the rock to settle into place. She remained still a few seconds, then placed the palm of her hand against the flat of the stone. Her fingers ached. The knuckles felt sore. A long, rough scrape beneath her index finger burned and felt soothed against the cool of the rock.

"Thank you," Trysten whispered to the dragon within. "Thank you for all you have done for us. We will remember you."

After a moment of listening to the wind whisper, she picked her way down the cairn. At the bottom, she approached her father. He straightened up but didn't resist as she drew him into an embrace. She buried her face into his shoulder, and he wrapped his arm around her, pulling her close. She took a deep breath and smelled the leather and wool and sweat of him.

When she let go, he wrapped his arm around her shoulders and drew her to his side. She looked away, to the cairn, so that she wouldn't see the tears brimming in his eyes.

"Are we ready?" Trysten asked no one in particular. A few nods from the men indicated that their work was done. A few cast their glances back to the cairn.

"Then let's go," Trysten said. She pressed lightly against the small of her father's back, urging him back in the direction they came.

He planted his staff before himself and leaned into it. "No," he said with a shake of his head. "That is not my place. You lead. The fallen bring up the rear."

"Who says?" Trysten asked.

Her father looked at her as if she had sprouted a second head. "Tradition. That is how it is done."

"No one has taken the time to explain these things to me, to tell me about the traditions that I am supposed to observe, so how am I to know?"

Her father glanced away, to some unseen point off over the horizon behind Trysten. "You learn as you go."

Trysten shook her head. "If it were that important, someone would have explained it to me. How was Paege expected to know any of this?"

"He was a hordesman. He's participated in burials before. He's seen it done."

"But I wasn't allowed to be a hordesman. How am I expected to know any of this?"

Her father continued to not meet her gaze, to not look her in the eye. It was odd, strange. It was unlike him to shy away from a challenge to authority or tradition.

"You will learn as you go."

Trysten shook her head. "Not good enough. If you can't bother to tell me what I need to know, then I'm making up my own traditions. And from now on, I walk with the fallen—No," she said with another shake of the head. "First of all, I'm getting rid of that word. There is no fallen."

"It is not within the realm of the dragoneer to choose which words we speak."

"I will not speak it. And you will walk by my side back to the village. That is my order."

Her father closed his eyes briefly. The look of pain in his expression nearly made Trysten backpedal, take away all that she said. But there would be no taking it away. What was said was out there, between them, never to be buried.

"Please," he said, then finally looked her in the eye. "These are the traditions that I have fought for. These are the traditions that Aeronwind died for. Allow me to have them."

Trysten took half a step back. She swallowed hard. The urge pressed at her to glance around, to see what the hordesmen were doing, to look at the expressions on their faces. She resisted, however. She didn't want to look like she was seeking their approval or support. This was about her and her father.

She nodded. In response, her father merely gripped his staff with his other hand.

Trysten turned away, and as the other hordesmen watched, she began to walk back the way they had come. Paege fell in behind her, just a step or two behind and to her right. Then she heard the boots of the other hordesmen picking through the stones.

As hard as she listened, she could not hear the light thunk of her father's staff probing the ground as he leaned his broken weight into it.

Chapter 28

When Trysten and the others entered the weyr upon their return, the villagers greeted them with a feast. A row of tables lined the center of the aisle. Plates and platters and bowls and tureens of food crowded the table tops and were filled with everything from mutton and fish to root stews and sweets. The villagers stood about their offerings and watched them enter in silence. Up and down the aisle, the dragons watched her. She peered into the eyes of each one, but when she looked to Elevera's stall, her heart stuttered to find it empty, only to then recognize the golden hide in the next stall over. In Aeronwind's old stall. There she stood tall and stared back at Trysten with her brown eyes.

A new sense of authority flooded through her, coursed across her skin, down and within her muscles. She was Elevera, the alpha. Trysten shook her head as if to clear it.

Paege stepped up to her and leaned close enough to whisper in her ear. "Sit. At the head of the table."

Trysten nodded her understanding even though she knew that. She recalled it from when her father had come back from previous burial processions. She had felt quite proud to sit at the left hand of her mother, who sat at the left hand of her father, who sat at the head of the table in a position of honor. He was important, special, and she was important and special to him.

And until he had died, Paege's father had sat to her father's right. She motioned at his former place at the table. "And you will sit there."

Paege didn't respond right away. She thought of him on Elevera, the time she had tried to work with them in secret. He had felt so closed off, walled away on the dragon his father had died upon. But she needed him, his help, and his experience. For the good of the horde and village, he'd have to be her commander.

He moved to the assigned place.

Trysten stepped to the head of the table as she had seen her father do. Across the weyr, the villagers moved to the tables and stood behind chairs and benches. Her mother smiled and stepped up to her place on Trysten's left. There Trysten stood and waited to see what her father would do. Finally, he and Galelin entered the weyr. Would he sit to her left, or do something ridiculous like go and sit at the foot of the table, next to the village overseer?

Caron stepped away. Trysten glanced over her shoulder and watched as her mother took her husband by the arm and tugged slightly. As Trysten feared, her father motioned toward the foot of the table. His wife tugged his arm again as she spoke to him, her voice too low to hear. Mardoc's shoulders heaved in a sigh of resignation. He then followed his wife back and stood to Trysten's left, between herself and Caron.

"Thank you," Trysten mouthed as he gave her a sidelong glance. Caron squeezed his arm. Mardoc straightened his back.

With everyone in their place, Trysten raised her hands as she had seen her father do, and then lowered them to the tabletop. With a bustle of rustling clothes and creaking wood, the people of the village sat at the collection of tables. Finally, Caron, Mardoc, and Paege sat before Trysten took her seat. Up and down the table, chatter erupted among the villagers. Utensils clinked as bowls and platters were lifted and passed around. The mouth-watering aromas overwhelmed the scents of dust and hay and leather and even the odor of herself and the hordesmen who had been bathed in sweat all day. Pitchers of water and mead and wine were passed around. Trysten filled a goblet with water and downed it all in one great draught. As she placed the cup aside, she looked over the villagers, trying to gauge their well-being. How were they faring in the face of all that had changed?

After dinner, as the crowd thinned out, and those that stayed began to clear the remains of the meal, Assina appeared at Trysten's elbow. "Are you ready for your fitting?"

Trysten looked at the young woman. She really wasn't ready. She stank like a goat, and every muscle in her body ached from the day's labor. She wanted nothing more than to head back to her cottage and collapse into her bed.

As if reading her mind, Assina touched the tips of her fingers to Trysten's shoulder. "Come on. It won't take but a few minutes, and the sooner we can get you measured, the sooner Talon and I can start on your uniform."

Trysten regarded the donated uniform she'd donned all day. She had begun to think of it as hers, but it would be nice to have one that truly was hers and fit like it as well. And following Assina would remove herself from the steady stream of villagers stopping at the head of the table and wishing her well on their way out.

Trysten agreed, then pushed herself up from the table. As she followed Assina out, several more villagers stopped and congratulated her. She accepted the well-wishes with grace and gratitude, but part of her wanted to point out that it wasn't her doing, that Aeronwind had died, and if it were up to her, Aeronwind would still be alive, and her father would still have the title.

But she smiled and shook hands and thanked each one of them. Between interruptions, she looked back at Elevera, who stood tall and erect, watching over all as Aeronwind had always done.

Outside, Trysten drew in a deep breath of the cool air. She swore half the day's heat had dissipated since she arrived at the weyr. She looked to the mountains. No horde of dragons from the Western Kingdom came streaming down. Instead, a dark band of clouds hung over the mountaintops.

"I hate social functions," Assina said suddenly.

Trysten lifted an eyebrow at her.

"No offense meant, because I understand the point of all that," Assina said as she waved a dismissive hand hand at the weyr, "but it's just too much for me, you know?"

Trysten thought of the dragons as she ran the palm of her hand over the emblem on the armor. How long would it be before everyone cleared out?

How long before she could get back in and see Elevera and the other dragons?

    Assina started for her cottage. Trysten waited for a second longer, then fell in behind her.

Chapter 29

Assina's cottage stood empty when they arrived. She lit a candle from the embers in the hearth and led Trysten back to the workroom. There she lit several more candles and a lantern.

The door opened. A moment later, Jalite and Talon stood in the doorway.

"I was about to get Trysten's measurements," Assina said as she looked up from a basket containing balls of yarn.

"I'll get this one," Jalite said to her son with a touch upon his shoulder. He nodded, glanced at Trysten once with an odd look, something that she didn't know how to interpret, and off he went.

Jalite shut the door behind her. "Those don't fit you, do they," she said with a nod to the garments Trysten wore.

Trysten shook her head. Her arms were too heavy, too weary to cross over her chest, and so they fell limp to her side feeling like lengths of old, worn-out rope.

"If you would, dear, please take that uniform off so that we may get an accurate measurement. Don't worry about Talon. He knows better than to poke his head in here when it's just us women."

Trysten glanced at the door. She was too tired to think about it much. She crossed her arms over her chest, grabbed the shoulders of the leather armor, then leaned forward slightly as she tugged upon the shoulders as she had seen her father do. Once she wiggled out of the armor, she pulled off the sweater and let it slip from her fingers. It fell to the floor in a puddle of wool.

"Your shirt, too, dear," Jalite said. "Your modesty will not help us get an accurate measurement. And again, you have my assurance that it is just us. Talon knows better than to walk in on us, or let anyone else in."

Trysten blinked at Jalite, and her eyes burned with sleep. Taking off her shirt suddenly felt like an unreasonable amount of effort. Still, the sooner they got her measurements, the sooner she could go home. She pulled her shirt out from the waistband of her pants, curled her fingers around the hem, and pulled it off.

Immediately, Assina approached with a length of yarn and a bit of charcoal. Despite her undershirt, Trysten felt an urge to cover herself, but again, she was too tired, and so her arms hung at her side.

Assina handed the end of the yarn to her mother, who pinned it to Trysten's shoulder with the tip of her finger. She drew the yarn across Trysten's shoulders, then marked it with a stub of charcoal at the other shoulder.

"Oh, I can't tell you how happy this makes me!" Jalite said, her voice near a squeal. "To think that a woman has not only joined the hordesmen but even become a dragoneer! I never dared to even dream that I'd be able to do this someday. Grandmother would be so proud."

"Grandmother?" Assina asked as she nudged Trysten to lift her arms, hold her elbows out.

"Well, not your grandmother," Jalite said. "Not my mother, but rather my own grandmother. She used to tell me tales of how *her* own grandmother once made a uniform for a lady dragoneer."

Trysten's head snapped around.

"Her grandmother made armor for a female dragoneer?"

Jalite nodded. "She was quite proud of that. She said she saw it. She was too young to do much other than be in the room, but she said she remembered it."

"Here," Trysten said, then pointed to the ground. "In Aerona?"

Jalite nodded again. "Yes. She was the last. Or at least the last here. The way people talk, I assume there are no female dragoneers anywhere anymore."

"Who was it? Why doesn't anyone talk about it—talk about her anymore?"

Jalite shrugged. "Times change, I guess. A man succeeded her, and he's been passing it down to his sons ever since until we wound up with your father, who was a fine dragoneer, it's just that I'm so proud to have a woman as dragoneer in my lifetime. To think that I get to be a part of that! That's quite exciting. Isn't it?" Jalite asked, then tapped Assina on the back of the hand.

Assina nodded, then pinned a length of yarn to the top of Trysten's shoulder with the tip of her finger.

"But, there is a rule. I saw it."

Jalite shrugged, then placed her finger on the end of the yarn to free up Assina's. "Rules change to suit the times, I suppose."

Exhaustion clouded Trysten's head. She had seen the rule. She had observed it with her own eyes in the book of rules. It was there. And the book itself was already how old? How could that be? How could there have been a female dragoneer, and not that long ago if Jalite's own grandmother had witnessed the construction of the armor and uniform? Could her father be lying? Simply mistaken? Could it possibly be true? What if it was nothing more than the fancies of Jalite's grandmother, who was a girl herself when this supposedly happened. That was a long stretch across time to account for. Who could she find who might confirm or debunk Jalite's claim?

Galelin. He'd know. She'd have to pay him a visit soon. But not tonight. As soon as Jalite and Assina let her go, she'd head off to bed.

The thought of another female dragoneer spun about in her head as if on a dragon of its own, the idea nothing more than a dole of doves to be herded into a fluttering ball of feathers.

Finally, Jalite and Assina allowed her to dress again after they had taken all of her measurements. Trysten brushed them off as they tried to wipe away Assina's smudges of charcoal. She claimed she was tired after such a long day and merely wanted to go home. Jalite and Assina reluctantly agreed, as if allowing her out of their cottage with any smudges left on her skin was a mark against their professionalism.

Once outside, Trysten took another deep breath and felt surprise at how much heat the air had lost. Though she couldn't say for sure, she also had the sense that the stars had grown brighter, larger, more vibrant since she had entered Assina's cottage. She took in another deep breath, and the air scrubbed the sleep from her, shook it off her bones as chills wracked her. She gritted her teeth and wrapped her arms around the armor and sweater, and she tried not to think about the previous owner and his fate. If there had been a female dragoneer, where was her armor? Who kept it? She had likely been buried in it, but frequently, there were two sets of armor, in case one set was damaged in battle.

And where was she buried? Was there a woman out there buried with her alpha, with her family at her side, in a place of honor? There was a book that held where each person, each dragon was buried. She could ask her father—No, she no longer had to. She was the dragoneer. Those books were hers. The den was hers, now. She could walk right up and sit in the chair behind the table, light a lantern, and pull the books down and read them until morning if it struck her.

She went straight to the weyr, but rather than climb the flight of steps to her father's—to *her* den—she paused at the foot of the them.

Night time had always been a special time to visit. The weyr was quiet, sparse, and empty of many of the people who would try and speak to her, or who would ask what she was up to. This night was a slight exception. A few weyrmen continued to sweep up the spaces from which the tables had been cleared. A few tables still remained, and a man and a woman negotiated fervently over who owned a particular table.

As she waited for one of the weyrmen to notice her and ask if her father knew where she was, the breathing of the dragons caught her attention. Many of them were still awake, and instead of singing their song of swooping, polyphonic breaths that rose and fell in waves and tempos, their breathing fell into a synchronous, uniform beat.

A weyrmen glanced up from a dark spot of some spilled liquid he was covering with dirt. His eyes widened briefly, and Trysten braced herself for the question. Instead, he asked if he could help her with anything.

Trysten blinked at the man. Her eyes burned again. Exhaustion numbed her limbs. A sense of loss settled into her, stretched her out as if she were an overburdened waterskin suddenly relieved of its load. She wished for something near with which to prop herself up, such as a staff.

"No," she said, then shook her head. "No, thank you."

The weyrman stared at her a few seconds longer, then went back to sweeping up the mess he'd claimed as his task.

Trysten turned her attention to Elevera. She stood in her stall and watched with quiet eyes. Curiosity flooded Trysten's senses. It collided with her own human sense of loneliness and swirled with bewilderment. She had what she wanted more than anything else in life. She was the dragoneer. She had bonded with Elevera. She had succeeded her father and kept the tradition alive in her own family. She had everything she could possibly want.

And so why did the sense of loss pile upon her so heavily, so oppressively?

She turned to the stairway. The thought of climbing those steps, lighting a lantern, and sitting down with the books to look for something she probably would not find was too daunting. Whatever was in those books would still be there tomorrow.

Trysten exited the weyr and walked home.

Chapter 30

After a bite of breakfast, Trysten returned to the weyr and found it empty except for the weyrmen who bustled about in their care of the dragons. A few of them glanced at her and immediately returned their attention to the tasks at hand, but most of them ignored her. The weyrmen had made their lives caring for the dragons and their equipment. Certainly, they knew about the song, about the synchronous breathing. Without looking up, they knew that the dragoneer had entered the weyr.

The stairs to her den beckoned. The books that might tell her of other incredible, brave women who were in her boots once waited for her there. How did they deal with the same issues, if they had to deal with them at all? If there were female dragoneers before her, then surely there had to be female hordesmen, if being a hordesman was how one got to learn the traditions.

She swallowed hard, then glanced at the end of the weyr, toward the hordesmen's hall. Research would have to wait. Her father had always been ready to work with the hordesmen at the crack of dawn. Even though a good bit of the village had slept in after the late night, she was still late to the weyr by comparison.

As she passed the midpoint of the weyr, she smiled at Elevera. The smile dropped away, however, when Trysten glanced to her left, to the wide door that opened up into the side yard. Out in the yard, her father leaned against his staff as he stared off into the cloud-swaddled wall of mountains. She stepped out to join him.

"Why are you late?" her father asked.

Trysten stopped. She dropped her gaze to the ground trodden with the footprints of people and dragons among the mud and stones.

"Everyone had a late night."

"Including the hordesmen of the Western Kingdom?"

Trysten looked to the mountains.

"Being the dragoneer means that you are responsible for the safety of this village. It also means that you are responsible for this stronghold against the Western Kingdom. The entire kingdom depends upon you now. The least you can do to honor that responsibility is to make the most of your time. You should have had the men ready to go by first light."

Trysten let out a long breath and crossed her arms over her chest. "And exactly how am I supposed to know that? I know that Paege would know all of this because he got to be a hordesman, but you wouldn't even allow me into the consideration, let alone allow me to fly with the hordesmen."

Mardoc swayed slightly as if challenged by a wind that only he could feel. "Part of being dragoneer is being clever. Being reasonable. If you don't practice during the daylight, when will you practice?"

"Is this why there are no female dragoneers? Because we're not clever or reasonable enough?"

This grabbed his attention. Dark sacks hung beneath his eyes. Her breath caught in her throat. His appearance had aged ten years since the previous night.

"You know why there are no female dragoneers. Or why there haven't been until now."

"Never? There has never been a female dragoneer before me?"

Mardoc returned his attention to the mountains. He regarded them a second longer. "Never."

"Why?"

Her father did not respond.

"Do you really believe that no other woman has ever wanted to be a dragoneer before me?"

"I believe you are one of a kind."

Trysten crossed her arms over her chest. She regarded the mountains as well. Hate for them welled up in her, rose up like an answering wall of mountains. So much of their lives were dictated by those brutes. By the wilds, if she could, she would knock them down, fly into them with Elevera and thrash them with her fist and dragon tail, send the rocks flying, scattering like the silk-weed pods that lined the pastures in fall. How different would their lives be if there were no mountains?

The mountains stood in utter defiance of her wish. They did not flinch. They did not stir. Clouds boiled off them like steam and dissipated in the winds aloft, leaving a pale blue that appeared to have arisen from the ice atop the mountains.

She heaved a sigh. "Excuse me."

Without waiting for a response from her father, she re-entered the weyr and continued to make her way back to the bunkhouse.

Much like the dragons in the weyr, the chatter and motion of the hordesmen in the dining hall came to a halt as Trysten stepped inside. All of the hordesmen looked at her as the remains of their breakfast lay before them.

"Are we riding today?" Trysten asked. She crossed her arms over her chest and lifted an eyebrow.

The hordesmen continued to stare at her. A few looked to their compatriots across the table, and a few suddenly found the crumbs on their plates, or their half-finished mugs of tea to be of interest.

One of the hordesmen, Rast, cleared his throat and straightened his back. "You never told us when you'd like us to assemble."

Trysten tapped her foot once. "I see that. I should hope that the Western Kingdom is a little more thoughtful than myself and gives you proper notice of their next attack, so that you may plan accordingly."

A few of the men stirred. Rast's face reddened. His back grew rigid.

"Let's go," Trysten said with a nod back at the weyr.

The men rose from their seats and followed Trysten to the weyr. Her jaw tightened as she found her father standing in the side entrance. He did not lean on his staff, but held it upright in his hand, as if it was the staff that needed his support.

At the middle of the weyr, as she stepped before Elevera's stall, Trysten turned to the hordesmen. They all stopped and regarded her. She folded her hands behind her back as she had seen her father do before giving the men a lecture.

"I need your help."

The hordesmen traded glances. A few shuffled their weight.

"I've not had the benefit of proving myself to the horde like each of you has. I've only proven myself to Elevera, and as alpha, she has chosen me as dragoneer. As honored as I am by her faith and decision, I still have a lot to learn about being a hordesman. You will teach me."

A number of the hordesmen glanced at her father, who must have remained by the side door, as she had not heard the shuffle of his lame foot if he had walked away.

"Yahi the cloud reader has said that the fighting season will start early this year. We have no time to waste. We have to be ready to defend ourselves, defend our village, and be the bulwark that stops the enemy from reaching the heart of the kingdom. That is our duty. That is our right. We will be ready, and from this moment forward, we will be ready by sunrise. That means we will be out here, our mounts saddled, our dragons ready to take to the air. Is that understood?"

Again, several of the men looked at her father.

Trysten's hands fell to her side. She drew her shoulders back. If she looked at her father, she would find him doing nothing more than staring at her with a solid, blank face, his attitude perfectly appropriate for a hordesman listening to the orders of his dragoneer. It infuriated her. It was almost as if he was mocking her. Why was he even standing there at all? Why wasn't he at home, relaxing, healing, helping her mother? Why did he have to be here, watching as if she were performing an imitation of him?

She reminded herself not to sigh in frustration. Stay steady. Rast leaned aside and whispered into another man's ear. The other hordesman looked to the ceiling as he stifled a grin.

She had to get them in the air. Her father couldn't follow them up there. Once they were in the air, she could act—she could command them as was her right and duty.

"Grab your saddles and mounts. I expect to find you all waiting for me in the yard when I get out there."

While most of the men glanced at her father again, Paege went for Leya, the dragon who had succeeded Elevera once she became alpha. A couple men remained still for a few seconds, then followed Paege's example. The rest watched Mardoc as if waiting for his daughter's orders to be confirmed.

"Now!" Trysten said, then slapped her palms together.

The men jumped to get their dragons.

She looked back at her father. As expected, he simply stared at her, his face as expressionless as the mountains behind him.

By the wilds did she envy his ability to do that, to make stone look expressive. She couldn't even hope to match him, so she didn't bother and try. Her face darkened with aggravation. When he continued to neither respond nor react, she started for Elevera. Her wings flicked up a bit, and her tail lashed with a sense of expectation that buoyed Trysten and lifted her over the irritation with her father.

Chapter 31

When she led the saddled Elevera into the yard, all of the hordesmen were ready to fly. Relief trickled through her, softened her muscles. She climbed onto Elevera's shoulders, and the hordesmen followed suit.

"We're going to go through the calls," Trysten announced. She nearly asked if the men were ready, but her father never did. He expected them to *be* ready. It was their duty.

"Release the dole," she called to the weyrman standing outside the door.

As the weyrman hurried inside to retrieve the cage of doves, Trysten raked her heels up Elevera's shoulders. As the dragon's wings unfurled with a snap, she grasped the lip of the saddle as Elevera rose on her hind legs, pitching Trysten back. Her knuckles blanched before Elevera shoved with her hind legs and beat down hard and fast with her wings. The world lurched as if yanked from under Elevera's feet. Dust and bits of straw fled the raw power, and the dragon rose into the air as she continued to beat her wings.

The other hordesmen followed Trysten into the sky before she ordered Elevera to level off and start a wide circle around the village. The hordesmen fell into formation behind her, the lesser dragons forming a *V* that streamed out behind Elevera as each dragon took advantage of the turbulence created by the wing beats of the dragon before it. Off her right flank, Paege and Leya kept pace.

Below, several weyrmen opened the cages. Doves streamed out and fled for the sky. Trysten thrust her left arm into the air and made a series of swooping motions to indicate what she expected the horde to do. As she made the motions, she pictured each one in her mind and knew that Elevera would execute her orders.

Off to her right, Paege repeated the orders for those who missed them.

Trysten pushed down on the left edge of her saddle while pressing with her right heel. Elevera dipped her left wing. The muscles in her back shifted as she lifted the leading edge of her right wing slightly. She dipped to her left and began to bank down toward the doves, who upon sight of the horde, elected to stay low and flee east across the open pasture.

Behind her, the *V* shape had broken into two columns, one on either side of her. It was a sight to behold; the massive, sleek dragons sailing through the sky. A grin spread across her face and stretched into the wind as she returned her attention to the fleeing dole. She lifted her left arm again and issued a series of orders for the left column, tracing each one in the air exactly as she'd seen her father do countless times, either in the air or while teaching new hordesmen inside the weyr.

They descended upon the dole. With a quick, curving gesture from Trysten, as well as a brief jab from her right heel, Elevera broke to the left and thrust her wings down and back to power past the doves. Upon sight of Elevera, the doves scattered to the right, only to be reined in by Leya as Paege pulled up even with her. Several of the doves broke off, either dropping down and veering off, or arcing up and peeling away. Most of them remained crowded in the dole, however. As they tried to climb up and away, two of the hordesmen pulled up overhead and kept the dole pinned close to the ground. Finally, with a sweeping motion followed by a grabbing hand and a jutting elbow, Trysten spurred Elevera on and broke right as Paege pulled Leya back. The doves swept up and out, through the hole that Paege and Trysten had created. Another hordesman swept in low over the ground, his dragon's claws nearly brushing the tops of the stone heather as she flew. Upon sight of her, the doves arced up.

Soon, Trysten conducted the horde through a series of maneuvers that had the dole of doves wound up in a tight ball, flying round and round as the dragons hemmed them in. Trysten grinned at the sight, at the doves flying in such a perfect, tight sphere of taupe feathers and pink beaks.

Furthermore, it was a delight to see the dragons circling the dole in perfect formation, each one equidistant from the other and forming a moving cage. With a pat on Elevera's neck, she signaled with her other hand for the riders to keep the formation up. For half an hour, they held the formation and lost not a single dove.

Finally, Trysten signaled for the horde to return to the weyr. They broke formation. The doves scattered and raced away in several directions. The horde flew back to the weyr and landed in the yard. As Elevera touched down, Trysten absorbed the sudden stop with her body and rocked forward and back in the saddle. She looked up to find her father standing in the doorway again. He nodded once, then turned into the shadows and disappeared.

After a break, Trysten ordered the hordesmen to prepare for a round of mock battle. Each one armed himself with a bow and a quiver of blunted arrows, then leaped back into the air on their dragons.

Trysten led her half of the horde around the village as the half commanded by Paege flew toward the mountains. After a distance, Paege's wing circled around and approached the village as if they were enemies from the Western Kingdom. Trysten ordered her wing to intercept. As they flew over the foothills, she glanced at the sun. It was barely beyond noon. The sun would serve no one any advantage at this hour, so she ordered the wing forward with speed.

As the two wings drew closer, Paege's split into two staggered columns, one slightly higher than the other. This move wasn't new. Trysten had seen it performed a number of times. Paege was going to spread the columns at the last second and try to force Trysten's wing to fly between the two, thereby taking arrows from the left and right, as well as above and below. It was a difficult maneuver to defend against. Both the rider and his mount's belly would be exposed to enemy arrows.

If Paege commanded a full horde, Trysten would have a hard time defending against such an approach. Fortunately, with only nine dragons, he couldn't react to one of the few defenses against the move.

In her head, Trysten practiced the series of motions needed to signal for the other riders to fan out wide at the last second as she and the dragon on her right rear flew through the middle. They would be exposed to the gauntlet, but her other riders would open with a volley of arrows meant to scatter, distract, and confuse Paege's riders.

She drew her left arm up against her chest. Her fingers twitched to give the orders. She drew in a deep breath, and as she began to extend her arm, a sense of anticipation, cunning, and a glee that was not her own swept through her.

Paege was ordering Leya to slow nearly to a halt upon his command.

He anticipated her counter-maneuver!

Trysten extended her arm and began to order the counter-maneuver.

Paege's arm flew out to signal his wing.

Trysten waved, canceling her order. She then commanded her wing to hold the *V* formation, dive, and let loose with arrows.

It was too late for Paege and his wing. The dragons fanned out quickly and came to a halt. Paege signaled wildly to change orders, but his hordesmen were already drawing arrows in anticipation of meeting Trysten's wing head on and in shock.

Instead, Trysten's wing slid underneath Paege's. The hordesmen behind her let loose with a volley of blunted arrows that pinged the bellies of Paege's wing.

Had it been a real battle, it would have been a devastating blow. It wouldn't have been enough to decide the battle, but it would definitely have put the enemy dragons at an immediate disadvantage as they were forced to fight with arrows lodged in their undersides.

Trysten ordered the *V* formation to split. Each leg would veer around and climb, taking advantage of the confusion while giving Paege's hordesmen a variety of targets and little to concentrate an attack on.

As Elevera banked and began to climb, Trysten caught sight of one of Paege's dragons descending, gliding in her direction. It was Woolyn, the dark red dragon carrying Rast. She barreled down right for Elevera.

Trysten hadn't even had time enough to formulate the collection of signals needed to communicate her wishes to Elevera before the gold dragon threw one wing up, closed the other, and rolled over backward.

A yelp of surprise escaped Trysten. The strap of her father's helmet pressed against her chin. She grabbed at the saddle's lip and clenched with her legs, even as the saddle's straps dug into her hips and waist.

Woolyn closed the distance. Claws clutched and flailed in the air as the two dragons grappled. A passing lash of Woolyn's tail caught Elevera hard in the chest. She roared, arched her back, spread her wings, and dove toward the ground before driving back up, wings beating, each flap like a blast of thunder in Trysten's startled ears.

She clutched the saddle's lip. If she wanted to, Trysten could take control, but at the moment, the alpha dragon was on her own. She banked, and with stunning speed, closed the distance between herself and Woolyn.

Rast's dragon banked hard and lined herself up for another pass at Elevera.

Trysten glanced at the rest of the horde. The battle had ceased. Her hordesmen circled with Paege's, their drill forgotten as they watched Trysten and Rast duel. Paege issued a half-hearted command for Rast to cease and return to formation, but the order went unheeded.

Woolyn's wings shoved the air beneath her, then she dove toward Elevera, picking up speed. Upon her back, Rast clutched at the saddle's lip.

Elevera continued to climb through the air.

Rast ordered Woolyn to turn over. He was going to try and either knock Trysten off her saddle or take the tassels streaming from her shoulders.

Before the thought fully registered, Elevera forced her angle up higher, faster, nearly climbing straight up in the air. It was an impressive feat, one that Trysten would think about and admire the moment she wasn't clinging to the saddle for dear life.

The sudden push upward forced Woolyn to draw up, to bleed off speed as she leveled her approach. Finally, at the last second, Elevera stopped and spread her wings out wide as if she intended to catch Woolyn.

They hung in the air for impossible seconds. The wind rattled through Trysten's ears, tugged at her breath. She forced herself to not look down and instead maintain eye contact with Woolyn.

With little other choice, Rast's dragon adjusted her flight and dove beneath Elevera to avoid colliding with her.

As soon as the red dragon committed to her maneuver, Elevera released a great roar and shoved her wings down and forward. She arched her back and swept her wings hard again as if to push the entire world over on its side to get at Woolyn.

Elevera flipped onto her back and began to glide down. Trysten clutched at the saddle and clenched her teeth as they streaked downward, plummeting with increasing speed toward Rast and Woolyn.

Rast glanced about, looking for Elevera. Finally, he twisted himself all the way around and saw the great, gold dragon descending upon him, upside down. His face grew wide. His jaw dropped.

Rast folded himself over onto Woolyn's neck, but not before Trysten released the saddle's lip. She stretched, reaching toward the red scales zipping past. With a flicker of movement, she snatched both of the tassels streaming from Rast's shoulders, one in each hand.

They came away with a slight tug, and then Elevera was rolling over, swaying through the air as if on the end of a great pendulum. Trysten shifted her weight with each swoop of the dragon. She clutched the tassels before herself, unable to believe or comprehend that she took them.

Above, the hordesmen waved their arms and cheered.

A grin spread across her face. Her father may never have had to face such an open challenge as Rast had just provided, but only because he had trained and fought beside the hordesmen before he became dragoneer. But then again, he also had the advantage of his grandfather naming him dragoneer, of making an open display of selecting him for the challenge. Trysten's own father had denied her that. He had left her to do just as she had done. Prove herself.

And perhaps that was what he was after.

Trysten tucked Rast's stolen tassels into a saddlebag, then ordered the horde back to the weyr.

Chapter 32

Back at the weyr, Trysten approached Rast as he dismounted. She held out the tassels, dangling from her hand. He lowered his eyes briefly, and a slight flush of red passed over his face as he took the tassels from her hand.

"You ignored Paege's commands," Trysten said.

"I didn't see them."

Trysten stared at him a few seconds longer. The tassels hung limply from his hand as if he had no idea what to do with them.

"You have to pay attention to the dragoneer. Always. If that had been a real battle, you'd likely have died."

Rast drew his shoulders back. A little more red flushed through his face. Though Trysten couldn't read the faces of men like she could dragons, it took no skill at all to see the turmoil in Rast's face. He knew she was right, but he wouldn't admit that *she* could have killed him.

"Another lapse in judgment like that, and you will be grounded. Understand?"

Rast nodded once, then stood stock still until after Trysten turned away.

For the rest of the day, she put them through their paces, and the horde grew more attentive, less stiff. She kept them in the air as much as possible, bringing them down to the weyr only to rest the riders and dragons. There, she watched for her father lingering at the edge of the yard or standing just inside a doorway, but he was nowhere to be seen.

As the sun lingered over the distant mountain peaks, Trysten called it a day. They returned the dragons to their stalls, and with the help of the weyrmen, the dragons were wiped down, checked for injury, and the riding gear was cleaned and oiled and put away.

Once the hordesmen retired to the bunkhouse, Trysten climbed the stairs to the den. She stepped inside, and the chill of the evening immediately slipped away as the fire in the stove warmed her bones. She ran her hands over her arms as if the coolness might be brushed away, then realized she was waiting on her father. If he saw her, he would call her into the inner chamber. But he wasn't there now. It was no longer his inner chamber. It was hers.

Trysten entered the next room. It was dark, and that seemed odd as well. The weyrmen kept the fire attended to, but they largely ignored the inner chamber. She retreated to the receiving room, lit a candle, and then carried it back to light several lanterns and flood the room with soft, warm light.

As she walked around the table, her fingertips lingered on the surface. Her lips softened with a smile. She sat in the chair that she had seen her father sit in so many times. Once or twice, while he was up or out, she had sat in this very chair and pretended to be the dragoneer, but now it was no longer pretend. It was her seat. She had earned it.

After a slight caress of the armrests, she gripped them and pushed herself up. From the shelf above the table, she plucked out the book that had the lists of previous dragons, hordesmen, and dragoneers who were all resting in the burial grounds. She placed the book upon the table, sat, and turned to the first page.

As she peered through the list and looked for the dragoneers, the door opened, and Paege stepped into the receiving room. She sat back in her chair as she had seen her father do each time she had stepped into the den and found him sitting at his chair, behind his table, poring over a book.

"Can I help you?" she asked.

Paege glanced around as if seeing the den for the first time, or trying to evaluate what he thought of what she had done with it, which was to change not a thing.

"How was it?" Paege asked from the doorway between the two rooms. "Your first day, that is?"

Trysten motioned to the chair on the other side of the table. It felt weird to do so. As soon as she did it, she realized she had issued a command, and that she was sitting on the other side of the table, clearly in a superior position, though it felt silly to think of herself as superior to anyone, especially her childhood friend.

Trysten swallowed, then nodded. "It was good. It went well, I think."

Paege sat. "I was really worried there, at the start. And I wanted to apologize for Rast. I tried to order him back."

Trysten shook her head. "Don't worry about it. I don't want to wish for that kind of insubordination, but I'm nearly glad it happened. I feel like it gave me a chance to prove myself. After that, the hordesmen all seemed to be a bit more..." She searched for the word.

Paege leaned forward slightly in his chair. "You really got their attention, that's for sure. Especially when you took both of Rast's tassels." He flicked the tassel on his own shoulder as he leaned back in his chair, grinning.

"I've never seen anything like that before. None of us have. To tell you the truth..." Paege leaned across the table as if to impart a secret. "The men are talking about you, the way you fly. You seem to have a connection with the dragons that they've never seen before. Not from your father. Not from anyone."

Trysten blushed. Relief surged through her. Her lips parted, then stalled before she confided in Paege about her connection to Elevera, and how she bested Leya and Woolyn. She was already on thin ice with the hordesmen. Though Paege wasn't likely to take anything she said back to the hordesmen's bunkhouse, still, it would be wise to keep her secret to herself for the time being. It wouldn't hurt for all of them, Paege included, to believe that she came by her talent naturally. But then again, how was her talent *not* natural? It was part of who she was, what she had always been. She was merely different, and her difference gave her a clear and distinct advantage over the other dragon riders.

Her gaze dipped to the book before her. Likewise, she should probably keep her peace about Jalite's claim that there had been female dragoneers in the past. If she was right, and there was any truth to that claim, then the truth had been buried for a reason. It'd be best to know that reason before sharing her suspicions, or better yet, any evidence she might discover to support the claim.

Trysten shut the book before her.

"What's the matter?" Paege asked. "I thought you'd be happy to hear that news."

"I am." She leaned back in her chair and rubbed at her brow with the tips of her fingers, then gestured at the book. "I wanted to see Aeronwind's name in the book. I'm happy with the way things have worked out, of course, but I still miss her. And I feel bad for my father."

Paege nodded. "I understand. To tell the truth, I know this sounds awful, but I have to stop now and then and remind myself what a sad week this has been. Losing Aeronwind was a terrible thing, all right. And I agree that it's horrible, what has happened to your father—I mean that kind of loss—but part of me is just so relieved that the burden has been taken from my shoulders."

Paege sat back in his chair, nearly slumped into it. The wood creaked as if the burden had been placed upon the chair instead. "I'm just pleased with the way things have turned out. You should be the dragoneer. You should have always been the dragoneer. From the start."

"Are you all right with being the commander?"

Paege appeared to consider it a moment, then nodded. "I suppose I must be. No, I am. I mean, yes, I am fine with it."

He sat upright in his chair again. "I'm glad to be flying at your side. I may not be the dragoneer, but I think my father would, in some way, be even more proud of me that I have followed in his footsteps altogether, being a commander like him."

It did seem to suit him, and Trysten was thankful for his presence, for his help, but it did seem that he was still living someone else's life, following his own father's wishes rather than his own. But then again, he was serving the village and the kingdom. He was a capable hordesman, and he was needed as such. It was unfortunate, however, that he couldn't serve the village and kingdom by pursuing his own wishes and desires.

Chapter 33

For several weeks, Trysten and the hordesmen practiced and drilled as the cloud cover over the mountains thinned with each passing day, and a knot grew in Trysten's stomach as she looked to the West and knew she was closer to being tested by the Western Kingdom.

On a clear day, as they performed another round of mock battles, Rast, on Trysten's team this time, suddenly broke formation and circled above. Woolyn banked and allowed everyone a chance to see him waving with one hand and pointing to the southwest. Trysten peered in the indicated direction. Against the gray clouds, a series of dark dots approached. They were too large to be birds.

It was another horde.

The knot in Trysten's stomach became a lead weight, and it was a wonder it didn't drag her and Elevera from the sky. She knew the day was coming, but she hadn't imagined it would be so incredibly soon. The Western Kingdom had caught them off guard. They didn't have time to fly back to the weyr and arm themselves with quivers of proper arrows. A few were kept stowed in each saddle for emergencies, and that would have to be enough. She peered into the distance again, squinted, and tried to count the number of dragons approaching. It didn't appear to be a full horde. A set of scouts, perhaps? Then it was even more important that they be intercepted. A missing scout party would be a far greater deterrent than word of how well-prepared they were.

The mock battle formation fell into a holding pattern. The dragons flew slow circles behind Elevera as all the riders turned their attention to Trysten. She peered up at the sun. It was far along the sky now and would present only a slight advantage to the approaching horde. The best thing to do would be to engage them quickly and fiercely, keep them from gathering as much intelligence as possible.

Trysten issued a series of orders. Practice arrows were stowed away and replaced with the three sharp arrows each carried for emergencies. Intersect the enemy with all available speed.

Elevera broke the holding pattern and threw herself in the direction of the approaching horde before Trysten could even command her to do so.

Behind, the rest of the hordesmen fell into the familiar *V*-shaped formation to conserve energy and conceal their true numbers. Trysten crouched behind Elevera's neck. Her heart hammered in her chest, thundered and threatened to launch itself from her throat like a stone from a catapult. How often she had seen her father go to battle, to take the village sword given to him by the overseer, and with it, order the hordesmen to follow. She had felt so proud of him when she had seen the ceremony, and she had hoped to have a ceremony of her own. The only way to accomplish that now would be to survive the coming battle.

Her heels dug into Elevera's side as she urged the dragon on.

Soon, they were close enough to count ten dragons approaching. It was a small horde, indeed. If they were scouts, they'd have a looking glass trained on her. She raised her left fist into the air and signaled for the others to draw their arrows and hold them at the ready. She lifted her bow from its hook on the saddle and drew an arrow of her own. As she nocked the arrow against the bowstring, the dragoneer of the other horde waved a white cloth in the air.

Trysten relaxed her bow arm. The horde was flying in a standard *V* formation. The hordesmen's bows were still stowed on the saddles. One of the dragons had no rider.

Trysten signaled for her horde to hold its bowstrings. The Aerona horde zipped over the other. The advancing dragons did nothing. As they passed, a great sense of weariness flooded her, warping her bones, then stretching them with a great longing. A longing for sky and something else. Shadows of what she had felt in the weyr right after Aeronwind died. She gasped and gripped the saddle lip. Her teeth and eyes clenched as sorrow and exhaustion threatened to overwhelm her.

It was an absconded horde.

Trysten tore a deep breath from the sky. She thrust her left arm up and gave orders for her horde to flank the other. As they broke into two groups, Trysten turned Elevera around and quickly caught up to the lead dragon. The rider waved his white cloth again.

A sense of yearning, pulling, like iron to a lodestone wracked Trysten.

"Who goes there?" Trysten yelled across the distance between herself and the lead rider. His colors were familiar. They weren't the same as hers, but similar. She had seen the uniform of the Western Kingdom dragon riders once. It had been on display briefly in the weyr after it had been taken from a captured rider. Her father put it up so that all might know their enemy upon sight. The Western Kingdom uniforms were plain, not as ornate as their own, but were still the basic woolen sweaters and leather armor.

"Nillard of Hollin weyr," the man yelled back. "We are of the Cadwaller Kingdom."

Hollin weyr. There was a village called Hollin many miles to the south.

"Well greeted, Nillard of Hollin weyr. I am Trysten, Dragoneer of Aerona weyr."

The man's head moved back on his neck. The surprise on his face was more evident than need be.

"Dragoneer?" Nillard called back. He turned in his saddle to peer back at the rest of the Aerona horde. "Did you say you were dragoneer of the weyr?"

"I am." She patted Elevera's neck. "This is Elevera, alpha of the weyr."

Nillard shook his head, then glanced at the ground briefly. By the wilds, what was his problem?

"Trysten, Dragoneer of Aerona weyr," Nillard called back, "we require rest, and we have news of the Western Kingdom."

A promise of news of the Western Kingdom tightened her chest nearly as much as the thought of flying into battle with them. Her grip on the saddle tightened.

"Follow me," she called, then signaled for her horde to return to the weyr.

Before they touched down in the yard, weyrmen were already spilling into the yard. Among them, Trysten brought Elevera to the ground. As soon as all four claws were in the grass, Trysten untied herself, slipped off the saddle, and hurried back to the pearl-colored dragon of Nillard.

"Where is your alpha?" Trysten called up before Nillard finished unknotting his ties.

"Our alpha?" Nillard's eyebrows rose in surprise, then dove beneath a furrowed brow. He scowled at the ties of his saddle.

"This dragon is no alpha. I can tell to look at her. Where is your alpha?" Trysten pressed.

"Our dragoneer was killed in battle. He went down with his mount. The commander and the beta fell as well."

Deep lines spread out from the corners of Nillard's eyes. Gray peppered his long beard. "I am the senior hordesman of the... I am the senior hordesman. May we speak in private?"

Trysten nodded.

Nillard passed a signal to the other hordesmen before dismounting. As soon as he hit the ground, he began to stalk toward the weyr. To Trysten's relief, several of the weyrmen entering the yard sported short swords strapped to their waists.

"Forgive me," Nillard said as Trysten drew up beside him, "but up in the air, did you not say that you were dragoneer of this weyr?"

Trysten nodded. "I did. I am."

Nillard looked her up and down. It was difficult to tell if he was disappointed, disgusted, exhausted, or all three.

"How long have you been dragoneer?"

Trysten held her posture as straight as possible. "Three weeks."

Nillard halted. "Three weeks? You've been dragoneer three weeks? How old are you?"

"Old enough."

Nillard shook his head. "Was there no one else to take the title?"

"Like it or not, I am the dragoneer of this weyr, and as my guest in this village, in my home, I would ask you to show me the proper respect."

Nillard glanced back at his horde, then bowed slightly at the neck. "My apologies, sir—ma'am. I meant no disrespect. It is just that in Hollin, a female dragoneer is unheard of. A dragoneer of your youth is also quite rare, and given the circumstances, I am, to be honest, a little disappointed not to find a more battle-hardened dragoneer before me."

"And I am a little disappointed to find that my honored guest is not a more respectful hordesman," Trysten said. "Now that we have that out of the way, you said that you had news of the Western Kingdom. I will have that news now."

Nillard glanced about. "In private. Away from prying ears."

Trysten ushered Nillard on. They climbed the stairs to her den. She gestured at the chair she used to sit in, and then sat in her chair.

"Your news?" she asked as she laced her fingers together and rested her hands upon the table.

Nillard sat, sighed, and leaned back in the chair opposite Trysten. His calloused hands dangled over his spread thighs. "Our cloud reader warned us that the peaceful season would be short this year."

"As did ours."

"But not even he imagined just *how* short," Nillard said. He leaned forward and rested his elbows upon his knees. "The Western Kingdom is on the move already. A horde of their dragon riders came screaming through the Bottoms Pass at the first break in the weather. They caught us unprepared. We were in the air within minutes of a watchman's warning, but by then, the Western horde was circling the village. They rained flaming arrows down upon us. It was a cursed thing, the way they flew, the dragons all lighting the arrows of the other riders. It was a thing of horror. Of beautiful horror, to see them forming those lines that slithered past each other, and the dragons puffing away, jets of flame writhing between the two lines."

Nillard shook his head. He ran his fingers through his beard. "We climbed up to meet them as quickly as we could. By the time we got close enough to let their bellies feel the sting of our arrows, they broke formation and rained wild wrath on us. Their first volley of arrows took out several good men. Then their dragons pelted us like stones. Several more men, including our dragoneer, were crushed beneath the weight of Western dragons."

Nillard let his head hang as if the memories of the event were too much for the muscles of his neck.

"I barely escaped. Leewind was hardly able to twist herself out of the way. She's a good beast. A mighty beast. I'll be wild if she didn't give the Western dragon after us a good, ripping gout on its way down. I could tell by the roar. But by then, it was too late. The Western horde fanned out through the village. Their dragons spread more flame, aimed for the thatch roofs. Set the whole village to blazes. Several of them even flew straight through our own weyr, setting fire to the whole thing. By the gods' breath,

Trysten, it was a level of fury and wildness that I have never seen in a fight with the Western Kingdom. They were unnatural. There was nothing they weren't capable of."

Nillard took a deep breath, then wiped his hands over his face. They fell to his lap with a clap. "Our dragoneer was dead. The alpha took to circling the village, crying and mewling with a broken spirit that set our mounts on the edge of panic. It was everything I could do to keep Leewind under my control. The commander mounted a defense, and we were able to bloody a few noses, but while we focused on half of the Western horde, the other half went after old Betalla, her beloved master broken upon her back. Poor thing didn't stand a chance. Them wretched westerners nearly did the old thing a favor by putting her out of her misery. By the time we realized what they were doing, we were pinned down. They filled old Betella with so many arrows that the weight of the arrowheads is what probably brought her down, twisting and screaming, roaring like the ground itself was crying before she smashed into a burning cottage in a crash of soot and flame."

Trysten gasped and covered her mouth with the tips of her fingers. Her body tingled with the thought of such a horrific death.

"The beta fell soon after, and once she hit the ground, I wouldn't have been able to hold old Leewind with the hands of the gods. The Hollin horde broke. Most of the remaining dragons followed Leewind north. She wasn't born of the line, but she is the oldest. And several of the males from the weyr took off as well. One came with us, you saw. Other dragons went east and south. For the wild gods, I have heard tales of hordes absconding, but let me tell you how terrible it is to be on the back of a dragon when she decides that she has nothing left to live for. We flew away from our village as fast as wind and wings would take us, and no amount of screaming, of cursing, of yanking on my saddle or digging my heels into that blasted beast's hide would stop her, would allow us to head back and do what we could for our village."

Nillard took a deep, gaping breath that showed a few gaps in his teeth. He stared at the ceiling and blinked hard. "I hope to the wild gods that you never have to sit upon your dragon's back and hear the screams of your friends, of your families, of the people you love and vowed to defend with your life as they are slaughtered in your shadow."

Nillard's gaze dropped to Trysten as if to pin her to the back of her chair. "The Western Kingdom is on the move. They are on the wing, and they are fighting like the wild gods gone mad. Sure as I am sitting here in your den,

Trysten of Aerona weyr, there are armies on foot ready to cross the Bottoms Pass as soon as the snow melts enough to allow passage. And I will further guarantee that an equally devastating horde is on the other side of the Gul Pass. If they aren't squeezing through right this minute, they are coming. If you are indeed a dragoneer, then ready your horde now, because the Western Kingdom seems intent on making this fighting season the last one. Why, if I didn't know better, I'd even go so far as to say they've had some help bringing about the early start."

Trysten lifted an eyebrow. "Help?"

Nillard nodded. "I am not a superstitious man, but to see the early end of the peaceful season coincide with that level of ruthlessness makes me wonder if there is a bit of truth in old tales."

Trysten leaned back in her chair. Old tales such as female dragoneers? "What old tales?"

"They say that not all the Originals were split into man and dragon. They say there were a few who were able to hide or resist the gods, and that they walk the ruins of their kingdom yet. Such... demigods are said to have influence over some matters, such as the clouds, and the hearts and minds of men and dragons."

Trysten leaned forward. "But you say you don't believe in such things."

Nillard leaned forward as well. The odors of smoke and sweat rolled off him. "I believe in what I see. And what I saw was an end to the peaceful season weeks before even the earliest recorded ending, and I saw men and dragons fight like beasts never before seen."

The table creaked as Nillard placed his elbows upon it and leaned in more. "They fought as if of one mind, as if a force was driving them back to what they once were. They fought in a way that put a man to mind of the Originals. To see the way they lit each other's arrows with fire breath made a man recall the tales of how terrible the gods could be."

Trysten's breath froze. Goose flesh pricked its way across her arms. Dragons and men of one mind? How in the wilds would Nillard and his men take it if they knew about Trysten's ability to understand the dragons on such a deep level? Keeping her secret was more serious than she had imagined.

Nillard leaned back and crossed his arms over his chest. "But why should I waste my breath with telling you? You will see first hand. In fact, I should like to see to my men and our dragons."

Nillard stood and placed the tips of his fingers against the tabletop, pressing down on them as if he expected the table to leap up, perhaps attack him even. He stared down at Trysten, his eyes hard and set in challenge, but she had no idea what challenge he was presenting. Did he expect her to call him on his story and claim that it was false? A lie?

"If you will excuse me, my men and I have a long way to go before we reach the mother city."

"The mother city?" Trysten asked.

"Yes, the mother city. Haven't you heard a wild word I said? The King has to know. We have to take word of it straight to his ear. He has to know that Hollin weyr has fallen and that a horde of Western wretches is loose in his kingdom. By the wilds, they must be hunted down. And on top of that, if little sprites like you are passing as dragoneers these days, then the King needs to send reinforcements as soon as possible."

Trysten stood.

A hint of a grin tugged at the corners of Nillard's lips.

"You think we need reinforcements here?" Trysten asked.

The grin came on. "Look, I like a spirited lady myself, the gods know, but regardless of what you got or haven't got in your trousers there, it doesn't matter in the face of your inexperience. How many fighting seasons have you fought in?"

"So you think we need more seasoned hordesmen?"

Nillard let out a warped guffaw. "Miss, you need a seasoned *dragoneer*. Follem, our dragoneer, fought four seasons as a hordesmen, ten as a commander, and then he fought another six as dragoneer before this very dawn. That man had spent more time on a dragon's back than you've been alive, I'll wager, and he didn't last five minutes in a battle with the Western Kingdom."

"So you think we need someone like you, then?"

Nillard gave a curt nod, then crossed his arms over his chest. "You bet you need someone like me. But I ain't got the bond of a dragoneer, and I'll be cursed if I'm going to play handmaiden to a green warrior princess. I'm afraid the kingdom would be better served if I made haste for the mother city."

"I disagree."

Nillard's eyebrows lifted in mock surprise. "Do you now? Well, that's a wild shame. I'll be sure to pass your grievance along to His Majesty when I see him."

Nillard started for the door.

"Nillard of Hollin, you and your men will fly in the Aerona weyr."

Nillard stopped. He turned around on his heel in a slow manner, one exaggerated to the point that he nearly wobbled like a top ready to fall over. "I beg your pardon?"

"You are conscripted into the Aerona weyr. Please ask for a man named Bolsar. He will see to your dragons and men. I will have him draw up a plan to expand the weyr as necessary."

Nillard's jaw dropped. He shook his head slightly. "I don't think you get it, young lady. There is a horde of berserker Western dragons and hordesmen loose in our kingdom. They burned down my village, *destroyed my weyr and my horde*, and they will not stop there. Whether they went north or east, I can't say, but I can tell you that the King must know now. Only he has the power to send the kind of reinforcements we need."

"A courier dragon can take your warning, and he can take it in two-thirds the time you and your horde can. Furthermore, a single male courier dragon is going to attract a lot less attention than half a horde, if the Western hordesmen are still out there. Finally—"

"Well, what if something should happen to that courier dragon? This is far too important to trust to a single dragon, a single rider."

"Then we'll send two, but you're needed here. Should the Western Kingdom travel north, or should the Gul Pass open early, and the Western hordesmen are as you described them, then I will need the might of your men, as well as your experience to turn them back here, to keep them at bay until reinforcements arrive."

Nillard shook his head. "By all that is wild and split! That is a *terrible* idea. This is just one, single village, and one hardly big enough to have a weyr as it—"

"I did not ask you for opinion, Nillard!" Trysten leaned forward and placed her palms on the table as she had seen her father do when ready to draw an argument to a close. "I am giving you an order. You came to my weyr on an absconded horde. By law, your dragons are mine. They belong to Aerona weyr now. You can either ride them in service to the King, or you can purchase a couple of mules at the livery stable and make your way to the mother city on foot. I am not asking for your opinion, I am telling you to make a choice, and make it now."

Nillard cocked an eyebrow then nodded as if confirming for himself what he thought. "We'll just see about that."

He stormed from Trysten's den. As the door slammed behind him, Trysten leaned her weight onto her palms and hung her head. She allowed herself one deep breath... then followed Nillard out the door. The man may have been an experienced hordesman, but he was as transparent as the summer river. He planned to take the remains of his horde and leave now.

Chapter 34

Trysten's feet hammered down the steps. Sure enough, Nillard stalked across the weyr, heading for the side door. His fists swung out in determined arcs, and his shoulders were hunched nearly about his ears with grave tension.

Trysten had almost closed the distance between the two of them by the time Nillard exited the weyr and entered the side yard. As soon as Trysten stepped out from the barn that housed the dragons, she took in the very sights she had hoped and expected to see. Troughs of water had been filled for the dragons of the Hollin horde. Fresh food was wheeled in on handbarrows and fed to the Hollin dragons. The hordesmen themselves gathered around a table with the hordesmen from the Aerona weyr to share their midday meal.

Nillard clapped his hands, then raised them over his head. "Saddle up, men, we must be on our way."

"But the dragons need rest," one of the hordesmen protested as he gestured to a dark green dragon who ate with gusto from the handbarrow parked before it.

"They need the rest, or you need to fill your gullet with drink?" Nillard called back. "Now, men. Up in the air with you! Now!"

The Hollin men shared a few looks of bewilderment and disappointment with their colleagues of the Aerona weyr.

Nillard turned to Trysten. His eyes squinted as if daring her to protest, to try and stop him.

She crossed her arms over her chest and stood with her feet apart as far as the breadth of her shoulders.

Nillard turned back to his men. "Now!" He clapped his hands together again.

The men placed cups and plates upon the table, and then after a few handshakes were exchanged, they trotted back to their dragons and began to mount them.

Trysten glanced at Elevera, who stood where she had left her. A weyrman held her reins as another wiped down her scales. Elevera turned her attention away from the commotion of the other hordesmen and dragons and peered directly at Trysten. She nearly gave a nod of her golden head, as if to provide the confirmation Trysten sought.

Nillard climbed into his saddle, patted his dragon upon the neck once, and then ordered her into the air with a verbal command paired with the motion of dragging his heels upward along the dragon's side.

The dragon shifted from claw to claw, then dipped her head and peered at Elevera.

Elevera held her neck high, her head rigid and commanding among the other dragons.

Around the remains of the Hollin horde, hordesmen gave commands for their dragons to take to the wing, to climb into the air. All of them acted slightly uncomfortable, shifting weight and bowing their heads. One dragon even staggered in a rough circle like a cat before stopping to stare at Elevera.

Nillard yanked on the edge of his saddle. He scraped his heels across his mount's hide, up and up, urging her into the sky. She did nothing in response but shuffle a bit, and stare at Elevera, who held her ground and commanded her horde to do the same.

A grin pressed over Trysten's face. She didn't deserve such a good friend. But then again, Nillard was being completely unreasonable.

"What's going on here?" Mardoc asked from behind Trysten.

She turned around. Her father leaned on his staff in the doorway.

She quickly explained the situation to him, how they had come across the remains of an absconded horde, and that they had already bonded to Elevera, much to the chagrin of the senior hordesman.

Mardoc smirked. "I bet he liked that."

Trysten turned back to the scene in the yard. Nillard was off his dragon and stomping across the yard, heading right for Trysten with a great scowl and his two fists swinging wildly to either side of him with each step. The man appeared to be ready for a fight.

He stopped short of Trysten, then looked back at Mardoc. His eyes traveled up and down the former dragoneer.

"I am Nillard, senior rider of the Hollin weyr. Who are you?"

"Fallen Mardoc of Aerona weyr."

The fight dropped out of Nillard's face as he inclined his head slightly and bowed at the neck. "Your service is honored."

Trysten worked hard at holding her tongue.

"As is yours," Mardoc said, returning the merest politeness.

Nillard glanced from Mardoc to Trysten. A light appeared to go on behind his dim eyes. "You are…"

"She is my daughter," Mardoc said with a nod. "And dragoneer of this weyr."

Nillard shifted his feet. He looked back and forth between father and daughter. His jaw dropped slightly, and he appeared to be working hard at trying to figure out how to word what it was he wanted to say. Behind him, the Hollin hordesmen began to dismount their dragons. They cast looks about, from Nillard to Elevera to their own dragons and then to each other. They were slowly catching on to what had taken place. Would they react as Nillard had, or might they behave with better sense?

Nillard appeared to find what it was he searched for in his head. He clutched his fist before himself as he turned to Mardoc. "Surely you know that it is forbidden to allow a woman to be a dragoneer."

Trysten's father stiffened. His knuckles blanched as his grip tightened upon his staff. "I invite you to take your argument up with our alpha dragon."

Nillard turned back to Elevera. His face narrowed, and his lips faded in obvious contempt.

"How can that be?" Nillard asked with a shake of his head as he returned his attention to Mardoc. "Dragons do not bond with women. It doesn't happen."

Nillard then turned his attention to Trysten. His gaze traveled up and down her as if to confirm for himself that she was indeed a woman.

Trysten stepped forward. "Obviously that assumption lacks some truth," Trysten said. "Elevera is the alpha of this weyr, and she has bonded with me. I am dragoneer, and I will not tolerate your ongoing disrespect. The fact of the matter is that you flew here on an absconded horde, and your dragons have since bonded to Elevera. She is their alpha. I am your dragoneer now whether you like it or not, whether you *believe* it or not."

Nillard shook his head again. He glanced to Mardoc, and his expression asked if he was going to allow his daughter to speak to him in such a manner. When Mardoc did nothing to respond to his unspoken question, Nillard turned away, to the dragons, to the hordesmen who had all begun to stare at them. He lifted his hands, then threaded his fingers together behind his head as he sucked in a deep, frustrated breath.

He turned back to Trysten, then to Mardoc. "This can't be. You can't allow a woman to lead a horde. Especially *this* horde, so close to the Western Kingdom." Nillard pointed at the mountains as if the others might have failed to notice the boundary between the two kingdoms. "They are coming for us. They are taking full advantage of the early end of the peaceful season, and they are fighting in a way that I have never seen in all my years. They are fighting as if they have a…"

Trysten's spine tightened. Her breath caught in her chest, and as if Nillard could feel her sudden tension, he glanced at her sideways.

"As if they have a dragon lord."

Mardoc tensed as well. "That is a legend," he said. "Nothing more."

"I have fought many battles in my days, and I tell you from the core of my heart, I have never seen anything like the battle that destroyed my weyr. The way those dragons flew, it was as if they were of a single mind, man and dragon. It was so much so that it has caused me to doubt the legends. And to top it off, I come here, and I find a horde bonded to a woman, which I also was brought up to believe could never happen. It seems to me that the unthinkable keeps happening, and so why can't dragon lords be real?"

Trysten forced a deep breath in. She shook her head as if to dismiss the whole idea of other people like herself. "It was probably an old horde smarting from defeat that invented the whole legend to begin with. It is easier to accept defeat if you think there was something mythical about your enemy, isn't it?"

Nillard nodded. "I used to think so myself. Sometimes it is easier to believe in the fantastical than it is to believe you can be bested, but I swear to you that what I saw could not be explained away so easily. With a decade of practice, I could not pull off the maneuvers I saw. No, I am telling you, what I saw, combined with the early end of the peaceful season, points to one fact. There is some magic about. Sorcery. Whether or not one of the Originals is involved, I cannot say, but the Western Kingdom is using some dark dealings to pull off what they have pulled off."

If Trysten's spine could have stiffened more, it would have at Nillard's suggestion. Part of her wondered about the veracity of his statement. Could there really be a dragon lord at work? Could there be someone like herself, someone who could know the minds of dragons as easily as she knew her own? But she bristled at the suggestion that there was any dark art to it as if simply being able to do what she did meant that she had to be evil by nature.

A man like Nillard could be dangerous. He would spread fear and suspicion through the horde. She had to figure out a way to get rid of him. But first thing was first.

"It's all a very fanciful story," Mardoc said, "but as a dragoneer, fallen or otherwise, I must say that you have done nothing more than report the presence of a talented dragoneer in the midst of the Western Kingdom. Dragons are highly intelligent beasts. There is very little that a dragon cannot be trained to do if ridden by a skilled rider. I know this first hand."

Nillard glanced to Trysten, then back to Mardoc. "To even be trained to bond with a woman?" He lifted an eyebrow.

Mardoc lifted his staff slightly and tamped it back to the ground in a small gesture of irritation. "You are speaking of things you know nothing about. What do you know of how a dragon selects its partner?"

Nillard shifted back on his heels. "I know enough. And more than that, I've been around long enough to know the lore, to know the laws, and I tell you that she cannot hope to withstand an onslaught from the Western Kingdom. This weyr will fall faster than Hollin did. The King must be made aware of what has happened—of what *is* happening. Both here in this weyr and along the mountains. Reinforcements must be sent, and your dragon..." Nillard drifted off as he turned his attention to Elevera, whose gold scales shone in the sun's rays.

Trysten clenched her teeth and fists rather than fly into the man and tear him apart, wrap his ridiculous beard around his throat and yank it until his face turned purple and his tongue fell from his mouth. She stormed away, leaving Nillard and her father. As she advanced out into the yard, the hordesmen from both hordes watched after her. Their chatter fell away as she approached Elevera, stopped, and turned around. Across the yard, she held everyone's attention.

"Let me welcome the new hordesmen to Aerona weyr." She held up her hands, her palms outward. "It is an honor to have each of you here to fight by our sides in the air."

Nillard took a step toward her. With speed and grace that reflected the man he used to be, Mardoc reached out and gripped Nillard by the bicep and dragged him to a halt. The man turned, then lowered his head in submission as decades spent in service to a horde forced him to defer to anyone—to any *man*—who held the dragoneer title.

"As most of you have heard, our new friends have brought news of the end of the peaceful season. Tragic news about the fall of Hollin weyr, about the loss of their alpha and beta dragons, about the death of their dragoneer and commander. Though we are saddened by what our brothers have lost in battle, we are also heartened by their appearance. We are honored by the choice of the remaining dragons to seek us out, to come to our weyr, to bond with our alpha and join our horde. We are not only honored, but we are strengthened as well."

Trysten let her left hand fall to her side while she clenched her right fist before her. "We are strengthened at a time when our kingdom needs steadfast and strong hordesmen like never before. An early end to the peaceful season means that we have a long, drawn-out fighting season ahead of us. On top of that, our new friends bring word of an emboldened Western Kingdom; one with new tactics and new maneuvers.

"The dragons of Hollin weyr have sought us out because we need their strength. We need their numbers. We need their experience to make us stronger and make us more resistant. With the two hordes combined, we will put up the kind of resistance that will stop the Western Kingdom. We will draw a line here, at this place, at this weyr, beneath our feet and beneath the shadows of our wings. This line will not be crossed. We will hold. We will meet the enemy when they come, and we will hold."

Paege let out a cheer that was quickly taken up by all the hordesmen of the Aerona weyr. The men from Hollin all glanced at Nillard, who stood before Mardoc, his arms crossed over his chest.

"The dragons from Hollin weyr have chosen Elevera as their alpha. It is the way of the dragons, and there is nothing that any person can do to change the hearts and minds of these magnificent beasts. It is now up to the riders. Will you join us? Will you become members of Aerona weyr? Will you ride your mounts by our sides, fly with us into battle to defend the kingdom and avenge your fallen brothers, your very families? Will you?"

The hordesmen from Hollin weyr glanced at Nillard again. A few of them stepped forward and echoed Paege's cheer. As they did, several more followed suit, leaving two, along with Nillard, to remain silent and stoic, arms crossed over their chests in defiance.

What cowards these men were, that would allow the destruction of their village, the slaughter of their families, friends, and hordesmen to go unanswered rather than follow a woman and her dragon into battle. To the wilds with them, then.

"Thank you," Trysten said with a nod to the Hollin hordesmen who had stepped forward. "I am emboldened by your courage. I am inspired by your desire to make the Western Kingdom pay for their atrocities. And we will do just that. We will make every one of their hordesmen sorry that they ever crossed the Cadwaller mountains, and we will do it this very season!" Trysten said, raising her voice to a shout as she raised her fist.

The men followed suit this time, not waiting for Paege's lead. Three cheers erupted from those gathered, and even one more of the Hollin hordesmen joined the ranks, leaving Nillard a single compatriot to join in his coward's stand.

A broad grin spread over Trysten's face as she stepped forward to meet the newly enlarged horde. Immediately she started handing out instructions to the weyrmen sprinkled among the crowd to begin plans on how to enlarge the weyr to accommodate the newcomers, both the men and the dragons.

Nillard turned to her father, said something, and after a nod from Mardoc, he slunk away, walking down the outside length of the weyr before turning the corner and disappearing. The remaining holdout jogged after him, but Trysten could not worry about it as she busied herself with getting to know the names of the new dragons and the hordesmen.

Chapter 35

After a long day, Trysten retired to her den and added the names of the new dragons and hordesmen to the weyr's chronicle. She paused and stared at her own handwriting beneath her father's. Below his inscriptions of new and lost dragons and men, there was her own mark on the weyr already. Ten new dragons and seven new hordesmen. New riders would be selected from the village population, and training would begin immediately. In the course of one day, she had increased the size of the village's horde by more than half and making it the largest horde in the weyr's history.

She slumped against the back of her chair. On the one hand, she was thrilled to have such a coup under her cap already, to have made such a mark within her first few weeks of being dragoneer. On the other hand, how in the wilds was she going to manage such a huge horde? She had made a lot of progress with the original horde in the last couple of weeks, but she had the legitimacy of her father to fall back on. They saw him as their dragoneer, and when he knelt to her on the day that Aeronwind died, it was as good as an order for them to honor her as they honored him. This new horde, however, had no loyalty to her, to her family, to the village or to the weyr. In her conversations with them, she found them to be a group of weary men in shock from the battle. She heard snatches and bits of stories that corroborated what Nillard had told her. It seemed that the Western Kingdom had attacked the village instead of the horde and completely overwhelmed them in a matter of minutes with tactics never before seen.

At least they had the benefit of experience from the Hollin hordesmen.

Among the flurry of activity, Trysten had dispatched a courier to the mother city with news of what had happened to the Hollin weyr, along with the names of the dragons and hordesmen that had survived the attack and joined the Aerona weyr. As Ulbeg and his courier charged toward the eastern horizon, Trysten dispatched two of the hordesmen on smaller, faster dragons to fly up and down the Cadwaller range, one north and one south, and report back with any news of hordes in the sky. She put Paege in charge of drawing up a regular rotation for watch, never leaving the skies unattended. Finally, she let the village overseer know about the events. He would establish a watch in the village and alert the shepherds to be on the lookout not only for hordes in the skies but also for signs of armies moving through the Gul Pass.

A knock at the den door brought her out of reviewing the day's events.

"Come in."

Her father entered, then shut the door behind himself. As his staff clunked against the planks while he crossed the room, she wondered how in the wilds he had gotten up the stairs without her hearing.

"You've had quite a day," her father said.

Trysten nodded, then rubbed her hands over her face. "I'm up for the challenge," she said as her hands dropped to her lap. Her gaze flitted to the log again, to her neat script below her father's.

"That's good," Mardoc said as he approached the chair on the other side of the table. "Because you are indeed in for a challenge."

"I'm not afraid of the Western Kingdom. We have good dragons, and a large horde now. We will turn them back should they show their faces in our skies."

Mardoc let out a little noise just before he dropped himself into the chair. It could have been a grunt, a start of a laugh, or some note of derision. "It's not the Western Kingdom that will challenge you. I have no doubt at all that you will win the day when the Western Kingdom comes, and they will come. It is the threat from the kingdom in the east that you should worry about."

Trysten swallowed as if to clamp down on the sudden skittering of her heart. She knew what he was speaking of, yet she asked the question all the same. "What threat is that?"

"I just returned from the livery stable. Nillard and his man traded a bow, a quiver of arrows, and a very finely crafted dagger for two mules and some supplies. They've already begun making their way to the mother city."

"What of it?" Trysten asked, then glanced at the top of the table. Her voice had betrayed her, high and tight and full of concern over what they would bring.

"Come now," Mardoc said. "I raised no fool. You know as well as I do that Nillard is off to tell the King about the weyr that took his horde and is commanded by a woman."

Trysten shook her head. "I had every right. It's the law." She nodded to the books above them. "He brought an absconded horde here. The dragons chose Elevera. There was nothing—"

"That law you are referring to also excludes you from being a dragoneer."

Trysten let out a long, low breath as she stared at the names in the ledger. Was the ink dry yet? If she ran her fingertips across the bold, black strokes, would they smudge? Or was it already fast, not to be altered? Not to be taken away?

Unless the page was ripped from the book, as perhaps it had been when it had recorded the presence of the first female dragoneer, as she was beginning to suspect.

Trysten sat back against her chair. "What do you think will happen?"

Her father's gaze fell to the ledger as well. He shrugged. "I have no idea. There has never been a situation like this before. It's good that you sent a courier upon Ulbeg. At least when Nillard makes it to the mother city, his news will be old. He will have a greater chance of appearing before the King as a sore loser. But he also might find an audience who will buy his story of nobility, of how he humiliated himself, how he lowered himself and rode into the mother city, a hordesman upon the back of a mule, rather than break the law he has sworn his life to defend."

"What can they do? Elevera has chosen. I am the dragoneer."

Mardoc tapped his staff upon the floor. "I heard a story once. I was a young man, still riding for my grandfather. He took me with him to the mother city for business with the Dragon Master. One night in a tavern frequented by hordesmen from around the kingdom, I heard a tale of a weyr on the northern shore, along the great sea. Their alpha dragon was caught in a storm. The winds blew her away from the shore and thrashed the strength from her. She fell to the sea and drowned, taking the weyr's dragoneer with her. The man set to be the new dragoneer, the man who rode the beta dragon, was overthrown by another hordesman who managed to bond with the beta despite not being her regular rider. The weyr honored the wishes of the new alpha and made this man the dragoneer. But his heart was wicked, and he had no loyalty to anything. Not to his horde, his village, or his kingdom. He used his power to threaten the villagers, to amass wealth. Fishermen had to pay excessive taxes directly to him, or he would not allow their boats upon the sea."

"How could—" Trysten began.

Mardoc held up his hand. "The other hordesmen wished to stop him. They knew what he was doing was wrong, but their mounts would not fly against the alpha. They turned on their riders, ignoring them in the best cases and killing them in the worst. New hordesmen were selected from the village to replace those who would stand against the crooked dragoneer. They became a force of terror along the northern shore that ran unopposed until the dragoneer's greed began to extend to neighboring villages. Finally, word made it to the Dragon Master of what was happening. The King sent several of his hordes north to rendezvous with local hordes. Together, they descended upon the village and destroyed the weyr, killing the dragoneer, the commander, and all of the dragons."

Trysten's eyes widened. "All?"

Mardoc nodded. "Every once in a while, there comes along someone who has the ability to know the heart and mind of a dragon. This person is said to be able to speak to the dragons, to know at a glance what they are thinking and to impart upon the dragons what is in their hearts. These people are called dragon lords. They are especially feared in the kingdom because of examples like this. Someone who can control a dragon horde so easily and so completely presents a grave threat to the kingdom."

Trysten's gaze fell to the book once again. If she could, she would crawl beneath it, push herself down below the table, through the floor, beyond the straw and dirt beneath them.

"When the King gets word of a dragon lord in the Western Kingdom, he will feel threatened. It took several hordes to destroy this one, for a single horde is no match for a horde commanded by a dragon lord, and already the Western Kingdom has destroyed the King's outpost in the southwest.

He will feel threatened. So when word of a female dragoneer reaches his ears a couple weeks later, he may feel compelled to react in a rash manner. I have never heard of a woman bonding with a dragon before. I must admit that if the King begins to look for his enemies behind every cloud, then he may see them whether they are there or not. Not only have you done what no woman has done before you, your command of the horde is quite exceptional, Trysten. It is unlike anything I've seen before."

Trysten gripped the edge of the table to keep herself from reaching forward, from running the tips of her fingers across the text she had so recently drawn. She wanted to know it was dry, that it was immutable, that it would never and could never be changed.

"Trysten?"

She met her father's gaze. Her lungs felt tight, like she had to suck her breath through a narrow reed.

"Do you understand the threat you are facing?"

Her gaze dropped to the ledger again. She gave a single, simple nod.

Mardoc shifted in his seat, pushed himself up with his staff. "Someone will come here seeking answers. I very much doubt that it will be the King himself, or even the Dragon Master, as Aerona is certainly a dangerous place to be all of a sudden. But the King will send a representative to see for himself what history is being made here. He will be seeking an explanation. What will you tell him?"

Trysten swallowed. "About what?"

"About your position. Why are you the dragoneer?"

"Because Elevera chose me."

Her father shook his head as if disappointed. "I raised no fool. You know what I mean. Why are you the dragoneer?"

Trysten pushed herself away from the table and stood as she had seen her father do when presented with a tough choice. She stepped to the window and looked out over the village. The warped glass hid most everything from her. The light of a few lanterns made it through the windows of cottages and then into the window of her den. The light seemed like such a feeble thing that could be snuffed out with nothing more than a slight motion from her cupped palm.

She drew in a deep breath. Now was the time to tell her father.

She turned away from the window, and as she opened her mouth to speak, her father pushed himself to his feet with the staff. "Someone is coming."

A knock announced another visitor.

"Come in," Trysten called before the echo died away.

The door cracked open. Paege poked his head into the room. "Am I interrupting?"

Trysten shook her head. "No. No, nothing at all. We were just... talking. What can I do for you?"

"I can come back," Paege said.

"Nonsense," Mardoc said. "You two have a weyr to run and far more of a horde than I ever did. You can excuse an old man and his silly stories."

He held Trysten's gaze for a second, then turned away to hobble out of the den.

As the door shut behind him, Trysten dropped into her seat. Her muscles fell about her like worn-out rope. As Paege began to tell her of the accommodations made for the newest hordesmen, Trysten's gaze anchored on the ledger and the neat rows of names she had recorded.

Chapter 36

Trysten knocked on the door, and a moment later, Galelin opened it.

"Ah, come for my report on the new dragons, have you? My! You are more eager even than your father ever was."

Trysten's practiced excuse for her visit fell away. She grinned. "You caught me. I'm sorry. I hope I'm not an imposition."

"Certainly not!" Galelin said, then opened the door and waved Trysten in. "An imposition would be if you summoned me to your den for the report as your father would have. If you come here for it, you save an old man a walk, and you grant him the extra favor of making a cup of tea for himself and his honored guest. Can I get you a cup of tea?"

"That would be nice. Thank you."

"Well," Galelin said as he pulled his kettle from the hob, "I'm pleased to report that the newest additions to the family are in good shape. There are a number of battle wounds to attend to. Nothing serious. Puncture wounds. A torn aerial membrane. It's nothing that can't be mended. I'd like to keep that brown dragon... What was he called?"

"Quella."

"Quella. That's right. Unusual name for a dragon, isn't it?"

"I suppose so. They're not from around here, though."

"Well, Hollin isn't..." Galelin stopped in the middle of scooping tea into a pot. His hand trembled a bit. "Or rather, it *wasn't* that far away."

"Are you all right?"

"Hmm? Yes. Where were we? Oh, dear me. I lost count. Confound it!" The old dragon healer dumped the tea leaves out of his pot and back into the cannister he had scooped them from. He began again.

"As I was saying, that Quella ought to remain on the ground for a few days. I noticed some swelling along the right angelic muscle. I think he may have strained his wing. I want to keep an eye on him."

"I appreciate your concern," Trysten said. "I will make sure it is addressed."

"Well, then, that is all there was to my report. There is nothing left but to drink the tea, is there?" He poured steaming water from his kettle.

Trysten took a seat at the table and refrained from picking at her nails.

"I was filling out the ledger this evening, adding the names of the new dragons and hordesmen, and I was wondering if there had ever been a female dragoneer before."

Galelin regarded her a moment. "You know as well as I do that dragons don't bond with women."

Trysten lifted an eyebrow.

Galelin grinned as he picked up the pot and began to fill two cups.

Trysten studied the old man and continued. "If it simply was a matter of women not being able to bond with dragons, then why is it forbidden by law? Why make a law to forbid something that cannot happen?"

Galelin placed a cup before her. "You are a very clever girl, aren't you? Sharper than your father, even, who is sharper than any ax."

"Thank you," Trysten said as she cupped her hands around the tea. The warmth seeped into her palms and fingers. "But that compliment is no answer. Can I order you to tell me? To tell me the truth?"

Galelin nodded. "I am a member of the weyr, am I not? Unless you got another healer from the Hollin weyr."

"Tell me the truth, Galelin. Was there ever another female dragoneer?"

Steam rose from the surface of Galelin's cup and dissipated, and he stared at it as if he expected the answer to blossom from the golden liquid like a flower.

"The truth, dear, is that I don't rightly know what the truth is."

Trysten sipped her tea. "What do you know, then?"

"I know that you have a good point and a keen mind. Why indeed forbid something that cannot possibly be? It seems to suggest that there was a female dragoneer at some point in time. There had to be one in order for some long-dead king to decide that it wasn't a good idea, that it should never happen again."

"In all your studies, have you come across something that might suggest who it was, and why she was... Why there have been no more up until now?"

Galelin shrugged. He considered his tea for a moment more, then took another drink. "Well, there is the tale of Adalina."

"Adalina?"

"Oh, it's an old folk tale. It's a legend. There's about as much truth to it as there is to any of the wild stories about the Originals."

"Tell me."

"I thought you wanted to know the truth?"

"Tell me."

"Very well." Galelin took a deep breath, then let it out as a sigh. He opened his mouth again, and then took a sip of tea. "You know the stories of the Originals, right? About how the gods grew to fear them, and so split them into men and dragons and destroyed the heavens in the process."

Trysten nodded.

"Well, there is a story that not all of the Originals were destroyed. A few escaped the wrath of the gods by hiding in a clever spot that is a whole other story unto itself. Needless to say, after the destruction of the heavens, the remaining Originals sought to rebuild them. But the destruction was so complete that they soon lost all hope that they could do it by themselves. A few of the Originals decided that the best way to proceed would be to take mates among human women. The idea of mating with a lower form of life was repugnant to the Originals, but a couple of them were desperate to raise an army that could rebuild the heavens and throw the gods from the skies."

Galelin brought his tea to his lips, sipped, and seemed to consider the story as if trying to draw the details up from a deep casket.

"One of the Originals took the form of a handsome young warrior, and he quickly seduced a young human woman. Before long, she bore a daughter and named her Adalina. Adalina grew up fast. She was fair, beautiful, strong and clever. The Original was quite pleased with his daughter, but being the offspring of an Original, she soon discovered that she could not only persuade her human counterparts with her charm and guile, she could also speak to the dragons and have them do her bidding as well.

"Armed with her father's abilities and her mother's ambitions, it wasn't long before Adalina married a king, and then had herself a kingdom. She led her armies into battle and soon reigned over a vast empire that stretched from one corner of the world to the other.

"This caught the attention of the gods, however. They feared exactly what they discovered, that at least one of the Originals had escaped their wrath. So they brought destruction to the lands. Storms and famine struck the empire. A plague rose up and swept the entire world, and those who contracted it were driven mad and spoke in tongues. Confusion spread across the land. Adalina's empire fell. It shattered like a dropped plate, and each one of those fragments became one of the kingdoms that exist today, and the inhabitants of each kingdom speak the tongue of their plague, even us. That is why we cannot understand those in other kingdoms. It was all to bring an end to Adalina's empire."

"And what of Adalina?" Trysten asked. "What happened to her?"

Galelin shrugged. "She died. I'm sure of it. The gods would not have settled for anything less than her head."

"And that is why women are forbidden from becoming dragoneers?"

Galelin shrugged again. "You must ask one of the chroniclers of the King's court. I'm just an old dragon healer who has heard too many fanciful stories to know anything of value."

Trysten took a drink of her tea, then regarded Galelin again. "There's something you're not telling me."

"Why would you say that?"

Trysten's eyes narrowed. "The Original. Did he try and have any more children?"

"The story doesn't say. But if you ask me, if a man—or at least a *human* man—is intent upon siring himself an army, then it doesn't make much sense to stop with one child, does it?"

"No. He'd want to have more. Many more. With a lot of different women, because he doesn't want to wait for a year between each child."

"Indeed."

"And if he had a lot more, then there would be a chance that the gods missed them, that they didn't get all of them because the Original would know where to hide them, wouldn't he? Because he hid from the gods the first time around."

Galelin nodded as he took a sip of tea.

"So then, assuming that the story is true, then there are a lot of people who are descended from the Originals."

"Perhaps. Or maybe only a few survived. And furthermore, it seemed that if they themselves had children, then their Original blood would get watered down, diluted with humanity until there was little left."

Trysten's head sank a little bit as if disappointed that she came to the end of the trail she had been pursuing.

"But you know, bloodlines are a funny thing. Before my hair went gray, it was red. A fiery red. But my parents both had brown hair. All of my siblings had brown hair. No one at all in my family had red hair, except for my mother's father, and my father's grandmother. Sometimes traits skip generations, and when certain people come together, then their children will have these traits that go back in the bloodlines."

Trysten sat up again. "So if two people who were descended from the Originals were themselves to have a child..."

Galelin took another sip of tea. "Especially in the families of dragoneers. I'm sure you've noticed how the title is passed from father to son, or grandfather to grandson in the case of your own father, but it always stays in the family even though there is that open charade called the consideration. Yes, anyone may audition for the title, but it is a pointless exercise; mostly just posturing on the part of the hordesmen. Everyone knows that the title will be passed to the dragoneer's descendants, almost as if there is something passed along in the bloodline. Like red hair."

Trysten sat up. She nearly asked a dangerous question.

Galelin gave Trysten a veiled look and continued. "I've heard rumors of a dragon lord since the new hordesmen came to our village. It seems that they are breathing life into a legend that many people have grown accustomed to dismissing. To hear their stories, it does make a person wonder if there is some truth to it."

Trysten's gaze fell to the tea before her. "*You* don't believe that, do you?"

"Our people's history is a chronicle of all the things we once believed, but believe no more. What history teaches us is that our beliefs are impermanent. They are shifting, changing things. They are spun from stories and facts. What if the stories of the Originals have an element of truth to them? What if there are descendants of one of the Originals walking among us? What if there are even Originals *still* walking among us. And if two of the descendants of the Original were to sire a child, then what is to say that that child might not have a trait not manifested in the family for generations, such as my former red hair?"

Trysten clutched her cup tighter to keep her hands from shaking. She focused on one breath in, one breath out in order to keep herself from blurting out her secret, from telling Galelin of her ability and asking if he truly believed that she was descended from one of the Originals.

But it was too dangerous.

She took a sip of tea to give herself time to think, time to recover. "My father says that the King will take exception to my position."

Galelin nodded. "That seems like a reasonable assumption."

"If I could have some precedent, some history, a story even to help secure my position, it would be helpful."

"The only story that will help you is the one you write."

Trysten regarded the cup in her hands. "I was hoping for a little more than that." She looked up at the old healer. "If you could look through your books and find some evidence of a previous dragoneer who was a woman, I'd appreciate it. It would be helpful."

Galelin shrugged. "I always delight in any excuse to look through my books, but I already know them pretty well. There is very little in them that would escape my knowledge or memory."

Trysten's shoulders drooped. She rolled the teacup slowly between her palms.

"Don't despair, young lady. If nothing ever changed, then there would be no point in keeping all of these dusty old books full of history. We record history to know what things once were. Things will change. They always do. You may count on it."

A weak grin struggled across Trysten's face. "Thank you."

"A good healer knows how to impress upon the spirit of all creatures, not just dragons."

She sat up and looked at Galelin. "How about the Dragon Master? Might he know more? Might he have stories and precedents to help my situation?"

Galelin shrugged. "He might. He might also have a greater understanding of why women aren't supposed to, or aren't allowed to be dragoneers. And after the men from Hollin horde reach the mother city, he will find whatever the King instructs him to find."

Trysten slumped back in her chair. She lifted the cup and swallowed the remainder of the tea. The pungent, rich odor of it overwhelmed her slightly for a second. She took a deep breath and inhaled the scent of smoke and wood ash.

"Thank you all the same," Trysten said. "For the tea and the stories. I must be off to bed now. I have a long day ahead of myself."

"Certainly. And let me tell you what a nice change it is to have the dragoneer call on me, rather than being summoned to the den each time I'm needed." Galelin slapped his hands down upon his knees. "These aren't getting any younger, you know."

Chapter 37

The following morning, when Trysten met the hordesmen in the weyr, it was hard to ignore Paege's black eye. She approached him. As she did so, he averted his gaze to her feet.

"What happened?"

"It was an accident," Paege said.

"I'm sure it was," Trysten said. "But that doesn't answer the question. What happened to your eye?"

The men near Paege shifted slightly.

"I had to use the latrine last night. I bumped into the door in the dark."

Trysten lifted an eyebrow. "You bumped into a door?"

"It was open. I didn't know. I mean, I didn't see that it was open. Because it was dark, you see? I collided with the corner of it. It caught me right in the eye."

Trysten studied the line of hordesmen that extended from Paege's right. All of them found something very interesting to stare at straight ahead. She returned her attention to Paege, then realized that something else was amiss. She counted the men.

"Where is Issod?" Trysten asked.

"Issod?" Paege asked. "He's in his sick bed today."

"His sickbed? And what exotic illness is he suffering from?"

"He... fell out of bed last night. Hurt his arm."

A choked snort came down the line as someone stifled a laugh.

"He fell out of bed?"

Paege nodded.

Trysten stepped back. "Do they have such different beds in Hollin?"

The men stared forward with stone-etched faces.

"I'm waiting on an answer, gentlemen."

One of the Hollin hordesmen slowly shook his head.

Trysten took a deep breath to squelch the heat building in her face. "Is anyone going to tell me what really happened?"

Paege stared straight ahead.

"All right, then. Saddle your mounts and meet me in the yard. All of you!"

As the men scattered, Trysten planted her hands upon her hips. It was bad enough that she'd have to integrate the two hordes as quickly as possible, but it was all the more challenging for the fact that the combined horde was composed of bull-headed men. How in the wilds would she get them to work together as one horde if she couldn't even get them to talk to each other or her?

Whatever it took, it would have to be done soon.

Trysten crossed the weyr to the hordesmen's quarters. As she entered the bunkhouse, Issod pushed himself onto his left elbow with a grimace. His right arm was held before him, cradled in a sling.

"What happened?" Trysten asked as she approached.

"I tripped and fell."

"Out of bed?"

Issod studied her face a second, then laid back on the cot. "I suppose so."

"What were you two fighting about?"

Issod stared at the ceiling. "There was no fight. I fell."

"And how was it that Paege got his black eye?"

Issod sighed. "You will have to ask him."

"I'm asking you."

"I can't say."

"I am giving you an order. Tell me how you hurt your arm."

"I already did."

"You are lying to me."

Issod continued to stare at the ceiling.

"On your feet."

Issod gripped the edge of the cot with his uninjured hand, but there he remained, caught between the two things he struggled with.

"On your feet, Issod, or I will have you tossed over a donkey's back and sent off to the plains."

Issod pulled himself to a sitting position with a grimace. After a second on the side of the cot, he rose to his feet and stared across the room.

"I will have the truth now," Trysten said as she clasped her wrist behind her back.

"The truth?" Issod glanced at her with a lifted eyebrow. "The truth is that none of this matters. The truth is that it doesn't matter one bit how I hurt my arm or how your commander got a black eye. I lost my family. I lost my friends. Everything I ever had and loved is gone now. Except for Verillium. The truth is that I owe her. I was a coward. I should have never allowed her to leave Hollin. I should have made her stay. I could have."

"What would that have accomplished?"

Issod shook his head as he turned his attention to the bunks across the hall. "We would have fallen and died there, alongside the other dragons, alongside my family. My friends. But now we are going to die out here, far from everyone, in a strange land where our bones will bleach under a strange sun. I was a coward. After seeing the way those men fought, I knew we were done for. Running has only postponed the inevitable."

"We are not going to die."

Issod scoffed. "My dragoneer was a good man. A seasoned man. The bravest man I have ever known, and as fierce as the most ill-tempered dragon. He fell within the first few minutes of battle. What hope has this bastard horde? A mismatched, motley crew of dragons and hordesmen led by a girl hardly stepped away from her mother's teat? What battles have you fought? What glories have you won?" Issod asked as a sneer writhed across his face.

Trysten took a deep, measured breath. The man deserved to be tossed out on his behind. He was a coward indeed, and his belief that they were goats in a pen waiting for slaughter was a dangerous position, as evidenced by the fight he likely started with Paege. The man was frightened to the edge of panic.

But if what the Hollin hordesmen said was true, then every capable rider would be needed. A large horde was an advantage, to be sure, but she was three riders short for their twenty-nine dragons, and on top of that, two of her hordesmen were always out on a scouting patrol. At any moment, she had twenty-three hordesmen ready to fly into battle behind her, which was hardly more than an average-sized horde. The village—the kingdom couldn't afford for her to lose another rider.

Trysten stepped up to Issod. His expression hardened, his mouth drew up tight, and his shoulders shifted back. Despite the busted arm, he appeared ready to step back and throw a punch.

"What battles have I fought?" Trysten asked in a calm, measured voice. "I have fought a battle for a dragon's heart. I have the glory of earning a dragon's trust and loyalty. And not just any dragon, but the alpha dragon. The same alpha dragon that yours now serves. If you have any respect at all for your mount, you will respect her wisdom, her choice. Verillium chose to follow Elevera, and Elevera has chosen to follow me. It is that simple. I am the dragoneer, and if you cannot trust me when I say we will be victorious, then you dishonor your own dragon as you dishonor yourself. Is your opinion of Verillium really so low?"

Issod flushed. His gaze dropped away, and his face tilted down slightly. It appeared as if Trysten had pierced him, vented some of the vitriol that he had brimmed with.

"Do you trust your dragon?" Trysten asked.

Issod nodded once but still refused to look her in the eye.

"Then you must also trust me. We will stop the Western Kingdom here. With the help and experience of the Hollin horde, and the strength and might of the Aerona weyr, we will stop them. But we are already a number of riders short. I need every capable person in a dragon's saddle in order to avenge the deaths of your friends and family, of your dragons and your dragoneer. Every person."

Issod finally looked at her.

Trysten returned his gaze for a second, then took half a step back. "You will go find Galelin. You will tell him that I want you patched up and ready to ride by dawn tomorrow. Is that clear?"

The color drained from Issod's face. For a second, it looked like he was about to crumble, to collapse into a ragged pile upon the floor. But then he straightened his back and hurried out of the bunk hall.

Trysten sighed and closed her eyes. By the wilds, managing the dragons was far easier than looking after the men. Would her father feel the same way?

Probably.

She took another deep breath to collect herself, to allow her frustration and concern to simmer down, and then she went to gather Elevera and meet the hordesmen in the yard.

Chapter 38

Over the course of the next few days, Trysten pushed the Hollin hordesmen for details on what they saw and experienced. She consulted with the village overseer and drew up a plan for a fire brigade. Blacksmiths worked around the clock. Their hammers became a metronome that echoed through the village day and night as they fashioned large, iron gates from whatever could be spared around the village. Carpenters recruited help from the villagers in order to build an extension on the weyr to house the additional dragons and hordesmen. Finally, the iron gates were suspended from tracks above the weyr doors so that the building could either be closed off from attacking hordesmen, or the weyr could be used as a trap to contain attacking hordesmen.

Jalite, Assina, and Talon had their work cut out for them as they organized knitting and leather-working circles among anyone in the village who had any skill at all. The tavern was empty of its regulars as they worked in the blacksmith shops or at the weyr, showing up only briefly for meals, so the armor guild moved into the tavern and spread out their baskets of yarn and needles, of leather and tools. The tables became work areas, and the proprietor made as much money as ever making sure that none of the knitters or leather workers went hungry or thirsty as they worked to outfit the new hordesmen in the colors and style of Aerona weyr.

Trysten saw very little of her family during the period as she worked from dawn to dusk with the hordesmen. With many people busy with preparations for the coming battle, her mother spent most of her time in the hills or along the river, hunting or fishing. Her father even gave up his habit of hovering around the weyr, and instead of grumbling about the addition, he surprised Trysten by staying home and devoting most of his time to preparing food for the weyr and the laborers working on it.

Each morning, as she stepped out of the cottage, she stared into the west as the first rays of the sun spread over the land and fell upon the mountains. Her chest tightened. More and more of the rocky, snow-strewn slopes became visible beneath the receding clouds.

It was a wonder they hadn't encountered a Western horde yet.

She proceeded to the weyr. There she met the hordesmen, and together they set out for another day of practice.

Toward evening, as the sun was about to set, Paege motioned and pointed to the east. A dragon approached. A small dragon. A courier dragon.

With several swoops of her arms, she ordered the horde back to the weyr before she, herself, flew out and found Ulbeg pushing through the growing dusk. Upon sight of Elevera, the little male perked up and found one last burst of speed. Atop Ulbeg's back, a village courier waved at Trysten, then pointed at the pouch slung across his shoulders before pointing at her. She was the recipient of the message he carried.

She nodded her understanding and searched the courier's face for an indication of what kind of news it might be. If it was for her specifically, it was unlikely he had read it, but he would know the flavor of the court, know what the mood was inside the King's castle. The stoic, emotionless look upon the courier's face did not bode well for the future.

As soon as their dragons touched down in the yard, the courier dismounted and approached Trysten in a stiff-legged manner that betrayed how many consecutive hours he had been upon the dragon's back.

"I bring a message from King Cadwaller," the courier cried as Trysten approached. Instead of removing the message from his pouch, he slung the pouch from around his neck and held it out to Trysten as if the whole bag had been sullied by its contents.

"How's the mood in the mother city?" Trysten asked as she took the bag.

The courier glanced to the east as if examining the city now, trying to decide how best to answer. He wiped the knit cap from his head and wrung it in his hands. "A far sight more dreadful since I showed up."

Trysten meant to press him for more details but then thought better of it. She was stalling, putting off what she imagined was in the scroll inside the pouch. She could talk to the courier later.

"Thank you for your service," Trysten said, then hurried off with the pouch.

She took it to her den, dropped the pouch upon the table, and stared at it as if a serpent might crawl out and bite her. She took a deep breath, pulled back the closures, and flipped open the leather flap. Inside, nested in the bottom, were a number of scrolls rolled up tightly and sealed with various seals. Different colored waxes indicated who sent them, and who they were for. The largest scroll and the one made of the finest parchment was the one intended for her. She need not pull it out and see the red cord and gold-colored wax to know that it came directly from the King's court and was addressed to her.

She broke the seal, slid off the cord, and as the edges of the parchment trembled in her grip, she unrolled the missive. In the large, ornate script of a court scrivener, she read the orders in which King Cadwaller the IV ordered Trysten of Aerona village to ground her horde until a prince of the court arrived, at which time, in accordance with the kingdom's law, he would take command of the weyr and send her horde back to the mother city. She herself would remain behind in Aerona, where she would be forever banished from setting foot inside the weyr or having any communication whatsoever with any dragon of any kind.

She read the words again.

The parchment slipped from her fingers. It curled up on itself as it fell to the top of the table, and there it lay, curled as tightly as any serpent ready to strike.

With a quick motion, she brushed the scroll aside, sent it skittering from the top of the table. She then shoved the pouch from the table as well. It landed upon the floor with a plop, the way worn leather bags do. The urge to stomp upon the scroll struck her. To just jump up and down upon it until she exhausted herself, and then pick it up and burn it in the flame of the nearest lantern and pretend she had never seen the cursed thing.

But it didn't matter. A prince was on his way. Surely. Ulbeg was a fast dragon, and by the appearance of him and the courier, they had made great haste on their return trip. It would probably be another day or two, possibly three before the prince arrived and ruined the rest of her life.

She shook her head. No. She was dragoneer. Dragoneers did not back away from challenges. They met them head-on. They met them with their hordes at their backs. She would deal with the prince, with the King. She had a day or two to come up with a plan.

Her attention fell to the scroll upon the floor.

She turned away and stormed down the stairs and out of the weyr. The river beckoned to her. Down there, with the breeze in the reeds and water on the stones, she could clear her head and begin to think about how to get out of this situation.

Chapter 39

After a few steps, a familiar voice called out Trysten's name. She stopped and peered into the gathering dusk. Assina approached down the lane.

"I was coming to get you," Assina said. "We've finished your armor, and we want you to try it on in case we need to make a few last-minute alterations."

Trysten's heart sank. Of all the days... "Now is not a good time, Assina."

Assina's shoulders drooped a bit. "Come on. We've been working so hard to get your uniform done. We've all been very excited to work on it! Please. Just try it on. It'll only be a few minutes. I know you're busy."

Trysten looked to the mountains. The sun had sank behind the clouds and stone. Only a brace of dark blue light remained in the sky, a melting barrier between the day and the starlight.

To the wilds. Why not? They had worked hard at it. She might as well let them have their excitement. Besides, it may very well be the only time she ever got to see herself in her own uniform. If the King took away her horde, at least he would never be able to take away the memory of herself in her uniform.

"All right," Trysten said.

"Wonderful!" Assina said with a clap of her hands. "Did I tell you how excited we all are?"

Trysten followed Assina to her cottage and into the room in back where Jalite presented her with the leather armor and the sweater in village colors. The sight of it brought tears to Trysten's eyes. She blinked them back, unsure of whether she was moved by the work and care that Jalite, Assina, and Talon had put into the uniform, or if she was simply gut-punched by the utter and complete unfairness with which the King was about to take it all away.

"I know," Jalite said as she clasped a hand over her chest. "Beautiful, isn't it?"

Trysten swallowed hard rather than make a comment about how surprising it was to hear battle armor described as beautiful.

"Try it on!" Assina urged.

Trysten undressed slowly and pulled on the leggings and sweater. They fit well. Snug, but not constricting. It would allow her complete freedom of movement in the air, but offer little for passing arrows or claws to snag. The thought restricted her throat again. What a conflict! It made her head spin to wish for battle so that she could wear the garments of a dragoneer, yet the battle would likely be bloody and destructive to her hordesmen, her dragons, and the village.

She passed a breath through tight lips, then allowed Jalite and Assina to help her into the leather vest that would protect her body from enemy arrows. As soon as the other women tugged it into place and tied off the leather laces, they ushered her to a corner of the room and angled her toward a piece of glass leaning against the wall. In it, Trysten regarded a slightly warped reflection of herself.

"How wonderful!" Jalite nearly squealed. "It's a perfect fit! That is *astounding* dear." She grasped Assina's shoulder and gave it a small shake. Assina grinned in response.

"Talon!" Assina called out as she turned around. "Come take a look."

Assina's younger brother entered the room. Upon sight of Trysten in her gear, he smiled and gave an approving nod.

"Oh!" Jalite said. "I almost forgot. Here." She reached into a basket upon a table and pulled out a leather helmet. Two braids of yellow wool cascaded from the temples of the helmet. Jalite placed it upon her head, then turned Trysten to the glass again. She picked up one of the helmet's braids and held it near Trysten's own. "Perfect!"

Assina nodded.

She looked at the braid still clutched in her hand, and then on into the glass. Tassels of the same color decorated her shoulder. That she could understand. She imagined it represented the long hair of the hordesmen as they flew through the skies, that they dared other hordesmen to try and grasp it, to capture it. But the braids? Why braids on the helmets? The men wore their hair loose or gathered behind their necks.

"Why?" Trysten asked. She gave the braid a little shake. "Why braids?"

A sly grin crossed Jalite's face. She exchanged a knowing glance with Assina.

"Talon," Jalite said as she turned her attention on her son. "Would you please give us another moment of privacy?"

Talon's eyes widened slightly as if surprised, as if things weren't going quite as he expected them to go. He took one last, long look at the handiwork of his leather armor, then left the room.

"It's a secret," Jalite said as the door closed behind Talon. "It's a secret that is usually passed down from mother to daughter in the armor guild. It's a right of passage, almost. We hand this secret off to the next generation as a way to show our trust, that we are handing off an important tradition to our children. But we'll make an exception for you, as it feels a bit like we've been keeping the secret just for you all this time."

"All this time?" Trysten let the woolen braid slip from her fingers.

"Generations," Jalite said with a nod. "As far back as anyone can remember."

Trysten's brow lifted in expectation.

"The braids are part of the uniform to remind us of the first dragoneers."

"The first?"

Jalite nodded. "The first dragoneers were women. Almost exclusively. There were men, of course, but it was the women who first bonded with the dragons, who opened themselves up to the dragons and rekindled a shadow of the bond once broken by the gods."

Trysten blinked. Blinked in disbelief.

Jalite's smile widened. "A queen arose from among the dragoneers. A queen so powerful that she threatened all the kingdoms surrounding her. She did not threaten them with malice, but with prosperity. Her kingdom grew so wealthy and prosperous that the surrounding kingdoms felt threatened by her, by her power."

"Adalina."

The smile fell away. "You've heard of her?"

"Stories. I heard she was the child of an Original."

Jalite shook her head. A grin crossed her face as if amused by a child's belief in superstition. "That is what the men say. It is easier to believe that a woman can rise to such power and prominence if she is touched by the supernatural. The truth of the matter is that she was simply good. She was loyal, faithful, smart, and above all, she persisted.

"But the surrounding kings couldn't abide by what they saw as a threat. It drove them mad to know that her might would allow her to overrun their kingdoms in a day should she see fit to do so, which of course she never would. But they were kings of small hands and minds. They suspected such treachery of her precisely because such treachery existed in their own hearts. They aligned themselves into a massive army and overthrew Adalina and her kingdom, and to protect themselves from similar perceived threats in the future, they outlawed women as dragoneers."

Trysten shook her head in disbelief. "But they say that women can't..."

Jalite cocked an eyebrow. "You going to believe that?"

"Of course not. But why would they spread that? Why would that story take root if it wasn't true?"

Jalite shrugged. "If you tell a woman enough times that she can't do something, then some will come to believe that. But you and I and Assina here, as well as many other women in the armor guilds across the many kingdoms know better. The braid is a way to keep Adalina alive, to pass along the story."

Jalite leaned in and lowered her voice. "You're the first female dragoneer in a long time, Trysten. A very long time. And when word gets out about you and your abilities, other women will be inspired to join hordes, to ride, to become dragoneers, to do anything they wish."

Trysten's insides wobbled. They quaked like a sheet of tin struck by a hammer. Her gaze drifted off under the weight of the story, the responsibility. Was it true? And if it was, then how much of Galelin's story was true?

"How did Adalina become a dragoneer?" Trysten asked.

Jalite smiled. "She was good at it. She had a connection with the dragons that few others were able to touch."

"Was she a dragon lord?"

"Dragon lords are superstition. When faced with someone possessing great talent and ability, men like to make up stories to explain their own shortcomings. How interesting is the story that goes, 'I was too lazy and not dedicated enough to become a good dragoneer,' as opposed to the story that by birthright, by sheer luck, someone else was able to be dragoneer without the same work and dedication? Did you not work hard for the title?"

Trysten opened her mouth, then stopped herself. She had worked hard. She worked hard still. Her sore muscles, callouses in places she never knew she had skin, her raw hands and aching thighs all spoke of the hard work she put in to being dragoneer and preparing a horde worthy of any that the Western Kingdom might throw at them. None of her abilities to know the hearts and minds of dragons had helped ease the amount of sheer, physical work she had put into *earning* the position.

"I did," Trysten said with a nod. "I worked *hard*."

"So did Adalina. So did all those who are said to be dragon lords. There are no such things."

Trysten nodded again, willing to step back from this line of conversation. As much as she liked Jalite's version of the story of Adalina, she wasn't about to accept her dismissal of dragon lords. No matter how hard she worked herself, it seemed that she still had an innate ability that others either lacked or had never developed.

"Thank you," Trysten said. "For the beautiful uniform. And for that story."

"You're welcome on both accounts. Remember, you must keep the braids a secret. If men were to get wind of why they are on their uniforms, they would tear them all off across the lands, and Adalina's story will be lost. You must promise us, and you must honor Adalina."

"I will. I promise."

As Trysten walked home, her mind wandered to the books in her den. Might she find something in there about the uniforms? She had never really looked into them before. And might her father know something? Would she dare ask him out of fear of revealing the secret?

The more she thought about it, however, the more frustration bubbled up in her. How dare King Cadwaller do this to her. She was a dragoneer. She had earned it. And she was a good one. Paege had even confirmed for her that he'd overheard the Hollin hordesmen speaking among themselves of Trysten's skill, the way she handled the dragons, how they seemed to follow her orders before she even finished giving them. The reluctance of the Hollin hordesmen to follow her became grudging respect with each day they trained together.

The day might come in which she would have to depend on the hordesmen to come to her aide, and that day might very well coincide with the arrival of the prince. Adalina, whether half-Original or just an amazingly skilled dragoneer, would not allow a man to sweep her out of power so easily. Trysten had earned the respect of the horde and the loyalty of her dragons. She would not be dismissed without a fight.

Chapter 40

Trysten stepped into the weyr and made a straight line for the den. As she approached the steps, a young woman stood from a bale of hay she had been sitting on. In her arms, she held a wad of clothing wrapped up in a ball.

"Trysten," the woman called as she rushed forward and stepped between Trysten and the stairs. "Do you remember me, Kaylar?"

Trysten stopped and smiled. "Yes, I remember you. You are the daughter of Sessus and Joachim, aren't you?"

Kaylar nodded. Her reddish hair was done in short braids, but they seemed out of place. She usually wore her hair swept up, pinned to the top of her head.

At the tavern. That is where Trysten had seen her. Kaylar was a barmaid down at the tavern.

"What can I do for you?" Trysten asked. She shifted her weight and tried not to glance up the stairs, to where the books waited and possibly held the salvation of her dream.

"I..." Kaylar clutched the bundle of clothing before her more tightly as she peered off in the direction of the stalls and the dragons in them. "I heard that there are a few empty dragons."

She glanced back at Trysten, her eyes wide. "I mean, not that they are *empty*, with nothing inside of them, you see, but I heard that they have no riders. They're dragons from the Hollin weyr. Such a tragedy, you know? Anyway, I work down at the tavern, and I've been helping out the armor guild with the new uniforms for the Hollin hordesmen, and I got to thinking that if you could be dragoneer, then there was no reason I couldn't be a hordesman. Or hordes*woman*. Hordeslady? Anyway, I want to ride one of the dragons. I want to follow you into battle. I want to do something more with my life than serve drink and food. I want to defend the village. I want to save the people I love. I want to make a *difference*, you know?"

Trysten's eyes filled up, brimmed, and nearly overflowed. She pressed the tips of her fingers to her lips. How horrible it would be to disappoint this woman.

Kaylar grinned. Apparently, she thought she had moved Trysten, and so she unfurled her bundle of clothing.

"Look, I already made myself my own uniform." She held up a sweater in the style of the hordesmen with the village colors and the cables along the sleeves. "I knit it myself. In my off hours. At night. I don't have the leather yet, but I'm saving up to get Talon to make me a set. I have half the money put away already. Can I? Please?"

Trysten forced herself to put her hands at her sides. She lifted her chin and swallowed hard. Did she dare break the news of her pending banishment, perhaps tell her to check in after the prince stopped by? Her gaze escaped her restraint, and her eyes flashed up the stairs.

"Oh," Kaylar said. "Am I keeping you from something?"

Trysten glanced back to the barmaid with dreams. She looked into the solemn, hazel eyes full of hope and fear, hanging her dreams on what Trysten would say. If Trysten told her no, told her that she would have the weyr taken from her in a few days, and the prince would take her place, would Kaylar persist? Would she bother the prince for one of the empty saddles?

Trysten straightened her back and pulled her shoulders tight. No. It was her job to make sure that women like Kaylar never had to find out how far they'd push themselves for their dreams, especially when their dreams were so reasonable, so respectable. They lived in the village. There was no reason why, if they could prove themselves in the battle sky, that they shouldn't be allowed to fly and fight with the hordesmen, to be hordesmen themselves.

Being dragoneer meant that her primary responsibility was to defend the village, and that meant defending the dreams of those who lived in the village.

Trysten nodded. "You're in."

Kaylar squealed, her face rocked in surprise. She lunged forward and clasped Trysten in a great hug. "Oh, thank you. Thank you, thank you!"

"Don't thank me yet," Trysten warned. "You can try out for the position, but you still have to earn it. Practice your archery, and hang out at the edge of the yard, especially at dawn and dusk. Watch us and see what you can pick up of the hand signals. It will give you an edge."

"I will," Kaylar said as she rolled her sweater back into a bundle. "I really will. I'll be there every morning. You'll see. Watch me."

With a grin and a nod, Kaylar took off. She glanced over her shoulder and flashed Trysten one more wide smile before disappearing through the doorway and into the night.

Trysten couldn't help but grin herself. Even if the King was able to stop her, even if he managed to wrench the horde away from her, Trysten at least had the satisfaction of knowing she had started something. Things would never be the same because of her. And it was good.

An exhaustive search through the books in her den revealed little about the origin of the uniforms, let alone the braids. The only time the books dealt with the uniforms was in describing them, what they ought to consist of, and that the armor guild would manufacture them at a fair price to be paid from the weyr coffers.

When Trysten shuffled down the stairs, all but a few of the dragons were curled up and asleep on the floors of their stalls. Without knowing precisely why, she walked down the aisle in the glow of the few remaining lanterns. The night watchman stirred, shifted, and propped himself up on his stool to better offer the illusion that he hadn't been dozing off.

As she passed each stall, she noted how they all breathed in unison, even in their sleep, as if their connection to her went beyond awareness. They knew the dragoneer was among them, and they were ready for action, ready for her command to wake and act on an instant.

The extension of the weyr was nearly complete. The odor of fresh lumber mingled with the dirt and hay. She inhaled deeply of the scent of pine, carted in from the foothills of the mountains.

Ahead, Elevera lowered her head and stuck her neck out in Trysten's path. She stopped and ran the tips of her fingers along the golden scales of the dragon's jaw. The dragon lifted her head slightly, and Trysten stroked the muzzle and ran her hand down past the side of her mighty jaw, to the top of her neck.

Elevera closed her eyes and let out a sigh in time with all the other dragons.

Shivers ran across Trysten's flesh. Goose pimples spread across her arm. Her hands stilled, and her eyelids drifted shut. She listened to the breathing of the dragons, and in the power and readiness of the sound, like a great waterwheel engine ready to turn the river into massive, grain-grinding power. The dragons waited.

It snuck up on her how much she missed their songs. She missed the individual patterns of breathing, the interplay between them. There was personality. Mood. A sense of life to the songs she used to hear.

It was all gone now. One dragon. One great horde of dragons behaving as one, all of them responding to her personality channeled through Elevera.

"It'll be all right, girl," Trysten whispered. She lowered her head and rested her brow on the tip of Elevera's muzzle. The dragon released a long, low breath. It washed over Trysten's face. It was warm and full of life and as much a caress as anything Elevera could manage.

Trysten patted the dragon's cheek. "I won't let them break us up. If they take the weyr, they cannot have you. You and I and the rest of the horde will go to the mountains if we have to. We'll live in the wilds. We'll be all right if we stick together. Understand?"

Elevera appeared to nod, then, with the tip of her muzzle, gave Trysten's shoulder a light shove.

"I should go home and get some sleep, right?"

Elevera stared at Trysten with her great, brown eyes.

"All right. All right, I'll do that."

She left the weyr, passing under the new construction on her way out, mindful of how much the fresh lumber looked like a scar upon the seasoned, darkened wood of the old weyr.

Chapter 41

A pounding on the door whipped Trysten from sleep. She sat up in bed. She heard her father and mother rising from their bed as well.

As she left her room, she noted the dim, low embers in the hearth. It was late. It had to be almost dawn. She cracked the door open. A hordesman stood in the dark, the sky behind him showing only the deepest blue traces of the coming dawn.

"Trysten," Rast said in his rough voice, "I've spotted the enemy."

Her heart jumped into the back of her mouth, and there, she knew, it would stay for the next few days.

As they hurried to the weyr, Rast explained that he had spotted an enemy encampment at the mouth of the Gul valley, where it emptied out of the mountains. He had spotted the glint of their fires and had landed discreetly at a small distance, then made his way along the edge of the woods for a closer look.

A horde of twenty dragons crowded a makeshift campsite near the edge of the woods, where the river widened out as it cascaded into the hills. They were definitely Western hordesmen with their blue-gray sweaters and the odd hoods of leather that they placed over their dragon's heads.

At the weyr, Trysten roused the night watchman from his nap upon the stool and set him scurrying with news of an impending attack. He hurried up the ladder at the back of the weyr to a small alcove where a bell waited. Trysten told Rast to ready the hordesmen to fly at dawn. As he rushed to the bunk hall, Trysten made her way to the overseer's cottage. She would meet him at his door as he flew out in response to the bell, which began to peal through the dark lanes of Aerona as if the stars themselves crashed down from above.

The village erupted into a flurry of activity. After speaking with Trysten, the village overseer went about organizing the village's defenses. Trysten then returned to the weyr.

The dragons themselves fell immediately into their synchronous breathing, and every dragon's head turned to regard Trysten as she stepped inside. The dragons knew what was coming. They were ready. They weren't eager for battle, lusting after it like the men would when displaying vulgar bravado, but the dragons knew that this was their lot, and it was a fact of life. They cooperated with the weyrmen and hordesmen and soon sported saddles laden with the instruments of war.

Every hordesman stood by his dragon and assisted the weyrmen as they readied the dragons for flight. All except for Issod, who was still out on patrol with Verillium. It would be a shame for him to miss the battle, as he, above all the other hordesmen, had come to live for the thought of vengeance. At the same time, he had a gleam in his eye that frightened Trysten from time to time. The man was haunted by his last battle.

Trysten made her way to her den, to her table. She sat and made a note in the weyr's log of Rast's report, then began to list the names of the dragons and hordesmen about to take flight. She scrawled the names with a haste meant to waste no time as well as hide the tremble of her hand.

The door to the receiving room opened without a knock. She looked up, then sat back as her father entered and picked his way across the room.

She placed the quill back in the ink well, then settled her hands in her lap as she waited for him.

Mardoc lowered himself into the seat across the table with a thud. He clutched the staff before him, then arranged it across his lap.

"Last minute advice?" Trysten asked.

Her father shook his head. "I wanted to apologize."

Trysten's breath caught in her throat.

"It was unfair of me to treat you as I did, in the time leading up to Aeronwind's death. I should not have stood in your way, but I was afraid for you. You have to understand that I know what it is like to do what we do. I have years of experience. I know the cost, the sacrifice, and the danger involved. And I didn't want you to have to endure what I have endured."

He grasped his bad knee.

She opened her mouth to speak but was unsure of what to say.

He shook his head. "It's more than that. As dragoneer, it was my duty to stand up for the village and the kingdom, to protect our king and his laws. I could not allow you to violate them so openly."

"I understand," Trysten said.

"No, you don't," Mardoc said with a shake of his head. "There is more to this than you know."

Trysten glanced to the door on the other side of the receiving room. She wanted to know what he had to say, but there was also a battle she needed to prepare for. Now was not the time to cloud her mind with distractions.

Mardoc raised his hand before himself. "Hear me out. I know you have a battle to prepare for, but I want to tell you this before you depart. I have no doubt whatsoever in my body, such as it is, that you will prevail, that you will rule the day. It is in your blood. It is who you are. And that is why I want to let you know before you leave. It is your right to know who and what it is you are putting your life on the line for."

Her heart had no place higher to climb in her throat, and so her stomach felt as if it were wedging itself up her ribs, crowding her heart. She tried to swallow in order to get everything back into its place, but her throat would not comply.

"You've looked over the ledger," Mardoc began with a gesture at the book. "You know that the weyr has been in our family since our ancestor laid the cornerstone. Our bloodline has mingled with that of war dragons since the beginning. It is the way of things. The dragoneers have passed the weyr on to their sons, who then passed it on to their sons or grandsons. Until now. And the reason for this is that there is a… talent. There is an innate ability to connect with the dragons that each dragoneer possesses. This ability is present in both the female and male lines, but it only manifests itself in men. So it has been since the beginning of the kingdom. When a dragoneer has more than one son, the younger sons either became hordesmen of exceptional skill and refrained from having a family of their own, or they traveled to different villages to start a weyr and a family. The reason for this is that dragoneers are prevented from marrying into families of other dragoneers. It is said that if this were to happen, there would be a chance that the offspring of such a marriage would possess the multiplied abilities of a dragoneer."

Mardoc took a deep breath as he leaned back against the chair. His gaze made tiny shifts, nearly imperceptible as he searched his daughter's face for something, perhaps recognition or realization. He appeared to be content with what he found, for he took another deep breath and went on.

"The notion of a dragon lord has taken on new life since the arrival of the Hollin hordesmen. It is an idea rooted, I have no doubt, in the offspring of forbidden marriages, of two parents who each carry the blood of dragoneers. As you have seen, men fear the idea of dragon lords, of anyone who can communicate with dragons on such a level as to accomplish the impossible, to rip through a kingdom's defenses as easily as we tear through a dole of doves. This is why certain marriages are forbidden."

Mardoc's gaze fell to the table, and such an incredible cloak of sadness descended upon his face that it tore the breath from Trysten's chest.

"Mother," Trysten managed. It came out as a squeak. She covered her mouth with her hand.

Mardoc nodded once. "Your grandmother, on your mother's side, came to Aerona as a refugee."

He looked up at Trysten. His eyes glistened.

"She and her brother fled a fallen village. As is the way of our people, we welcomed them into our homes and made them part of our families. Your grandmother married a stone mason and had a family. Unfortunately, accident and disease took most of them, until only your mother remained. She was beautiful—a fierce thing. I had never seen a woman as brave and relentless and true with a bow and arrow. Your mother challenged my heart like no other woman. Soon we were betrothed, and when news of our betrothal came out, her uncle approached me. He revealed that they were the children of a fallen dragoneer. That he had been unable to bond with the alpha after his father's death, and that the horde had absconded. As the enemy approached, he and his sister fled, and they hid their identity in order to conceal their shame."

"Galelin," Trysten whispered.

Mardoc lifted an eyebrow. "How did you know?"

"He told me. Well, he told me about how he was the son of a dragoneer. That he wasn't able to keep the horde from absconding. He never said anything about a sister, about my... grandmother."

Her father chuckled as he shook his head. "He's a hard man to gauge. He came to me and me alone because he didn't want his niece to know what shame she had descended from. He came to tell me his secret so that I could break off the marriage before we broke the law. But it was too late. Our betrothal was hastened because your mother was already carrying you. I told Galelin to keep his tongue and never breathe a word of it to anyone, or I would make sure that his shame was known by all."

The matter-of-fact nature of her father's admission startled Trysten. He spoke of such things as if speaking of a meal that didn't quite agree with him. Trysten's heart beat hard and loud. She heard it in her ears and felt it in her temples, pounding and pulsing as it sank in that her father knew. Her father knew about her. He knew all along.

"When you were born, I took measures to make sure that your mother and I would have no more children together. I could not part from your mother any more than my hand could part from my arm. We were a horde, the three of us. I could no more leave the two of you than Elevera could leave any of the dragons in the weyr.

"I had hoped that Galelin was mistaken or exaggerating, or altogether lying about your mother's heritage. But as you grew up and expressed an affinity for the dragons, I grew more certain of the man's story with each passing day."

Mardoc lifted his staff from his lap and planted the end of it on the floor beside him with a thud that startled Trysten.

"Be honest with me now, Little Heart. How far do your abilities extend?"

Trysten sat back in her chair. The whole weyr felt unmoored, loosened as if it had been lifted up during the story and placed on the back of the largest dragon ever to live. It was spreading its wings now, and all that had been solid and dependable was nothing more than air, a simple distance between Trysten and the hard stone of truth.

"Quick, now."

Trysten drew in a deep breath and glanced at the shelf above the table. The scroll from the King lay flattened and folded and stuffed into one of the drier, stiffer books that never seemed to be of much use.

"You see," Mardoc continued, "I must know about your abilities. You should have never been born. I should have never courted your mother. And when you tried to become dragoneer, I knew it would invite hardship and sorrow for you. That is why I stood in your way. I wanted to protect you from my indiscretions. If you were to become dragoneer, and word got out, then I knew it would not be long before word spread that Aerona weyr had a female dragoneer. And once word reached the mother city, the King would send someone to investigate. If the investigator discovers the truth, we will lose everything. The horde. The weyr. Everything.

"I tried to get Paege to be the dragoneer because the two of you have always been close, and I fancied that you might marry someday. In that way, Paege would have a son to pass the weyr onto, and it would remain in our family, if indirectly. But again, life was to show me what a blind fool I am. Your powers are far greater than I suspected. I doubt there was anything that could have prevented Elevera from bonding with you. I deliberately withheld information from you in the hope that a little humility would season your powers. At that point, I was thinking of the legend of the dragon lords, and I was feeling quite concerned. And every time I saw you in the air, I knew with greater certainty that the legends are true. My daughter is a dragon lord."

A tremble shook Trysten. She blinked away tears as her father leaned forward onto his staff.

"I had hoped that word of you, and your abilities wouldn't make it back to the mother city until Galelin and I could figure out what to do, but that cad Nillard has undoubtedly upset things. The fact that the King has yet to respond is causing me great concern. I suspect that he is sending another horde up here to replace ours. And I fear for what will happen to you, Little Heart."

Her father leaned forward, opened his hand, and rested it palm-up on top of the table as if asking, waiting for her to hand him something.

"Please. Tell me."

Trysten leaned forward. She extended her hand and took her father's in her own. He clutched her hand, and a hot tear rolled down her cheek as if he had squeezed it from her. All the strength and might she knew of her father before the accident was there once again. It ran beneath his flesh, simmered through his muscles and rang off his bones as he stared at her with a wall of intensity and concern.

"I have to go," Trysten said, her voice hardly over a whisper.

Her father's hand tightened around hers as if he were deciding to never let go, never release her, keep her and protect her from a world that never understood them, that feared them for no good, sensible reason.

He nodded, and his hand slipped from hers. He sat back in his chair, clutching his staff, and once again he was Fallen Mardoc of Aerona weyr.

"When you return, then," he said. "And you will return."

Trysten stood and wiped her palms over her cheeks. How many times had she sat where he sat now? How many times had she watched him rise from behind his table after dismissing her, ready to head out of the den and on to some important matter? How horrible it was to see the tables turn. At that moment, in that very second, she would have given it all up, every bit of it to wrench the table back to the way it had been so that he could sit on the other side once more and be strong and vital again, the dragoneer lecturing the daughter he feared would be greater than even his imagination, someday.

"When I return," she said, and lest she say anything more and completely uncork the dam of tears, she stalked past him and out of the den. She thundered down the stairs and took a deep breath. She drew in the calm courage of the dragons. By the time she hit the bottom step, she was almost as much dragon as human in her demeanor, solid and collected as the dragons who patiently waited to be underway.

Elevera stood ready. The weyrmen had saddled her. Her bow and quiver each rested on its appropriate hook. Rations and a bandage kit waited in a small pouch. Bags of water sloshed like a whisper in their skins as Trysten took the reins and nodded thanks to the weyrman. She led her dragon out into the yard where the other hordesmen waited, all standing next to their mounts and staring at Trysten. Issod, having returned from the watch, stood with Verillium's reins in hand.

The entire village had gathered around the yard. The overseer approached with a sword and scabbard balanced upon a large, plush pillow of gold-colored felt.

"Trysten of Aerona weyr," the overseer called out, "our village is in jeopardy. May we call upon you? May we place our lives in your hands and upon the wings of your capable horde?"

The overseer halted at the end of his question.

And as she had seen her father do, Trysten led her dragon to the overseer.

"Overseer Tuse of Aerona, it is my honor, as it has always been my family's honor, to take your lives into my hands and onto the wings of my horde. I can no more turn you, or anyone in Aerona away, than I can turn away my own kin. You are my kith. Your life is mine, and I will protect it as such."

As the words passed her lips, she pictured her father speaking them, standing tall and strong and handsome in his riding uniform with the dark gray Aeronwind behind him like his massive, winged shadow as if he were far more than a human body could ever contain.

Overseer Tuse lowered himself on one, cracking knee. He lifted the pillow. "Take this sword, Trysten of Aerona. It is the fighting spirit of our village. May it call the wind to your wings and the aim to your arrows."

Trysten released Elevera's reins to lift the sword and scabbard from the pillow. She buckled the scabbard to her side, then drew the sword and held it before her. She had never seen it unsheathed up close before, and the detail etched into the blade arrested her heart. Each side was engraved with a motif that resembled the cables that ran up the sleeves of their sweaters. In some places, the cables appeared to be twining rivers. In other places, they appeared to be twining dragons, all running together before disappearing at the point.

"Rise and cheer!" Trysten called out, her voice loud and solid. "Your voice is our wind!"

The villagers stood. All around the yard, cheers erupted from the people she had grown up with. They raised hands and fists to the sky. They shouted wishes of luck and victory. Among them, Trysten picked out Jalite and Assina and the rest of the armor guild. All the guilds-women had their hair done up in hasty braids. Kaylar, in her hordeswoman sweater, waved from behind them.

Trysten nodded to them, then turned to Elevera, who knelt without a word of command. Trysten placed a foot into the stirrup, and with her free hand, grasped the edge of the saddle. Holding the sword made things difficult, but she'd seen her father do this a number of times. She counted to three, then pulled herself up, swung a leg over the saddle, and landed in her seat, the sword still held aloft and weighing heavily on the muscles in her arm.

Trysten peered ahead to the mountains. The sun had climbed over the horizon. Light lit the lowest peaks as the taller ones disappeared into the gray cloud cover. The gray band grew shorter each day as if it were a drape slowly being lifted to reveal some ghastly surprise, the first hints of which awaited them now.

She glanced back at the weyr, and in the doorway stood both her father and her mother. Her father stood tall, a hand on his staff. The other hand was wrapped around her mother's waist. She smiled, full of encouragement despite her worried eyes. Trysten smiled back, then felt a flash of pain at the realization that she didn't know. Her father and Galelin had kept her heritage from her. Would she dare break it to her?

It was her right. She deserved to know. Just as soon as Trysten got back.

With a flick from her heels, she urged Elevera across the grass. She leveled the tip of the sword at the mountains ahead. "Hordesmen! Your bravery has been proven beyond all doubt in these last few weeks. All of you are seasoned veterans who have flown in the fighting season. I know that I can trust my life to each of you, that I can trust this village to each of you. You have proven in seasons past your courage, your skill. Even those who have not started their lives with us have proven both, for you have survived against incredible odds to fight again, to take vengeance as well as put your lives on the line for this weyr and this village. Your bravery and courage are not in question. What makes you among the finest hordesmen to ever ride is that you have not only proven yourselves in battle, but that you have the courage to resist any prejudices that our society may have heaped upon you. You see me, and you see generations of tradition cast aside. But you also see a new future being born. Our new brothers have told us of an enemy that fights like no other. And so to defeat them, we will defend ourselves like no other. Your courage is greater than any hordesmen before you. Today, we will make sure that each of your names is forever known to the hordesmen behind you. You are the finest people to ever take to the saddle, and you ride the finest dragons who have ever flown. The day will be ours. Victory will be our light. Legend will be our shadow!"

With relief, Trysten let the sword sweep down, past Elevera's shoulder.

Buoyed on a great cheer, Elevera spread her magnificent wings and pushed down as if to wrap them around and protect the entire village. Trysten struggled to stuff the sword back into its scabbard as her dragon propelled them upward, but after she replaced it, she peered over her shoulder. Behind her, twenty-five dragons leaped into the glory of the sky. To her right, as a *V* formation took shape, her gaze lingered a moment on Paege. His face was set and unreadable. He was a stone, and whatever he felt at the moment, it was hidden behind the wall that men build to protect their emotions.

As Trysten turned back around, she thought of her father's wish that she should marry him.

She shook her head.

Chapter 42

As the village fell behind them, Trysten's mind raced, charged forward in starts and stops. She thought of her father's revelation, of her heritage and what it meant. Her father had called her a dragon lord. She then cast the thoughts aside and forced herself to concentrate fully on the landscape ahead between the hills and mountains.

Below, the rising sun glinted off the rushing, tumbling waters of the River Gul as it wound through the hills and often ran white as if trying to shake the mountain chill from its shoulders. Her gaze followed the river until she lost it behind a set of hills.

The thoughts lunged back. What would she do about the approaching prince?

That question had a simple answer. She would protect the village.

Ahead, movement crested a large hill covered in stone and heather. A horde of dragons approached.

Every inch of Trysten tightened. Elevera grew tense like a bowstring, ready to snap the horde behind her into the heart of the enemy. Trysten crouched against her dragon's neck and surveyed the situation. Twenty dragons. Twenty Western hordesmen against twenty-six from Aerona weyr. A pleased smiled tugged at the corners of her mouth. Those were good odds. Also, meeting them out in the open, on hills with air currents familiar to her dragons, gave them several advantages. Too much confidence could be dangerous, but so much in their favor should hopefully steady the nerves of the Hollin hordesmen, who were undoubtedly a bit jittery with the memories of their last battle against the thought of facing the same enemy again.

Trysten lifted her arm into the air and whirled it in two wide circles before pointing at the enemy. She thrust her arm into the air, then angled it back toward the sun. With a flick of her heels, Elevera began to climb and gain altitude. In addition to everything else in their favor, the Aerona horde would attack at the sun's angle, blinding the enemy until after the first volley of arrows.

The landscape dropped away as they climbed. Undoubtedly, they had been spotted, but the enemy horde did not appear to change its tactic. They picked up elevation as well, but they weren't trying to out-climb the Aerona horde. Trysten's brow tightened. If they had to fight with the sun in their faces, then they should be trying to climb above the Aerona horde. The sun wouldn't be at a direct angle, and gravity would help guide their arrows while shielding them somewhat from Aerona's own.

Were they trying to slip beneath? If they flew under the Aerona horde altogether, it would force Trysten to order pursuit. They would turn around and suddenly find the sun in their faces. Also, with fresher dragons, the Western horde might try to run for Aerona and duplicate the attack strategy that brought down Hollin.

As she watched the Western horde for a hint of their strategy, a shout snagged her attention.

Issod waved wildly at Trysten. He then motioned to the south. In the distance, just above the horizon, another horde of dragons sailed along. They couldn't be the prince's dragons. They would approach from the east, not the south.

The horde's shape changed. It shifted, leveled out. It had spotted the Aerona horde and had turned to an intercept course.

Trysten's jaw tightened. She couldn't count the individual dragons at this distance, but it appeared to be a normal-sized horde. The Western horde's plan drew into sharp focus. Such sharp focus that it cleaved away her numerous advantages. The two hordes were to rendezvous, but when the first horde saw what she was trying to do, they kept reeling out enough rope for her to hang herself and her horde. Her plan of gaining elevation and keeping the sun to their backs had only served to reveal their presence and intentions to the second horde. Soon it would be forty dragons to her twenty-six. By the wilds.

Her knuckles blanched on the saddle lip. They were now outnumbered nearly two-to-one. On top of that, at least one, and possibly both, of the Western hordes was led by a dragon lord such as herself.

Her eyes drifted shut. She took a deep breath. The cold air sank to the core of her. Elevera's powerful shoulders shifted and moved beneath her. The air whooshed about her as the dragon cupped it in her expansive wings and pushed it down and away from them. Trysten leaned forward and placed her palms against the cool scales of her dragon's neck. The breath she held passed through pursed lips, slipped through her, from her, and was whipped away by the wind in her face.

The odds were against them, but she had a good horde, a solid crew of riders and dragons who knew the landscape. The Hollin hordesmen had the experience of a previous battle. The Aerona hordesmen were fighting for their friends and family. All of them were fighting for the kingdom. They had far more to gain, far more to win than the Western hordes.

Trysten opened her eyes. Her gaze narrowed on the horde ahead of them. The advantages still belonged to Aerona weyr. The day would be theirs. The Western hordes were separated by several miles. The Aerona horde had a handful of minutes to engage the first horde before the second one intercepted them. That would be enough time. It had to be.

Trysten waved her left arm in the air, then made a forward, pinwheeling motion to indicate that the horde should charge ahead at all available speed. She kicked Elevera in the shoulders with her heels several times. In response, the gold dragon surged ahead, wings beating hard at the air as if to shove the sky behind them.

As they approached, the beating wings of the first horde began to slow. They were stalling, angling for time to allow their reinforcements to arrive. Bravery belonged to the Aerona weyr. It was perhaps the greatest advantage they held. She pinwheeled her arm forward again and urged Elevera onward.

The second horde began to push hard as well.

Trysten's heart beat faster. They'd have very little time to deal with the first horde before the second fell upon them. She thrust her arm into the air again and ordered a concentrated attack on the Western dragoneer. If they could take out the rider or his dragon in the first pass, then they could take advantage of the resulting confusion and possibly neutralize half the horde before the reinforcements arrived.

What should have been minutes felt stretched into hours as Trysten watched the two hordes approach. The one before her didn't seem to move fast enough while the one to south screamed toward them. Finally, as they drew within range, Trysten ordered a maneuver designed to focus a barrage of arrows upon a single target. As Elevera dropped to form the base of a *U*, Trysten grabbed her bow and slipped an arrow from her quiver. As the other dragons filled in around her and formed the stems of the *U*, Trysten gasped as Verillium sailed over, then began to drop in a spiral that was not part of the plan. As the dragon came around, she revealed Issod, who pulled his bowstring back and took aim at the Western alpha.

"Issod!" Trysten called out.

Verillium twisted around, her wings bent back. Gravity had embraced the dragon as she fell toward the hordesman's target.

Trysten jabbed her heels into Elevera's shoulders as she slammed her bow back onto its hook. With her other hand, she clutched the saddle lip and shoved downward. Elevera, however, hadn't waited for the command. The golden dragon hunched her shoulders, arched her back, and with a swoop of wings, dove after Verillium.

What a fool she had been for allowing Issod to fly! His loss had indeed been too much for him to bear. But what was done was done. Her only chance to save him was to order Verillium down, to allow Elevera to assert her dominance and force the subordinate dragon to ground where she would largely be ignored by the fray.

Issod's arrow flew. It missed by a wide margin, hampered perhaps by nerves as much as the injury to his shoulder. In response, an arrow arced up from the bow of the Western dragoneer and disappeared behind Verillium as she continued her spiraling dive. Her pale belly flashed before Trysten, and then as she spun back around, a bow dropped away.

Issod lay back against his dragon, limp and leaning into the momentum of Verillium's fall. An arrow protruded from the young man's neck.

Trysten gasped.

A barrage of arrows erupted from the Western hordesmen.

Elevera whipped around. Pain punched Trysten in her stomach and hammered blows upon her arms. The ache and throbbing fizzled away. Elevera had taken a number of arrows in her belly and wings to shield

Trysten, and their connection, their bond allowed her to share in her every sensation.

A long, pained growl escaped Elevera's throat. Trysten grasped the saddle lip and prepared to pull Elevera out of the dive as soon as they slipped beneath the Western horde. As she watched the speed with which the Western hordesmen fitted arrows to their bowstrings, it seemed unlikely that she would clear them before taking another volley. She held her breath as Elevera raced the safety of their enemy's shadows and tails.

Arrows suddenly streaked past her from behind and above.

The Western horde scrambled to avoid the onslaught.

Gratitude lit Trysten's face as she glanced back at her horde, diving behind her. Pain exploded through her again. She lunged forward and gripped the saddle lip. Her arms howled with pain. Her head tingled. A blow sent her back arching, her fingers digging into the leather of the saddle.

She turned toward Elevera but knew immediately it had not been her dragon that had been injured.

A dark orange dragon flashed by underneath with an arrow protruding from her back, near her left haunch. The rider glared at Trysten, his face wrenched into anger, hatred, hurt, as if the whole war had been her idea, and he and his dragon were nothing but innocent bystanders.

Horror exploded in her. By all that was wild! She not only experienced what her dragons felt, but she felt what those of the enemy horde experienced as well.

And then she was out of time.

Elevera spread her wings wide. Pain ripped across Trysten's arm as a hole in the dragon's wing widened under the sudden punch of wind. She roared as they slid beneath the Western horde.

Several arrows streaked past them, but with the Aerona horde close behind her, the Western horde didn't have time to bank their dragons and get a clear aim. A rash of roars exploded behind her as the two hordes collided.

Trysten gasped, clenched her eyes shut, and then pushed it all down, blocked it all out as if shoving every arrow's blow and blast of fire breath into a leather bag that she cinched tight and dropped from the heights. Now was not the time to lose herself in the sensations of the dragons. Was this why her father had told her of the dragon lords before she went into battle? Did he know she would experience this? Then why not flat-out say so!

There wasn't time to wonder. After a flick of her heels and a tug on the saddle, Elevera banked hard to the left and began to flap in great, downward thrusts as she climbed back up to meet the Western horde.

The Aerona horde passed behind her. They flew out and banked as well, struggling to curtail their momentum and fall in behind Trysten and Elevera.

The Western dragoneer gathered his horde and banked in the opposite direction, turning to challenge them.

Trysten glanced at the second horde. Why weren't they racing forward, coming to reinforce the first horde? That would have been her tactic if she had been in their position.

It didn't matter. What mattered was that the first horde was coming about for another pass. She nocked another arrow as the Western hordesmen did the same. She gritted her teeth. This had to end now. She didn't have time to fly back and forth, exchanging arrows and swipes with claws and tails. The second horde would be on them soon. If Trysten weren't ready for them, the Aerona horde would be overwhelmed within minutes.

She pulled back on her bowstring. She flicked her heels against Elevera's shoulder, but the dragon already knew to aim for the dark gray alpha dragon with the fiery plume of feathers sweeping back from the crown of her hood. Upon her back, a man in a matching headdress took aim at Trysten with his own arrow.

They rushed at each other. Trysten recalled Issod, the arrow in his throat. She pulled back her bowstring just that much more, then let the arrow leap from her aching fingers. Fire erupted from Elevera's maw, chasing after it. The arrow slipped right over the dragoneer's head. He loosed his own arrow, but not before the Western alpha folded her wings and dropped as if ordered to ground. The arrow streaked away, uselessly spent as Elevera soared over the Western alpha, carried by her gliding momentum. Trysten clenched the saddle lip with her free hand and braced herself as she sensed what was coming. Elevera jerked as her claws grasped the saddle on the Western alpha's back.

Leather straps snapped.

Pain ripped through Trysten. She arched her back and sucked in a tight breath as Elevera's claws dug through the Western alpha's scales.

Elevera released her claws. A man screamed, and his scream fell to the stones and heather below.

Trysten collapsed forward, drawing the bow close to her body. Several arrows whizzed past. One struck Elevera in her flank. Her scales held and deflected the blow. They cleared the enemy horde, then Elevera banked hard to the left. The Western alpha spiraled downward toward her fallen rider. Bright red rents stood out among the ripped-away scales along her back.

A shudder wracked Trysten. The Western dragoneer was dead. The Western alpha's spell over her horde was as broken as the fallen master she chased after.

Mere minutes remained before the Western beta established command over the remains of the horde, then a minute or less beyond that, the second horde would be upon them.

Chapter 43

Trysten peered over the battle and tried to pick out which dragon was the beta. The Aerona horde had passed through the Western horde behind Trysten and was continuing to shadow her as she came about. One of her dragons struggled to keep formation and had already fallen to the back of the horde. Something was wrong with her wing.

Beyond, the Western dragons should be falling behind the beta, drifting into place for the beta to establish her new rule. Instead, the dragons flew about in disarray, left and right, forming more of a disorderly cloud than a fighting regiment. Something was wrong with their horde.

It was imperative to know which was the beta, where to focus their attack. Trysten closed her eyes and clutched the side of Elevera's neck. Pain flicked her side, her legs as her mind picked up on all the injuries taken by the dragons in either horde. Most keenly felt were the ache in Elevera's belly and the gash in her wing where she had taken a few arrows. Still, Trysten took a deep breath, opened herself up, and tried to imagine the currents between the dragons, the series of subtle cues oblivious to humans that the dragons used to communicate. Which Western dragon was the beta? If they could get the beta, the rest of the horde would abscond and flee. She rubbed her palm over the rough scales of Elevera's neck and tried to feel, to know, to be but a silkweed seed on the wind of the dragons' thoughts and feelings.

The neck beneath Trysten's palms tensed.

Her eyes flicked open wide as Elevera let out a great roar. A roar that shook Trysten, quaked her. She clutched the edge of the saddle and glanced about. The Western dragons, in unison, dropped and slid down through the air and approached Elevera. Their riders shouted at each other in their strange, barking language. They gestured wildly. A few drew back their bows and aimed at Elevera's exposed belly, but the moment Trysten saw them, their mounts twisted over, flipping the riders upside-down before diving out of their bows's range.

A gasp escaped Trysten.

Never. Never had anyone spoken of a dragoneer taking command of an enemy horde before. It was an impossibility as far as Trysten knew or understood. Defeated hordes absconded and fled, as the Hollin horde had. But, with the exception of the wounded alpha, the Western dragons were taking up a position behind and beneath Elevera. It was clear that the size of the Aerona horde had suddenly expanded. Just how far did her powers as a dragon lord extend?

Around her, the dragons from Aerona and Hollin fell in behind her. Most of them banked slightly as the riders peered over the sides of their dragons at the scene below. The two dragons that remained steady, level, betrayed the severity of their rider's injuries. Trysten's heart tightened as she thought of the fallen riders slumped over their saddles.

There was no time to mourn those who had bravely fought with her and gave their lives for the village and kingdom. Their sacrifices would be in vain if they didn't prevail over the second horde, which would be upon them in a moment. There, in battle, she would honor their sacrifices, and hopefully, find just how far she could push her powers.

With a thought, Trysten ordered the Western dragons out and ahead. The astonished riders continued to shout back and forth in their foreign tongue. They fought to wrest back control of their dragons, but they were no longer their dragons to control.

As the Western horde flew out to meet the second horde, Trysten pulled up on the edge of the saddle and flicked her heels in an upward motion. Elevera climbed into the sky. The Aerona horde followed, except for one dragon, the one with an injured wing. She tried, but then fell back and circled downward to seek safety among the stones.

As they flew out to meet the second horde, Trysten ordered her own to fan out and form a straight line. The second horde needed to see exactly what they were dealing with, and how many dragons. As they approached, Trysten gave an order to prepare for an attack on a dive. The captured horde would fly straight at the second horde and force the second horde into a dive to avoid a collision. Once they flew out from underneath the captured horde, the Aerona horde would greet them with a hail of arrows.

Trysten patted Elevera on the neck. The ache in her stomach grew. It grew with that of several other dragons that had taken arrows in the softer scales of their bellies as well. Off in the distance, she sensed the ache in a shoulder of one of the captured dragons.

A bevy of shouts erupted from the captured horde as they tried to warn to the second horde. Trysten lifted her arm and signaled for all to be ready. She took up her bow and pulled an arrow from her quiver. Her legs tightened with tension, waiting to give the order. She drew in a deep breath, held it, then wished for the captured horde to spread their wings and make a screen of themselves.

As they responded to her wishes, their wings snapping out in a breathtaking, colorful display, the second horde flew up and over the screen formed by the captured horde. Trysten's trap lay empty. Worse yet, the second horde released a hail of arrows.

The line held for a brief second as the Aerona horde answered with their own arrows. As soon as Trysten released her bowstring, a punch of pain struck her in the left side of her belly. Unlike the pain broadcasted from the dragons, this hit her a hundred times harder. She glanced down long enough to see an arrow lodged in the leather of her armor. Though the armor had done its job, the tip of the arrow was buried far enough for Trysten to know that it had broken skin.

As she batted the arrow away with gritted teeth, the second horde drew into a *U* and headed straight for her. As she peered at the hooded faces of the dragons bearing down on her and Elevera, she could not only sense the dragons but sense the dragoneer as well. It was a distant feeling, like knowing that someone else was in a cottage with her, even though she couldn't say why she knew.

This was the horde that had taken out Hollin weyr. This was a horde commanded by a dragon lord.

Before she could issue the command, Elevera drew her wings in close to her body and plummeted out of range of the arrows. Without having to look up, Trysten knew the other dragon lord had ordered pursuit. The entire second horde fell through the sky behind her. As the stone-broken and heather-strewn ground raced and spun toward her, Trysten recalled Nillard's story of how the Western horde had taken out the Hollin dragoneer so quickly. They would crush her. They would drive their dragons straight into her in order to kill her. And if she could sense the presence of a dragon lord... Her throat tightened at the thought that he could sense her as well. What would he *not* sacrifice to stop a dragon lord who took control of an enemy horde while their riders remained on their backs?

Arrows flitted past. Trysten and Elevera fell with such speed that the velocity of the arrows looked unreal, as if they were feathers born on a stiff wind rather than propelled violently from bowstrings.

As the ground appeared ready to swat them from the sky, Elevera's wings snapped open. Agony ripped itself from Trysten's throat. She clutched her left arm as the wound in Elevera's wing widened under the sudden change in air pressure.

Elevera tilted into her momentum and zoomed over a set of stone cairns. There were dozens of them, perhaps more. The amount of growth on them indicated that the burial ground was old, ancient.

Trysten hunkered down over Elevera's neck to minimize the air's drag on them. She glanced back. The entire second horde swooped down in pursuit. Their dragons were in better shape, were not as tired or beaten as Elevera, who still had several arrows still lodged in her belly along with a growing rent in her wing. The other dragons gained on them easily.

Far above, the Aerona horde twisted in a wide, steep spiral. Instead of pursuit, they appeared to be aiming for where they expected the second horde to be. Trysten imagined a half-moon flight pattern, and Elevera immediately began to fly along the course pictured in Trysten's mind, leading the second horde back into the path of the Aerona horde. The Aerona horde responded by shifting their spiral to bring them down where Trysten wished to meet them.

Trysten and Elevera hugged hills of stone and heather and swooped through a shallow valley in an effort to shield themselves from arrows, should the second horde come close enough. Once they emerged from the valley, she glanced back to see how much closer her pursuers were. The second horde was no longer in pursuit. They had shifted to their left. Instead of coming for her, they were heading straight for the point that

Trysten had told her dragons to descend upon. Her teeth ground together. By all the wilds! Why hadn't she thought of that? If she could sense what the other dragons were doing, then the other dragon lord would know what her dragons were doing as well. He was going to cut the Aerona horde off when they leveled out of their dive, and the riders would be gripping their saddles instead of pulling on their bowstrings.

With few options ahead of her, Trysten ordered Elevera to bank sharply to the left. She then imagined the Aerona horde diving at full speed.

Trysten held her breath. The Aerona dragons began to fall. To her relief, the riders were pulling back on bowstrings and taking up aim, ready to release a few arrows and cover themselves before breaking the dive. She glanced to her left. The second horde readied arrows of their own. But every arrow tip pointed at her atop Elevera.

As soon as the thought popped into Trysten's head, Elevera peeled upward before the other dragon lord and his horde could react. Up Elevera went, straight into the sky before twisting back and over, leaving Trysten hanging upside-down in the saddle to watch as the Aerona horde snapped its wings open and streaked across the landscape, barely clearing the ground. The two hordes collided as if approaching at the angle of the arms of a *Y*. Arrows flew. Pain seared across Trysten's body. Gouts of fire erupted as the two hordes clashed. Screams escaped the men. The world nearly shattered as she watched Paege's dragon fly into the copper-colored alpha of the other dragon lord.

Wings and necks and tails intertwined before the dragons bounced apart. A bright green dragon twisted hard to avoid the collision, but managed to clip it with her wing. Paege's dragon and the copper alpha crashed to the ground as the green dragon collided with the stone and heather and began to roll end-over-end, broken wings flapping as the rider was crushed over and over until his mount came to a stop on her side.

Trysten cried out. She clenched her eyes shut and fought to shove away all the pain of the two hordes colliding and exchanging blows. She pulled in a deep breath, then snapped her eyes open and forced her focus on the scene below. Elevera executed a quarter barrel roll and banked toward the fray as the two hordes scrambled to regroup.

The copper alpha lay upon her side. Her head lashed at the air. A whine warbled from her as the dragon lord stumbled away, his back toward Trysten. He unslung his bow from his shoulder and pulled an arrow from his quiver. Leya's broken wing dropped against her side as she struggled to rise to her feet. Paege lay several yards away, still tied to his saddle, which had broken free of his mount. He struggled to right himself but appeared to have a problem with the straps meant to secure him to the saddle during aeronautic maneuvers.

The dragon lord lifted his bow and took aim at Paege.

Trysten pushed hard on the saddle and dug into Elevera's shoulders with her heels. Elevera dove hard. Another roar erupted from her as they swooped down.

The dragon lord spun around and took aim. Trysten crouched over Elevera's neck. Her hand drifted to the hilt of the village sword.

As they swept down upon the dragon lord, he released his arrow. Elevera answered with a stream of fire as Trysten pulled the sword from its scabbard. Flames engulfed the arrow before it whizzed past Trysten's ear. The rushing gas and fire had offset the arrow's course the tiniest bit, enough to spare her.

The dragon lord dropped into a crouch, but it was too late for him. Trysten swung the sword down and forward as if trying to strike a ball on the ground. On instinct alone, she missed nicking Elevera's wing, then tensed when the blade found its home.

She tightened her grasp on both the hilt and the saddle lip as she buried the blade in her target, and it tugged at her arm before the sword slid free as Elevera lifted back into the air.

Behind them, the Western dragon lord lay crumpled on the ground. Further back, the two hordes circled to take another pass at each other, arrows nocked and ready.

"Stop!" she screamed.

It was too late. If she ordered the dragons of the Aerona horde off, it would only upset the aim of the riders and open them to attack.

With horror, she realized she must open herself to all that was happening around her. It was the only way to take the second horde as her own and stop the bloodshed. She forced the muscles in her body to relax, her mind and heart to drift out and embrace the onslaught of pain and suffering about to hit her on behalf of the dragons. She gasped, shuddered, then yelped as she saw in her mind's eye what was about to happen. The dragons of the second horde knew what was coming.

The riders of the second horde cast their bows aside. They rained from the air in what appeared to be an act of surrender, and it was enough to throw the Aerona horde off. They held their own bowstrings as the second hordesmen each pulled a long sword from a scabbard. The swords were longer than anything Trysten had seen, and they curved sharply like a dragon's claw. As the two hordes swooped into each other, the second hordesmen turned their swords so that the blades pointed downwards. As Elevera roared and called the dragons to her horde, the hordesmen thrust the swords into the shoulders of their mounts.

"*No!*" Trysten screamed as the dragons of the second horde roared. They dropped from the sky, colliding with several Aerona dragons as they fell.

The second horde slammed into the ground. The hordesmen had not only pierced the hearts of their mounts but had managed to sever the straps for their saddles as well. The riders themselves lay broken among the stones.

As the initial shock waned, Trysten lifted her face to where the first horde they had engaged continued to fly in a wide, slow circle in the distance. Those dragons had no sense of impending death, and not one of the riders appeared to be making an effort to slaughter his mount.

What in the wilds had just happened?

Trysten returned her attention to the scene below as Elevera banked through the air. The Aerona horde had lost a couple more dragons and riders in the final pass. Her loyal hordesmen lay broken or writhing among the stones and cairns of a long forgotten village burial ground. No movement at all was spotted among the fallen Western hordesmen.

The remaining Aerona hordesmen doubled back and took up position behind Trysten and Elevera. They banked left and right as the riders peered down at the carnage, as stunned as she was even without the benefit of her dragon lord sense.

Chapter 44

The instant Elevera landed, Trysten cast aside her restraints and slid down the shoulder of her dragon. She landed in a crouch and turned to survey the underside of her mount. Several arrows poked out from her more tender spots, but the arrows' shafts and fletchings were coated in dried blood. Upon their return, Galelin would certainly have his work cut out for him.

Not far away, Leya, the beta dragon, lay upon her side. Her chest heaved, then stopped. Trysten held her breath, willing Leya to draw one more. With a whoosh, Leya's breath started again, fast and steady. It was not a good sign. Despite the healing powers of dragons, she was soon destined for Aerona's burial grounds.

Rather than attending his own dragon, Paege stood over the body of the fallen dragon lord. He held the long sword of the dragon slayers at his side not as if it were a weapon, but rather as if it were nothing more than an item he needed to transport home or to the market. He looked over his shoulder and stared wordlessly at Trysten as a wind tousled his hair, drove it into his eyes where it covered some of the red and swollen flesh on the right side of his face.

As Trysten started for him, he began to limp toward her, his face curled into a grimace of pain.

"Are you all right?" she called.

Paege nodded. He glanced at Leya, then shook his head. "She will have died in service to the village and kingdom."

"She saved my life," Trysten said. "You and her."

"You wasted no time in returning the favor."

They stopped before each other. The black eye on the left side of his face had begun to turn yellow and lighten up over the last couple of days. The whole right side of his face would be a bruised mess by tomorrow. Hair stuck in dried blood that had run down from a gash on his cheek, near his ear.

Trysten wished to throw herself at him, wrap her arms around him and pull him close, feel him against her and know he was alright, that they were both alright. Or at least they were among those who had survived. Instead, she turned from him and surveyed the carnage. It seemed so much greater and ghastly from the ground. Perhaps it was just the additional bodies, the able riders and their mounts who rushed to the injured, and those who stood about in shocked awe at the fallen Western hordesmen.

"Can you believe…" Trysten began, but her words trailed off.

"These swords," Paege said. He drew from its scabbard the one he had taken, then held it out for her to see. Up close they looked impossibly vicious. She had seen cutlasses sported by a few of the village men who fancied weapons. They were shorter, curved blades made for slashing, and so sharpened on one side only. This sword, however, was brutal. The length was typical of a broad sword, but it curved like a cutlass, and it was sharpened on both edges, which tapered to a finely-honed point. The curved nature of it, like a talon, and the length, both spoke loudly of the blade's intended purpose, which they had all seen with terrifying clarity.

"Who would do such a thing?" Trysten asked.

"Better yet," Paege said as he carefully sheathed the sword and presented the hilt to Trysten, "why did these riders slay their dragons, yet those up there did not, or have not?"

The first round of Western hordesmen remained imprisoned upon the backs of their dragons. Trysten watched them for a seconds, until the loss she had witnessed that day threatened to overwhelm her. It was senseless that these men should slaughter their dragons and end their own lives. She wasn't sure what would become of the men imprisoned aloft, but they would not be harmed. Their dragons would be cared for, held in as much esteem as any of Elevera's horde.

She approached the body of the fallen dragon lord. He wore leather armor stained to black. Strips of black leather had been sewn down the length of the top of his sweater's sleeves. His leather helmet had a flap on the back of it that protected his neck, but it was not adorned with the feathers that the Western hordesmen typically sported. This man was different. Very different. Was he even from the Western Kingdom? If he wasn't from the Western Kingdom, where did he come from, and why had he attacked them? Surely his horde was from the Western Kingdom. The first horde had slowed up once spotting her. Why would they have done so if they weren't buying time?

She peered at the men above again. Perhaps they were doing nothing more than conserving energy. When they saw her dragons approach at full speed, maybe their instinct had been simply to allow her horde more time to wear itself out.

They might have some answers if she could find a way to communicate with them. Answers might come, but first, the injured needed to be seen to.

Chapter 45

Clanging bells greeted Trysten upon her return. Below, villagers scrambled. Archers took up positions behind freshly-made berms. Bucket brigades formed near stores of water. The readiness of the villagers was pleasing, even if they had mistaken her for an enemy, which was understandable. She was, afterall, returning with more dragons than she had left with.

Elevera's strength was fading fast, but she still had it within herself to spread her golden wings in a display that would be easily recognized by all the archers watching over the tips of their arrows. The dragon then soared over the village and landed in the weyr yard. She came down a little too hard and stumbled forward. Thoughts of Aeronwind and her father flashed through Trysten's mind, but then Elevera found her footing and came to a stop, lifted her head high, and flashed her wings once more in a flourish before tucking them at her side.

"Good girl," Trysten said with a pat on her neck. "I'm so proud of you." She blinked away tears with a bat of her eyelashes, then turned to the villagers rushing out to greet her. She pointed back at the approaching hordes. The captured horde flew in a tight knot surrounded by the remaining Aerona hordesmen, who held arrows at the ready should the Western hordesmen offer any resistance.

"Take those riders into custody," Trysten called out to those gathered around her.

Many of the villagers glanced back and forth, openly astonished, unable to make sense of what approached, and the strange orders that accompanied it. But as the first of the Western dragons sat down, they rushed forward, arrows and swords drawn, yelling uselessly at the Western hordesmen to get down.

As Trysten dismounted, her father stood at the open door of the weyr, leaning on his staff as if he'd been standing there since she left. He nodded at her once as Galelin rushed out from his side and ran at surprising speed toward Trysten and Elevera. Uncle Galelin. She shook her head in disbelief.

With her feet on the ground once again, Trysten crouched and peered underneath Elevera. The arrows remained in her, and it seemed that Elevera's belly pooched out more, slung lower to the ground, heavy with exhaustion and pain.

"Oh, Elevera," Trysten cooed. She pressed her palm against the dragon's side and started to lower her brow to the dragon's heaving chest when a pair of hands grasped her about the shoulders and pulled her to her feet.

"Are you all right, my child?" Galelin asked as he whipped her around. His gaze dropped to the hole in her armor.

"I'll be fine. See to Elevera. She has arrows in her ventral side."

Galelin lowered himself on a cracking knee and peered beneath. He nodded, then motioned a weyrman over to help him stand back up.

"Get this dragon into her stall immediately," he said as he clutched the weyrman about his shoulders. "Keep her standing until I can clip off the arrows. Lots of water. Clean linen. I must perform surgery."

The weyrman voiced his understanding and immediately took up Elevera's reins.

"Don't you worry, my child! She'll be as good as new by tomorrow morning."

"I know she will," Trysten said as she peered up into the brown eyes of her dragon. How calm and resolved the dragons were, especially Elevera. It was her strength. It was her will. All that was good about Trysten was in that dragon, and she would be all right.

A commotion broke out at the edge of the yard. A few of the captured hordesmen put up pointless resistance. Village archers took aim at the Westerners, and then at their dragons, and then at the riders again, unsure of what to do in such an unprecedented situation.

"Hold up!" Trysten called to the weyrman who had taken Elevera. She ran forward, patted Elevera's side, then undid the scabbard of the village sword from the saddle. As it dropped free, the weight of it threatened to yank her to the ground as she recalled the sensation of it swinging in her arm, the force of it pulling against her as the blade sank into its target.

"What is going on here?" the village overseer asked from behind Trysten.

"There are injured on the field of battle still. Several of our riders stayed behind to see to them. They were in too bad of shape for flight."

She turned from the oversee and to the nearest weyrman, who stood about wide-eyed as if waiting for someone to explain everything. "Outfit several dragons with supplies. Rations. Linens. Water. Have one of the hordesmen lead them back to the field of battle to collect the survivors who... who will need a ride back."

The color drained from the weyrman's face, be it from the weight of Trysten's words, or his sudden involvement in this historical event. He nodded with understanding and hurried away.

Trysten turned back to the village overseer. "I have defended the village from those who would have what is ours. I return your lives to you."

With a struggle, Trysten knelt and presented the sword.

The overseer lifted the sword from Trysten's palms. "Rise, Trysten of Aerona, and receive our ceaseless gratitude and praise for your service."

It was good to hear his words, but hopefully they were more than simply from a rote script recited by the overseer. The entire village's gratitude would indeed be needed once the prince arrived.

She struggled to her feet, refraining from pressing her palm to the wound in her abdomen. She then motioned at the prisoners. "Keep them secured for a few days. A prince from the mother city will arrive soon. Turn our prisoners over to him. The dragons are ours. They belong to Aerona weyr. They are bonded."

The village overseer's jaw dropped. He peered out at the Western dragons and the hordesmen who were on their knees now, hands behind their backs as their wrists were bound.

"A prince?" the overseer asked. "Why is there a prince coming? When was this arranged? Why didn't I know about it before now?"

Trysten moved away from him without an answer so that she might survey the dragons of the horde. Verillium stood at the edge of the crowd. A group of people worked to unfasten Issod's body and pull it down. All told, four men had been lost for certain. Two men remained at the field of battle to look after another who was too injured to fly, and another man was unaccounted for when his dragon broke formation and went to ground in a fit of exhaustion as they made their way back to Aerona. Assuming that the dragon who fell short recovered after a rest and returned home, then she would have lost two of her own dragons. It was a small price to pay considering that she came back with sixteen more dragons than she had departed with.

But each wound, on both sides, was etched onto her bones, stitched into her muscle. She felt every one over and over as she crossed the yard. A small crowd gathered around her. They shouted congratulations and encouragement, well-wishes and gratitude, but they all wanted to engage her and ask about the captured horde and riders. They wanted the story, wanted to hear first hand what would eventually be passed down from ear to ear and recorded in scrolls and books, especially once the tales of the dragon slayers filtered through the village. Such horrors were unthinkable in a place like Aerona, and not a man, woman, or child would be ignorant of the story by sunset. Nothing like this had ever happened in Aerona before, perhaps never in the entire kingdom, and as such, they were all witnesses to history.

At the entrance to the weyr, Trysten's mother stepped forward only to be restrained by her husband's hand. She stopped, her wrist held behind her.

"Are you all right?" she asked. Her gaze dropped to the hole in Trysten's armor.

"I will be," Trysten said struggling to keep the pain from her voice.

"She has a duty to see to yet," her father said.

Caron stepped back, not quite to her husband's side. She covered her mouth with her hand and nodded. Tears dampened her eyes.

Trysten passed down the aisle of the weyr. Ahead, the courier dragons shuffled with impatience, nearly ready to go. Weyrmen hurried about, stuffing saddlebags full of supplies that might be needed. The breath of the courier dragons came in unison as they watched her pull herself up the stairs. She stepped inside her den, sat at her table, and dipped her quill in the ink well. Her hand hovered above the ledger and trembled. It shook and quivered as the battle came back in flashes. Every blow. Every arrow. Bones into the stones. A cairn exploding with the collision of a stricken dragon. All of it played across her as if she herself was the ledger.

How could the Western dragon lord put himself through all of that? For herself, it was a matter of duty. She had to defend the village and kingdom, and now that she knew what it entailed, knew the cost of that battle, the thought of going off again made her want to curl into a ball beneath the table and cry until she turned to dust and slipped through the cracks in the floorboards. It was an awful, horrible thing. How could anyone willingly participate in it? It was one thing to have to defend her kingdom, but another to be the one who instigated this terror. What kind of monsters were these Western men? What kind of ghastly things sought out battle, sought out injury and death? How could any dragon lord do that?

She breathed deeply, closed her eyes. In the midst of it, as every blow echoed through her bones, she drew on Elevera's strength. It kept her going. Even with a rent in her wings and a belly full of arrows, each taken in order to save Trysten's life, Elevera had kept a calmness about her. She held a stoic attitude as if the battle was as inevitable as the storms that rolled down from the mountains. She lost members of her horde, and the ones that she had gained, the captured Western dragons, she regarded them in the same manner that she viewed her own. The very dragons that had carried the Western hordesmen and had clawed and bitten her brethren were now her own, and she would look after them and protect them as much as the dragons she grew up with in this weyr.

Such amazing creatures. She was not worthy of Elevera's loyalty. None of the humans were.

A drop of ink fell to the blank page. Trysten lowered her hand and wrote out the names of the fallen and those unaccounted for. She then dipped her quill again, and her hand hovered over the remainder of the page, unsure of where to begin in her written record of the battle.

A knock came to the door. Before she could tell the intruder to go away, her father entered.

"Put down the quill," he said as he closed the door.

Trysten sat back in her chair, shocked. "It is my duty."

Mardoc shook his head. "Record the names of the fallen, but do not write your account of the battle yet. What you say may be used against you."

"What?"

"The prince. When he arrives, he may read your entry, especially after a visit to the tavern fills his ears with all the stories of today's battle."

"But if he hears about it—"

"Tavern talk is not as reliable as the written word." Mardoc collapsed with heavy bones into the chair on the other side of the table. "Tell me what happened. Tell me first."

The quill slipped from Trysten's fingers. The tip of it made a mark across Issod's name. She picked the quill up and attempted to brush the ink away with the tips of her fingers, but only succeeded in smearing it further.

"Oh, Father..." Trysten began. She slumped back in her chair. "You can't even begin to imagine."

"I can't," he said with a shake of his head. "In all my days, I have never seen a dragoneer capture an enemy horde and bring it back. I have never heard of such a thing. Before today, if one had even told me such a thing was possible, I would never have believed it. Until today."

He leaned forward and rested more of his weight upon his staff. "How far do your powers go, Little Heart?"

The pet name nearly shattered Trysten. She was no longer Little Heart. She was no longer that young girl who had merely wanted to be dragoneer.

"It was awful. There was another dragon lord—"

"Another?" Mardoc leaned back, his eyes wide and face long with surprise.

"A Western dragon lord. The Hollin men said it was the same horde that attacked them. But they had these swords. And after I..." Trysten took a deep breath.

Mardoc held up his hand. "Start from the beginning."

And so Trysten started from the beginning and told him everything that had happened since they left the village that morning. She told of the two battles, of capturing the first horde and of how the second was lost. Once she finished, her father merely shook his head in disgust, or perhaps disappointment.

"What kind of men do such a thing?" Trysten asked, then found she had run out of breath.

"They rode with a dragon lord," Mardoc said. "They knew the cost of loss."

Trysten shook her head. "But we... If anything... We would *never*."

"But we are not a people of war. War is a way of life for the Westerners—"

"But how could they know?" Trysten asked. "If they had a dragon lord, they had to know that they would be virtually unstoppable. Why carry those swords, then? They look forged for one purpose, and one purpose only. Why would they think they needed to carry them? How could a normal horde ever hope to beat them? Look at how quickly they defeated the entire Hollin weyr. It's almost as if they had to know…"

She couldn't bring herself to say it.

Mardoc nodded. "As if they knew they might go up against a dragon lord. And not just any dragon lord, but one that could take their horde."

A chill shook Trysten. Her gaze dropped to the ledger.

Mardoc tapped the floor with his staff. "It's enough to record the names of the fallen for now. Let's see to others—"

"But it's the custom—"

"There is nothing customary about being a dragoneer. Not anymore. Not since you have taken the title. Come. We must see to other things." He stood to indicate that the discussion was over.

Trysten slipped the stopper into her ink well, then followed her father onto the landing. She surveyed the weyr beneath them. People ran about, seeing to the injured dragons and seeking out the last few people in the village who hadn't heard the story of the battle as undoubtedly told to them by one of the Aerona hordesmen.

As they descended, she paused and glanced back at the den. If her father, a man who stood by the customs of the dragoneers so steadfastly until the end, could tell her to wait to write the record of battle, then what was the chance that things had been left out before? What was the chance that all the dragoneers before her had been selective in what they recorded of their history?

Once on the floor of the weyr and found Galelin overseeing the work of an apprentice who patched up a rent in a dragon's wing.

"How's Elevera?" Trysten asked.

Galelin issued a few commands to the nervous apprentice before ushering Trysten and Mardoc to the corner of an empty stall. Trysten's gut tightened as she braced herself for terrible news.

"Elevera will be fine," Galelin said in a hushed tone. "A day or two in the stable, and she'll be terrorizing doles of doves like old times."

As relief passed, puzzlement settled onto Trysten's face. Galelin leaned forward and glanced from Trysten to Mardoc as if about to include them in a conspiracy. "I saw one of those swords brought back from the battle. One of the hordesmen was waving it about, showing it off, spoils of war and all that, as if this whole wild fighting season was nothing more than a matter of sport."

Galelin spat into the corner.

Trysten's back tightened. She hadn't forbidden the men to plunder the bodies of the fallen hordesmen, but perhaps she ought to have.

"I recognized it," Galelin continued. "In one of the calmer moments, I slipped back to my cottage for some particular herbs, and oncer there, I looked it up in a book of myth."

"Myth?" Mardoc asked.

"Myth," Galelin confirmed with a nod. "It is the sword carried by the hordesmen of The Second Horde."

"The Second Horde?" Trysten asked with a cocked eyebrow. She had begun to think of the horde as the second horde and was a bit incredulous to think it was what it was actually called.

"I've heard this tale," Mardoc said. "A long time ago. From my grandfather."

"You never told me," Trysten said.

"The Second Horde was the elite guard of one of the Originals. When he took human form and searched for a mate, he became vulnerable, mortal. To protect himself, he personally trained a weyr of hordesmen to act as his personal guards. As he had offspring, he raised them—"

"Wait. I thought he had one daughter: Adalina," Trysten said with a shake of her head.

"You cannot have an army with one child," Galelin said.

"It seems that I do," Mardoc quipped.

"But the swords… They are… They have one purpose that I can see," Trysten said.

"Make no mistake. They are deadly to anyone who takes their blows. But it is not humans that the Original needed protection from. Even in human form, he was far mightier than even the strongest man to have ever lived."

"He needed protection from dragons?"

"Other Originals," Galelin corrected. "Those swords were meant to slay other Originals."

Trysten glanced from Galelin to Mardoc. "What does this mean, then? That those men had those swords?"

Galelin cleared his throat. "It means that when those men fail to return, whoever sent them will know that they encountered someone mighty enough to slay the Original's personal guards."

After Trysten had seen to the rest of the injured men and dragons and had her own injury treated, she served the village once again as a guest of honor at a banquet. She forced herself to smile and say the appropriate things throughout the dinner. But as soon as she could, she retired to the weyr. Most of the villagers remained in the square, celebrating with drink and music. Only a single night watchman greeted Trysten when she entered. He eyed her with open awe as she walked down the aisle and looked into the eyes of each dragon. Their breath came slow and steady and matched her steps. She stopped at Elevera's stall and peered up at the dragon. She was on her feet already, and though Trysten wanted to step inside the stall, crouch, and peer at Galelin's handiwork, she couldn't bring herself to tear herself from her gaze. Trysten took a deep breath with the rest of the dragons, and then lifted her palm up and out.

Elevera lowered her head and rested the side of her muzzle against Trysten's hand. She recalled the song, the subtle shifts in the dragons' breathing patterns. She remembered the different rhythms, the rising and falling, the swelling and crashing, and it seemed as if entire conversations, whole storied songs were passed between the dragons with nothing more than the changing rhythms of their breath. She had been able to sit and listen to it all when she was a girl. She could take it in with rapture for hours on end until her father came in and all the dragons fell into unison as if they were every bit the edge of a blade, nothing more than a tool waiting for the warrior's command.

And now she was the warrior, and these dragons were a weapon for her to wield.

The pit of her stomach hollowed out in grief. She gritted her teeth, and her throat clenched closed at never being able to hear that song again.

Trysten took a deep, trembling breath as a tear dropped down her cheek. Her fingers curled, clutched at the golden muzzle of Elevera. She pulled the dragon closer, then rested her brow against the dragon's nose.

"Sing for me," Trysten whispered. "Please."

Elevera's breath slowed as it swept over Trysten's face. Down the aisle, the breathing of the smaller courier dragons picked up. Across the weyr, the dragons altered their breathing, swung their patterns, rolled low, grumbling breaths. Crescendos of high, quick breaths made a staccato rhythm up and down the aisle. The weyr brimmed to the rafters with their quiet song as the dragons sang for their dragoneer who wept for all that was lost and what was yet to come.

The Complete *Dragoneer* Series

The Bonding
The Prince
Aerona Stands
Outposts
Between Kingdoms
Couriers
Emissaries
Elevera

The Complete *Untethered* Trilogy

A Dragon in the Forest
A Dragon on the Sea
A Dragon in the Mountains

The Complete *Wisdom of Dragons* Series

Dragon's-Eye View
Letting Go
Fighting Chance
Hordesmen

The Complete *Dragonjacks* Series

The Shepherd
The Flock
The Wolf
The Champion

About the Authors

Yes, they're married. Together, they write fantasy fiction featuring strong female characters and hopeful, adventurous stories appropriate for most ages. And of course, dragons.

If you enjoyed the book, and you wish to be notified of future releases from Vickie and Danny Knestaut, then please visit the link below and sign up for the newsletter. You will be notified when new books are published.

www.knestaut.net

Printed in Great Britain
by Amazon